Elizabeth Speller lived in Berlin, Rome and Paris before reading Classics at Cambridge. She has written for publication as the *Independent, Financial Times* at the universities of Cambridge currently holds a Royal Literary University and divides her life between Gloucestershire and Greece.

Her debut novel was the bestselling *The Return of Captain John Emmett*, which was both an Orange New Writers pick and a Richard & Judy Summer Book Club selection.

'Reprising his role as amateur detective from Elizabeth Speller's compulsively gripping debut, *The Return of Captain John Emmett*, Laurence Bartram begins to delve into the Easton's sinister history. Speller's flashbacks to the war, and its traumatic effects on the individual and the community, are incredibly moving, a sophisticated blend of compelling research and resonant emotion: while Bartram's musing on the significance of mazes adds an intriguing level of erudite complexity to the familial mysteries at the heart of the novel' Eithne Farry, *Daily Mail*

'An absorbing read . . . Speller is movingly effective at handling some of the terrible aftermaths of that war, especially the sense of guilt among survivors . . . There is much to enjoy. The unravelling of Edwardian hypocrisy, the intricate relationships between the classes – these are sensitively handled, together with the creation of interesting characters' Jane Jakeman, *Independent*

'Elizabeth Speller's novel works exceptionally well as an absorbing mystery story but it has a depth of characterisation and a psychological acuity that is rare in crime fiction. As she unveils the strange fate of Kitty, she also creates a highly convincing portrait of a small community still in thrall to the losses, cruelties and betrayals of its recent past' Nick Rennison, *BBC History Magazine*

'A novel about sorrow — post-war grief, a bereaved mother, mutilated men and dysfunctional families — and secrecy . . . A beautifully written, leisurely analysis of loss, sorrow and the influence of a numinous place' Jessica Mann, *Literary Review* Books of the Year

'Well-researched and written, this is a welcome addition to the Virago imprint . . . Speller's Captain Laurence Bartram, caught in a slipstream of grief, is a solid creation — observant, non-judgemental, and all too human in his sexual desires . . . Like Wilkie Collins, Speller affords her seemingly peripheral characters an equal weight and importance' Sarah Crowden, *The Lady*

'Bartram unravels the dark history of the Easton family, to get to the heart of what happened [to Kitty]. The wistful ending will haunt you' Kate Saunders, *Saga Magazine*

THE STRANGE FATE OF
KITTY
EASTON

Also by Elizabeth Speller

Fiction
The Return of Captain John Emmett

Biography
Following Hadrian:
A Second Century Journey Through
the Roman Empire

Memoir
The Sunlight on the Garden:
A Family in Love, War and Madness

THE STRANGE FATE OF
KITTY
EASTON

Elizabeth Speller

virago

VIRAGO

First published in Great Britain in 2011 by Virago Press
This paperback edition published in 2012 by Virago Press

Copyright © Elizabeth Speller 2011

The moral right of the author has been asserted.

A CIP catalogue record for this book
is available from the British Library.

ISBN 978-1-84408-633-7

Typeset in Centaur by M Rules
Printed and bound in Great Britain by
Clays Ltd, St Ives plc

Papers used by Virago are from well-managed forests
and other responsible sources.

MIX
Paper from
responsible sources
FSC® C104740

Virago Press
An imprint of
Little, Brown Book Group
100 Victoria Embankment
London EC4Y 0DY

An Hachette UK Company
www.hachette.co.uk

www.virago.co.uk

For my sister Susannah and my nieces,
Georgia and Daisy Cannell

While the world is full of troubles
And anxious in its sleep.
Come away, O human child!
To the waters and the wild
With a faery, hand in hand,
For the world's more full of weeping than you can understand.

W. B. Yeats, 'The Stolen Child'

PART ONE

CHAPTER ONE

*L*aurence Bartram was waiting for a late connection at Swindon station. It was a bright April day and he had been glad to leave London: a city teeming with the crowds drawn in by Empire Exhibition fever. Now, as he looked beyond the water tower towards the vast marshalling yards and busy workshops of the Great Western Railway, the metallic clangour, the smell of oil and coal, and the distant shouted exchanges of railwaymen filled the air. There was order in the rows of trains in their cream and brown livery and then the tidy terraces of railway cottages, but behind them the sweep of the hills to the south-west rose, bigger than all of it.

Once settled on the train, Laurence felt in his pocket for the three letters he had brought with him, all of which he needed to respond to. It was the one from William Bolitho, an architect, asking him to look at Easton Deadall church that had intrigued him and brought him on this journey. Alongside the church, Lydia Easton, who had the small estate of Easton Hall, hoped to create a maze to remember the many men from the village who had died during the war. It was an odd sort of memorial Laurence had thought, re-reading William's letter. But Mrs Easton was also improving the estate workers' cottages. William had been sanguine; he wrote that the job was basically roofing, painting and installing water closets. But planning the geometry of a maze had evidently been some compensation for the more mundane improvements and recently Mrs Easton had raised the possibility of a new window in the church to commemorate her late husband. 'I've sketched ideas — found a London man to do the practical stuff — but I'd really appreciate it if you could come and take a look at the church itself,' William had written. 'The building has charm. But it's an odd sort of a place, clumsily restored last century but recently one of the workmen was scraping off some decaying floor covering, when he started to expose quite an elaborate geometric design beneath. I sense it's very old and don't want to damage it with our rather basic skills. Do come and share your expertise.'

Laurence pulled out his watch as the small branch line train finally approached Marlborough. It was twenty-five minutes late. As the engine slowed, Laurence's eyes fixed on a single woman who waited on the platform with a boy beside her. Eleanor Bolitho was hatless and coatless. Since he'd last seen her her long red hair had been cut into a thick bob. Her son, Nicholas, was pulling her towards the engine, but Eleanor's eyes were passing up and down the carriages, her hand shading her eyes from the spring sunlight.

Three or four other people got off the train and an elderly porter moved purposefully towards him. Laurence handed over his suitcase just as Eleanor saw him and waved heartily, pointing him out to her son. She reached Laurence and flung her arms around his neck, almost knocking his hat off.

'William will be so pleased you've come,' she said. 'What a stroke of luck you have so many breaks and that you know everything there is to know about churches.' She made it sound as if his being a schoolmaster had been an intermittent pastime, but her enthusiasm was flattering.

'Laurence is a teacher,' she said to Nicholas, 'so I expect he'll want to practise on you and will be very strict.'

The boy, slim and dark, looked up at Laurence and smiled tentatively.

'David – he works on the estate – has driven us over,' Eleanor said. 'As the train was late he's gone off to deliver something for Lydia but he'll be back any minute. I'll tell you all about the place, on the way, but I know you are going to like Easton. Later you can start to think about the church – William thinks it's jolly old. Don't let him make you do it today. He tends to sweep everybody up into his enthusiasms. See, even I'm doing it.'

'I hope I can be as useful as he thinks.'

Laurence was very keen to see the church for himself. He didn't know the village and the church was not in any books, perhaps because it had been deconsecrated for many decades before Mrs Easton's dead parents-in-law had petitioned their bishop to bring it back into use. According to William Bolitho's letter, there were rarely any services now.

'How's Mary?' Eleanor asked, with what she probably thought was nonchalance.

'Committed,' he said, wryly, thinking of one of the other letters he had with him. 'Tell me what lies ahead,' he said, changing the subject.

'Well, I can't tell you what a blessing it's been, Frances and her sister inviting us here,' Eleanor said. 'You'll like Frances – she's clever and straightforward – but she's a bit stuck at Easton Hall, I think. She ought to be making her own life not hanging around like a Victorian spinster on the edge of somebody else's, but ...' She shrugged.

'And her sister, Mrs Easton?'

'Lydia.' Eleanor sighed and then spoke in such a low voice that he could hardly hear her at first, but he realised it was Nicholas she was trying to protect although the small boy had moved away to watch house martins feeding their chicks in a nest under the platform roof. 'She's lovely. Gentle, kind, frail. Seems ... a bit detached at times, not in a cold way, but just not part of us all, increasingly so in the last few weeks. She's not forty yet but she's slightly rheumatic and with her poor health and of course her beastly, tragic life, she looks older, poor woman.' She stopped as if expecting an immediate response. 'You remember the Easton case of course?'

He didn't.

'Lydia's quite a bit older than Frances — they're only half-sisters. They were both born in America, not that you can tell — they've been in England most of their lives. She must have married Digby Easton twenty years or so ago. They had just one child: Katherine — Kitty. Before the war, when Kitty was five, she disappeared.'

She shook her head. There was a sudden exhalation of steam and the train started to pull out. Nicholas was jumping with excitement. Eleanor turned and smiled as she watched him but then her face changed. 'It's unimaginable, losing your only child and never having any idea of what happened to them.'

As the train disappeared, the stationmaster let Nicholas wave the flag. Eleanor's eyes never left him.

'But that's how it was,' Eleanor said, turning back again. 'They left her in bed, asleep, and in the morning she was gone.'

'Good God,' Laurence said, the whole overwhelming story taking time to sink in. 'William said they'd lost a child, but I'd assumed there'd been some illness. I can just remember the case now I think. I suppose I was at Oxford.'

'Poor Lydia,' Eleanor said, standing up. 'She never saw Kitty again, never had another child and then war came and in 1917 Digby was killed.' Eleanor stopped, as if still shocked by the enormity of Lydia's loss. 'Did William mentioned the memorial maze? Most of the men in the village were lost in France as well,' she continued eventually. 'The usual stupid thing: they all joined together. Solidarity. Brotherhood.' Her voice was simultaneously scornful and perplexed.

'Many of them were probably in reserved jobs, too,' Laurence said, following her down the platform. 'Farmworkers and so on. Though indoor servants and keepers – I suppose they had to go.' But most of them were also probably bored with their small lives, he thought. It had all seemed such an adventure at first.

Eleanor reached Nicholas and took his hand. 'Digby was company commander, I think. Julian in effect was his number two. As in life, so in death. The youngest brother – Patrick – has had a minor problem with his heart since childhood and despite his efforts was passed unfit for active service, I gather. The Easton men went to war together and died together.'

'But Julian Easton came back?'

'Frances says much changed. And I think they're struggling to work the estate. Easton Deadall is a village of widows, children and old men. They only really have David – he's our driver today – to lend a pair of strong hands around the house and gardens.'

'He survived too?'

'Well, yes, obviously.' She gave him an amused look. 'Local, but not one of the Easton boys. He was a sapper, I think. Apparently he saved Julian's life under fire. Of course neither man talks about *back then.*' She glanced at him. 'Rather like you.' But she patted his arm affectionately. 'The only other survivor was a chap called Victor Kilminster who couldn't face returning and ran off to New South Wales. Julian helped him resettle, I think. But I heard he's due to come back soon. Julian's rather grumpy about it.'

But Laurence was scarcely concentrating as his mind returned to Kitty Easton and he slowly recalled more of the story of the disappearance. It had been front-page news for a while but then international tensions had consigned the Easton child to history everywhere but Easton Deadall.

'And the little girl – they didn't think she could have gone off by herself?' he said, very quietly. 'Five isn't that young.'

'Possible I suppose.' She let her son go ahead. 'But she was in an upstairs room in the middle of a corridor. Her nanny slept in the next bedroom. The house was locked up and Kitty was frightened of the dark apparently.' She bit her lip. 'So, possible, but unlikely. And they searched everywhere. How far could a five-year-old have got in the middle of the night?'

While Laurence was serving in France he had lost his wife in childbirth and the baby had died with her. For the last months of the war he had not cared whether he lived or died; he was probably a liability to others, but the cynic in him believed his survival was certain once life had no value for him. But to lose a living child and never know what had happened to her was, as Eleanor said, hard even to think about.

They walked from the station forecourt onto a small road, with Nicholas skipping ahead of them. A car was parked outside and a man perhaps a little older than himself was leaning against it smoking a cigarette. He was gazing down the street and didn't hear them approach until Nicholas ran up to the car.

The man put out the cigarette, put on his cap, and swung the boy into the air with a laugh and then lifted him into the car. As Laurence approached he put out his hand.

'David – Captain Bartram,' Eleanor said. She looked at Laurence. 'Do you still call yourself Captain, Captain?'

'Not really.'

'Anyway, David helps with all the jobs at Easton and there are plenty around the place. He keeps things going and the car running and stuff like that. Lydia and Julian would be lost without him. Easton as a whole would.'

'Pleased to meet you, sir.'

The man had a slight west country accent. His floppy, light brown hair fell forwards over a lean face. His gaze was steady as he shook Laurence's hand, his grip rough and warm. Dressed like any countryman with his open-necked old tattersall shirt, moleskin waistcoat and worn corduroys held up with a wide belt, he looked strong and at ease. His military boots were dusty.

As they bumped along the road Nicholas looked at a book with pictures of steam engines while Eleanor continued to chatter intermittently, despite the noise and vibration. But Laurence found it hard to stop thinking about the little girl. He imagined every visitor to Easton Deadall had their arrival prefaced by the ritual telling of this story and he began to feel apprehensive about meeting Lydia Easton.

They were passing between banks of twisted roots and in the shade of the huge beech and oak trees of the ancient Savernake Forest before he spoke again.

'So, what about the others?' he asked.

'Well, you'll like Frances. She's thoroughly modern and very sound. And handsome.'

He stopped himself from smiling at Eleanor's assumptions as to his taste in women.

'Then dear old Julian. He's a rock. Has an absolute passion for the estate. Wanders around with his dog – tries to make the whole thing work. The widows and children adore him. I think he took it badly that he survived the fighting that killed most of the boys locally and, indeed, his brother. Anyway,' she said more cheerfully, 'apparently the famous Patrick is arriving at the end of the week. I've never met him.'

She paused to see if Laurence was with her. 'He's an archaeologist.' He was about to respond when she added, 'Sir Arthur Evans's assistant. From Crete.'

'Knossos,' Laurence said, relieved that he had finally recognised the name. 'Of course.' He thought with slow delight what a bonus it would be to hear of the excavations of the Cretan ruins.

As Eleanor had been talking, they had turned off onto an open road through pasture into a narrow lane. Now they passed an empty barn. Beyond it he could see houses.

'Tarantara,' Eleanor said. 'Behold, Easton Deadall.'

They drew closer to a cluster of cottages, two or three had canvases laid over damaged roofs. Heaps of new stone, sand and lime were piled up by a shed. A bony cow was tethered near by, cropping at the verge. On a tiny village green two white ducks swam in a pond under a huge horse chestnut tree. Children were playing. One of two women sitting on a bench beneath the tree raised a hand as they passed. It was a gentle and timeless scene.

As they left the village Laurence said quietly, 'Mrs Easton still owns the house? Why didn't Julian inherit on Digby's death?'

'The estate is entailed. You know how these ridiculous systems work? Asking for revolution.' She tossed her head but then returned to explaining life at Easton and the home of her landed friends, as if this was something quite separate from her political battles. 'In the case of Easton Deadall, Kitty's the problem,' she said. 'She would have inherited and Lydia absolutely refuses to have her declared dead.' She shot a knowing look at Laurence. 'In the normal run of things, apparently, Lydia would have held the estate until Kitty reached her majority. She would be – what?

Rising eighteen? – now, so not an issue for a few years yet. Julian's next in line after Kitty.' As she spoke, the drive led between stone gateposts, along a gently rising avenue of lime and elm and there, suddenly, was the house.

'Hideous,' Eleanor said, matter-of-factly. 'But better inside.'

Whatever he had envisaged – and knowing it had been mostly rebuilt in the previous century he'd expected a solid, slightly grandiose country seat – the first glimpse of Easton Hall was startling.

The cluster of buildings and styles was extraordinary, but not because of the accretions of time: rather it was as if the Victorian architect had incorporated every architectural style into one building, with little thought of how such a building might sit in the beautiful Wiltshire landscape. Or at least Laurence presumed it was beautiful but the house blocked out the open land he thought must lie beyond it. The effect of it all was part Scottish castle, part Tudor palace, part Venetian palazzo: more operatic set than family house. Above its turrets and crenellations small clouds moved swiftly across a palest blue sky and to one side, its proportions dwarfed by the house, stood a tiny church. Even at a glance he could see that the church was ancient, just as William had said.

Eleanor led the way through a cobbled gatehouse on the eastern side of the yard. A small dog came bounding up. Nicholas looked delighted; he patted it and then knelt down and let it lick his face until Eleanor intervened.

'Run and find Daddy,' she said. 'But don't go far.'

To Laurence she said, 'I expect William'll be in his office.'

But Laurence had stopped dead, transfixed by the view, so different to the one he had just seen that it was as if they had emerged through the gatehouse into a different time and place. The lawn, for as far as he could see, was divided up by long gravel paths, between which lay broad beds. Spikes of new growth were pushing through the earth and bright green tendrils curled up a pergola. At the far end of one of the paths was a spreading mulberry tree and under it thousands of tiny spring flowers were in blossom. To the right the grass fell away steeply, and the distant sound of water suggested that there was a lake below, in the deep depression, out of sight. From a terrace the lawns ran to a haha which formed the boundary of the new maze: Laurence could just make out the low dark curve of spaced plants.

The terrace, broken by three sets of steps, each elaborately decorated, gave on to the garden. Laurence was fascinated by the perfectly realised small stone creatures, each different and not yet worn away by time, carved at the corner of each step of the flight nearest him. They were so exceptional that he could only wonder at who had created them. Voices behind him cut short his speculation.

Two dark-haired women came towards him. That they were sisters was obvious but their colouring was very different. Lydia, he assumed, as she looked older and carried a slender walking stick – was very slim with a pale complexion. Her long hair was streaked with silver. By contrast, Frances was darker skinned, with almost black hair and eyes. Her hair was short and she wore what looked like a man's Norfolk jacket. Eleanor gave him a conspiratorial look, which he thought Frances caught. Both sisters were smiling warmly and Lydia took his hand in hers.

'It's wonderful you could come. So very good of you to spare the time.'

Frances shook his hand only briefly but seemed to watch him more closely, he thought.

He was led through the main entrance, its heavy door was already open. The floor inside was paved in red, white and grey lozenges and warmed by the sunlight coming in through large windows to both sides of the door. A console table bore a large vase of narcissi and irises.

Laurence's first impression of the interior of the house was entirely at odds with the forbidding building he had seen as the car came down the drive. His spirits lifted in response to the light and ease around him.

At the far end broad stone stairs rose and curved round to the gallery of an upper floor with a green baize door half hidden below it. Almost immediately a young girl in a print apron appeared from behind that door. She nodded her head shyly, pushing her mousy hair out of her face.

'Laurence, this is Maggie. Maggie Petch,' Frances said. 'She lives on the estate and we're lucky enough to have her help with the house. She'll show you to your room and David will bring your cases up. Perhaps you'd like to join us in the library when you've rested?'

Laurence's bedroom, on the south side of the house, offered a fine view over the garden. Opening the window he could just see the edge of a churchyard and a few small gravestones. To his right a flash of water indicated the lake he'd guessed was there, although most of it was hidden in a dense thicket of trees. In the far distance he could make out a narrow river, presumably the Kennet. But what took his interest was the delicate pattern of the maze. From up here it looked as if it might have been painted on to the lawn but its symmetrical convolutions were quite clear.

His case was already standing at the end of his bed. He unpacked his paltry belongings in case a maid came up to do it for him while he was downstairs, exposing the limitations of his country-house wardrobe. Apart from anticipating possible surprises in the weather, packing a dinner jacket and a country tweed suit that he rarely wore and which he now noticed smelled strongly of camphor, he had brought little. He placed William's letter in a drawer along with the other two: a note from his former lover, Mary and one he had received the day before confirming the offer of a tutor's position with an aristocratic family in Italy. He had made no decision yet, but would use his stay at Easton Deadall to consider it.

His compass, measuring tape, batteries, torch and military field glasses, all of which he might need to assess the church, he placed on a small writing desk and he took out three books. One was a volume on Saxon and Norman church architecture; the second was Cary's translation of Dante, the third was a present from his old school friend Charles, who had a passion for detective novels. This one was called *Murder on the Links*. A sinister-looking figure in overcoat and hat crouched in trees overlooking a bunker on a golf course. The title looked as if it had been daubed in blood. As he put it down he looked closely at a small photograph hanging above the nightstand. A handsome man and a smiling young woman stood outside the Hall. He took it down and turned it over. 'DVGE and LTE October 1906'. The late Mr Digby and Mrs Lydia Easton, he supposed.

Leaving his room, he stopped to look around and orient himself in the comfortable, slightly old-fashioned house. Despite its charms, it was from somewhere near here that Kitty Easton had gone missing over ten years ago. How, he thought, could Lydia Easton bear to remain in a place that must once have been filled with the sounds and traces of her daughter and husband, and which was now a monument to their absence? He had left his own marital home as soon as he could after the death of his wife and child. Being there had felt suffocating, as if it had already become a museum. Yet here Lydia stayed in the company of ghosts.

Maggie appeared when he reached the bottom of the stairs.

She led him across the hall in the direction of voices. He hesitated in the library doorway, but Lydia Easton saw him at once, stood up, although he noticed it was with some difficulty, and drew him in.

She didn't look like a woman who was shut away with horrors. In fact, when she smiled as she did now, her face had beauty; more so, he guessed, when she was approaching forty, than she might have possessed as a very young woman. The fullness of her mouth, the tiny laughter lines radiating outwards from her eyes, and irises that were almost amber in colour, were combined with a fine bone structure that would keep her striking into old age. The one anomaly was that the pupil of one eye was much larger than the other but that only made her eyes seem more luminous. She seemed too thin, he thought, and her skin was almost translucent, giving her a fragility that was entirely absent in her sister.

Frances was sprawled in a battered leather armchair in stockinged feet, one leg under her, the other dangling. With her muddy hem, she had the look of a schoolgirl. She and Eleanor had broken off a conversation as he came in. A tea trolley stood between them.

'Tea, Laurie?' Eleanor reached for the teapot and strainer as Frances uncurled herself and waved a book at him.

'Well done,' she said. 'Really interesting.' She held it up so that he could see the jacket. 'Eleanor gave me your book a while back. What an incredible amount of work.'

He felt ridiculously pleased. In the years after the war, the writing of his work on London churches had seemed as stagnant as his life. He had long, solitary days at his disposal, yet somehow the manuscript never moved forward. When he had finally started work as a history beak at Westminster School, it was only then, when he no longer had any free time, that he was suddenly driven to finish it and he was surprised how gratified he'd felt with the result.

'What I love,' Frances said, as he took the fine china cup and saucer from Eleanor, 'is that your own passions come through too. Like the bit on Chelsea Old Church. I used to know it and I could feel you hadn't just ticked off its architectural features to show how clever you are, but sat and got the feel of it.'

'It's one of my favourites. I used to escape there rather a lot.'

He caught Eleanor's approving look and stopped, suddenly self-conscious, as she offered him a plate of sandwiches, saying innocently, 'Cucumber or anchovy relish?'

'And now you're a schoolmaster?' Lydia said.

'Well, I have been. But I'm actually considering something new.' He had no chance to explain because Lydia added, eagerly, as if he needed to be encouraged to stay, 'There's plenty of history around here for you – not just the church.'

'That's the sort of thing Patrick – Lydia's brother-in-law – is awfully good on,' Frances said. 'He's been out in Crete. He's an archaeologist.' Leaning forward, she looked animated. 'Wouldn't you love to be there? Making history and revealing it all at once?'

'I'd like to see Egypt,' Lydia said. 'The thought of buried treasure – all that gold and lapis lazuli – chariots and statuettes and goblets. That pharaoh nobody can pronounce. I read in my newspaper that Mr Carter and Lord Carnarvon said it was the first thing that hit them when they peered in: gold as far as the eye could see.'

Eleanor responded, though with a smile that saved her from sounding critical: 'Slaves building tombs for pharaohs then, and aristocrats disinterring them now, still ordering local peasants to do the hard work for them. I suppose that's progress. Less flogging, anyway.'

Frances laughed. 'She was like this at Cambridge,' she said to her sister. 'She's a fiery Amazon, always fighting for the rights of man. Well, woman, actually, on the whole.' She looked fondly at her friend. 'She's all of our consciences.'

'Not really.'

'*Yes*, really.'

A large portrait of a man in uniform caught Laurence's eye: Digby Easton almost certainly. The man was pictured sitting side-on in front of a window. The garden stretched out behind him. Easton already had a captain's pips. His boots shone, one hand, loosely holding leather gloves, lay on his crossed leg and the other held a riding crop. He seemed the picture of confidence, privilege and good health, with high colour and a clean-cut profile, yet when it was painted, he had, Laurence guessed, no more than a year to live. He looked around to see if there was a picture of Digby and Lydia's daughter, but could see none.

Noise from the hall interrupted his thoughts. A rumbling and a child's laughter preceded William Bolitho's entrance into the room with Nicholas at his side and a man who must almost certainly be Julian pushing the handles of William's wheelchair. An excited Jack Russell ran in circles around them. William broke into a broad smile.

'Very good to see you, old chap. You've obviously met Lydia and Frances and this is Julian.'

Julian Easton stretched out his hand over William's shoulder to take Laurence's. He had the look more of the countryman than of the gentry, though his gaze was intelligent and his grasp firm. Light-brown curls were just beginning to recede on his hairline and he had an odd puckered scar running along and under his jaw, but it didn't detract from his pleasant face.

'Welcome to Easton. You seem to have brought fine weather with you.'

Laurence had felt gnarled flesh as he shook Julian's hand and now he caught sight of both of the man's hands resting on the wheelchair. Julian wore a signet ring on his little finger, but he appeared to have been injured here too: there were stubs of flesh and old scar tissue showing pale against his tanned fingers. A war wound, Laurence imagined. The injury didn't seem to bother him.

'We've been all over the place,' Julian said, his eyes on Lydia. 'Now William's got the bit between his teeth, there's no stopping him. We've been up to the village, making sure the mortaring started while the weather's good.'

He turned back to Laurence. 'I hope you'll be comfortable. Do you have everything you want? I have to see David about the generator before dark, but feel free to wander about. Use my bicycle at any time – it's in the stables. Take a peek at St Barbara's.'

'The church was only reconsecrated fifty or so years ago,' Lydia said. 'The first service was the marriage of the boys' parents.'

She picked up a small silver frame from the mantelpiece; Frances took it from her and handed it to Eleanor. Laurence could swear Eleanor's mouth twitched in some private amusement as she passed it to him. A plain young woman in swathes of lace and pearls and with an alarmed expression was almost hidden behind her massive bouquet. Towering over her, her groom looked like the handsomest possible version of Julian.

'It will come as no surprise that Mama brought a sizeable dowry with her,' Julian said, cheerfully. 'My mother was actually a Catholic, but Papa certainly wasn't having any of it, and being so biddable, she was married in a Protestant ceremony. At twenty-six she was worried that no one would marry her at all but her charms appealed to Papa, given the family had nearly bankrupted themselves over the previous century rebuilding this pile after a fire. My father led her a merry dance. The handsomest man in Wiltshire, they used to say.'

'Actually you look very like him,' Frances said, and to Laurence's surprise Julian blushed slightly.

He seemed about to protest but Lydia said, 'Of course he does' and smiled at him, holding out a hand that Julian crossed the room to take. Then, after a pause as she set the picture back in place, she added, 'Kitty does too, especially around the eyes. Especially when she smiles.'

CHAPTER TWO

*J*ulian went off with his dog at his heels to find David.
Lydia, saying she had a headache, to lie down.

William, who back in London had seemed genial, relaxed, even bored in face of his disability, was now a man defined by his work and keen to get back to it.

'I have only until late summer this year, because Nicky goes back to school in the autumn and we have to return to London. Then I'm not back until the following spring.'

He made the comment lightly, but it reminded Laurence that wherever Eleanor needed to be, William had to be too.

'They've set aside a room – it used to be the gun room – for me to spread out in. Anyone else can come and go: workmen, family. It works perfectly. Why don't you come along after you've seen the church? Before dinner, say? The church has an electric light so you should be able to see a bit if it's dark in there. Meanwhile I'll make sure Nicholas isn't being too much of a nuisance in the kitchen. Eleanor will show you where to find me.'

Holding the rim of the wheels, William hauled his chair over the wooden floor on to the smooth stone of the passage.

Looking at him from behind, Laurence could see how strong his shoulder muscles were, even under his jacket, as they strained to propel the chair over the uneven wooden surface. Eleanor stayed behind.

'He prefers to move himself about when he can,' she said quietly to an unasked question. 'But at home, since you last saw us, he has this marvellous electric chair from Garroulds, though it turns out he's not as keen as we thought to go very far.'

She watched William until he disappeared. Then her face lightened.

'See, I told you you'd be out looking at the church before you'd even settled in.'

Frances glanced up from the tea trolley, where she was helping herself to fruit cake. 'Are you sure you really want to?'

'Actually, I'm intrigued by what William has told me. And how long have they had electricity? It's not William's doing?'

'Oh, we're thoroughly modern here,' Frances said, pointing upwards in the pose of a medieval saint revealing the abode of God.

He noticed that what he'd assumed was a central candlelit chandelier was an electrolier.

'Easton's had electricity since the end of the last century,' she said. 'Julian's father was very keen on novelty and his mama was a nervous woman, so she was all too willing to indulge the Colonel, once he'd persuaded her that many families perished horribly in fires caused by gas lighting or were suffocated by invisible fumes. Apparently Easton was one of the first houses anywhere to have it installed. The whole house runs on the power of water diverted from a tributary of the Kennet. It channels through the generator house – you can walk over and look tomorrow if you want, but it's only really a sort of cowshed with a cistern underneath – and that sends power down cables in iron pipes to the battery room in the house. And then it goes to the rooms. Don't ask me where it goes when the lights are off. I don't quite grasp it all. Julian and David understand the generator. They love it, care for it like a rare creature. And apparently the house isn't going to go up in some apocalyptic conflagration.'

Then she smiled.

'One incinerated Easton Hall might be unfortunate but twice in two centuries would look like divine criticism.'

'And the water from the cistern feeds to the lake?' Eleanor asked.

'Exactly. Everything is controlled by sluices. Utility is our byword here.' Frances laughed. 'But if Julian or David should ever leave us, we should slip back into the darkness and have to light our way with flaming faggots.'

'So even the church,' Eleanor said, 'is lit by mysterious power.' As he knew she would, she then added, 'I don't understand it either but as a former atheist my faith now lies in electricity.'

Frances shook her head slowly. 'One day you'll get into trouble,' she said, then grinned. 'In this world or the next. Anyway, you pop off to the church and I'll check on Lydia. She seems very tired today. I might come over in a while if I can find some shoes.'

She gave a mock wave.

'Enjoy yourselves. Don't freeze.'

With Eleanor at his side, Laurence went out along the terrace. It was a fine evening but getting chilly. Eleanor had picked up a knitted jacket, which she now belted around her.

'Let's sit down for a minute,' she said, 'before it gets really cold.'

She indicated an ornate bench. Two stone ammonites supported the stone seat and what looked like newts had been skilfully carved into the arms. Eleanor sat close to him and she stretched her legs out in front of her.

'It's beautiful here,' she said. 'So much space. So much peace. Even I can enjoy pretending nothing's changed or needs to change.' She looked down towards the distant lake. 'And with all that's going on, everyone's focused on something outside themselves. I was thinking over tea that everyone here has lost things, important things – even poor little Maggie is as good as an orphan, with her father dead in the war, her mother gone off with a fairground gypsy – and yet we don't feel like a gloomy crowd when we're together. Perhaps we're all going to be all right?'

'Lydia seemed—'

'Not at all right, you're going to say. No; although she has been awfully keen on the maze and the window, she's just not well. Not in spirit, inevitably, and not in body now. It's as if she's ageing all at once.'

'Like the woman in *King Solomon's Mines*?'

'It's *She*, the book you mean, actually,' Eleanor said, airily, but then gave him a mischievous smile.

'Does she often talk about her daughter like that? In the present tense?'

She nodded, more serious again. 'Yes. Lydia believes – she *knows* absolutely that Kitty is alive. Perhaps that's how she stayed sane all these years, why she's never left. But it's hard when you first hear her do it. And very hard to know what to say in return.' Her expression was rueful. 'You watch how everybody's eyes move away from her. Even Julian's.'

'Is she religious?'

Eleanor looked surprised. 'Why do you ask?'

'Well, she's wanting to add this window in the church, and her parents-in-law obviously were, as they went to all the trouble of restoring the place and applying for reconsecration.'

She laughed. 'None of the Eastons is, I think. Or possibly just Julian? But I gather Marianne Easton — Lydia's mother-in-law — was pretty devout. Even if forced by her husband out of the arms of the Pope and into those of the Church of England.' Her face took on an expression he had come to know well. 'I expect marriage to Colonel the Honourable George Easton gave her the opportunity to offer up her suffering. Anyway, I gather that the price of using her fortune — it was in soap — to put the estate back on its feet was to start with the place of worship. It was in the marriage settlement.'

'Lydia must have money too?'

'Not masses but quite a bit, I think, since her parents and aunt died. But it's only now she's really doing what she wants with it.'

'Her parents-in-law died a while back?'

'They've been dead for years,' she said casually. 'Poor Marianne Easton died when the boys were young. She was never well after having Patrick, apparently. All nerves. Some problem delivering the baby and he wasn't healthy. Fine brain, though, so they say. So at least that was saved from fertilising some French field. Marianne died when Patrick was a child.'

After a pause she said brightly, 'Old Colonel Easton's buried over there,' and nodded towards the churchyard.

'Was he very difficult?'

'Anything I know is through Frances and my guess is he was simply typical of his class.'

Laurence waited for Eleanor's prejudices to get to work on the late George Easton but she was surprisingly mild.

'I expect he was a not very clever, not very sensitive, rather spoiled English gentleman . . .'

She broke off as footsteps crunched on gravel. Frances was coming towards them, still in her Norfolk jacket, a bright-coloured scarf wound turban-like round her head. Laurence jumped to his feet.

'Lydia's fine,' Frances said. 'Anyway, I thought I'd join you after all.'

'We were talking about Lydia's parents-in-law,' said Eleanor. 'Was the old man still alive when Lydia came here?'

Frances nodded. 'Hunting was the old man's real love apparently. He kept trying to make Lydia ride and she hates horses. They make her wheeze. But when Kitty was born – I'm sure Eleanor's told you about poor Kitty – he became quite the doting grandfather. Got her a little pony, took her out on a leading rein. He died when she was only three or so.' She looked contemplative rather than sad. 'Kitty loved horses then, so perhaps she would have grown up to become a true Easton. It's hard to imagine; life at Easton was always so manly.'

'You say, "would have grown up"?'

Eleanor turned an anxious face towards Laurence but he returned a reassuring glance. Frances had brought up the topic of her niece as if she wanted it out in the open.

Frances looked at him but without surprise. 'You're asking me if I think she's alive?' She shook her head, very firmly. 'I'm not Lydia. After all these years, the prospects for poor little Kitty alive would terrify me more than accepting she's dead.' She pulled up her collar with an ungloved hand. 'It's getting cold.'

Getting up, she walked ahead of them through the lych-gate, past a few worn gravestones. The church was set back slightly from the line of the house; it looked very small against the elaborate solidity of the Hall.

It was substantially Saxon, he could see that straight away; squat with a short, square tower and runs of herringbone brickwork. The near wall showed the shape of a blocked-up arch. Two large old yew trees near the door reached as high as the gutters. Behind them the stone was rough cut and the few windows little more than slits.

He took two or three paces and then stopped in amazement by the entrance to the porch. He could feel himself smiling at the sight in front of him and he intercepted a look between the two women. They had all been careful not to tell him what he would find.

The curved archway almost seemed to move, covered as it was with creatures, both real and fantastic, as well as fruit, leaves and vines. He could make out a boar, a horse, a bear, a dragon and a griffon, a strange, spotted sort of cat and a pelican with its chicks gouging its own chest to feed them. There were two capering round-faced imps and, on either side, as capitals to slender columns, two fierce male faces gazed outwards, their hair curling into vegetation, leaves sprouting from their mouths. Not an inch of stonework was undecorated.

'Extraordinary,' he said. 'Absolutely wonderful.' He moved back a couple of paces and pointed. 'Green men. There's a whole medieval bestiary here. And yet I've never heard of this church.' Even in his delight he was puzzled. 'There's something like it, I think, on the Welsh borders but ...' He looked at Frances. 'It's a real treasure. Unique.'

Gazing at the forest of pagan creatures, he understood why William was so keen for him to see the church.

They pushed open the heavy door and came into a space still just lit by daylight. After the external arch, it was a disappointment. The Victorian additions William had mentioned were all too obvious. They dominated the church: a heavy Victorian Gothic pulpit and lectern, some highly varnished pews and, in rich blues, golds and reds, a stained glass window of a penitent Magdalene with her rather masculine jaw and extraordinary waves of luxuriant red hair protecting her modesty. Her rich light threw a crimson wash over the white walls and stone floor.

He gazed around; there were only two other, very simply

coloured windows. The west window was just a chequerboard of pale blues and yellows, and to the side, near an octagonal font, was a small glass bearing the Easton coat of arms. A framed painting behind the altar showed another female saint, standing by a tall tower, sparks fizzing between her feet, her face peaceful despite the lightning that crackled in the black clouds above her. It was the church's patron saint, St Barbara, he realised after a second, and it was the only time he had ever seen her in an English church.

He looked down. The floor had a strange, thick black surface, with patches of decay. A few inches around the edge, the material was in the process of being stripped away, presumably the work William had temporarily interrupted to get Laurence's opinion. He took out his penknife and stuck the blade in a short distance, then pressed it with his finger. It was some sort of bitumen. Where the surface had been removed, parts of a few slender rectangular tiles in white and black had been exposed in an unusual woven pattern. The tarry application might have been a cheap way of covering damaged paving but it would probably be worth removing; it was not in good condition and to strip it away would be more labour- than cost-intensive. If necessary they could replace the cracked stones beneath. Whatever the result it would look less gloomy than the present surface.

'Where is the memorial window going?' he said to Frances.

'It's replacing the chequered window at the back.'

Frances indicated the large west window. Afternoon light shone obliquely through it.

'William's sketched out an idea,' said Eleanor. 'It's extraordinarily good. Beautiful. Very different. Possibly the best thing he's ever done. I hope you'll go and see it.' Then after a pause she added, 'He still needs reassurance after not working for so long.'

He remembered visiting the Bolithos in London for the first time and how struck he had been by the startling modern art in the room. He wished William's own tastes would prevail here, so that hope in the face of immense loss and the terrors of the unknown might be represented in something abstract and mysterious. The window faced west, so the memories embodied in it would always be illuminated by the setting sun.

CHAPTER THREE

When Laurence returned to the house, Eleanor directed
him to William's makeshift office beyond the butler's
pantry. The old brick floor was worn smooth and William
seemed able to manoeuvre around it with ease.

William's delight at Laurence's reaction to the porch of St
Barbara's was tangible. 'It's breathtaking, isn't it? Gloriously
pagan. I was determined to drag you down here without letting
on. I've found no record of it but I'm limited to the library here
of course.'

He spun his chair and pointed to a large plan of the village
pinned on the wall.

'And now to the mundane. These are the cottages we're working on. No repairs since the last century. No running water.
Outdoor wells, earth closets. Even the old vicarage,' and he waved
a snooker cue to indicate a larger property in its own garden
standing back from the others, 'was frozen – and I use the word
aptly – in the 1850s. Little wonder they couldn't find a new
incumbent. It's completely derelict now, though it must have
been quite a fine building. Elsewhere, some decaying thatch.

We've had to wait for a thatcher and his lad from Avebury. Generally: well, glad as I am to be here, nothing really needs an architect — a good foreman could see to it. Severe damp mostly. Rotten timbers. There was one place in one of the cottages where we might have had a lethal accident any minute. We lifted worm-eaten boards at the foot of the stair to find a deep well. Nobody had known about it. The two little boys there were given to jumping from halfway up the stairs to the ground. They could have gone through any minute. We blocked it up. There was a nasty moment when they hauled out some bones. Julian was ashen — and we never told Lydia. But they were identified as the remains of a dog.'

Laurence nodded. 'The well wasn't found in the search, then?'

'I'm sorry?'

'For the child? For Kitty Easton before the war? They didn't discover the well then?'

'Evidently not.' William sat back in his chair and shook his head. 'You know, everybody talks of what a thorough search it was — with lakes drained, ponds and rivers dragged, every barn and outhouse scoured. Melancholy business. But for all that, they will have overlooked as many places as they explored.'

He appeared to be considering his own words even as he spoke.

'The child — what's left of her, if anything — might not be very far away at all. Easton — the house, the village, the surrounding land — is full of forgotten corners. I've seen some even without leaving this chair. Disused buildings. Sealed spaces. Water. The well we revealed was just one of them.'

He gestured to the other side of the room where three maps, apparently of different ages, had been pinned up.

'The plans are pretty rudimentary. I can tell you that any excavation here carries its own grim dramas.'

Laurence said, 'Is Julian aware of the possibilities?'

'All too aware, I think, though in some ways I suspect finding her now would be a relief for him.'

Laurence could understand that. He wondered whether the shadow of Kitty Easton would ever lift while the current occupants of Easton were alive. They might have stood a chance if a body had ever been found, but her unknown fate prompted constant speculation. He had been guilty of it himself since he first heard of her disappearance.

Suddenly William leaned forward, eagerly. 'Enough of that. Now for the symbol of restoration. The maze. A little mystery, a small challenge, a need to engage the mind as well as the eye, is as good a thing in gardens as it is in architecture. Or, indeed, in women.'

His face looked almost boyish. Laurence laughed in contemplation of the challenging but unmysterious Eleanor.

'I mean, I know you will have seen it but this is the thinking behind it.'

William flung back a baize cover with a magician's flourish, to reveal two drawings. The largest was a plan of the house and garden. Paths, terraces and kitchen garden were all drawn to scale. Between the rear terrace lawn and the ha-ha was the new maze, geometric and drawn in dark pencil. A second, straight-on view had been done as if the viewer were standing on the far side of the ha-ha in years to come. The maze flourished, with Easton Hall in the background beneath a summer sky with small clouds. Flowering shrubs bloomed along a path leading to the arched maze entrance. Two marble statues, carrying urns, marked the way in.

'Naiads,' said William. 'Water nymphs, given that the power for the house and the beauty of the gardens all come from water. They symbolise the meeting of old and new.'

'Marvellous,' Laurence said.

William's drawings were pretty but he was fascinated by the diagram of the maze itself and found himself wanting to follow its sinuous lines with a finger.

'Well, none of us here will live to see the maze as mature as I've drawn it here. But it's a bit of encouragement ... for Lydia mostly.'

'How long ...?'

'Fifty years. Certainly it will take that long until the walls become impenetrable. But if all the plants take, it should look fairly substantial in ten to fifteen. It needs a lot of watering. By the time the fatherless children of Easton are old, they should be looking at a fine memorial. By the start of the next century, it may be a fact of life and nobody will remember the events that inspired its commission. But even now the intention is clear.'

William laughed.

'Foolish, really. Immortality in a well-pruned hedge.'

He backed his chair away.

'Before the war I designed buildings. Small buildings mostly. I was, as I believed then, right at the start of my career, which I fully expected to be a triumph.' He beamed. 'Or I would be asked to tackle tiny details on some important project. As a student I worked under C.W. Stephens on Harrods – my bit is the skylight over the staff tea room. But this feels different, a collaboration between me and nature.'

He was watching Laurence to see whether he understood.

'And not just because it is *something*, frankly. It's come after years of doing nothing, with Eleanor and me both pretending that I would work again, because the second we conceded I might not was the moment we would condemn ourselves to a narrow life in a few tiny rooms – a cripple with no legs and the cripple's nurse, not the promising architect and his wife the bluestocking fighter for political change.' He paused, looked away. 'Now, with this: escape.'

'This is going to be a long project?' Laurence said, with an awkwardly overemphasised sweep of his arm to embrace the plans and the lists, knowing he had cut William off. They had been young officers in the same war, the same area of France. They had both survived, which was more than many had done, but, apart from a bad back, all Laurence's wounds had been to his mind; he could walk into the future when he was ready. William's life, and Eleanor's, had been irrevocably changed and diminished by events.

William remained silent, sucking at his pipe. Small sounds seeped into Laurence's consciousness: the rattle of waterpipes, a dog barking, right at the edge of audible sound. Someone walking about on an upper floor and coming downstairs. Laurence smelled soap and steam near by. Someone, Maggie or the cook Mrs Hill perhaps, was doing the washing. The footsteps drew nearer. William looked up just as Eleanor looked round the door.

'Hello. Is this strictly a chaps' conversation or can anyone join?'

William's face lit up. 'Gardening, actually, we're on to gardening.'

As Eleanor came through the door, Frances followed her. Eleanor smiled, 'I love this room,' she said. 'It feels properly old.'

'It has the original floor, I think,' Frances said. 'But I like it much better now it hasn't got all Digby's guns.'

Laurence was surprised that he hadn't noticed that the small part of the room not covered in drawings and maps held empty gun racks. Only two guns were left, high up, both old Purdeys.

'Julian's,' Frances said, following his gaze. 'He inherited them from Digby. He rarely shoots now and there's no keeper any more, though David takes the fatherless Kilminster boys out for rooks and rabbits for the pot. He's an amazing shot, the boys say. Julian never enjoyed shooting. Country sports were Digby's passion. Patrick's too when he was young. But Julian says his hands were always a bit stiff from the scars.'

'His war wounds?' Laurence said.

Frances looked slightly embarrassed. 'The scar on his neck was from the war, but not those on his hands. Julian had the so-called Easton fingers. Kitty did too.'

Laurence was lost. 'I'm sorry?'

'He was born with an extra finger on each hand. His father removed Julian's. He said it was no different to docking a puppy's tail. But apparently it was awful. Digby once told us Julian screamed and screamed and one hand went septic.'

'Do you mean that he did this with no anaesthetic?' Eleanor said, looking appalled. 'On his own child? What a vicious man.'

William made a face. 'Unbelievably barbaric.'

'Lydia absolutely refused to have Kitty operated upon,' Frances said, 'even by a doctor. She thought the idea of mutilating her child was much more monstrous than two tiny extra fingers.'

Eleanor still looked shocked. 'Little Tich, the music-hall man, has extra fingers,' she said. 'It's far from unknown. And it often runs in families. It's possible Patrick's heart trouble has the same origin,' she added. 'They're sometimes connected.'

'Then Julian got off best, I suppose,' Frances said.

Eleanor nodded, but Laurence thought that Julian's scars had accompanied him to the battlefields of France, whereas Patrick's problem had seen him honourably kept out of harm's way.

William cleared his throat and gestured to his plan with his unlit pipe.

'Laurence wanted to know what we'd planted. Or at least I wanted to tell him.'

'Yew,' Frances said. 'We put in thousands last November. Millions, it seemed like,' she said, clearly happy to move away from the Eastons' childhood.

William looked cheerful. 'We laid out the design with pegs and string, then everybody set to: David, Walter Petch – that's Maggie's grandfather, Ellen Kilminster, her lads, Mr Hill and even Maggie helped. And Frances, of course.'

'Bluestockings, green fingers,' Eleanor said, tucking her arm in her friend's.

'Yew is the right choice here, I think,' William said. 'There are the two splendid and ancient ones in the churchyard so we know it can prosper in this soil. It's the plant of resurrection too, of course, although I'm keen that the maze shouldn't be a sad place. Entering it should be more in the spirit of hide-and-seek. It's for children or lovers, with voices heard but not seen.'

'That seems very jolly,' Laurence said, in an attempt to cover up his own instinctive aversion to entering any maze, 'and a link with the druids, or whatever went on in these parts.'

Eleanor gave him a cool look. 'All Victorian make-believe,' she said.

'Actually the early communities here were undoubtedly pagan,' William said. 'They may have worshipped the sun, or horses, or mistletoe, but very few societies don't worship something. Ask Patrick when he comes. He's bound to know.'

Frances bent over the plan.

'It's likely there was an earlier maze at Easton Deadall.' She looked up at Laurence. 'There've always been stories of the Easton Deadall maze. People getting lost for ever. Digby swore there'd been one originally.'

'From before the war?'

'Much longer ago than that. Some prints of the old house show it. William's seen one ...'

William said, 'It's visible only in two very early sixteenth-century prints. In all later ones it's gone. It's hard to see quite how it was or where it was.'

He spun his chair around, niftily avoiding both women.

'There's a copy here somewhere.' He started moving a pile of papers on a long wooden dresser. 'Its scale is wrong for its depicted position but we're talking about very old draughtsmanship. It might not have been a maze like ours — it could have been a parterre or a knot garden, of course, so the walker could see where they were going.'

Finally he pulled out a small print and pushed himself back to the table.

As he laid it down, Laurence leaned forward. It was the first time he had ever seen the old Easton Hall. It looked Tudor or earlier, and it was smaller than he'd imagined.

'Perhaps the old maze was burned down in the house fire?'

'Possibly, or it simply went out of fashion. Or it was neglected and ran amok. Or the plants caught a disease. Who knows? But I like to think I may be following an old tradition connected with the house.'

'Did you take your design from this?'

'No. I liked the idea but when I looked closer, I saw it wasn't realistic in its proportions and as far as I could see it couldn't work. It was extraordinarily complicated: all the paths appeared to be dead ends. It was basically an island maze—'

'An island maze?'

'One that has several paths to the centre and islands within it. It's the hardest sort to navigate. I didn't want visitors to my maze to get lost. I didn't want anybody to be afraid.'

'I always found Digby's stories rather beastly,' Frances said. 'Julian pooh-poohs them, says nobody could get truly lost inside a hedge as they could shout and be heard, or break their way out, or, in his case, use a pocket knife. Which he, as a man, carries at all times of course.'

Laurence slid his hand deep in his pocket and felt the small knife he had always kept with him since he had been given it as a boy.

'When Lydia first came up with the idea,' Frances was saying, 'I really wished she wouldn't. Why not restock the rose garden or build a fountain or something? Heaven knows there's enough water round here.' She looked appeasingly at William. 'Now, of course, I can see the new maze isn't a trap, it's just . . . a game.'

'It's still about disorientation, I think,' Eleanor said. 'You change direction so much you become dizzy, your head spins, so although the sky is above you and you aren't shut in, you get muddled and in some people that leads to panic. And the paths can be quite narrow. And then, finally — escape. Euphoria!'

As she spoke, Laurence was recalling the twists and turns of trenches: some newly dug raw earth, some with explosives set to destroy any intruder, some stinking with the rotting corpses of men and horses, or simply lethally deep in water and mud. He didn't think anyone would have chosen a maze as a memorial, whatever its long association with Easton Hall, had they served in the infantry.

'Julian says that nobody's ever found a skeleton at the centre of a garden maze any more than they've found a dead cat up a tree,' Frances said. 'Though actually he wasn't that keen at first. But Lydia had her imagination piqued by the old maze pictures and because Digby had this fancy there'd been one. Julian always wants her to be happy.'

'My maze is a branching maze,' William said, his eyes on Laurence. He, too, had remembered France, Laurence thought. They had first met when investigating the post-war death of a friend who during the war had been trapped in a collapsed tunnel where the other soldiers had died slowly of suffocation.

'And that's why. It's not like an island maze; you can't get lost. Well, not if you stick to simple rules.'

Eleanor smiled. Laurence sensed she had heard it all before, but Frances was leaning forward, listening intently.

'A branching maze would be like a tree if you unrolled its curves,' William continued. 'And I like that too – another symbol of new growth. But there's a simple trick to finding your way in. You put out your right hand and keep it on a maze wall, turning right when paths lead off. That way, you come to the heart of the maze, and you can sit there peacefully – because there'll be a bench in the shade – knowing you can just do the whole thing in reverse to walk out.'

'So if you keep a calm head, you can just stroll along, sit in this leafy bower and stroll out again?' Eleanor said.

William nodded.

Frances said, 'I feel I have a stake in this maze, anyway. I check my treelets quite often but they aren't showing much sign of ambition yet.'

Laurence was wondering how they'd even got started with William scarcely mobile and such precise geometry at stake, when William answered the unspoken question.

'David was invaluable,' he said. 'He's got an extraordinarily good eye. It would have been impossible without someone like him to be my legs, as it were. The others helped, but he was at the centre of it all. He took my drawings, understood the measurements, then laid the pattern out in string and it worked, with very few adjustments. Maggie tried it out – walking through it. I watched like a stern overseer.'

Laurence glanced down at the design. The path was two feet wide, too narrow for a man to negotiate in a wheelchair. Was this just adhering to conventional measurements or had William no desire to enter his own maze?

'I first came here last summer,' William said. 'I'd done a bit of research on labyrinths and mazes. I knew a couple – Hampton Court, obviously. The Stanhopes' one at Chevening. Before the war I'd actually seen the wonderful stone labyrinth in Chartres cathedral. I was always fascinated by them but they were completely out of fashion in gardens and rare within architectural design. I spoke to a man at Kew, who said several more mazes may have been destroyed or lost in the war. They need shaping, feeding, upkeep. Manpower.' He looked around. 'Frankly, that may be a problem here. We have to hope adult men will eventually live again at Easton Deadall and care for it.'

'Labyrinth?' Frances said. 'Is there a difference between a maze and a labyrinth? What's at Chartres? Are labyrinths enclosed while mazes are open to the sky?'

'In churches, usually it's a labyrinth. Just a pattern on the floor or wall, no raised boundaries,' Laurence said. 'Chartres is very old – twelfth century or thereabouts – but there were others in important churches. They must have been quite common once.'

William was nodding. He must have known as much about Chartres as Laurence did.

'See,' he said, 'you're already earning your keep in matters ecclesiastical.' He smiled in pleasure.

Laurence waited for William to take over but when his friend remained silent, he said, 'A labyrinth isn't meant as a puzzle: it's a journey, a conduit. You enter it and you move along to its end. Perhaps the idea was to slow the walker down, to allow spiritual reflection, but the outcome is in no doubt.'

'Patrick will have something to add, I expect,' Frances said thoughtfully. 'In Crete they found some kind of maze. It seems to fit the legend of King Minos. It's possible it's actually the place where the monstrous Minotaur was fed on young Cretan men and girls.' She paused, looking ruefully at William. 'Not that that's quite the association you're after, of course.'

'The very maze of ancient myths,' Eleanor said drily. 'How convenient for the archaeologists that it should be right there.' But she took her friend's arm and squeezed it. 'Come on, let's go and find Nicholas. William, do you want to change for dinner?'

'I'll be along in half an hour.'

When the women had gone, William lit his pipe. Laurence had noticed before how Eleanor made William both more relaxed and more alive.

'I ought to go,' he said.

'Of course.' Laurence started to rise to his feet.

'But while you're here, perhaps you'd like to see the design for the window in the church. You'll need to use your imagination – it relies upon light, and changing light at that. I'm no expert. But I've had long exchanges with a man who will actually put it together and I've told him to be as critical as he likes. Don't worry if you can't see anything in it,' he said. 'It's quite a modern concept.'

Laurence recalled again the pictures, in abstract blocks of colour and line, in William's rooms in London.

The design for the memorial window lay on a table by the window. It was a surprise, but Laurence had expected to be surprised. Darker lines indicating the lead contained planes and rectangles, with each segment marked 'yellow', 'red', 'white' or 'gold'. Over it all was a delicate tracery of what would presumably be incised patterns.

'The fine lines are etched with silver nitrate,' William said, his finger moving gently across the paper.

In the centre was a lozenge containing entwined initials: Laurence could identify the D of Digby Easton. From the shield, rays shot outwards, shattering into shards of light, with the effect

40

of a starburst. In each corner was incised a fragment of Easton: a meandering stream, a standing stone, a galloping horse and, a master stroke, he thought, a tiny version of William's new maze. The border was a slender column of flowers, birds and insects, echoing the spirit of the carvings on the church porch. Several of the tendrils here were initials, each, he guessed, one of the fallen. In pencil, it was beautiful; in illuminated glass, he thought the effect would be stunning. For a second he was too moved to speak.

William was looking at him intently.

'It's extraordinary,' Laurence said, relieved that it was so good and that he didn't have to dissemble. 'It's so full of life and grace and detail. Not at all sombre.' He looked at his friend, shaking his head. 'I don't know what to say. Brilliant hardly covers it. What does Lydia think?'

'She feels as you do, I believe,' William said with animation. 'She said she wanted something true to Digby, because it's first and foremost dedicated to him. I never knew him, of course, but he sounds like a man with a certain vigour for life. I hoped this might carry that spirit.'

Laurence weighed his next words carefully.

'Depending on the colours you choose, the red and gold,' he pointed to William's tidy writing, 'it's also going to feel quite ... explosive.'

William nodded, looking pleased. 'I'm so glad you saw that. It's not easy to look at a pencil drawing and imagine height and changing colour and light. But I intended there to be movement, even violence, at the core of it; I wanted it to carry a truth as well as beauty.'

Laurence had a sudden sense of what William had lost in the terrible catastrophe of his war. What kind of visionary architect might he have been if he had remained whole-bodied?

'I didn't want it to offend her or, worse, hurt her,' William went on, 'but it's not just that the volatile energy hints at how these men died. It's also a nod to the church itself: St Barbara.'

'I think it's the first St Barbara I've seen in England,' Laurence said, 'although I looked it up and there are three others: a newish one near Coventry, one in Worcestershire and one in Lincolnshire.'

'She's more common in the orthodox Church,' William said, 'or so I'm told.'

'And in Catholic churches,' Laurence said. 'There's one in Rome. She's the patron saint of explosives and lightning and, indeed, violent death, which you obviously know.'

William said, 'So, you see, it all connects, which is satisfying. People who look at the window might just see pretty images or they might think they understand its deeper associations – it doesn't matter. They'll be there.'

Laurence understood William's contentment. Easton had its dark past and its sorrows, but now perhaps goodwill and hope were being rebuilt.

William tapped his pipe, looked at the bowl doubtfully and took out some more tobacco.

'For those who believe in such things it's also a plea to St Barbara to keep us safe from any more disasters. I wouldn't suggest that to Eleanor, or she'd have me locked up.'

Laurence smiled.

'She'd think it was the most appalling superstition,' William said. 'She's already explained to me that Barbara was simply a manifestation of the heathen god Nertha or Thor the god of storms. A desperate fantasy constructed by oppressed and starving peasants. So I've rather blurred that bit in discussing it with her.'

He clamped his teeth round the stem of his pipe and somehow managed to smile.

'But, extraordinarily, she also turns out to be the patron saint of architects.'

CHAPTER FOUR

The next day, on his way through the rear of the hall and through the green-baize door to find William after lunch, Laurence had stopped to look at a framed photograph on the wall. It showed the servants at the end of the previous century, when there were at least fifteen of them. Now, as far as he could tell, there were no live-in staff. Maggie and Mrs Hill seemed to be up at the Hall most of the time. David, with the help of Maggie's grandfather, apparently took care of the house and garden, and acted as chauffeur if necessary. Certainly the Hall was no longer the grand establishment it once was.

On most days, Frances had explained, Mrs Hill just left out a plate of cold mutton or beef for luncheon, with pickled beetroot, eggs and pickled onions for anyone who wanted them. Today, although six places were laid, Laurence was alone in the dining room. Eleanor had taken a picnic and gone off with Nicholas to fish for tiddlers with a jam jar.

When he joined William in his office, William greeted Laurence with a broad smile while doing a calculation on paper. As he put down his pencil to speak, they heard footsteps approaching. Julian was preceded by Scout, bounding in and jumping up at Laurence. Julian wore what looked like old riding breeches and his socks and shoes were muddy. Even the elbow patches on his shapeless Norfolk jacket were coming adrift. Restraining Scout, he felt in his pocket for a dog biscuit, which Scout took from his hand.

'Lydia's not well at all,' Julian said, quite gruffly as if he was speaking to the dog, but looking up at Laurence and William. 'Just came to see if you chaps were getting on all right. I've been with David, checking the sluices.' Now his face lightened. 'When I was a boy I used to go and watch the miller upstream from here, clearing the wheel and the cogs. It would have been done like that for centuries. It used to fascinate me, seeing the water kept back and then the power of it teeming through the gates when he'd finished. We used to send corn to be ground there. Now we're using an almost identical system of sluices and wheels to make electricity.' He seemed to find this as astonishing as the millstream had once been.

'Pull up a chair,' William said. 'I'm only working out some costs for timber.'

Julian remained standing, shifting a little from foot to foot. He was a good man, Laurence thought, and an intelligent one, but awkward. He suspected he was far happier doing practical jobs than making conversation.

As if to bear him out, Julian started to speak, then stopped, narrowing his eyes as if concentrating.

'I'm driving to Marlborough any minute with Frances and your wife and Nicholas, for paint and Lydia's medicine. The boy's keen to go for a ride in the motor car.'

He thrust his hands in his pockets. The dog looked at him hopefully.

'It's Kitty.' He rubbed the scar on his jaw as if it irritated him. 'I've been thinking, since that well turned up in the end cottage.'

William nodded but said nothing.

'She was only little,' Julian said. 'We looked everywhere. But it's not impossible if you're clearing stuff or lifting floors ...'

William exchanged a brief look with Laurence before speaking.

'It was a very long time ago,' he said. 'Not that it probably feels like that for you—'

He was interrupted by Julian. 'The thing I can't let go of is that she is *somewhere*. She wasn't just magicked away. She was a real child.' His voice was carefully controlled but the look he gave them was of pure bewilderment. 'Either she wandered away or someone took her. Either she's dead or she's alive. Either she is still in Easton or she's not.'

'Even if she were once here, there might not be anything to find,' Laurence said, quickly. He knew how fast bodies broke down in certain conditions, especially if they had been injured before death.

'But if you should find anything, not Kitty necessarily—' His hand went down to the dog. 'Anything a bit queer. I need to be the first to know. Think what to do.'

'There was never any clue, though?' William said. 'No rumours? No reason to think she never left here? Nothing said to the police?'

'Things were different then. Local people might well have kept their mouths shut. Back then, estate business was kept on the estate. There were one or two who muttered that the effort wouldn't have been made for a cottager's child, one or two who thought the police were hard on Jane Rivers, the nanny, a local girl. Maybe some foolish talk that Lydia was a foreigner. And Frances too. But it was between themselves. They weren't keen on talking to strangers.'

Laurence's gaze went to Julian's disfigured hands, one finger nervously tracing the damaged flesh as it must have done countless times.

William moved slightly and his chair creaked. The dog panted, her eyes watching her master. Laurence noticed for the first time that it was cold on this side of the house. Out in the yard stood the car that David had driven to fetch him from the station, obviously newly polished. A pony trap stood upended against a side wall. As far as he knew, no horses were kept now.

The dog barked sharply. They glanced up to see Frances in the doorway, holding a tray. Julian seemed embarrassed.

'You all look as guilty as sin,' Frances said airily. 'I've obviously stumbled on a nest of plotters. But Mrs Hill insists you need tea and Lydia has sent me to fetch Julian.'

'Of course, of course.' Julian clicked his fingers for Scout to follow him, but his eyes were almost pleading with them.

'We'll take care,' William said to him. Frances raised an eyebrow at Laurence as she went out.

When Julian and Frances were out of earshot, William spun his chair over to the battered dresser and pulled out a drawer. Leaning over the arms of his chair, he reached down with a practised arm and pulled out a silver flask, which he held up to Laurence.

'A mind sharpener,' he said. He tipped the liquid into Laurence's tea and then, more generously, into his own. 'Irish forebears,' he said.

His face was suddenly serious.

'Given that Lydia's clearly not strong, would Julian tell her if Kitty's fate did come to light?' He picked up his cup and drank. 'Would it help, when she's survived so long by believing the child's alive, to find a few pitiful bones? Possibly it would help, perhaps she'd like to bury her properly, but it depends on the circumstances. Anything that suggested she'd been trapped would be unendurable. If it were Nicholas, I think I'd go mad.'

The first sip of tea almost made Laurence gag and he swallowed hastily.

'I thought at first as he was talking that Julian was desperate to know,' he said, 'though it seems a hell of a long time to still be wanting – or expecting – an answer.' He reflected on the intensity of Julian's request. 'But then he didn't actually say that. I think it's more that he genuinely believes we might find her and was warning us. And that he's scared of that happening.'

'Because of the effect on Lydia?'

'Possibly.' Then Laurence added, 'Do you think he wants clarification? So the estate can be properly his?'

'Easton?' William said. 'I think it's hardly entered his head. Unless he's uncommonly disingenuous and I don't believe for a minute that he is. In fact, I suspect he didn't even realise it might look like that to us. He's not stupid but until just now I wouldn't have said he was a complicated man. He simply tries to do the right thing.'

Laurence nodded. 'Do you think she's dead?'

William shrugged. 'What's the alternative?' Then he said slowly, 'I saw a painting once. Well, a print. My nanny had it in her room. It used to terrify me. A gypsy family stripping the clothes off a wealthy child they'd abducted. Would someone steal a child for profit?'

'How would they chance on Kitty Easton? A child who lived deep within a rural estate?' Laurence said.

William's idea was the most appealing of the options, largely because it left her alive, but it was also far the least likely.

'And it would hardly be a spur-of-the-moment thing. How would they get her away? Or, indeed, if they killed her, dispose of the evidence?'

47

'A grudge, then?'

'A child isn't a pet mouse. It needs care, concealment. If it was a grudge, then her chances weren't good from the start. And she was old enough to tell someone where she lived, surely? And what her name was?'

'Yes, I suppose so,' William said. 'If she was killed here, then it had to be somebody local. Somebody who already knew of a place where they could hide her body.'

'But a place that other people didn't know about ...'

The sound of footsteps echoed down the stone corridor. Their eyes turned to the door. It was Eleanor.

'We've probably emptied the Kennet of tiddlers. I've dissuaded Nicholas from having them fried for high tea.' She regarded them with mock suspicion. 'What are you two actually up to?'

William looked amused. 'Up to?'

'Laurie? My husband may be happy to blur the line between truth and fiction but I'm sure you'll tell me?'

She perched on the end of the table, gingerly moving one of William's plans to the side, with an ominous air of having settled.

'God damn it,' William said with affection. 'You see what I have to put up with? A woman who can read my mind? Who would hang a man on a thought?'

'Actually I wouldn't hang anybody. It's inhumane. It's corrupting. It's just vengeance ...'

William raised his hands in the air in mock surrender. 'See, here I am, a poor cripple, and a sitting duck for political lectures.'

Eleanor went over to him and kissed him on the forehead, then assumed a villainous face and a vaguely foreign accent. 'But ven the day comes you vill do vat you know to be right, my darlink. Anyway I'm off to Marlborough.'

She gave a theatrical wave goodbye, then suddenly spun around.

'Still, you smell of whisky. And in the middle of the day. Tut tut. Tell me if it's all going to be downhill from now on.'

William laughed. Laurence thought how lucky they were, despite everything. Outside in the sunshine once more, Eleanor pressed her face up against the window and made a face before walking away. She was in such good spirits these days. The country life seemed to suit her and company, of course. Was it difficult at home, with just her and William and Nicholas and their restricted life? Was she lonely?

He turned back to look at the house plan again.

'So Kitty slept here,' he guessed, pointing to the bedroom nearest the one labelled 'Nanny' in the east wing. 'Nursery, bedroom, nanny, nursemaid's room, schoolroom. All in a row.'

'I imagine so.' William was next to him. 'So from there she left the house by either the front or the back stairs.'

'The back, I imagine,' Laurence said. 'Much nearer.'

'You are probably right, except . . .' William stroked his moustache. 'If she simply woke up and wandered off, she might be more likely to try to find her mother.'

Laurence was about to agree when William said, 'Except personally I much preferred my nanny to my mother.' He smiled. 'But then I was the fourth child of six – five boys and my sister, Lilias, and I think the novelty of motherhood had worn off by the time I arrived. My mother longed to be an artist and was rather perplexed by all these children around the place.'

'Is she still—?'

'Yes. Seventy-two. Indomitable. I think I went up in her estimation when I captured Eleanor. Military heroics rather passed her by but she was a great one for the modern woman.'

'And your father?'

'We lost him a few years ago,' William said, more sombrely. 'My eldest brother was gassed at Ypres. Died, rather slowly, in

49

a convalescent home at Hastings not long before you met us. Bad year. My father had always suffered from bouts of melancholia. He never really got over losing his first-born and went into a decline. Set out walking one January day, fell through the ice on a nearby pond and drowned. The rest of us all made it through. Well, the youngest, Gordon, was still at Harrow, but it had never seemed to console my father.'

'I'm sorry.'

'My mother seems to have an easier time of it without him. She has a gallery near Berkeley Square.'

Then, more briskly, he returned to the plans in front of him, waving away the smoke from his pipe.

'Once she was downstairs, there were any number of ways Kitty could have left the house.' He tapped the various entrances and french windows. 'She could even have been bundled out by a window.'

'I assume the doors were locked?'

'Julian's certainly a stickler for it now.'

They both looked up as David opened the back door and smiled tentatively.

'Ah, forgot the time,' William said. 'We're going to check the maze.'

David seemed relaxed as he stepped behind William and moved to manoeuvre the chair over the step. 'The yew's shoot-ing up. We've lost only four plants,' he said, 'and a couple of maybes. I reckon by the time my little one can walk, there'll be a proper hedge there. I wish my ma could have seen it.'

'Was she from West Overton? Isn't that where you come from?' William asked.

'Born, bred and buried,' David said. 'Never even been to Swindon – and proud of it.' He laughed.

'She must have missed you when you went to London.'

'It would've broken her heart or had her take me for a lunatic, but she was dead before then. Perhaps that's why I went. It took a war to make me see I'd been a lunatic to leave.'

Laurence remained behind, looking at the plans stuck to the wall. The two men were still chatting easily as David rolled the chair unevenly across the stable yard. A dog, presumably Scout, barked in the garden. Somewhere in the house there was the muffled squeak of a sash being raised.

He thought that while he was alone he would go over to the church and make a more serious assessment of it. Going up to his room, he fetched his torch, measure, compass and a small notebook, and stuffed them in his pocket. As he came downstairs he found a man standing in the hall, holding his hat in his hand and looking around as if trying to recognise where he was. A battered leather case stood by his side. In the split second before the stranger realised he wasn't alone, a certain wariness crept over his face. Even though the man was unknown to him, his expression was one that Laurence had seen before.

He went over to the stranger with his hand out.

'Laurence Bartram,' he said.

The stranger smiled and his face was transformed. 'Patrick Easton,' he said, shaking Laurence's hand warmly. 'Which you may have guessed.'

'I'm awfully sorry,' Laurence said. 'I think everybody was expecting you this evening. Lydia's resting. The others are on some jaunt to Marlborough.'

Patrick looked amused. 'I am much earlier than I said I'd be. Actually it's rather good to make my entrance undeclared. If we could rustle up some tea I'd actually treasure a rest. It may be a lovely day here but the crossing was rough yesterday and the car I've borrowed was rougher still.'

'I think Maggie's gone home,' Laurence said, 'but I'll go and sort out some tea. Why don't you sit in the library?' Then he added, 'It feels rather strange to be inviting you to relax in your own home.'

'It's not my home,' Patrick said. 'It was never mine, Mr Bartram. But I'll tell you what, I'll leave my case here, then come and play kitchen maids with you in the scullery.'

Rather to Laurence's relief, tea turned out to be a complicated process which did away with the demand for instant conversation. Vast kitchen cupboards contained fish kettles, huge jelly moulds and silver chafing dishes — a culinary armoury from times long past — but failed to reveal any china suitable for a simple tea. Between them they eventually unearthed an ancient teapot, black with tannin inside, two delicate but chipped cups and saucers and, under a beaded muslin in the larder, a large jug which held what Laurence hoped was fresh milk. As they brought the rather battered tray into the library, Laurence looked out; he could just see William and David moving out of sight at the far end of the maze. He thought David was laughing.

Patrick shivered theatrically, although he still had a thick woollen scarf wound around his neck. He moved to the fireplace, which was laid for the evening, kneeled down and took some matches out of his pocket. Laurence watched him light the paper spills.

Later, Laurence came to think of Patrick's default expression as sardonic and often challenging, possibly defensively so, but his first impression was that there was something ascetic about him. He looked like a man who did not eat enough — his cheeks were hollow, his shoulders slightly stooped, his skin sallow. Patrick's hands, long fingered and tanned by the sun, seemed incongruous when holding a small teacup decorated with yellow roses. As he sat, his eyes moved perpetually, apparently taking in the room. His gaze stopped at the portrait of a uniformed Digby and an odd expression, partly affection, Laurence thought, but tinged with some other, more complicated emotion, crossed his face.

'Old Digby,' Patrick said. 'It's certainly not the same place without Digby. Or, indeed, my father. Back then the whole place hummed. They'd be out with the guns, riding to hounds, throwing dances, hatching glorious schemes – mostly disastrous – going on escapades and excursions, with cavalry men, racing drivers, actors, bounders, swooning girls. My father's style was consuming prodigious quantities of champagne, while a queue formed at the back door of tailors, local traders, blacksmiths, wine merchants and irate husbands wanting satisfaction. Digby just loved life and loved company. He hated being alone. And he had the sort of charm that could persuade a fish to fly.'

Laurence wondered how Digby's exuberant spirits had altered after Kitty disappeared.

'And then he bagged a beautiful and rich wife,' Patrick said, 'and before he could get too bored – and he was never at his best when boredom set in, to be honest – a hero's death.'

After a very long pause while he drank his tea, he added, 'I miss him. He made me laugh more than anyone I've ever met. Still, Mr Bartram, to be frank it's better the estate be in the hands of Lydia and the loyal Julian.' He made a rueful face, defusing his slight sharpness. 'That's if there was to be anything left of it at all.'

'Are you glad to be back?'

'I am back, so I suppose I must be. No, I'm not being entirely truthful. Families – well, in my case what remains of them – you know how it is: it can be damned awkward. And I already miss Crete.' He gave another quick smile. 'But I'm fortunate in that what I have been doing is something that gives me enormous pleasure and Sir Arthur Evans's enthusiasms tend to sweep one on.'

Was it arrogance that led Patrick to assume that Laurence knew his profession already or merely an accurate assessment of family talk?

'Working with him must be extraordinary,' Laurence said and meant it.

For over a year the papers had been full of Howard Carter and Tutankhamun's gold, but to Laurence the idea of stripping back the earth in Crete, layer after layer, not to discover glittering treasure but mysteries — walls, paths, fortifications, which needed patience and imagination to reconstruct — was far more thrilling. Not in order to stock museums, but to try to discover how these ancient people lived, what they hoped for, what they feared. He knew that on Crete they had found inscriptions in an unheard-of language, a tantalising, unreadable clue to these long-gone people.

'I wasn't there for the crucial bit, sadly. The excavations started at the turn of the century. The most famous finds — the tablets, of course, and the figurine of the snake goddess — were early on.'

Patrick stopped and waited to see whether Laurence understood what he was referring to.

'I read Sir Arthur's account,' Laurence said.

Patrick nodded. 'I went out there once in the vac but not full time until I left university. I missed the boat really because all that soon stopped in the war, of course, so I only managed a month or so. I went back to Sir Arthur's house near Oxford to help write up the finds. Since then, the last five years, it's mostly been reconstruction.' He got up and went over to the fire. 'Some of it more like getting the decorators in,' he said as he poked the coal into life.

'But to be right there. At the heart of such a great discovery—'

Patrick turned back to him. 'I know who you are now,' he said, almost as if they were at a Belgravia cocktail party. 'You're the churches man. The expert. You wrote a book.'

Laurence must have looked surprised as Patrick said, 'Frances wrote. There was a letter waiting in Paris. She said you were coming down to give St Babs the once-over. You're a friend of the architect chap who is trying to sort out the cottages.'

'William Bolitho.'

'Bolitho, yes. And his wife? A clever friend of clever Frances?'

Laurence nodded. 'William is in a wheelchair,' he said. 'He lost his legs in 1917.'

Patrick nodded. 'I gathered. Difficult. I'm glad he's here. It was good of him. But what do you make of our church? Beyond the extraordinary carvings round the door?'

'They're astonishing. The best I've ever seen.'

Patrick was nodding vigorously as Laurence continued, 'As for the interior, I've scarcely had more than a quick look but there are certainly some intriguing anomalies. Actually that's where I was going.' He took his compass out of his pocket and held it up.

Patrick put down his cup, which he had been almost nursing in his lap, suddenly alert.

'Anomalies? I'm always drawn to anomalies.'

'It's nothing much, possibly odd orientation, and the floors have been resurfaced rather clumsily and I can't see why.'

'May I come too? Watch for a while? Before everybody gets back?'

Patrick had dropped his guard and looked genuinely interested.

Laurence's heart sank. He preferred to think in peace, especially when trying to make sense of a puzzle, but it was he, not Patrick, who was really the stranger here. Patrick had every right to visit his own family's church.

'I won't interfere, I promise,' Patrick said, still sounding enthusiastic. 'Back in Crete, Sir Arthur is possessed of a magnificent certainty and has rebuilt the palaces of the Minoans so that they'd feel quite at home if they returned tomorrow. I don't have his great gift of faith. I like the standing and silently sensing the invisible. You too, I imagine?'

Laurence was surprised by Patrick's frankness and perception. He was about to reply when he heard voices.

'Ah, my hosts,' Patrick said, 'my *family*. No rest for me then.' Turning to Laurence, as the voices drew closer, he added 'Later perhaps,' just as Lydia called out from the corridor, 'Hello. Patrick? Is that you?'

She came in just a little ahead of Frances looking unwell but as animated as Laurence had ever seen her, taking Patrick's hand in both of hers. From behind her, Frances, who had looked watchful at first, stepped forward.

'Patrick,' she said, giving him a hug. 'How awful of us. I had no idea you were here until I saw that strange old car outside and realised it must be yours.'

'Your telegram said you'd be later ...' Lydia said.

Patrick grinned. 'The car. Dreadful old thing. Somehow suitable for an archaeologist, but I rather wondered whether I was going to make it at all. I set out early, simply so that I stood a chance of getting here in daylight.'

His glance lingered on his sister-in-law and Laurence fancied he could see concern in Patrick's eyes but he swiftly turned to Frances, regarding her too with real warmth.

'You look so well, Frances.'

He turned back to Lydia, who was holding on to the back of a chair. She blinked a couple of times, almost as if she were trying to focus.

'Sit down,' Frances said gently, taking her arm again. Lydia's skin was greyish and she closed her eyes briefly, but once sitting by the fire she brightened again quickly.

'So where's my big brother?' Patrick said. 'Out beating the bounds in true squirearchical fashion?'

Lydia smiled. Frances stood behind her chair, gazing down at Lydia with her hand resting on her half-sister's shoulder.

'He must be with David and William,' she said, looking up.

'Ah, yes. Turning old Easton into a model estate. Before scouring the mop fairs for tenants.'

Frances's eyes narrowed but Patrick appeared not to notice.

'It's really very good to be here again, Lydia.'

'You should come more often,' she replied but without any tone of reproach. Then, turning to Laurence, 'We haven't seen Patrick for five years. I fear he has weathered those years better than we have.'

'Nonsense, you look well!'

'It's not nonsense, despite everybody's care, but you were always gallant,' Lydia said.

Laurence was struck by the long interval of time. Five years' absence?

Maggie came into the room carrying the tea things. The girl looked flustered, her eyes opening wide when she saw Patrick, who stepped forward to take the tray from her. Putting it down, he shook her hand. 'Well, I think I can certainly say that you've grown. How old are you now?'

Maggie's cheeks were blotched with embarrassment or pleasure. 'Fifteen,' she said. 'I'll be sixteen come July. I'm sorry I wasn't here, I was seeing to my grandad and I didn't know we'd have people for tea,' she said, all in a rush. Then she added, 'Mrs Hill is teaching me to cook. I did half the cake.'

'I'm glad. I'll have to come back more often when you're in charge of the kitchen.'

Maggie's expression was uncertain. She stared down abruptly at the cup still in his hand, then around the room like an animal seeking cover, her eyes seeming to fix on the tray Laurence had brought in earlier. Suddenly she seized Laurence's teacup from the table beside him and snatched Patrick's from his hand, putting them next to their ancient teapot, and picked up the tray. For a second Laurence was startled. Muttering 'servants' crockery,' she half bobbed, something he'd never seen her do before, and headed for the doorway, nearly bumping into Eleanor, who was closely followed by Julian.

Maggie hovered, awkwardly, trying to get past the new arrivals.

'It looks as if my brother's already been availing himself of your fruit cake,' Patrick said, giving Maggie a pat on the back as she left the room.

Julian looked impassive but a spot of colour burned on each cheek. Compared with his younger brother, he did look a bit solid, despite his hours walking the estate, Laurence thought. Julian's movements were slower too, his features more amiable but less classically handsome.

Eleanor stepped forward and shook hands with Patrick. Laurence had seldom seen her so demure.

'My husband's just sorting out tomorrow's plan of work,' she said. 'He hopes you'll forgive him.'

Eventually Julian moved forward and shook hands with his brother.

'Patrick.'

Both seemed to be gauging the other's reaction. Frances was pouring tea but, as she straightened up and handed a cup to her sister, she too was watching the two men.

'Good journey?' Julian asked.

'Not bad. Warmer here than Greece, funnily enough. Outside, anyway. This house was always so damned cold.'

Patrick rubbed his hands together in an exaggerated fashion, taking a fresh cup of tea from Eleanor.

Julian bent down and rubbed Scout's ears.

'Is that Otter still, or son of Otter?' Patrick asked.

Julian fiddled with the dog's collar. 'Daughter of Otter,' he said. 'Scout.'

'He's always had the same breed of dog,' Patrick explained to Eleanor, 'as did my father before him. A single dynasty of small but indomitable terriers. Inbred and not very bright. But fearless.' He reached down to pat the dog but Scout bared her teeth.

'Give her time,' said Julian. 'She doesn't like strangers.' He ruffled her neck again. 'Well, I've promised to help William – but we can talk at dinner perhaps?'

Without waiting for an answer he walked out. Scout shot ahead, her paws skidding on the flagged corridor. They heard Julian's footsteps retreat and the baize door at the end of hall thudded shut.

Lydia seemed nonplussed, her eyes following Julian to the door. Patrick sat, seemingly relaxed, in the window seat, one leg crossed over the other, looking out for some minutes as if putting some distance between himself and the rest of them. Eleanor raised her eyebrows and Frances shook her head, almost imperceptibly. Eventually Patrick turned back to the others.

'You've really made some changes, Lydia. You've done marvellously well.'

'Well, it's tidy, at least, but in another month—'

'The first time I came back after the war, I wished I'd never come back.' He directed his gaze at Laurence. 'It was February. The whole place was still in mourning. As for this,' he pointed towards the garden, 'except for the small borders by the house, they hadn't been able to keep it up in the war. It had grown and rotted year after year. It was bitterly cold when I arrived, I remember that clearly ... Your new man?'

'David,' said Frances. 'Not very new now.'

'He picked me up. Didn't talk much. He didn't have to. We passed through the village. Some chimney smoke. Some bare beanpoles. An empty wood store. A couple of boarded-up windows. Two scared-looking children peering from a doorway. A woman in black trudging up the lane. David slowed to pass her. She looked like a witch, with her arms wrapped round herself and bent over in the cold, but when she raised her head she was young under her shawl and must have been beautiful. Perhaps I'd known her once – I used to know everyone in Easton – but she just stared at me. I'd left the Hall and Digby and the village, all unchanged and prospering, and I'd come back to a landscape of death. Even the drive was overgrown. Dead trees, branches we had to swerve around. When I got out, blackened weeds crunched underfoot.'

Frances interrupted him. 'We know, we lived through it.' But Patrick didn't seem to hear her.

'Silence. Nothing lived, not a bird, not the smallest creature in the undergrowth. Paint peeling off doors and windows. Nobody came to the front door. I remember walking round to the terrace. Last autumn's dead leaves had blown against the french windows, and the urns by the steps had cracked open and black earth spilled out. The remains of our wonderful wisteria had been ripped away by wind, lying broken across the flags.'

When he ran out of words, Eleanor said with surprising gentleness, 'It must have been a shock.'

Patrick looked at her. 'Everything was gone, you see. Things I'd dreamed of from a Crete blasted by summer heat. My mother's rose garden. I especially remember that. The croquet lawn ... I know, I know. I expect you're thinking: what about old Digby? What about the gallant men of Easton? Here Patrick is, with a melancholy tale of dead flowers and, as Julian would be the first to point out, Patrick would be less horticulturally sensitive if he'd been through what the other Easton men had in the war.'

'Julian has never once even thought that,' Frances said sharply. 'You couldn't fight. That's all there is to it.'

But Laurence thought, watching, that that wasn't all there was to it.

'And, selfishly, how glad we are that you didn't,' Lydia added. 'So that at least you are here today. Part of Easton again.' After a long pause she said, 'We did try, you know. Especially at first.'

'We burned the rose arches because we were cold,' Frances said fiercely.

Patrick shook himself. 'I'm sorry, Lydia. I was being abominably ill mannered. It was meant to be a tribute to you. I could never have imagined how hard it had been for everybody at home until I saw Easton. It was my yardstick, all the years I was away.'

Eleanor seemed about to say something but she bit her lip. Frances stayed silent.

'I really should go and unpack,' Patrick said, when the silence had dragged on too long.

'Of course,' Lydia said. 'We've put you in the blue room. Your old room. I hope you'll find it comfortable.' Some spirit returned to her eyes as she added, 'And pleasingly unchanged.'

Patrick stood up and looked around at the others. 'I'll see you all at dinner,' he said. 'And, Laurence, I hope you'll tell me about our church.'

'I'd forgotten how rude Patrick can be, ' Frances said when the door was hardly shut. 'Where was he in the war when we were desperate for help? Not thousands of miles from home, reading "Home Thoughts from Abroad" in Greece. He was just thirty miles away, cataloguing broken pots in Oxford.'

CHAPTER FIVE

*L*aurence had agreed to meet Patrick the next morning at the church. He went the back way, intending to have some time there alone, and passed a pretty woman sitting at a table in the butler's pantry, cleaning silver. As he paused in the doorway she started to rise. On seeing that she was very pregnant, he said, 'No, don't get up,' but she was already on her feet.

'Susan Eddings, sir. David's wife,' she said, and gave him a smile.

He went out into the stable yard and crossed to the church. He paused at the carved arch and marvelled. There was such life and mischief in it. Once inside, with the door thudded shut behind him, he felt he was in his own territory. He ran his hand over the stones by the door and found a switch. It was by no means dark but when the light came on, although he could see clearly within its circle of illumination, it seemed to cast the corners into deeper shadow.

He stood just inside the door, getting the feel of the place. He could mentally remove the accretions of the last half-century and see the simple barn-like stone building this had once been. There were no tombs visible and, more unusually, no wall plaques. He walked towards the altar and lifted up the corner of the linen cloth covering it, revealing a faded green damask one underneath. Below that the altar stone was battered but there were remains of carving on the corners. He let the cloth drop and as he did so wondered who had put the simple vase of flowers on it, given that the church was rarely used now. He pushed a faded carpet aside with his foot, then checked his watch. When he had seen the church before, he had noticed the setting sun had not shone directly through the west window. Now he got out his compass. As he did so, he heard a noise behind him and went to open the door. Patrick stood in the porch, putting out his cigarette before entering. Once inside, he stood still and looked around.

'It's a pity we lost our rector. There was something about this place when I was a boy: Mama, Papa, the village, every Sunday, week in, week out, with Morning Prayers by rote and the schoolmistress on the organ, a beat behind in the hymns. Yet my father believed only in himself and my mother remained a secret Roman Catholic all her life, with her missal hidden in her dressing table. I once found her rosary on the floor under the bell here. It was very old – I'd never seen it before: ebony, I think it must have been. She was horrified when I asked her if it was hers. Poor old Mama. Always so frightened of Father, when really he was just a bit of a bully, but something in her meekness, or perhaps his resentment of her money, used to spur him on to goad her. And he was a bit of a one for pinching servant girls' bottoms. He would probably have thought the rosary was a necklace. He wasn't terribly up on theology, apart from insisting that Catholicism was somehow treasonably foreign, like most other loyal English gentlemen at the time.'

He looked around him.

'Are they going to restore the organ?'

It stood almost out of sight to one side of the nave, a small instrument, probably dating back to the restoration of the church. Pipes filled the arch around it. The dark lid was scratched and dusty. Patrick opened it and made a face, then sat at the organ stool, turned on an electric switch and pulled out a couple of stops. As he did so the church door opened again and a woman's figure was silhouetted in the doorway. As she walked forward Laurence could see it was Eleanor. She came and stood next to him. Patrick played a chord; the sound was thin but not unpleasant. He followed this with a few bars of what Laurence thought was Bach but the organ seemed too small for the piece and some keys were sticking. Patrick, an unlit cigarette now clamped in his mouth, turned to look at Eleanor and then, with his eyes half shut, launched into some dance music. She laughed. Laurence could see that he'd be a good performer, given a piano. His face was animated and he tossed his floppy fringe out of his eyes. Then, almost as soon as he had got going, he stopped with a burst of 'The Man Who Broke the Bank in Monte Carlo'. Eleanor clapped. 'Bravo,' she said. 'Encore.'

'No. Laurence wants to give the church a once-over and I promised I would be as silent as an Easton revenant.'

Laurence's heart sank at the thought that he would now have an audience of two, but in fact Eleanor moved away and sat facing the altar, while Patrick leafed through a hymnal. When Laurence walked to the base of the bell tower, Patrick turned to watch him, but Eleanor, apparently deep in thought, did not. A single rope was fastened to the wall and the solitary bell hung not far above him. At the west window he opened his compass again. He tapped it twice and it was as he thought. The orientation was not east–west as churches usually were, but north-east–south-west. The floor at this end was stone-flagged, with the marks of earlier dividing walls.

Patrick, who had moved closer, asked him, 'What were those, do you think?'

'Probably a tiny chapel, a Lady Chapel, I imagine. Removed at the Reformation, probably.'

Patrick said, 'I like to think of Mama worshipping in a church which had been Roman Catholic for centuries before we Protestants got hold of it.'

Most of the interior walls had been whitewashed but one retained a painted design in a dark madder. Stylised flowers filled a pattern of squares over an area perhaps three feet by four.

'Quaint,' Patrick said.

'Old,' Laurence replied. 'Very old, I think.'

'Lucky to survive my mother's improvements,' Patrick said. 'How old?'

'Medieval, I would imagine. The same sort of age as all this.'

He switched on his torch and shone it upwards. The ceiling was formed from simple wooden trusses, but the stone corbels that supported the beams were as elaborate as the entrance archway, with clusters of leaves, flowers and small animals, including a hedgehog, a field mouse and a slow-worm. Deep among them was an impish face sprouting leaves. It was easy to see what had inspired the man who much more recently had sculpted the creatures on the garden steps.

Laurence shone the beam into the corner near the long table under the window. To the right was what appeared to be the top of a rudimentary arch with a column, about four feet high, incorporated into the wall. Above it was a carving, about a foot square. It looked hacked at, rather than eroded by time; either way, its original subject was lost but could possibly have been some kind of head and body.

After a minute, he said, 'I think there might have been an earlier building here.'

'Before the church? Or part of it?'

'Hard to tell.'

With anyone else, he would have expected them to push him but Patrick just nodded.

Eleanor joined them. 'Interesting,' she said.

'Interesting, but probably not significant. People did use the foundations of old buildings to raise new ones from time to time, or areas that had some sacred connotation would acquire various structures over the centuries.'

Patrick was thoughtful. 'My father used to say that the altar had been a standing stone. Perhaps it was true and some doughty Christian hauled it here to purge it of its heathenness.'

'It's just as likely they built the whole church round it,' Laurence said. 'Churches are enclosures for altars – the altar's not furniture for the church.'

Patrick said nothing but he looked at Laurence with respect.

Dinner that evening was more formal than the night before. It was not completely dark outside when they sat down; from the nearest windows it was possible to see beyond the terrace but the maze was hardly discernible. A clear violet sky tinged with green promised a cold night, although the day had been beautifully warm for late April.

The tarnished silver, which had appeared at every other meal, was now clean and bright; crystal glasses stood on a newly laundered tablecloth. The women had dressed up too. Lydia looked serenely beautiful in what he thought must be a pre-war dress, which fell to her ankles and sparkled with thousands of tiny beads. She was walking with a silver-topped cane and was evidently finding it hard to put her weight on one leg. Frances was watching her. She wore an equally old-fashioned long crimson dress, with her hair caught back in a small jewelled clip.

From everything Eleanor had told him about Frances, Laurence doubted she ever left Easton much or had any call for fashionable evening dress. He thought that at least Lydia had known marriage, even if followed by tragedy, where Frances had only escaped briefly to Cambridge. Eleanor alone wore a modern evening dress, with a low waist and a silk fringe bouncing on her knees. A long pearl necklace was knotted on her chest. She had obviously seized any old cardigan to throw on over it but the effect nonetheless made her look young.

William was already at the table. Julian pulled back Lydia's chair for her. Lydia handed him her stick and laid her hand on the table edge to steady herself as she lowered herself into the chair. Laurence ran a finger under his dress collar. It felt a great deal tighter than when he'd last worn it in London a few months ago. Patrick gave him a rueful smile. He had failed to bring evening dress altogether and, the last Laurence had heard, was going through the wardrobes, looking for Digby's clothes, which Lydia had told him had been put away in one of the spare bedrooms. Digby had been, Laurence thought, looking at Patrick now, shorter and wider than his younger brother, as well as smaller than he looked in his fine portrait. The jacket gaped slightly at the front and Patrick kept pulling down his cuffs. There was something defeated in the limpness of his bow tie.

Susan brought in the soup, followed by Maggie carrying a jug of water, her face set in concentration. Maggie served Lydia and then went straight to Patrick. He made some pleasantry that Laurence didn't catch and patted her on the arm. Susan indicated the two other women with a nod of her head and Maggie blushed but, as she poured out a glass for Frances, she was still gazing at Patrick. Laurence was amused. The girl was obviously sweet on Patrick. He could see Eleanor was trying not to smile as Maggie allowed water to run down the side of Frances's glass.

When Maggie and Susan had left, Julian filled their glasses with wine.

'Some of the last bottles of Easton's cellar at its finest,' he said. 'I think my father must have put this down.'

Laurence was in no haste to drink. He was warm, comfortable and glad to be among friends. The mock-turtle soup was excellent.

Eleanor said, 'This must be Susan's cooking?'

Lydia gave a quick, small smile. 'Our main challenge is how to persuade Mrs Hill to let that aspect of her duties be taken over by Susan. I don't think Mrs Hill really enjoys cooking—'

'And those who eat it certainly don't,' Patrick chipped in. Eleanor made a small sound, which she covered by dabbing her mouth with her napkin. Julian frowned at Patrick.

'She does her best.'

'That's the worry. What would happen if she took against us?'

Lydia said, quite firmly for once, 'Susan, however, is a very good cook and I know she'd like to continue after her confinement. Maggie's longing to look after the baby.'

There was a warmth in her voice that was usually absent. Laurence thought that the prospect of a child around the house again, far from distressing her, seemed to animate her.

'Was Susan a cook before her marriage?' Laurence asked.

Frances put her spoon down. 'No. Well, only vaguely. She made biscuits. She worked in a factory during the war. Near Reading.'

'How did she meet David?' Laurence had sensed a great closeness between the couple. David's reserve fell away when his wife was around and she fussed over him as if he were an invalid, rather than a strong man.

Frances looked at Lydia, who just shook her head. 'She told me but . . . I can't quite—'

'She's got no family,' William said. 'David told me that neither of them had. His widowed mother died years ago and Susan spent most of her life in an orphanage, then a couple of years in service, after which she went into a factory.'

'I think she was a kitchen maid,' Eleanor said, 'in a big household, because she told me she shared a room with two other girls, and she talked about the shooting parties they used to have. Presumably that's where she learned her cooking.'

'Lord,' Patrick said. 'Must be a bit of a comedown, being at Easton. Only the obsequious shades of butlers and footmen, tweenies and still-room maids in our servants' hall. In fact, only the ghost of the Hall itself.'

'She wasn't happy there,' Lydia said. Her voice dropped as the door opened. Maggie stood on the threshold.

'Shall I take the plates, ma'am?'

Maggie piled them up carefully, with Lydia's bowl, which had hardly been touched, on top, walked towards the door and then looked perplexed to find that it had shut again. She gazed around, her arms full, biting her lip. Julian had to jump up and open it for her.

Patrick, his eyes sparkling with amusement, then said more seriously, 'I feel sorry for her.'

'Susan?' Frances said in surprise.

'Maggie.' Patrick was looking at Julian. 'Stuck here with no one her own age and just Mrs Hill, queen of gossip, talking about the dead and the war and the old days, and no doubt whispering to Susan about Maggie's mother and the gypsy.'

'Maggie's living with her only known relative,' Julian said gruffly. 'Walter's all she's got and she's never known anything else but Easton. Not everyone is desperate to travel the world to escape.'

The door opened again. This time Susan came in, carefully pushing the door fully back with her foot and carrying a tureen of potatoes. Behind her Mrs Hill, still in her apron, carried a joint of gammon, and in the rear Maggie bore in the cabbage as if she were an acolyte at some ritual.

'Thank you, Mrs Hill, Susan.' Lydia smiled. 'And Maggie, of course.'

They trooped out, Mrs Hill's feet thudding heavily.

Julian was filling the glasses once more, this time with an exceptionally dark wine. Patrick drank heavily.

Lydia leaned forward. 'I hope you're enjoying Easton, Laurence,' she said. 'It can be very beautiful in summer. When I first came I thought it was the most lovely spot in all England.' She looked at him as if willing him to see it as it had been.

'I love the downs – I always did when I was a boy.' But he knew she meant Easton, not the county of Wiltshire. 'And the church has great charm. I'm not sure what's emerging where the tarry surface near the altar's been removed, but it looks old and interesting and anyway much better than the existing surface, which would need replacing in any case.'

'Of course,' Lydia said. 'Perhaps we could get one of the Kilminster boys to lend a hand. The older boy's very willing and we could give him some small payment. And Walter if he's up to it.'

Julian said, 'I agree. If we don't like what you find, we'll just cover it up again.'

'I was wondering if we could go and explore a bit?' Eleanor said. 'I'm the one who knows the area least and I'd love to see it properly, given I find myself among experts.'

'Splendid idea.' Patrick's face lit up. 'The next really fine day we'll walk to Avebury, see a few things on the way.' He leaned forward. 'I know everybody's beavering about at Easton but I had an idea. If you can face going a little further afield,' he looked at Julian, pointedly, 'what about the exhibition – at Wembley? We should go, don't you think?'

Eleanor, amused, seemed about to reply when Julian spoke.

'I'd been thinking about visiting it. There's a whole section on advances in agriculture – not just displays, but free advice. And its patriotic, don't you think?'

Patrick glanced at Eleanor, but she shook her head and picked up her glass.

'You'll come?' he said, turning to William.

'I don't think it's feasible,' William said but before his demurral could cast a damper on Julian's enthusiasm, he added, 'But I'd like Nicky to see it.'

The door opened and Maggie started collecting dishes.

Patrick looked pleased. 'Then you'll come? Laurence? Frances? Lydia, would you come if we went by car?'

There was something in his tone that carried the expectation that Lydia would refuse. She'd started shaking her head even before he'd finished, but smiled as she said, 'No, but you can bring me toffee tins with pictures of threshing machines and cowboys and coolies.' Looking at her sister, she added firmly, 'And Frances should go.'

'Yes, you should,' said Eleanor. 'See what our country stands for. Not to forget our loyal dominions.'

Patrick gazed at Eleanor enquiringly. 'You don't approve?' he said. 'Or you really don't want to go?'

'Oh I'd like to see the sideshows,' Eleanor said sweetly, and Laurence's heart sank. 'But I'm afraid all that colonial claptrap is a bit too rich.'

Laurence watched William try to hide a smile.

When Maggie put a clean plate down in front of Patrick, he looked up at her.

'Now *you'd* like to see the King and Queen and go down a coalmine at the big exhibition in London, wouldn't you Maggie? And go on the enormous funfair?'

Maggie coloured. She managed to put the next plate down on top of a fork, which flipped on to the floor. She struggled under the table to pick it up while Lydia raised an eyebrow but with a half-smile. Maggie stood up, brushing her hair out of her eyes. She rubbed the fork on her apron and put it down by Patrick's plate.

'Susan says she'd go but she can't because the baby might come. It was in her magazine. She was trying to get David to go with me but he said over his dead body and Mrs Hill said she'd never been to London and never wanted to. David said it was a hell-hole and he wasn't never going back.'

Lydia looked startled, but Eleanor said, 'So you've already got secret plans?'

Maggie blushed an even darker red, her eyes meeting Frances's almost pleadingly. 'I'd like to see the Queen's Doll's House and the beautiful ladies dressed up as people from the olden days.'

'You're not alone there,' Patrick muttered theatrically. 'Right, if Mrs Easton is willing, why don't you come? I'm sure you deserve a day off.'

'Actually if we go it would be terrifically decent to have Maggie along to help look after Nicky,' Eleanor said. 'Would that be all right, Lydia? And then, given he's going back to my sister's anyway around then, we could stay overnight and drop him off.'

Lydia nodded, then said, 'Thank you Maggie,' and gently inclined her head to the door.

When the girl had gone out she added, 'I think it would be a wonderful plan. Susan can't go, obviously, and I'm sure she or Ellen Kilminster would be happy to keep an eye on William and me. Perhaps David could drive some of you up? I expect he'll want to return at the end of the day, given Susan's condition, and he can bring Maggie back, but the rest of you could stay in London.'

'Frances, you're very welcome to stay with us. Oh, do say you will.' Eleanor, turning to William, said, 'If you don't mind, darling? It would all be quite jolly.'

Patrick said, 'Mind you, I'm surprised the government managed to bring the exhibition off at all.'

Eleanor glanced up sharply.

'Mr MacDonald inherited the idea from the Liberals,' Laurence said. 'I don't suppose they had much choice. And there's a general feeling it would cheer us all up. The newspapers are full of it. Londoners talk of little else.'

Patrick looked sceptical. 'Chaos with the workmen, though. It near as dammit – sorry, Lydia – didn't get built at all, from what I hear.'

'What *do* you hear?' Eleanor put her knife down. 'Out in Greece?'

Something in the way she held her jaw made Laurence nervous. He turned to Julian. 'Could you pass the wine?'

'Well, inevitably the minute Mr MacDonald and his Independent Labour Party get in, the workers down tools. They thought they'd found their champion. Nasty shock, though. They found that once in government, the new lot carried on much as the old lot.'

'It was an impossible situation,' Eleanor said. 'I doubt Mr MacDonald would have started such a white elephant of a project with so many other more worthwhile calls on the budget, but once started they wanted to make a go of it. They're not amateurs. And it gave people jobs. Lots of people who were out of work.'

'Jobs that they promptly turned against the government by going on strike. And then your Mr MacDonald – I presume he is yours?' Patrick raised a eyebrow, '– promptly crushes them by calling in the soldiers just as quickly as his predecessors would have done. The purity of ideals meets the reality of power.'

'No,' Eleanor said, her cheeks burning. 'That's just not fair.'

'Hard on the soldiers, I imagine,' Laurence interrupted, hoping to divert her. 'I doubt ordinary soldiers ever like intervening against men who might have fought beside them a few years earlier.'

'Quite like Russia, though,' Patrick said, picking up his glass, but Laurence noticed his other hand, resting on the table, was clenched tight.

'That's an idiotic comment and ill informed,' Eleanor fired back.

'Eleanor,' William said and she shot him a furious glance before glancing around the table.

'I'm sorry,' she said tightly, 'I'm being very rude.' She looked at Patrick as if to indicate that the rudeness was entirely his responsibility, then said, 'It's only because it's not a parlour game to me.'

'I'm sorry,' Patrick said. 'I've been too long out of polite society.'

Lydia said brightly, 'Well, I think for you all to see the replica of King Tut's tomb would be an awfully good adventure.'

'I read that they're having a mass of trouble with our cowboys,' Frances added quickly. 'From America. They're cruel to horses apparently.'

Julian looked concerned. 'Questions asked in parliament. Quite right too.'

'I'm afraid our Wild West lacks refinement,' Frances said, reaching for Lydia's hand. While engaged with the conversation at the table, she continued to stroke her sister's swollen joints.

Laurence had often noticed this apparently unconscious gesture of care. 'But at least we don't *eat* horses like the French.'

'Got offered them in France,' Julian said. 'Digby wasn't having it. Stuck to potatoes.'

'The men ate it,' William said. 'My lot, anyway. 'Though I don't think *cheval* meant much. Hunger's hunger. Stew's stew. I felt rather the same at the time.'

Laurence regarded Eleanor out of the corner of his eye. She had stopped eating and was gazing at her lap. Patrick was watching her too but it was hard to tell what he was thinking. William, usually adept at steering his wife away from controversy in public, had a fixed smile on his face as another silence fell.

Laurence searched wildly for a less contentious topic. 'I've been thinking about going abroad myself in the autumn.'

This did get Eleanor's attention and the others' too.

'At Westminster I took on the job of a chap who was badly injured, but he's returning soon, and although the school has offered me a different post, I've been considering something else. I thought being down here would give me a chance to think it through. I've been offered a year of private tutoring. A foreign diplomat whose son was briefly at Westminster.'

He could hear himself almost parroting the phrases he'd used when he had been interviewed in the fine Belgravia house. Signor della Scala had sat among his books, his almost perfect English and his Sackville Street tailoring at odds with his dark colouring and black eyes. He was serious but businesslike, and his earnest wish to do well by his only son was evident. After the interview he had shown Laurence some ancient cameos, exquisite pieces of work, kept in a locked case. The man had done his research on Laurence's past: at one point in the interview, Laurence had been disarmed to see a copy of his book on the desk. It looked as if it had been read.

Laurence had warmed to the man and his dignified eagerness, yet as he left the house he had felt unready to take such a giant step. On some days, the war and the life he had led before it seemed very far away; at other times dreams woke him, or the sudden intrusion of memories he hoped had gone for ever stopped him in his tracks. In France he had promised himself that, in the unlikely event of his returning safe home, he would never leave his country again. However, in the last few days at Easton he'd occasionally felt that the post offered exciting possibilities and that, having lost every element of his former life so utterly, just following its almost vanished trails was more dispiriting than making a new start.

Eleanor was looking at him as if ready to strike but he plunged on, already seeing where this diversion might lead and knowing that the details he was omitting would soon be forced out of him.

'I like the family. The boy is clever but not very strong.'

'Where is this?' Frances said, with what he knew was deceptive lightness.

'Rome,' he answered while deliberately avoiding her gaze.

Lydia spoke. 'My mother-in-law would have approved.' She smiled with more animation than she usually showed.

'The Roman Church,' Julian said. 'Poor Mother.'

'Father made all sorts of promises when he married her that he would respect her beliefs,' Patrick said. 'But once he'd got her, he had no time for it, had he?'

Julian cut up the last mouthfuls on his plate with great care, as if it took all his attention, and made no reply. Patrick looked exasperated at his studied silence. Laurence often thought that in his way Patrick did want a relationship with his brother and half the goading was to get a response, any response, from him. It was Julian who wouldn't engage.

'Rome was Mama's dream in every sense,' Patrick said. 'I'm surprised she didn't want her heart buried there.'

Frances made a face.

'Anyway, Laurence, you may go as her posthumous emissary,' Patrick went on. 'Astonishing country. It has all the beauty of nature, from mountains to hills purple with vines, to the grottoes of Capri, the ruins of Pompeii, and then there is all the art that tyranny and patronage can produce. And the Italians are a beautiful race, at least when young. Of course even as adults they're like children — excitable, sentimental, imbued with religious superstition — but things are beginning to be turned around. There's a new sort of politics.'

'Do you mean Signor Mussolini?' Frances asked, glancing at Eleanor.

'I'm sure the man's the very devil,' Patrick said, 'but he's got the measure of the country. They can either continue as struggling peasants and hot-headed revolutionaries, or they can take a bit of discipline and join the modern world.'

'His party have overthrown the elected government,' Eleanor said quietly. 'His only real opponent has just been murdered.'

'The Deputy? What's his name? Matteotti?' Patrick said. 'He's only disappeared. Who knows where he is? It might be a Socialist stunt. And Mussolini's not been implicated. It's a new system, and it's early days. Power struggles are to be expected. It's not far off the situation with Zinoviev and Trotsky in Russia, except far less dangerous for them and for us.'

'A stunt?' Eleanor said, her voice clipped.

'It's a different culture,' Patrick replied. 'They've been soaked in blood for their entire history: think of Tarquin, Emperor Augustus, the Borgias, indeed, most of the popes, Garibaldi. That's what they understand. Italy is in chaos. Mussolini's giving it a future.'

'His Fascist Party are militaristic brutes,' Eleanor said. 'And he's a swaggering oaf who thinks he's Caesar.'

Even Patrick looked impressed by her vigour. Julian glanced anxiously at Lydia but she seemed fascinated. Laurence kept his eyes on Eleanor, her face pale and her shoulders tense, her napkin clutched tightly. He felt a flash of guilt that his horizons and his passions were so limited.

'It's men like that who threaten everything people have died for and everything we've lost,' she said. 'They like war. You think we fought the war to end all wars. Well, wait and see what Signor Mussolini and his cronies have up their sleeves. Their own *stunts*. Lethal ones.' Her voice wobbled.

Frances said gently, 'But if you go to Italy, Laurence, perhaps you can see these things for yourself.'

Julian cleared his throat. 'They were our allies.'

'Eventually,' William said.

'Well, if you're going, you'd better check your host's political credentials first, or perhaps you can just subvert the heir?' Patrick said lightly but without a smile.

Laurence's eyes remained on Eleanor, who stared fixedly at her lap. Only the slight tremor of her hand betrayed her emotion. From where Patrick was sitting, he wouldn't have seen it. William put his own hand over hers and squeezed.

'I loved Italy,' Lydia said brightly. 'Digby and I went to Florence for our honeymoon. What a wonderful start to a marriage.'

CHAPTER SIX

*O*ver the following weeks, while William dealt with the thatcher and had two visits from the stained-glass craftsman, Laurence had been working with David, the older Kilminster boy and Walter Petch, clearing the church floor. It was a larger area than he'd initially realised. Although the first strips had come off quite easily, the surface that had been underneath the pews had become denser and more thickly layered. David and the boy even seemed to be enjoying it, David speculating on why it was apparently so hurriedly and so badly applied. Walter remained dour and never once looked Laurence in the eye.

'Don't mind him, sir,' David had said quietly. 'He misses the old days.' He smiled. 'I was two villages away at the time so I get to hear a lot about how much better things at Easton were then.'

One day, when he went to see how work was going, Laurence found Eleanor and Frances on their knees, scraping the floor, scarves tied round their heads.

'Aha,' Eleanor had said. 'Women at your feet. Every man's dream.'

'You should probably wear gloves,' he said, looking at her red knuckles.

'It's fun,' Frances said, 'and besides, we think there's a pattern underneath.'

She sat back on her heels and pointed to an area about eighteen inches square. Some geometrical shape was emerging, although the residue of tar made it hard to see it clearly.

Later, Lydia had come down, leaning heavily on Patrick, and then Eleanor helped William over in his chair.

'If you're happy, Laurence, I think it's going to need solvent to clear it completely.'

'The under surface looks good,' Laurence said. 'Solvent should be fine if we go slowly.'

Since then they'd been using petrol to dissolve the remainder, but it meant nobody could stay working there very long as the church was full of fumes.

Today it was so fine that when Patrick suggested taking a break and going for a walk, which would allow William and the stained-glass man to make final measurements in the church, it felt good to escape into the fresh air.

Frances and Eleanor accompanied Patrick and Laurence as they cut diagonally across the lawns that ran steeply down to the lake. Julian had said Lydia avoided going there and the hidden green-black waters were certainly uninviting. There was something artificial about the planting too. Ever since Laurence had arrived, William had been intending to visit the lake to see whether it was possible to fulfil Lydia's hope of taking out the impenetrable thickets of evergreen shrubs that made it such a claustrophobic spot. However, the path was too muddy and narrow to take a wheelchair and somehow the visit had never happened. Laurence felt a pang of guilt.

The water level must have dropped recently and two dry

bronze spouts, covered in verdigris, stuck out from the surface.

'Does it fill just from those?' he asked Patrick.

'It looks stagnant, but actually it's very clean water, hence the lilies. There are culverts bringing water from the Kennet and, of course, principally from the generator. But there is a sluice,' he pointed to the end nearer the house, 'which can shut off incoming water. It's centuries old but with a couple of strong men it can still be made to work. Or it could before the war. And under the lilies there's a drain, which empties out down the slope.'

The glossy leaves of the water lilies covered a quarter of the pool's elsewhere smooth, obsidian surface, and patches of bright duckweed speckled the dark water.

'When we drained it ...' Patrick faltered. 'To see whether Kitty ... before the war ...' Then he said more firmly, 'When we were looking for my niece, we found the lining had been painted black. Possibly it was to seal it, but I'd guess my forebears intended to create this rather Gothic effect.'

'But you can't swim in it,' Eleanor said, coolly. It was the first time Laurence had heard her talk directly to Patrick since the row at dinner. It was almost a question, but she was looking at the lake with apprehension.

'I do,' Patrick replied. 'Or I used to a lot. So did Digby. Julian replanted the lilies after the old ones were lost when we emptied it – you'll have noticed that Julian likes things to stay the same – but he's not so keen on going in, as he had a bad experience with water when he was a child. Our father believed that, like puppies, we'd swim if we were thrown in. It worked on Digby, but very nearly drowned Julian.'

Eleanor seemed about to speak, but Patrick continued, 'Wait until a really hot day and you'll be raring to go in.' For once he lost his calculatedly careless tone. 'Or by moonlight – when it has a certain atmosphere – slipping into its Stygian waters by night.'

Eleanor appeared unconvinced.

Frances was silent and when Laurence glanced at her she was looking away. It was not hard to imagine the men struggling to open the drains and close the sluice gates – in search of Kitty. He could visualise the scene as the water churned out of the lake, its usually motionless surface turned to mud and debris, and the tension as the level dropped, the waiting to see whether a small body lay in the dark slime on the lake bed. He could not imagine the effect on Frances, watching her sister's despair, and the fear of the desperate searchers of either finding the little girl dead or of not finding her at all.

Laurence was glad to leave the sunless spot, while Frances and Eleanor seemed to come to life as they emerged into the sunlight. They all passed through an open stone gateway on to a country lane. The downs swept up to their left. Hawthorn hedges, distorted by the wind, cut along the valley, and sheep were grazing on the nearest hill. As they left the lane and followed a grass track, the ancient turf felt springy underfoot and the air smelled fresh as if after rain.

Eleanor looked around her. 'What a glorious day,' she said. The long tassel of her tam-o'-shanter swung as she turned her gaze from side to side. 'Now to mysteries of iron age forts and standing stones and pagan deities.'

Laurence wondered what future historians would make of the landscape of death they'd created in France and Flanders and Turkey: the fortifications, the bones, the weapons. Would somebody stand in those places in centuries to come, excited at the extraordinary nature of what lay around him? Would he puzzle over what its creators thought they were doing as he sifted through fragments of men and metal, horses and ruined timber?

Would he think these early twentieth-century people had been trying to appease some particularly cruel god?

Frances said softly, 'You're miles away.'

He realised he had stopped walking and started forward again, intending that they both catch up with Patrick, and with Eleanor who kept a few paces behind him, just out of earshot. She had not yet forgiven Patrick for the row, he thought.

'Patrick truly loves all this stuff,' Frances said. 'He's in his element. This is where you see him with his guard down.'

'He looks pretty fit,' Laurence said, watching Patrick stride out down the track, with Eleanor still a little way behind him.

Frances looked sideways at him. 'You're thinking if he can dig up palaces in Greece, he could have fought?'

Laurence felt defensive. Had he been thinking that?

'He does have some quite serious heart problem,' she said. 'He wasn't well enough to go to Oxford when he first left Eton. I once saw him collapse and he looked ghastly. I thought he was having a fit but it's something to do with his heart valves. And I don't think he actually digs. He looks after the things they find. Identifies them,' she said, lowering her voice slightly although Patrick was too far away to hear.

Ahead of them Patrick had come to a halt. He pointed to a tidy mound, with a tree on top, about half a mile away.

'That barrow was one I dug with Digby when we were about eleven and fifteen. We weren't supposed to, of course, and we didn't find much — not the fabulous treasure we were looking for — but there were a few bits and pieces, which we had to hide in the stables or there would have been trouble with our father. We dug straight down at right angles to the surface in our haste to find gold, and we were lucky it didn't all cave in on us.'

'Are we going to Silbury?' Frances asked.

Patrick nodded. 'Why not? The last resting place of the strangely elusive King Sil.'

'Are we going the usual way?' Frances asked, sounding puzzled.

'I thought we'd show Eleanor and Laurence a fine long barrow first.'

He pointed to what looked like a cairn of stones just showing at the top of the hill. As they drew closer it was revealed as a partly turf-covered hump, rising a few feet out of the ground. Patrick led them round the far side, where large stones stood upright, not quite blocking what appeared to be an entrance.

Patrick bowed slightly. 'Eleanor?' he said. 'Ladies first.'

Eleanor and Frances exchanged glances, looking reluctant. Laurence stepped forward to the blackness of the opening and bent to clear the keystone. His heart was thudding. The inside was dark but there were tiny specks of light, evidently coming through the stonework. He stood up straighter and found he was holding his breath. He let himself breathe; he dreaded smelling something terrible but it was nothing more than earth. Every instinct told him to turn and clamber back to the open hillside and the light. His eyes strained to make out the dimensions of the chamber and he stood to one side to maximise the light coming between the entrance stones. He looked around him. It was essentially just a long, narrow room, constructed out of dry-stone walling with a beaten-earth floor.

'Laurence,' Patrick called, and he turned to see Patrick at the entrance, holding out a candle, already lit. 'At the far end there are ledges you can rest this on.'

Laurence took it gratefully and held it out in front of him. The space was not large. Carbon coated the rock above the ledges Patrick had directed him to. He was evidently not the first person to light the barrow. He half expected to hear rats, but to his relief it was silent and not even especially damp. Behind him

Frances rustled as she came in. She looked around her, slightly fearfully, then looked relieved as no horrors presented themselves. She stood very close to him and he could hear her breathing quickly. He could still catch Patrick talking outside and then Eleanor laughing.

Frances said, 'I think I've seen all I need to see.'

She turned and for a moment her body blocked the exit. Again, he felt a wave of panic, but she was soon outside, with him close behind her. Patrick stepped into the chamber and Eleanor, with a wry smile, followed him. Laurence focused on the landscape around him and took a long, deep breath.

Patrick and Eleanor emerged, Eleanor also looking happy to be out once more.

'Are they certain people were buried here then?' Frances asked. 'If they haven't dug it all out?'

'Oh, they found bodies here all right,' Patrick said. 'Four or five adults and a child.'

Laurence saw the look that passed across Frances's face but Patrick hadn't noticed. In many ways Patrick seemed much less sensitive to the tensions around Easton, but perhaps as the member of the family least often back home, he was simply determined not to join them all in stasis.

'They were found in the last century,' he said, 'and buried millennia ago.'

Frances's expression relaxed.

'One odd thing: there were tiny bones, finger bones, mostly, in the interstices – the little gaps between the stones. Too many for it to be coincidence.'

Eleanor made a face. 'I don't like the idea of somebody rooting through my grave in two millennia, waving my femurs about, putting me in a case in the British Museum and deciding I was a serf on the basis of my lack of jewellery.' Her face lightened as she spread out her fingers, revealing only the thin band of her wedding ring.

Frances looked at her, apparently amused. 'But you don't believe in an afterlife, Eleanor, and you do believe in knowledge, so I would have thought you'd be thrilled to come to such an instructive end.'

'Of course she believes in an afterlife,' Patrick said. 'Everybody does at heart, every culture, whatever the intellectual fashion. We're far too selfish to believe all our worldly endeavours only come to this.'

Eleanor turned sharply and Laurence expected her to flare up at Patrick, but she simply said, 'Actually, Patrick, I'm rather surprised that an educated man like you is so superstitious.'

'Actually you don't know what I believe.'

'By inference I do.'

'You should work with evidence, Eleanor, not prejudice.'

Laurence watched Eleanor's face but she appeared surprisingly placid. Although Patrick was watching her too, he noticed, Eleanor turned away.

'Shall we walk on?' she said, brightly.

They strode downhill in single file, but not before Frances rolled her eyes at Laurence. He tried not to laugh.

A breeze had got up and there were currents moving over the silver sweep of grass that lay before them. From the field rose the huge and abrupt mound that Laurence knew to be Silbury Hill. Patrick called out to Eleanor as they got closer. She turned her head to reply but Laurence couldn't catch their words. As they moved into the lee of the hill, Patrick stopped again, looking at the hill almost with pride.

'Somebody's done the calculations for how many man hours it took to build this. It's much the same size as the pyramids of Egypt, the smaller ones anyway. Makes you think.'

He sat down in the grass as if to do so, and the others followed suit.

'What is it for?' Frances said.

'A tomb, presumably,' Eleanor said.

'No, apparently not. There are plenty of myths: is it King Sil still on his horse? An ancient reservoir? A ziggurat? A place for human sacrifice?' Patrick replied.

Frances looked startled. 'You don't believe that?'

'No. I don't *not* believe it, but I don't believe we have evidence for it either. That's not the same.'

'Perhaps it was the sort of community sacrifice that sent soldiers to their deaths?' Eleanor said.

If she meant it sarcastically, Patrick still answered her seriously. 'If you mean a sort of cenotaph, like that of the Greeks, I think we would have found traces. But elsewhere around here,' he made a broad gesture with his arm, 'there was certainly conflict. Arrowheads embedded in skeletons. Skulls crushed. That kind of thing.'

'If we go on sitting here we'll all have lumbago,' Frances said, 'that I do know.'

She jumped up.

They all followed her. Laurence struggled to rise. He had injured his back in 1917, in the same disastrous attack that had wiped out so many of his men and had seen him decorated. He had never even opened the box in which his Military Cross lay, and never consulted a doctor about his back.

'Give me your hand.' Frances stood in front of him. 'Come on, Laurence, we American-born girls are fearfully strong.' She grinned. 'Our grandmothers hewed logs and rode bareback.'

She braced herself and pulled him up, although for a second it seemed more likely that she would fall on top of him, than that he would get to his feet. Her beret fell off and her hair was in her eyes. She brushed it back and pushed the woollen hat in her pocket.

'I thought you were born in New York,' Laurence said teasingly. 'Not a lot of hewing there, I imagine.'

'No, but there's a hewing culture, you see. America's still building, growing. There's a sort of energy.' She sounded quite earnest, then added, 'That's why your aristocratic Englishmen were stealing our womenfolk as brides before the war . . . and at least our girls aren't your cousins.' Her lips twitched.

Eleanor and Patrick had pulled ahead of them and were climbing the mound. Patrick turned and beckoned to them, then continued to scramble upwards with Eleanor.

Frances seemed disinclined to climb the steep slope.

'At least they've stopped rowing,' she said. 'I sometimes think Patrick enjoys it but Eleanor feels genuinely passionate about her ideals. He shouldn't play with her.'

'Have you ever been back to America since you were sent here as a child?' Laurence asked.

She shrugged. 'I always meant to one day. But then everything happened.'

They had reached a fence and she leaned back against a post.

Laurence said, 'It must have been hard.' He meant it but it sounded inadequate.

'Well, none of our lives are what we thought they'd be.' She paused. 'Eleanor said your own wife died?' When he didn't answer immediately she seemed embarrassed. 'I'm sorry—'

'No. It's quite all right,' he answered quickly. 'It was a long while back. She died having a baby and he didn't survive her.'

Frances looked at him. 'I didn't know you'd had a child. I'm so sorry. Were you there?'

'No. I was in France. After I embarked I never saw her again and I never saw our son at all.'

They resumed walking.

'But compared with Lydia—' he began.

Frances said quietly, 'Do you know, I still wonder what happened to Kitty almost every day.'

'Did you ever have a sense of it?'

'Not then, perhaps. I was almost hysterical. It was all more ghastly than anything you can imagine. Lydia was ...' She blinked quickly. 'And Digby went from bewilderment to fear to rage and nights of heavy drinking. But later, with time to think, years to think, I'm sure that if she had wandered off we would have found her. A huge mass of people looked for weeks. How far could she have got? Other children who've disappeared like that have been found in the end. I kept thinking of the Saville Kent case.'

She glanced at him to see if he knew what she was referring to. He nodded, although he remembered only the name, not anything connected with it.

'My aunt used to talk of it,' she said. 'But then that little boy was killed by his own sister.' She seemed to be gauging his reaction. 'And they found the body.' Eventually she added, 'And with us there was a kidnap note. Digby did everything he could to pay off the kidnappers but perhaps it was the wrong way to deal with it. I think, being Digby, he wanted to try to catch the kidnapper, rather than simply handing over the money. But he may just have sealed her fate.' She stopped. 'No. I'm being awfully unfair. I didn't always find Digby easy, but Lydia adored him. Perhaps I prefer that scenario to her being taken for any other reason.'

'Like what?' It was the first he'd heard of a note.

'I don't know.' Her eye caught Laurence's and she looked away. 'Something darker than mere greed.'

He looked up to see Patrick trying to descend Silbury Hill

slowly and carefully, but eventually the steep sides forced him to run in order not to lose his balance. He was gasping for air and pale but laughing. He held his hand out to Eleanor who was edging down sideways, using her hazel stick. She was windswept and looked happy.

'You should have come up,' she said. 'You have a sort of aerial view of this whole odd world. You can see Easton and everything.'

'How old is all this?' Laurence asked.

Patrick was looking north, where Laurence could just see the standing stones at Avebury. He didn't answer.

'Thousands of years, Lydia says,' said Frances.

'Three millennia before Christ,' Patrick finally said. 'But of course it took hundreds of years to build. It would be like asking how old is London?'

'I like it here,' Eleanor said. 'I like all the layers: people living on top of the past. It makes me feel like an insignificant speck. A rather cosy insignificant speck.'

'You're not intimidated by all that lies behind and beneath you?' Patrick asked. 'Nor proud to see how far we've come — out of our caves, beyond witchcraft and superstition, to all the achievements of the modern age?'

Eleanor stared at him unbelievingly. 'Achievements? Cutting a swathe through a whole generation? Tanks and aeroplanes and barbed wire and chlorine gas?'

Patrick, half smiling, held up a defensive hand.

Frances said, 'I'm the sort of American who likes the past in a sort of aesthetic way. I'm probably very superficial. When I got to Cambridge, I could hardly believe the beauty of it. When I first arrived here, Easton was like a picture in a storybook: this strange old house, the avenue, the family and the village sharing a name. It was the England we were brought up on. That was before ... everything, of course.'

Eleanor moved closer to her friend and tucked her arm through hers. Patrick looked slightly embarrassed. Eleanor turned to him. 'Perhaps Patrick likes unpicking it all, so that he can feel in control of it. Identify, measure, label and prevail.'

'You might be surprised to know that what I always liked about the ancient past was the mystery,' Patrick said, his voice a tone higher. 'I'm not interested in possessing the stuff. I gave up treasure hunting when I was thirteen. And actually I don't want to have definitive answers. I prefer fragments to reconstructions.'

Instead of biting back, Eleanor said, 'We ought to be cutting back home, you know. Nicholas will be driving Maggie mad.'

'Of course.' Patrick gave a little bow. 'We'll go straight back across the fields and be home in time for crumpets.'

They were relatively silent on the way home. Laurence listened to their footsteps, Patrick's breathing, rooks cawing in a stand of trees and the breeze just catching the hedgerows. Patrick opened a gate, which creaked loudly as it swung back. The smell of hawthorn blossom was quite noticeable as they passed through. When he was in France, Laurence had feared he would never enjoy times like these again. Yet he had never belonged anywhere, as the Easton brothers did. He felt momentarily sorry for Digby, who had known this territory all his life, who had once been, in his own way, a tribal chief like the skeletons in the barrows, but who would never return to his small realm.

Suddenly there was Easton, standing in its slight depression, sheltered from the elements. To the far side he could see the avenue of limes, a part of the church, the lake hidden in its shrubbery and the ha-ha marking off the formal gardens from the fields. From here William's choice of position for the maze seemed inspired. Even in its rudimentary form its precise geometry was visible from the surrounding land, its design seeming to draw together all the components of the landscape. Lydia's idea for a living memorial had been simply but perfectly interpreted. And yet William could never have seen it from up here on the downs. From the prison of his chair, William's vision had created all that now lay below them, just from his imagination, using black marks and contour lines on paper.

By the time they returned, David was waiting for them with Nicholas, who seemed indifferent to whether his mother had come back or not. He was hopping exuberantly on one leg.

'Daddy let me go in the maze but David says I can't go in the church because it smells,' he said. 'So I've been cooking. Susan and me did biscuits. I put on silver balls. Soon I'm going to go on the helter-skelter at Wembley and see the biggest steam engine in the world.'

Julian had complained that David was fretting about taking the car to London for their trip, and plainly thought it was an abuse of a good engine to push it. Patrick had laughed, saying that David's dislike of the city evidently now extended to objecting at the car he loved being exposed to its dangers. But the David who appeared now seemed completely relaxed, even excited.

'Mr Bartram, we can see something. The pattern's coming clear in the church. I've told Mr Bolitho and he said you might want to go there as soon as you got back.'

'Go back to the house with David and help Mrs Hill,' Eleanor said to Nicholas.

'I don't want to see an old church anyway,' Nicholas said, looking cross but following David across the grass.

Laurence, Patrick and Eleanor walked slowly towards the church. The petrol fumes were still lingering and they waited between the hefty yews until David arrived, pushing William.

Inside the church, Laurence dropped back to let William go first.

'Good heavens,' William said.

The last veil of floor covering had now been completely removed and what was revealed was unmistakable in white stone on grey.

'A pattern. It's a sort of big geometrical knot,' Eleanor said. 'It's beautiful. And perfect.'

After a second Patrick said, 'It's a maze.' He looked at Laurence for confirmation. 'Isn't it?'

Laurence nodded, thinking that this one small church was rewarding him with so many surprises.

'Actually in a church it's usually a labyrinth. And it's very rare in England,' he said. 'There are several in France and Italy. There's one at Ely but that's a cathedral, whereas this little church is ... nothing. But I'm almost certain the pattern must be medieval.'

'There's a labyrinth in Cambridgeshire,' William said, 'an old one. The only other similar thing I've heard of is in Lincolnshire but that's actually a replica of a garden maze near by.'

William was excited despite himself, Laurence thought. In the last few years, boredom, rather than the Germans, must have been William's worst enemy.

'What's it for?' Frances said. 'Is it just a decoration?'

'You either walk along them or meditate upon them,' Laurence said. 'Some people think they are just intended to focus the mind on God; others say they represent Christ's trials on the way to Calvary or the human journey through life.'

Patrick, who had just stood looking intently at the floor, was already turning to leave. 'I'd like to draw it,' he said. 'I'm going to fetch some paper.'

Eleanor said, 'Bother. I really need to get Nicholas's tea.'

She made an expression of regret as they all turned to go.

David followed them too, but not before he'd stood for a moment, looking down at the pattern. When he realised Laurence had seen him, he gave him a wide smile before turning and walking swiftly after the others.

When the church fell quiet, Laurence lingered, taking it all in. The pattern in front of him was unlike pictures of continental mazes that he had seen and it clearly extended under the font and front pews. What puzzled him was why anyone had chosen to cover it up.

He didn't bother to put on the electric light, preferring to look at the maze as it would have been seen over the centuries. The monochrome design remained clear even as the light began to fade. After a time, he wasn't sure how long, he heard the door open and close behind him. It was Patrick, with a pad under his arm. He stood next to the altar and gazed at the maze.

'I find I don't want to walk on it,' he said, 'although it must be perfectly robust to survive under the bitumen.' He took out a pencil and gestured towards the light switch. 'Do you mind?'

Laurence shook his head. 'Not at all.'

As Patrick drew, they sat in companionable silence. Finally he said, 'Mind you, it's not a labyrinth.' He tipped his drawing towards Laurence. 'Not a smooth conduit to God nor a final redemption through travail. Nothing like William's jolly maze either. It's a mass of dead ends and false junctions. More like the fabled maze of the Minotaur that dear Sir Arthur keeps seeing in every crooked passageway at Knossos. There is only one way out and if it had walls you'd exhaust yourself long before you succeeded. It's ... a trap, a prison.' Then he added, more bleakly, 'It's a perfect symbol for Easton.' He took out a cigarette. 'Do you mind?' he said. 'It being a church?'

Laurence shook his head.

'Julian would mind,' Patrick said. He inhaled deeply.

They dined early because they needed to make a very early start to Wembley the next morning. The discovery of the floor seemed to have excited everyone.

Lydia said, 'Do you think we should tell the bishop?'

Eleanor said, 'They'd probably dig up the maze and take it to Salisbury.'

'A secret Easton maze,' Julian said rather earnestly. 'And to think it was under our feet all the time.'

Patrick looked at him and seemed about to speak but he paused as Frances spoke to William.

'I'm not like Lydia. When she came here she thought it was quaint, but I find the name Easton Deadall a bit sinister. When I was little in London and I first heard Lydia was coming to live at a place called Deadall, I was scared.' She opened her eyes wide in mock fear. 'The more so when I knew I'd be coming too. I thought the names of English villages went back to the medieval Church and were things like Barking Abbots or Priests Worthy, or were in Latin: Parva, Regis or Nowhere-cum-Nowhere. All those impossibly rural names dripping mud and madness, like Cold Withers or Sheepscurvy.'

'There's nowhere called Sheepscurvy, Frances,' Eleanor said with an assumed sternness. 'You made that up.'

'There is a jolly-sounding place called Cold Slad,' Laurence said.

For once, he thought, the small ghost of Kitty Easton was not hanging around the conversation and people could be normal, light-hearted, themselves. He had been here only a few weeks but sometimes he felt exasperated by their frozen memories: not by Lydia, in whom it could only be expected, but with the others.

'Well, Sheepscombe then,' Frances said. 'There is a Sheepscombe. But Deadall—'

'It's unlikely to have anything to do with death,' Julian said. 'It will be a version of something perfectly innocuous because English place names are very old.'

He had reverted to the sort of pompous defensiveness that Patrick's presence seemed to bring out in him.

'It's probably from the word "deed" — land deeds or something.'

'Actually,' Patrick said, sitting forward, 'I was thinking about that as I drew the maze in the church. Tutankhamun's tomb in Egypt, Evans's work on Knossos on Crete: what do they have in common?'

He looked around, more to see that he had got everybody's attention than expecting an answer, Laurence thought.

'Each has a labyrinth, a maze. And what is a maze? An architectural mystery? A place of arcane ritual, a hiding place? Even, if complicated enough, a fortification?'

Patrick looked directly at Julian.

'I don't know why it never occurred to me before, regarding Easton. But I think Deadall is a variant on Daedalus.' He ended on a slight note of triumph.

'The father of Icarus?' Eleanor said.

Patrick nodded more vigorously.

'Daedalus the craftsman,' Frances said, slowly. 'But I don't see how that links with—'

'In ancient myth, Daedalus created the Labyrinth,' Laurence said, seeing Patrick's pleased expression. William was nodding.

'He made it to keep the monster — the Minotaur — in,' Laurence said. 'In Crete.'

'Fortunately here at Easton we have captured only Aphrodite,' William said with a small smile.

Patrick said, 'There have always been rumours that there's been a maze at Easton. Maybe it was never a hedge maze. Or maybe, if there was a hedge maze, the idea was taken from the church. Possibly one of our papist ancestors had seen one in a French cathedral and copied the idea. It's more than likely.'

Even Julian looked interested, his sceptical expression fading, and Eleanor was leaning forward, resting her chin on her hands.

'And the ones in France could have been inspired by ancient settlements,' William said. 'They have standing stones there as well as at Avebury and Stonehenge.'

Maggie, who had slipped in almost unnoticed, removed some dishes and handed Julian a new bottle of wine, but he simply set it on the table. He was frowning slightly, in perplexity, Laurence thought, not displeasure.

'Once it was probably Easton Daedalus. Or something Daedalus. As Julian says, back in the mists of time, villages took the names of landowners or were named after any distinguishing feature.' Patrick looked at Frances. 'Hence Sheepscombe. Simply Sheep Valley. It's the same principle with Bridgwater, or Blackpool. With us it's the family who owned land around here, Easton, plus Daedalus, after the maze.'

Julian looked puzzled. 'Are you saying they named it after a maze or the maze was designed because of the name?'

Laurence thought it a good question. William had referred to one example of a church copying a hedge maze in eastern England, but Patrick shrugged.

'Not a clue, Jules, old chap. It's only a notion. We'll never know, although,' he paused, 'my guess is it may be some kind of folk memory of the prehistoric remains roundabout. For all the strange structures and the digging and the wild guessing over the last two centuries, we haven't a clue what else was involved, or what else they built that wasn't as durable as the Welsh granite they brought to Stonehenge. They may have made wood henges; they might have used hedges for mazes. We really have no idea.'

It seemed to Laurence that Julian and Patrick were actually not so unalike. Julian's interest in agricultural innovation and Patrick's passion for the distant past were not dissimilar; he'd even glimpsed physical similarities between the brothers as Patrick had spoken. For once, Patrick was not lecturing in a manner that suggested he was cleverer than everybody else but, rather, wanting to share an idea.

'It does make me think that the story of mazes associated with Easton has real substance to it,' Patrick said, and then added, almost an eager schoolboy, 'don't you think?' His eyes moved from one face to another.

Frances said, looking at her sister, 'It makes what Lydia's doing seem inspired, putting a maze at the heart of Easton again.'

'But it is only a theory,' Julian said firmly, although he seemed intrigued almost in spite of himself. 'As you say, we'll never know.'

'It's a good theory, though,' Eleanor said. 'It feels right. Labyrinths, mazes, whatever you call them – stone patterns or ancient hedges, they're part of the whole history of the area.'

Julian flushed. Did he think Eleanor was contradicting him, Laurence wondered. Did he not see Eleanor might want to emphasise the importance of William's work?

'I like the idea,' Lydia said. 'Kitty loved the story of the Minotaur. She thought he was only bad because he was lonely. She wanted to rescue him and feed him clover.'

The room was suddenly a place of clanging knives and forks, gulps of wine and clicks of forks against teeth. A momentary shifting of logs in the fire. The creak of a chair. Nobody spoke. Then, as if they'd all been suspended in time for a few seconds, William asked Julian if he could revisit the generator shed and whether in time it would have the capacity to drive electricity for the cottages.

Patrick turned to Laurence. He spoke quietly.

'You should consider coming out to Knossos one day. I shan't be there for much longer but I think you'd find it interesting, if a little startling in its current incarnation. Spring or autumn's best. Summers are abominable. Searing heat and the Meltemi, a wind that drives men mad and covers the site in grit, blows incessantly ... But in spring, with the snow still on the White Mountains, and olive blossom blowing like fine, pale-green snow, and the sea still cold ...'

Laurence felt instant excitement, his customary caution set aside. Perhaps Patrick Easton was just making conversation but to see these great palaces and this faraway island with its heat and strangeness, whose ancient people, Evans had revealed, were entirely peaccable, would be the journey of a lifetime.

'I'd like that very much.'

'The thing is, what you feel there is that these people were alive. They weren't setting out to be mysterious. They were just living their lives: whether nasty, nice, ugly, beautiful, successful or unlucky. Their world was coherent to them, just as ours is to us.' He paused. 'Or to most of us, away from Easton.'

'When I was on honeymoon,' Lydia said, and Laurence felt a sudden sadness for her as the room tensed again, 'we saw a labyrinth in a church.' Embarrassed by the sudden attention her words had caused, she faltered. 'I think it was in Italy, near Milan. Maybe. Or Florence – my memory is not too good these days.' She pressed her fingertips to her temples. 'It wasn't at all religious, though, and despite being in a church it had a

Minotaur – one like Patrick's – in the middle. It said so in Latin. Digby read it to me.'

Patrick looked triumphant. 'Exactly, Lydia. Exactly.'

Lydia gave him a brilliant smile.

'I wish Digby could have been here to share all this,' she said.

CHAPTER SEVEN

$\mathscr{T}$he day began full of promise. Even first thing it was already warm and bright. While David drove Eleanor, Nicholas and Maggie to London, Laurence had agreed to travel by train with Patrick, Frances and Julian. When he went down to breakfast, Eleanor and William were nowhere to be seen, but hearing a giggle from the butler's pantry he put his head round the door. Nicholas was kneeling on a chair in the kitchen, watching Maggie putting crockery in one of the picnic baskets.

'Isn't it exciting?' she said.

He noticed she had put a ribbon in her hair. Animated and with her eyes shining, she looked more childlike than usual. He thought that although everybody was perfectly kind to her, she could never have had much fun in her life. Her best hope was being useful.

'Mrs Hill says they've got Chinamen with pigtails and Wild West cowboys and the King and Queen might be there and Miss Frances says there's a great big tent full of chocolate. And a sugar mountain.'

Nicholas's eyes had widened. 'And Not Stop. Mummy says there's a Not Stop.'

'Not Stop?' Laurence said.

'It's Never Stop,' Maggie said, like a big sister. 'Never Stop, Nicky. Give me that plate.'

She looked at Laurence as if he were half-witted. Lifting up the side plate, she turned it to the light and rubbed it with the sleeve of her cardigan.

'It's been in the papers, Nicky's mother showed us. It's a bit like a train but it doesn't have a driver or anything and it just goes slowly and doesn't stop and people get on and off.'

Laurence nodded. 'Right. Right. Well, I hope I can have a go on it.'

'Nicky will have to be very careful getting on,' Maggie said firmly.

'And Red Indians and an elephant,' Nicholas said.

'It's just its head,' Maggie said. 'But there's an ostrich and a whole statue of Prince Edward with his horse in butter. How do you think he doesn't melt? Will they eat it after? How do you think you do a statue in butter?'

'I've really no idea,' Laurence said. 'We'll have to try it. We'll need a lot of butter, though.'

Maggie's face fell a little. 'Not of the prince, though, as Nicky's mother says he's weak and ind—indolent . . . even if he's quite handsome.'

Laurence set his face in what he hoped was a serious expression. 'Well, I'm sure she's right. Nicholas's mother is something of an expert on the royal family.'

Nicholas beamed. For a second he looked extraordinarily like his father. Laurence watched him pick up a teacup and hand it to Maggie.

'Good boy,' she said approvingly, then turned to a rack of biscuits and started to load them into a tin. Nicholas touched one with a finger.

'All right,' Maggie said. 'You can have one. Just one, mind, and don't finger them all.' Then she looked at Laurence. 'I made these, Susan taught me. Susan is the best biscuit and cake maker in Easton.' She giggled, and Laurence thought he had never heard her laugh before. 'Susan says biscuits were the way to David's heart. Do you want one?'

He was about to say no when he caught sight of her eager expression.

'Absolutely. Just one. And I won't finger the others.'

He bit into it. They were ginger biscuits, soft and fragrant.

'Well, Susan's certainly taught you well,' he said. 'He'll be a lucky man who marries you.'

She blushed a deep red almost immediately and he hoped he hadn't offended her but then she looked up and smiled shyly.

'I was actually looking for Mrs Bolitho,' he said. 'Nicky, do you know where your mother is?'

'She's gone to the maze with Daddy,' Nicholas answered. 'She'll be back in ten minutes. Then we're going in the car.'

Laurence walked down the passage, past the laundry room with its boiler and two big Belfast sinks. Sheets were hanging from an overhead rack. A disintegrating hamper was pushed to one side under the half-open door of a laundry chute, and three irons stood ready for heating on the range next to a packet of Reckitt's Blue.

Although it was not washday and the fire was out, the lingering smell of washing soda and starch took him back to childhood. His more modest home had had a separate washhouse and a woman who came in to do the family laundry. She was so fat that when she waddled down the garden in her pinafore, her arms full of washing, it was hard to tell where sheets ended and woman began. He would stand in the doorway, watching her huge arms force the dirty clothes down into the suds and wring the sheets out with thick red hands. She chatted all the time but with such a strong Irish accent that he scarcely understood anything she said to him. His mother had put a stop to it all when she'd arrived home in a new hat one day and he'd looked at the waving feathers and said, 'Jaysus, but you're a sight for sore eyes.'

He passed through the baize door, which thudded softly behind him. The house was completely silent. He peered into the drawing room; its careful formality appeared unchanged from the previous century except for a solitary copy of *Country Life* left on a side table, its pages curling, and a plaited brown strand of wiring running to a lamp. He tried the latch on the right-hand french window. It opened easily. He stepped on to the terrace. The sky was virtually cloudless, the blues, pinks and lilacs of June flower beds fresh in the early-morning air. Unseen birds were singing and he could even smell the old roses that clung to the wall.

He was glad, as much for Maggie's sake as anything else, that the day looked set fair. He could see David, Eleanor and William by the maze at the far side of the upper lawn. David had put planks down so that he could wheel the chair as close as possible. Eleanor saw Laurence as he approached. As she waved, the brim of her deep-brimmed straw hat bobbed.

'Are you all set?' she called. 'We're going to be off in five minutes.'

David and William were in earnest discussion but broke off as he reached them.

'Morning,' William said. 'We're just sorting out the watering. Almost all the plants have taken but the ground here is drying out much more quickly than I expected and we're going to need some organised irrigation.'

'We can run hoses from the stables,' David said. 'We might

need a pump but the pressure should be enough. We could use the generator. Though Mr Easton says the levels on the river are already so low this year, we might have to switch off if we don't get rain. First time in twenty years, he says, because of the dry winter.' He surveyed the maze with satisfaction. 'Good strong plants. Give them some water, they'll do fine, I reckon.'

As Laurence looked at David, he found it hard to imagine he had ever lived in a city. Despite the man's initial reservations about driving to London, he had made an effort. He was wearing a suit, well worn but clean, a tie, his shoes were polished and his hair was slicked down. He was holding his chauffeur's cap in one hand, but he looked every bit the countryman he was.

'David, Julian and I are the only ones praying for a cool summer,' William said. 'I'd expect to replace some if there are gaps, but I hope they're putting down good roots.'

The pattern of the maze was increasingly clear. The plants had become bulkier even since Laurence had first seen them and there was bright new growth on almost all of them. In the centre was a statue of a half-draped woman.

'William's a romantic,' Eleanor said. 'Meet Aphrodite.'

'Actually it was Eleanor's suggestion,' William said, 'and David's execution. She saw poor old Aphrodite lingering forlornly by the lake.'

As William paused, Eleanor said, 'You know, we do need to set off. Nicky is terribly keen that Maggie should go with us in the car so I've said she may, though I think she was really quite excited about the train.'

'Righto.' William looked quite cheerful. 'I'm going to make the best of the day. Work without interruption.' He smiled, then reached out and stroked Eleanor's arm. 'It's all right, Ellie, I'm going to be fine.'

'You know Mrs Hill is coming in to fix your lunch soon after midday. And Susan will be checking on you, to see if you need anything.'

'Oh dear.' William smiled. 'I'll try to think of something.'

'Lydia's had a bad night,' Eleanor said. 'Frances thinks she'll sleep today.' She shook her head almost imperceptibly. 'What she needs most is a doctor but she just won't have it ...'

Laurence pulled out his father's old watch. His father had been dead for nearly fifteen years, yet the watch kept perfect time. It was five to eight.

'I'd better find Patrick. Enjoy your peaceful day, William. Eleanor, we'll meet you by the roaring Lions of Wembley.'

Laurence took the path around the house. The Daimler was parked on the drive, ready to go. By the stables, Patrick was leaning against his Morris, lighting a cigarette. He held a silver cigarette case out to Laurence.

'Frances has gone back for her gloves,' he said. 'Or probably to tell Lydia something else. You'd think we were going to the French Riviera for a month.'

The kitchen door opened on to the yard and Julian came out.

'We need to get going,' he said. 'The train leaves before nine.'

'Then we shall,' Patrick said, tapping his cigarette on the bonnet of his car. 'But perhaps we should wait for Frances?'

Even as he spoke, Frances appeared. She had on a loose summer dress and carried a coat over her arm. A green cloche hat made her face look elfin and the effect was increased when she smiled.

'Sorry, Patrick.' She waggled some cream gloves in his direction. 'Hardly worth it because I shall undoubtedly leave them in the car, or on the train, or drop them at Wembley, but my Aunt Lavinia's precepts stay with me. A lady without gloves is a lady on the brink.'

'Aunt Lavinia?' Patrick looked amused.

'And anyway, I bite my nails.'

Laurence hadn't seen her so relaxed. He had worried that both she and Eleanor would have their day overshadowed by anxiety about those left behind, although both Lydia and William claimed that they would rather stay at Easton. He thought it was probably true in Lydia's case – since his arrival he had never seen her go further than the upper garden – but there was so much that he thought William might enjoy at Wembley, not least observing Nicholas's excitement.

They made the train just in time. It was fairly full. The first-class compartment was already very warm, with a middle-aged woman and a vicar comfortably established. Patrick opened the window a little.

At one point Frances whispered, 'Are you seriously going to see His Royal Highness immortalised in butter?'

'I don't think you can be immortalised in butter,' Laurence said. 'Not when the next day you'll meet oblivion between the toast and the marmalade. It's not exactly the Colossus at Rhodes, is it?'

The vicar gave Laurence a stern look over his spectacles, while the corners of Frances's mouth twitched as she tried not to laugh, but after that conversation felt inhibited. Julian, in the seat nearest to the corridor, read his *Morning Post*. Patrick sat on the other side between the vicar and Laurence, armed with a newspaper and a small book on Mesopotamia. Eventually and slightly self-consciously, Laurence brought out the mystery novel his friend Charles had given him. Frances raised an eyebrow and he held it upright so that she could see the cover. She seemed amused. From time to time over the next hour he looked up to see Frances with her forehead against the window, gazing out, her face almost hidden by her hat. Some instinct caused him to look up just as they passed the White Horse and she had leaned forward to get a better view. He watched her but she never noticed.

Despite himself, he was soon caught up with Mrs Christie's ridiculous Belgian detective. By the time the ticket collector opened the door to their compartment, Julian was apparently asleep, although his fists were tightly balled. The misshapen scars showed clearly against his taut skin. Patrick was reading his *Times* and Frances was talking quietly to the woman next to her. Laurence looked out at the western approaches to London: on every journey there were new roads and new houses and more being built by the look of things. The train was slowing now. A billboard announced: 'Thrift, security, healthy living. Your own home in the country.' A big key and an acorn at the centre were obviously the symbols for this new life.

The vicar rifled among the papers in an elderly briefcase. Julian opened his eyes, uncurled his hands and stretched. Awake, he thrust his hands in his pockets. As they passed a gasometer, the sweet smell of gas seeped through the window. The long vistas were soon blocked out as they came to a stretch of soot-stained factory buildings following the line of the railway.

At Paddington they took a short ride to Marylebone and within minutes had caught the LNER train on the loop line to Exhibition Station. Each train was more crowded than the one before. Laurence found himself standing jammed in a corner away from the doors, his head slightly bent by the curve of the roof. A Wembley Lion snarled from a poster six inches from his face. Next to it the word Metroland was imposed upon a garish stylised sunrise, a boxy house and solid lupins. He felt slightly giddy. If he leaned further forward he could just see Frances, who had been offered a seat, but Julian and Patrick were out of sight.

After a few minutes, he began to feel the first stirrings of an anxiety that he had not faced for a couple of years. He took a couple of deep breaths, gripping the back of a seat. He tried to fix his eyes on a line of rivets across the carriage but his neck was prickling and he was beginning to sweat. The carriage was getting very warm, he could smell male sweat and women's perfume. He had no idea how long this last bit of their journey would take; surely it was meant to be not much more than a quarter of an hour. He forced himself to focus on an imaginary map of London and ran a finger around his collar to ease its pressure.

Just when he thought he must escape or pass out, the train took a curve to the left, and the standing passengers swayed. Through their slight shift of position he suddenly saw Frances, watching him with concern. He attempted to smile at her but it felt forced and he looked away. She got up from her seat and moved towards him, squeezing through the passengers standing between them. A woman near him tut-tutted, but, smiling brightly and pushing determinedly, Frances reached him. She was immediately forced right up against him but she also placed her hand on his upper arm. It was that action that seemed an act of intimacy. He wanted to cling to her until the dizziness had passed.

'It's all right,' she said, not even bothering to ask for confirmation that something very much wasn't all right. 'We'll be there in five minutes.'

Although he still longed to escape, he felt the panic subside.

The train drew in a few minutes later. They let the other passengers get off, noisy and urgent.

'You'd think this was the last day,' Frances said. 'Look, there are Patrick and Julian waiting for us. Are you sure you are all right? We can stop for a while.'

'No. I'm fine. It was just the heat.'

She looked at him but did not reply and he felt churlish for not showing his gratitude.

A quarter of an hour later they passed through turnstiles into the exhibition. Patrick and Julian were studying the map. Laurence gazed about at an extraordinary landscape of domes and towers, pagodas and massive archways, as far as the eye could see, each building wonderfully unrelated to its neighbour, with flower beds, rivers and terraces, even a lake with pleasure boats. Around them a flow of humanity moved slowly and sinuously along paths and avenues. Immediately in front of them were two hefty neoclassical buildings – the Palaces of Industry and Engineering. He had seen pictures in the newspapers and had thought them rather grim. William had pronounced them unimaginative, but in the sunshine their severe lines were softened by the gardens and waterways around them.

Despite himself, Laurence felt exhilarated by the mood of the crowd, the fine early summer's day and by Frances's company. He could smell burnt sugar, grass and roses, hot oil and horse manure. Above the chatter and laughter, the wails of a nearby baby and people shouting to each other, he could hear an assembly of noises almost beyond what his brain could process. A crash of cymbals and trombones at a distance, a hurdy-gurdy, a tinkling of bells from a pavilion on his right, water rushing and some animal bellowing. A tall man in uniform, rather strangely of a major in the Scots Guards, walked past with a beautiful young woman on his arm. She caught Laurence's eye and held it for a minute before dropping her gaze. He looked after her; she was dressed all in black and white, with the palest blonde hair he had ever seen. He had a feeling that in this unreal place anything was possible. Patrick noticed her too.

'What a looker,' he said. 'Do you think she's his wife?'

On the train they had decided to split up for the hour or so before they were due to get together for lunch at the Grand.

'We don't want to look like a Methodist church outing,'

Patrick said as they arrived. Clearly he wanted to be free of them though he gave them no hint of what he had planned.

Julian was keen to see the monolithic Palace of Industry and was undaunted by the queues.

'My *Times*,' Patrick had said, consulting his newspaper just before they all dispersed, 'calls it "the ripened fruit of all the wisdom and invention of the ages".' He looked at his brother. 'Could have been set up just for you. Enough wisdom and invention to keep you topped up for another decade or so at Easton.'

Julian, who was dressed in his country suit and already looked hot and uncomfortable, flushed.

'But then a quick restorative nip to see the most beautiful negress in the world, do you think?' Patrick said. 'Or into the Palace of Beauty? Think of it as art, Jules. Fruits of the empire. The sort of thing you fought for.'

Julian didn't even acknowledge Patrick's comment. He took out his map again and scanned it briefly, before nodding and saying brusquely, 'I'll see you at the Grand for luncheon then.' With that, he strode off.

As Patrick himself turned to go, he passed his folded newspaper to Laurence, pointing to the inside-page headline. It read: 'Italian opinion shocked.' Underneath were details of the abduction and murder of the Socialist Signor Matteotti and the arrest of the presumed assassins. Patrick raised an eyebrow but made no comment. He lifted his hat to Frances and walked off in the opposite direction with a sense of purpose.

Laurence skimmed the piece. 'The charges have no relation to Signor Mussolini or the honesty of the Fascisti generally,' it continued. He looked around for a bin and pushed *The Times* deep into it.

Laurence was glad to have Frances to himself but now he felt he should offer suggestions as to what they should see, when in truth, faced with the huge scale of the exhibition, he had no idea where to begin. Julian had told him it was spread over two hundred acres. Now he was here, the chaotic reality of its size hit him.

Frances flicked through the exhibition programme and then, rather randomly he thought, opted for Underwater World. 'We'll impress Nicky, at least,' she said.

The aquarium was only five minutes' walk away. From the outside a huge painting promised a vast if rather complicated marine world. Octopuses waved from behind a coral reef and malign-looking sharks lurked on the seabed near a treasure chest and what looked like a smiling skull still in a pirate's hat. Bubbles rose prettily and homely crabs lingered at the water's margin. They went in. After the glare outside, the room was cool and dark, the ranks of glass aquariums observed by quiet spectators. Presumably no single aquarium could contain the sort of peaceable undersea kingdom portrayed outside or one very fat creature would soon have the place to itself.

There was an uneven thudding noise and a faint bubbling of pumped water but otherwise it was almost silent. They paused to watch tiny jewel-like creatures flicker through a glassed-off pool, then crossed the floor to a big aquarium, faintly illuminated from behind. The noise they'd heard since they entered turned out to be three boys thumping excitedly on the pane of glass. The greenish water seemed to contain nothing more than a large black rock. The largest boy banged hard with a swing of his fist. His friend was opening up a penknife.

'You know what's in there?' Laurence asked, peering at the label on the glass.

They looked at him suspiciously.

'A Madagascan carnivorous sea slug,' he said. They were

watching him closely but had stopped banging the glass and he felt as much as saw Frances nodding her head beside him.

'It holds the record for the fastest flesh consumption of any living creature.'

The smallest boy stepped back and the other two shot a suspicious glance into the dark water.

'It does nothing but sleep and eat,' he added. 'Only fresh raw meat, of course. It's fussy. That's why it has to work fast.'

'I'm surprised they haven't taken more precautions,' Frances said, wonderingly. 'A special guard or something. If it should get out it could reduce half this room to bones in five minutes.' She looked at the container apprehensively.

Laurence shook his head. 'Quite careless really, although it would be something to see. Apparently they start with the face, the soft bits. It gives them a way in.'

None of the boys had answered but all three rapidly moved on to the next exhibit, which seemed to contain an unhappy eel.

Frances gave his arm a squeeze. 'Let's go,' she said.

Outside she walked ahead to a display of tropical plants and then called him.

'Oh smell this. This is definitely frangipane.'

She held a spray of waxy flowers between two fingers, stained with pollen. The small blossoms were perfect, shaped like small propellers, cream tinged with blush pink and a yellow crater at their heart. He could smell them without having to lean close.

'We had flowers like these in London when I was a child.' She suddenly looked wistful. 'This huge conservatory full of flowers. I used to hide in there. Pretend it was a garden.'

She didn't wait for a response but walked on, slowly. Laurence hung back and watched her. She looked paler, smaller and more delicate among the huge, vulgar blooms and the sky above them looked inadequately blue.

'I wonder how Julian is getting on?' he said, when she came back towards him. 'Rather him than me queuing in this sun. But he's a determined man.'

For a second Frances made no response, then she said, 'Why does Patrick tease Julian all the time? It's not fair. It makes him look stupid. '

Laurence instantly regretted the remark he'd intended as light-hearted banter.

'Jealousy?' he said.

'Julian's such a different man since Patrick got here. This gruff, wary person I scarcely recognise has eclipsed the kind man I know. He was almost rude to Ellen Kilminster when she told him Victor was coming back from Australia, even though, heaven knows, we need strong young men at Easton.'

'I suppose he worries about Lydia?'

Her face fell. 'We all worry about Lydia.'

'She's not well at all, is she?'

Even in the time he'd known her, Laurence thought she had become more frail.

'I think for a while she was buoyed up by all the schemes to improve Easton, creating the maze and the window, and some-how that's no longer enough,' Frances said. 'She's obviously more tired, and she gets muddled, and in a funny way she's becoming withdrawn from us all.'

'Yet she has a core of something stronger, I think?'

Frances nodded.

'She doesn't talk much about her husband,' Laurence said, carefully, and he regretted his comment when Frances stopped and turned to face him.

'I think it's more that after what happened to Kitty nothing else could really touch her. She lost two other babies, a little boy, stillborn, and a miscarriage. Her life was all about loss long before the war. She remembers our parents too, which I don't, and when Digby died I think she didn't have any emotion left. He'd swept her off her feet. He was impulsive like that. And she felt guilty about Digby, because she couldn't live up to him.'

'Yet she is the last to be blamed, I'd have thought,' Laurence said. 'She's very much the sufferer in this.'

'Lydia would forgive him anything,' Frances went on as if she hadn't heard. 'We'd had this careful, orderly upbringing and she was always the more reserved of the two of us. Then along comes Digby and he bursts into her little world. Everything he did was larger than life. He was inexhaustible and impulsive. He had oodles of charm and a fiery temper but it was all quickly forgotten too. He was not an easy husband but probably an entertaining one. Certainly at first.' She stopped, then turned away.

Laurence thought it was a decidedly qualified compliment.

'I came to join her not long after they'd married,' Frances said, 'when my elderly aunt in London died; I was still quite young, Kitty was a baby.'

She shook her head, as if unable to believe Easton had once been so different.

'Digby was wonderful to me, made Easton my home, but there was always another side to him and that emerged more and more as time went by.'

She was obviously thinking how best to describe her brother-in-law.

'I think he wasn't very good when things didn't go his way. There would be explosions of temper or frustration, sudden and soon gone. Lydia always believed in the Digby she'd first loved, but it made everything so tense, her trying to head off Digby's rages. An exhausting sort of love.'

Laurence noticed her unconsciously flexing her fingers.

He hadn't realised that Lydia had tried to have other children. No wonder she sometimes seemed remote behind the polite smiles and well-mannered concern.

'If she didn't hang on to this apparently foolish, even embarrassing certainty that Kitty, at least, wasn't dead,' Frances said, 'I think she'd have gone mad years ago.'

She didn't look at him as she spoke but walked on, bending to smell a flower from time to time.

Not for the first time, but with increased foreboding, Laurence wondered how on earth Lydia might react if William's restorations did come up with absolute proof that Kitty was dead. That she had been dead for more than a decade.

Frances turned at the end of the border. 'Could we get a drink?' she said. 'I'm dreadfully thirsty. There's a place over there, I think.' She pointed to a red-and-white striped stall.

'Of course. Stay here, I'll fetch a lemonade.'

She sat on a low wall as he queued at the lemonade stall behind a noisy family; the smallest boy, in grass-stained knickerbockers, scuffed the ground with his foot. When the father turned round to pull him away, Laurence saw that all that was left of the far side of his face was pitted and tautly ridged skin. Their eyes met.

As he looked away swiftly, Laurence caught a glimpse of red hair and a light-coloured dress. Something about the woman's movement made him think it was Eleanor. Trying not to spill the lemonade, he eased his way between couples and families walking along the main drive. There she was, holding her son's hand and gazing at the same exotic gardens. She didn't seem nearly as surprised to see him as he was to see her.

'They're beautiful, I suppose, but there's something a bit frantic about them,' she said, hardly looking at him.

'Eleanor . . . Hello, Nicky.'

'What do you think?' she said.

'Frances loves them,' he said, pointing across the central bed before returning his gaze to Eleanor.

'All these stiff lilies, they remind me of funeral flowers,' she said. 'They're too much. Artificial. Give me forget-me-nots and delphiniums and larkspur when I die.'

He had a brief vision of his mother, dressed in crape with a veil over her face, touching the flowers that lay on his father's coffin. He had not thought of it for years. Her hand in its black kid glove brushed the white blossoms, which seemed to him then living things already condemned to death by being cut. He was fourteen and had kept very close to her, with his sister crying noisily on his other side. As his mother leaned over the coffin, the acrid smell of the crape was repellent. It had rained as they stood by the grave and when they were home, his mother had pushed back her damp veil to reveal the horror of her stained face, black streaks running down it as if she too were decaying. A year later, she too was dead.

'Laurie,' Eleanor said, 'you're miles away.'

'Sorry. Thinking of my mother,' he said, and smiled ruefully.

'Did she like flowers?'

'Yes.'

It was not really true. They had an elderly gardener who kept things neat, his mother's main requirement for a garden. All he remembered were some rather tortured rose bushes.

'Carnations,' he said, feeling it was expected of him.

'Despite what this all stands for,' she gave a small smile as she gestured around her, 'it is lovely to be here. But it breaks my heart for William. He wouldn't want to see the organised spectacle: the choirs and the jamboree and the rodeo and the whole circus element – they're not his thing. But he'd love to see the mad collision of building styles and the engineering pavilion. And just people. People enjoying themselves at last.'

'Perhaps you can come back——?'

'I shouldn't think so,' she said. 'It's virtually impossible. It becomes a humiliation for him. You'd think with all the men who were crippled just doing their duty ... Anyway,' she paused. 'I expect the statue of the Prince of Wales will have melted by then.'

'I want to see the Battle of——' Nicholas interrupted but he clearly couldn't remember the name of the battle.

'Zeebrugge?' Laurence said.

'We're not going to see a make-believe battle,' Eleanor said. 'A battle's not entertainment.'

'The *Flying Scotsman* is a Gresley Class-A engine, Daddy says.' He stumbled over the words.

'It's wonderful, darling. And very, very popular.'

'I wish Maggie was here,' Nicholas said disconsolately.

Eleanor raised her eyebrows at Laurence.

'Actually she could have come but she was very keen on staying with David and putting out their lunch, although David was obviously equally keen to stay by himself with the car.' She looked exasperated. 'I know he doesn't like London and I know he didn't want to leave Susan, but it's a dreadful shame for him not to enjoy all this. But Maggie will make him join in. She seems so excited that I worry the real thing's going to be a great disappointment.'

'Ah, motherhood,' he said, 'with its secret vocabulary: the virtues of joining in. You're not worried about its politically corrupting influence?'

'I think David's his own man, don't you?' she replied crisply. 'Still, I hope he keeps an eye on Maggie. She's never been to London before. I told him to bring her and Nicky to the Tomb of Tutankhamun at two-thirty and then we can have an early tea. She's awfully keen on seeing Queen Mary's Doll's House.' Nicholas screwed up his face, but Eleanor didn't see it. 'I might go with her.'

'She wants to go to the fair,' Nicholas said firmly.

Laurence looked up, still holding the lemonades. Frances had obviously seen them and was walking towards them.

'You were much quicker than we'd expected,' Frances said to Eleanor. 'What a stroke of luck. I suppose if we stay on this main avenue, sooner or later we'll see everyone we know.'

Frances was giving Nicholas a kiss. He wiped his face when she straightened up.

'I saw a soldier with brown skin and a turban,' Nicholas said. 'And a beard.'

'They'll all be part of the show,' Eleanor said, 'grateful children of the Empire.' But she smiled sweetly.

'What on earth's the Palace of Beauty?' Frances said. 'Patrick was ribbing Julian about it.'

'Women,' said Eleanor, 'in glass booths. Like in the aquarium, only without tentacles. Not visible ones, anyway.'

Frances looked at her with slightly narrowed eyes.

'It's supposed to be a tableau,' Laurence said, watching Eleanor's face. 'Pears Soap set it up. A couple of dozen actresses and mannequins dressed up as famous beauties ...' He faltered as he caught Eleanor's eye.

'Like who?' Frances said.

'Helen of Troy ... er, Nell Gwynne ...'

'Just the two?' Frances looked amused. 'Or are you hiding your encyclopaedic knowledge of historic beauties?'

'Cleopatra?'

'All men's possessions,' Eleanor said, 'or women of expensive virtue, depending on your view.'

Frances seemed about to protest but then said brightly, 'Shall we go past the Burma pavilion? I mean, we've got time and it's supposed to be very fine – Patrick said the entrance is a copy of one of the gates of Mandalay.'

'Why not?' Eleanor took Nicholas by the hand. 'Sorry, darling, I know you're a bit old for hand holding but I don't want you to get lost.' The fine day seemed to have slowed everybody down and most people were gazing about them, apparently as keen to look around this fantasy world as to hurry into the next attraction.

'I never dreamed it would be so busy,' Eleanor said. 'It really would have been very hard with William.'

She was watching a woman with a perambulator struggling to pull it up some steps. Two young men in bowler hats stepped forward to help her. The baby started to cry.

The Burmese Pavilion now came into full view.

'Oh goodness,' Frances said, 'isn't it heavenly?'

Despite a couple of incongruous lime trees, the building was as fantastic and graceful as the Palaces of Industry and Engineering were grandiose. The delicate ornate spires, the pagodas and the fretted roof edging were all in teak, which in the sunshine almost seemed to glow.

Nicholas had broken away from Eleanor and ran ahead, stopping by the gates. Frances pursued him right up to the elaborate gateway and the fantastic winged creatures guarding them. The boy stood gazing up at them.

'Shall we go in?' Frances asked.

Eleanor looked at her watch. 'We won't have time to do Burma as well as India. I said we'd take Nicholas back to David and Maggie in forty minutes. Any preferences?'

'I want to go on the swing boats,' said Nicholas firmly. 'And the donkeys and the helter-skelter. And see the ostriches. And have an ice cream. And Maggie says there's real seaside. With sand.' He looked eager.

'You'd be sick,' Eleanor said without looking down at him. 'But we'll go to the fair after tea. Before I take you to Auntie Charlotte.'

'But I want to go back to Easton with Maggie and you and Daddy,' Nicholas said with a wobble in his voice.

'You'll see Maggie in the holidays, I promise.'

Frances was by Laurence's side again, her face tipped up to his, watching him.

'Would you like to see India?' She looked at him anxiously. 'Or would you rather walk around outside? It's such a beautiful day.'

'I'm all right. It was just the train.'

She smiled, obviously slightly embarrassed at her concern being so transparent.

Sometimes he wondered whether all the men he saw, apparently living their ordinary lives, still had moments of secret terror. Did the blacksmith lie in bed with his sleeping wife breathing softly beside him and the screams of limbless horses in his ears? Did the solicitor hold his napkin to his nose and mouth at the smell of roast pork being brought to the table? Did other men remember train floors slippery with blood and vomit, or compartments thick with the stench of fear, sweat and cigarettes, or were they better than he was at putting it all behind them?

'I'm happy to do whatever the others want to do,' he said finally and smiled to put her at her ease.

Chapter Eight

hey had found their table at the Grand by the time Eleanor got back from taking Nicholas to the car to have his picnic lunch with David and Maggie. The room was large and not yet full. Despite a hum of conversation, it felt peaceful and cool after the mêlée outside. Julian had arrived before them and was uncharacteristically elated; even before Frances had taken off her gloves, he was talking.

'I've never seen anything like it. It's far better than I'd been told. There's even a chap filling fountain pens for free. But the agricultural section is quite extraordinary. If we had harvesters and tractors like that at Easton, we could really turn things around.'

He waved some printed sheets at Laurence, almost hitting the waiter who was filling Frances's glass.

'I've got some details for Lydia. In ten years the Easton Deadall boys will be men. In fifteen years those men will marry, have children. If they feel they have something to stay for, bring their brides to, Easton will go back to how it was, except that it will be looking forwards.' Laurence had never heard Julian talk at such length nor seen him so animated.

Frances looked up and waved vigorously to someone behind him, her lips slightly parted. Laurence turned around but not before he'd seen all the excitement in Julian's expression extinguished.

Eleanor and Patrick were standing together just inside the double doors. She had obviously met him on the way and both of them were in spirited conversation as Patrick handed in his hat to the cloakroom girl. Eleanor's gaze swept over the tables until her eyes caught Frances's just as a waiter came to show her to their table. Eleanor looked pretty: her nose was slightly pink and her hair had sprung into tight curls in the heat. Patrick pulled her chair back for her and she sat down next to Laurence.

'Phew,' she said. 'I'm quite glad to be relieved of motherhood for an hour or so. Nicky is absolutely determined to see anything with a motor, any large or freakish living creature, or to cadge some kind of present to take away, however unsuitable for a child. I had to buy him a plaster of Paris replica of the British Lions to divert him from endless lemonade, humbugs and barley-sugar twists. He was even petitioning for an exhibition Bible. A *Bible*.'

She spoke as if he'd wanted to lay hands on some racy pictures.

'In the end I threatened to take him to Kiddies' Dreamland – now there's a sinister thought, with visions of infant opium dens. Mind you, they'd be thoroughly biddable children – and leave him with the Old Lady who Lived in a Shoe along with all the five-year-olds.'

Patrick and Frances were laughing.

'Are Maggie and David having a good time?' Laurence asked.

Eleanor looked slightly irritated. 'David just isn't interested. He just seems to believe the place is a thieves' playground and his duty is to protect the car. When I took Nicky back to them, Maggie was raring to go but so far she'd only got as far as some

New Zealand sheep-shearing display because it was the nearest exhibit and David, rightly, didn't want her to stray far. She wasn't very impressed, but she's enjoying organising their lunch.'

'She'll like the Queen's Doll's House after lunch,' Frances said. 'She was looking forward to that.'

'Hmm,' Eleanor said, 'that was this morning. When she left Easton, she was a child. Things change in the face of this saturnalia. Now she's discovered there's dancing at some kind of palais in the amusement park.'

'Does she know *how* to dance?' Frances asked, looking surprised.

'It's not really dancing, is it?' Patrick said. 'More a sort of mutual leaning.' He leered theatrically.

'Well, whether or not she can dance, she's got nobody to lean on,' Eleanor said. 'I'm certainly not taking Lydia's kitchen help dancing.'

Mock-turtle soup was followed swiftly by mutton and capers. It was all a bit grey in colour, as Eleanor was swift to point out, but Laurence was hungry.

'Patrick was telling me about his work on Crete,' Eleanor said between mouthfuls. 'It sounds quite marvellous – I'd love to see it all.'

'You must have been sorry to leave it in the war?' Laurence asked Patrick.

He knew instantly he had said something wrong. Only Eleanor appeared not to notice. Frances dropped her eyes. Julian's fork stopped midway between his plate and his mouth, only for a fraction of a second, then he too fixed all his attention on his plate as he carefully cut a boiled potato in two. Patrick simply didn't answer at first.

'None of us could stay in Greece,' he said eventually. 'Sir Arthur returned to England when war broke out, so I came back to help him collate his papers at Boars Hill and do some research at Oxford.'

Nothing he had said sounded at all problematic to Laurence but those at the table remained silent. Even Eleanor looked perplexed now as her gaze travelled from Frances to Julian.

'I volunteered in a hospital there,' Patrick said, slightly defensively.

Eleanor said, 'Was that at Wingfield?'

Patrick gave her a small smile. 'Yes,' he said. 'They were good people there. I bicycled over. It used to make me feel exhilarated and guilty to cycle because so many of the men at Wingfield would never walk, much less freewheel down Boars Hill. I'd come back along the river. When I got back in the evening I'd read "The Scholar-Gipsy".'

He was animated again, but a glance at Julian's grim face seemed to stop him in his tracks.

'I love Matthew Arnold,' Eleanor said, quickly.

Frances looked up. 'Me too,' she said. '"Thyrsis". It's in the library at Easton.'

Conversation remained awkward for the rest of lunch, Julian commenting only on the spotted dick, which he ate with gusto, and otherwise talking to Frances about Lydia and Easton.

Eleanor asked Patrick, 'When did you return to Oxford?'

'Quite early on. I went there at the beginning of Michaelmas term 1914, virtually straight from Crete, when the war started.'

He was peeling an apple as he spoke, his movements neat and economical. Laurence could imagine how carefully he would handle fragments of unknown antiquity newly dug from the earth.

'The days we spent puzzling over statuettes we'd found on the island. The evenings we spent talking to old men, the young ones having taken commissions in the main.'

The waiter was hovering by the table, wanting to be paid. By the doors to the restaurant two or three people were already waiting. Laurence fumbled in his inside pocket for money.

While they waited for the waiter to bring back their change, Eleanor checked her watch.

'Oh Lord,' she said, pushing back her chair. 'I'm going to have to hurry. I told David to bring Nicholas and Maggie to Tutankhamun's tomb at two-thirty and it's almost that now. And I have to find the place first.' She looked anxious. 'It's crowded out there.'

Julian unfolded the map and pulled out some spectacles from a battered case, the first time Laurence had seen him do this, but it was Patrick who pointed at the page.

'The amusement park.'

He indicated a large arc of land occupying most of the east side of the site.

'Tutankhamun is here,' he said, his finger on the bottom boundary, 'on the edge of the roundabouts and the coconut shies.' He gave a wry smile. 'Which puts us would-be archaeologists in our place.'

'You all go ahead,' Laurence said. 'I'll wait for the change.'

'We can use the Never Stop,' said Frances, picking up her gloves. She and the other two men followed Eleanor out.

As he stood just outside the restaurant five long minutes later, Laurence looked in the direction that they had gone. He could see the curve of the screw-driven railway but the carriage that held them had already disappeared around the bend.

Increasing numbers of sightseers seemed to have filled the paths and drives since the morning. The broad avenue offered little cover from the sun and, unlike Laurence, most people were strolling along with no obvious purpose in mind. Laurence could hear the noise of the funfair. To his right lay a large lake, dotted with rowing boats and gondolas, and surrounded by ranks of green deckchairs. Layers of distorted sound bounced off the water: laughter and squeals and one man singing as he rowed.

Something about the heat and the sparkling water, even the splashing of inept rowers, took him back to the Henley regatta before the war, more than ten years ago now. Was it 1911, that long, hot summer when it was inconceivable that anything could ever change? It was there he had met his wife, Louise, and the woman he still loved, Mary. Perhaps if he had been more forward, more courageous, then, their story — his, Louise's and Mary's — might have ended differently.

In his memory the Oxfordshire sun shone every day. A haze shimmered on the river and on the immaculate lawns. He saw again the excited public-school boys, the Oxford and Cambridge crews, and the rowdy Leander men in their bright blazers and boaters, with the proud parents looking on.

He had shut his eyes only for a second and mostly because of the sun, but when he opened them he was momentarily disoriented. It was all gone: the rowers, his wife, the innocence of that distant time.

The music was louder towards the south-eastern side of the Wembley ground. The crowds were even thicker here, the notices more garish. A man loomed out in front of him, swinging some kind of bladder, more like a medieval jester than a gypsy.

'Tickle the monkey?' he bellowed. 'Come on, sir, you look a sporting type. Try the monkey-teaser.'

As Laurence ducked under his outstretched arm, the air-filled bladder bounced lightly on the back of his head.

Ahead lay the painted wooden cap of a roundabout, with lurid scenes of the Wild West. As Laurence entered the huge enclosure, the horses with their flared red nostrils and streaming wooden manes began to move. Mothers holding their children on their laps, young men with their sweethearts, finding an excuse to squeeze them tight, and pairs of nervous children began to shout with excitement and fear as it gathered speed, clinging to the gold barley-sugar poles. One young woman was already having trouble keeping her skirt down and two spectators – young men with glasses in their hands – were slopping beer all over themselves in mirth. Watching the up-and-down motion made him feel dizzy. He leaned on the rail for a second.

'It's a galloper,' a thick-set, swarthy man next to him said to nobody in particular. 'My dad worked on making horses before the war.' He was nodding to himself with satisfaction. 'His horses gets everywhere. Paris, America even.' Finally he turned to Laurence. 'See them saddles – double-scalloped carving round the edges with royal blue and crimson stripes? That's my dad.'

He pointed with an oil-grimed hand, tendrils of blue ink climbing up his muscular forearm.

Laurence found himself nodding back. The horses were beautifully done but when he was a child he'd always found their fierce expressions a bit sinister. He had some sympathy with a small child, tear-streaked and wide-eyed, who shot past him and swung away. The stranger wandered off, gesturing at the name on the painted boards. 'Scudamore, Devizes,' he said over his shoulder. 'See. My dad. Just the ticket.'

Further on at an intersection, a sign on the broadest path carrying the thickest crowd pointed to *Beach and Donkeys*. *Madame Isis Fortune-Teller* a handwritten notice proclaimed on a striped booth.

He felt relief as he spotted King Tut's Kingdom looming ahead. In view of the noise, the candyfloss, the whelk stalls and the rides, he could see why Howard Carter had tried so hard to get the exhibit banned. It didn't speak of scholarship and derring-do, or even ancient dynasties.

As he was approaching what seemed to be the end of a long queue, he was surprised to see Julian moving in the opposite direction, pushing with some determination through the crowds. Julian saw Laurence and veered towards him.

'The children aren't there,' he said, his voice tight with tension. 'I'm going back towards the car, in case they're still with David. It makes sense for Eleanor and Frances to stay put. They're near the ticket booth. Patrick's just gone across to the Queen's Doll's House in case David misunderstood where they were meeting. That was where Eleanor had agreed to take Maggie later.' Julian's tone was businesslike but his eyes were anxious. 'I'll be straight back. Why don't you wait with Eleanor and Frances?'

Laurence ignored the long and fairly good-humoured queue to take a closer look at the Egyptian attraction, decorated with pictures of palm trees, the Sphinx, a serious-looking pharaoh and a large notice saying *King Tut's Treasures*. Pillars, on either side of the entrance, were covered in hieroglyphics, flanked by statues of Nubian slaves and the inevitable image of a mummy. Eleanor and Frances were standing right by it, dwarfed by its size. Neither saw him immediately. Frances, whose gaze was raking up and down the queue, noticed Laurence before Eleanor did.

'We were only five or ten minutes late,' Frances said. 'I'm sure they would have waited.'

Eleanor turned around. 'It's not like David to be late,' she said, 'unless they've got lost.'

'There was probably just a misunderstanding,' Laurence said. 'And, frankly, it looks clear on the plan but it's hellish hard to get through the crush.'

He pulled out his watch. It was nearly half an hour after they were supposed to rendezvous. He tried to hide the first stirrings of alarm.

Eleanor said, 'David lived in London for a while, so he's not going to be troubled by crowds.' It sounded more like a question than a statement. 'I just hope he and Maggie are keeping a tight hold on to Nicky. He can be an awful dawdler, especially if he sees something that takes his eye. Although an Egyptian mummy should be quite an attraction.' She gave an uncertain smile.

Frances, who seemed more obviously anxious than Eleanor, kept looking back to the queue. 'Shall I just make sure they're not at the far end?' she said.

Laurence watched her follow the line back round the building and out of sight. Eleanor gave a big sigh.

'By the time they get here, we'll be queuing until nightfall.' Her eyes were flickering away from him. 'I just wish they'd get a move on.'

Frances was returning. 'No sign,' she said from a few yards away and bit her lip.

Behind her, Laurence saw Patrick appear but he was alone.

Eleanor, who had seen him too, said, 'Well, that was a bit of a long shot,' even before Patrick reached them. 'I didn't really think David would have taken them up to the Doll's House,' she said, brightly and fast. 'And I think there would have been protests from my son.'

Laurence had a feeling she was trying to soothe Frances.

'Do you think we should get in the queue?' Eleanor said, turning to Patrick. 'So that we're ready to go when the children turn up?' Her words were tumbling over each other.

A group of young men and girls came out. As they passed, laughing, one man said in a strong London accent, 'It's not real, silly. The real stuff is locked up – it's worth a fortune. King Tut's still in India or somewhere.'

'You'll be laughing on the other side of your fat face, Stanley, if the mummy's curse does for you,' said one of the girls. One of the men laughed and another girl cuffed him on the arm.

'Everybody's dead who dug it up, any rate,' the first girl said. 'Everybody. The pharaoh might not like us all gawking at his things. We wouldn't like it if they went and dug up our Queen Vic. It's rude.'

They moved on noisily. Even Frances looked amused briefly. Then Laurence turned around and saw Julian, looking hot and pushing his way towards them. The others hadn't turned round yet but he caught Laurence's eye and shook his head. As he reached them, Frances turned and saw him. Her face drained of colour.

'What's happened?' she said, putting her hand on Julian's arm. Julian looked cross rather than worried.

'I don't understand it. David's been an utter fool. He was at the car. Said he brought the children round the perimeter because of the crowds, left them at the eastern gate, from where he says you can clearly see this spot, and pointed out to Maggie where they should wait.'

Eleanor's alarm was almost tangible. 'Why didn't he stay with them?' she asked. 'What on earth was he thinking?'

'He had some damn fool idea – sorry, Eleanor – that there were some unsavoury types eyeing up the car.'

Patrick looked exasperated. 'I thought he was supposed to be so reliable,' he said to no one in particular.

'Where's David now? ' Laurence said.

'I left him back at the car. It's possible that if Maggie and Nicholas got lost, Maggie might have the wit to get back to the motor park.' His tone of voice suggested that he doubted this and it certainly didn't seem to reassure Eleanor, who was scanning passers-by as if she might see Nicholas at any minute.

'They must be set up for this here.' Laurence found he was loath to say 'lost children'. 'Children must get parted from their parents all the time. They're not just going to disappear.'

'Maggie's a sensible girl,' Patrick said, his eyes fixed on Eleanor.

'But she's scarcely been out of the village – Marlborough

would seem like a busy metropolis to her, Swindon like a city. There must be thousands of people here. Hundreds of thousands.'

A note of panic was entering Eleanor's voice and for a few moments they all stood, uncertain what to do.

Eventually Laurence said, 'I suggest somebody stay here with Eleanor, in case they simply turn up. One of us can go and find out what they do about children who've wandered off.'

He thought it might be a mistake to leave Frances with Eleanor as her own anxiety was so palpable.

'Patrick, why don't you stay with Eleanor?'

Patrick was sweating lightly, although he, of all of them, should be used to the heat. It occurred to Laurence that Patrick's weak heart, so easily forgotten when Patrick was on form, made him the least suitable for racing all over Wembley.

'If Julian doesn't mind going off to speak to a policeman, simply so that they can keep an eye open?'

As he said this, Laurence looked at Julian, who said, 'Of course.' Julian pulled out his watch. 'Perhaps we could all rendezvous here in half an hour?' He looked first at Laurence, then at Eleanor, who said nothing but nodded slowly. Julian nodded once and strode off, against the flow of people.

'Meanwhile, Frances and I could stay together and go round the area between the eastern gate and here. It's not impossible that somebody will have spotted them,' Laurence continued. 'What's obviously happened is that they missed this exhibit, or even thought the queues were too long, or simply got lost.'

'Especially as we were late,' Eleanor said. Frances blinked a few times, apparently bewildered.

Eleanor added, 'Perhaps Maggie's lack of familiarity with cities might be just why she felt safe to go off, with no idea of how confusing it might be.'

'Maybe they decided to fill in time by looking at the beach or having a ride on a roundabout?' Patrick said.

Just as Laurence was about to speak, he saw the young woman who had been selling tickets for King Tut's Treasures leave the booth and an older man take her place. They had tricked up the girl to look Egyptian with dark lines around her eyes and a heavy black wig, which she was scratching underneath with a finger. Before she could walk away Laurence went up to her.

'Excuse me.'

She looked wary and stepped back; her hand dropped away from the crooked wig, exposing a very fair hairline.

'I was just wondering if you'd seen someone I'm looking for.'

She gestured towards the booth. 'Not bleeding likely. I bin in that steaming box all morning.'

'I just thought you might have seen two children – well, a small boy and a girl of fifteen. They might have been waiting to come into your show.'

She made an incredulous face. 'There's lots of kiddies, all day. They all looks the same by dinnertime. And they'll all be nicking stuff if you don't keep an eye out.'

He turned back to Eleanor, shaking his head.

'Where do you think they might have gone first, if they didn't stop here?' he said.

Eleanor raised her eyebrows. 'The beach, I suppose. That's where Nicky would have headed.'

It seemed to Laurence that she was struggling to maintain her composure now.

'I can't think of anything worse myself.' She sighed. 'Maggie was keen to see the beauties of the world or whatever they're called, but I hope she would have thought twice about taking Nicky there.'

'Right. Frances and I will brave the beach. We'll return in

twenty minutes, no more, by which time I hope the two of them will be back with you.'

Eleanor gave a rueful smile and leaned back against the slatted wall of a booth, as if exhausted.

'Shall I get us a lemonade apiece?' Patrick said. She only nodded. Although her smile was determined, her shoulders were slumped. Laurence and Frances set off, Laurence with some relief at doing something.

'He can't swim,' Eleanor called after them just as they were about to go out of earshot and this time Laurence could clearly hear a tremble in her voice.

Frances was tense and alert. Despite the day's warmth, she had wrapped her arms around herself while they were talking. Now she walked on without saying a word.

Out of the corner of his eye Laurence saw that the fellow who had talked to him by the roundabout was now manning his own ride. It seemed popular, although it was neither as huge nor as spectacular as some others: just eight or ten great fat cockerels on gilded poles, rising and falling jerkily.

He nodded to the man who didn't seem to see him; his eyes appeared fixed as he studied passers-by. Thousands of strangers must go by every week.

As they passed the little terminus of the miniature train, the man shouted out from behind them, 'Roll up, roll up. Kiddies go free with their mums or nanas. Cock-a-Hoop. Only ride like it in England.'

He must have pressed some kind of button because suddenly an ear-splitting metallic cockcrow screeched out. Laurence's heart raced and he almost ducked. It had been six years, yet noises like that still meant danger.

Only now, as they turned left towards the beach, did Frances speak again.

'You do think we'll find them?' she said.

'I'm sure we will,' he said and he believed it. 'I know it's difficult. But between us we'll find them.'

'Maggie's nearly grown up but she's very young for her age,' Frances said. 'And Nicky's only a little boy. He couldn't look after himself for very long.'

'Well, for one thing he's got Maggie, so he's not on his own and, do you know, I think any son of Eleanor's would probably be able to give quite a good account of himself.'

When she didn't respond he added, carefully, 'It's nothing like what happened to Kitty. She disappeared from her own bed.'

She stared down at her feet and for a minute he thought he might have misjudged the origin of her anxiety but then she looked sideways at him.

'Thank you,' she said. 'Eleanor always said you were perceptive about people. I just couldn't bear to see Eleanor go through what Lydia went through. Even if it was only for a day. And Nicky's only a year older than Kitty was.'

To Laurence the beach was depressing as much in its attempts to be sea-like as in its surroundings. On the other side of the exhibition's perimeter fence lay a vast landscape of mud and crushed rubble. Pegs and intersecting lines for positioning future houses and roads covered acres of what must once have been fields. London was swelling even as he watched. Dark-clothed men swarmed over the ground, carrying materials or knocking in staves. Across this huge building site a section was already covered with rows of small, identical houses, faintly Tudor in style with black-and-white timbering. A handful of nearer ones, more finished than the rest, had leaded windows and hanging pantiles. The half-dozen lines of building works stretched almost as far as the eye could see into a shallow declivity, then disappeared over the top, with the roof of the exhibition railway station just visible to his left. There was no sign of anything green and grow-ing.

Almost as unreal was the huge curved stretch of sand in front of him. How would they ever clear it up, he wondered. Artificial coves had been constructed. Deckchairs sagged with the freight of grandmothers and spinster aunts. Men with their jackets off and rolled-up sleeves led small daughters, their dresses tucked into their bloomers, towards the water. Some children had come better prepared and were already wet, standing in the shallow and slightly murky water, their woollen swimming costumes sagging on their skinny frames. The bodies of both adults and children were so white, so unused to sunlight, he thought. All the time his eyes ranged back and forth, hovering for a minute over any girl of Maggie's size and age and every small boy.

A man trudged up and down the sands, leading a donkey by a halter, two little girls in pinafores sitting impassive on its back. The donkey man's other arm was absent, his sleeve pinned neatly to his chest. On the far side of the donkey track, between the beach and the sea, was a low cement wall, making the beach look more like the nearby Grand Union Canal than a south-coast resort. But there was laughter and excitable shouting, boys run-ning about and being told off. Cooling down in the water was obviously so attractive on a hot day that adults were standing in it, fully clothed but having removed just their stockings or socks.

Laurence walked behind a young couple with their arms around each other and a child beside them. He turned to look at the small dark-haired boy, just as the child lifted his face to his parents and asked, 'Is it like the real sea, Mam? Is the real sea this big?'

'I think so,' said the mother, plump and pink faced, herself scarcely older than a schoolgirl. 'Bigger, even. Mebbe.'

When he reached the end of the long stretch of sand,

Laurence retraced his steps, again scanning the crowds. He already sensed that neither Maggie nor Nicholas was here and he could see Frances, walking slowly towards him from the other end. She shook her head as she did so.

'It was never very likely,' he said. 'Let's give the sea monsters a quick look.'

As they walked towards the rest of the amusements, they paused on the edge of a group of excited cross-legged children and a row of women in deckchairs in front of a Punch and Judy show. A couple of men in collarless shirts and braces were watching, grinning. Punch was thumping Judy and the baby with a stick.

'The bobby'll come and nick you,' a boy shouted. 'See if he don't.'

'Shhhh,' said several of the women.

They continued walking between further amusements. Laurence was startled when a band struck up, playing 'The Soldiers of our Queen'. The bandstand was out of sight but obviously close at hand. Hoping to avoid the crowd immediately around it — he didn't think either Maggie or Nicholas would linger to listen to a band — he indicated a narrower side path to Frances. Behind the front line of huts and tents, it was less easy to navigate. Laurence took Frances's hand and guided them out between two striped tents. He was back at the fortune teller. Two girls came out, their expressions worried.

Frances said quietly, 'This could have been such a happy day. Do you think really they'll be all right, Maggie and Nicholas?'

'Yes. Absolutely. They'll just be lost. The day may be interrupted but the show is open until autumn; we can come back. Perhaps without children?'

He smiled at her, trying to reassure her without sounding glib.

'Still,' she said wearily, detaching herself from his arm, 'they're not here.'

'Let's go back to Eleanor and Patrick,' he said. 'It's possible Maggie will have found her way back to them or back to David. And Julian should have spoken to the police by now.'

'I suppose for them it's all in a day's work,' Frances said. 'Probably people lose their children every hour.'

'Probably,' he said, nodding. 'I'm sure they must.'

'I can't imagine what David was thinking,' she said.

'Perhaps he just couldn't see it through their eyes — how huge the space is, how vast the crowds. Even Nicky will have seen more crowds than Maggie.'

He could see Eleanor, now sitting on a bench a few yards from King Tut's Treasures, and Patrick leaning against the palisade beside her. Julian had joined them and looked more alert, though scarlet-faced. None of them had yet seen Laurence and Frances. Patrick was smoking. Eleanor had her head back, eyes closed, but even as Laurence watched, her head snapped forward and she looked around her, spotting him immediately. He started shaking his head from a distance and hated seeing a brief look of hope leave her face. Frances took both Eleanor's hands as she reached her, but again it seemed as if Eleanor was the comforter. Patrick had lost his usual air of confidence.

'The police have told their patrols to look for Nicky,' Julian said gruffly, 'but they weren't the slightest bit bothered by Maggie having gone astray, once I'd convinced them she was unlikely to have kidnapped Nicholas. They say she's fifteen and not their concern. And quite obviously they think, given that Nicholas is likely to be with her, there's not much to worry about.'

As he spoke Julian glanced uneasily at the two women.

'They seem quite certain they will turn up, saying they have twenty or so missing children every day.'

It seemed to Laurence that once Maggie and Nicholas had failed to rendezvous here, looking for them was more or less like searching for a needle in a haystack. He was about to suggest that the women went to have tea when he caught the eye of the man on the cockerel roundabout. The ride was just stopping and children were being lifted off. As he crossed the worn turf, he knew the man had seen him. As he stepped up to the booth, the man came out of it. The armpits of his shirt were dark with sweat as he swung himself down; his forearm revealed that his badly executed tattoo was a regimental crest. Laurence wasn't sure whether the man recognised him from his brief exchange earlier, but he looked ready to speak.

'Summat up?' he said.

'We've lost a child. Two children ...' Laurence began.

'Kiddies always going missing here,' the man said.

"I just wondered if you might have noticed them. They were supposed to meet us here but we were late and they've gone. A small boy of six. An older girl, fifteen.'

Even as he spoke, two children of much that age hovered, examining the price board. He realised how impossible it would be to identify Nicholas and Maggie. There were hundreds of Nicholases and Maggies here. His mind had moved on and he almost missed what the man said next.

'I might just have done.'

Laurence was instantly alert. The man was obviously trying hard to remember. Laurence didn't want to push him.

'Yep,' the man said. 'Nicely spoken lad in a sailor suit, young woman – I thought she was his nursemaid – west country by the sound of her?'

'Dark-haired? The boy?'

The man shook his head a little less certainly and Laurence's heart sank. As he half turned away he could see Eleanor and Frances watching him.

'Tell you what, this lad, his name was Nicko. Nicholas – I'm sure of it. My boy's called Nicko so I notice it. They sat where your lady friends are sitting now. Then the boy came over and wanted a ride. That's when I heard his name. The girl was telling him he'd have to ask his ma and to keep his sunhat on. In the end she let him have a ride. She only had two bob on her, no change. I let him ride for free.'

Laurence, his attention fully on the man, felt in his pocket for coins. So this was just an attempt to get money. But to his surprise the man held his hand up, palm outwards.

'Nah. It's done.'

'And then what?'

'Then he got off. They went back to sitting.' He nodded towards the bench. 'He did, any rate. Next time I looked, he was on his own. Next time.' He pushed back his grimy cap. 'Nah, I didn't see him again. Talking to a gent, maybe? Maybe not? The afternoon rush. Queuing for my fine birds, they were.'

He reached out to the massive flank of the nearest cockerel and stroked it tenderly.

'Lads aren't great ones for sitting long, are they?'

He looked over to a pair of anxious mothers who were pushing forward reluctant children. A hefty boy was already climbing on a stationary creature.

'Nothing else to tell you,' the man said, walking away. He gesticulated at the boy. 'Geroff with you, yer too big.'

Then, just as Laurence was about to walk back to Eleanor, the man seemed to remember something.

'Hang on. He *was* talking to a bloke. Not so much talking as the man was shouting. He sat down on the same bench. I was staring meself. He had one of them masks.' The man touched his own face with stained fingers. 'Creepy, I call 'em but you can't help but feel sorry for the blokes who have to wear them. You know ... metal things? Painted with eyes and all.'

Laurence did know. Of all of war's ugly legacies, the copper masks with their exquisitely painted features covering the most ruined faces, where nothing remained to shape flesh around, were the most grotesque. When he had seen men in them, he had thought they were as brave to go out in them as to deal with whatever devastation lay beneath. To know yourself repellent: how could a man live with it?

'The boy was scared. He was staring and then he was moving away. The bloke noticed and shouted at him and the lad ran off. Up there,' he pointed between two rows of stalls, 'I think. Like I say, things got busy.'

'It must have been them surely?' Eleanor said when Laurence had repeated the account, leaving out the man's memory of the masked man's anger at Nicholas's fear. 'But why did Maggie leave Nicky by himself? Why did David leave both of them?' Before anyone could answer she exhaled deeply. 'Why did I leave them? Nicky could have come to lunch with us.'

Frances turned her head away.

'I mean, I was taking him to my sister's to go to the seaside with them, and coming back to Easton without him.'

'He would have been bored stiff,' Patrick said. 'It was probably boredom, which sent him, or them, wandering off.'

Frances's eyes were screwed up against the sun.

'If Maggie had gone off for some reason – it might even have been to the lavatory or something quite run-of-the-mill – and Nicholas had got bored, where would he have gone?'

'Can he read well enough to get around?' Julian asked.

Eleanor's usual spirit flared up. 'He's six. Of course he can read. But not signs. Just little books ...' Her lower lip moved slightly in a tiny spasm.

Laurence and Patrick exchanged glances. Patrick peered at his watch.

'We have to decide how long we're going to stay here,' he said. And when Eleanor and Frances looked up, startled, he said, 'It's been over an hour and a half now. Should some of us stay here and some of us go on home? Sooner or later we'll have to decide.'

For all his calm words, he held his cigarette case in his hands, snapping it open and closed while making no effort to remove a cigarette.

Laurence glanced at Eleanor. Her pupils seemed huge.

'Let's have one more walk,' he said, 'in case you see anything we might not. Something that might take Nicholas's eye. The others can watch out for him here.'

She looked dazed but she followed him as he took the route Nicholas had apparently taken when scared by the injured man. They came out in a circle of food stalls and souvenir kiosks.

'He didn't have money for any of this,' Eleanor said despondently.

'Let's go as far as the main buildings. Perhaps he tried to find you. Would he know where you were lunching?'

'No. Yes. Perhaps,' she said. 'Yes.'

'That's easy then,' Laurence said, guiding her forward.

By the gates of the funfair was a tent advertising a magical show: *DeVine and Maguire. Magicians to the crowned heads of Europe.*

Eleanor gave a weak smile. 'Before or after the war, do you think?'

Two sides of the tent had been half raised, presumably to allow circulation of air, but it also enabled a handful of onlookers to peer in without paying. A fat, shiny-faced woman was remonstrating with them as she turned to let down the canvas. The gawpers moved away. Laurence bent and looked through to see a man in evening dress and a woman in satin tunic and tights, with feathers in her hair, spin a box over a void. There was a rather feeble drum roll and the front fell open. A small boy was standing inside.

'Good Lord,' Laurence said, standing up straight. Eleanor took one look at him and then ducked into the tent, despite the fat woman shouting, 'Not without a ticket, you don't.'

'Please. It's my son. That's my son.'

The satin-clad assistant lifted Nicholas down from his box and at her nudging he bowed deeply. The crowd clapped. Before Eleanor could reach the stage, Nicholas had bowed again.

As she returned to the open air, pushing her son before her, the crowd was still clapping. Laurence could see that, although she was close to tears, Nicholas looked cross.

'I'm a saucer's apprentice,' he said.

'Sorcerer's,' Eleanor said, squatting down to his level. 'Oh Nicky, where have you been? What happened? Where's Maggie?'

'There was a nice man who bought Maggie and me an ice cream and said where were we from and talked about cars and what car we had and could I drive it. But then there was a nasty man,' Nicholas said, suddenly holding on to his mother. 'He had a face like a bad puppet and he shouted. So I ran away and then I was trying to see magic so I went in the tent and I was watching disappearing balloons and the lady getting sawed but she wasn't and the pretty lady said I could be in the next trick. And everybody liked it and clapped.' He looked resentfully at Eleanor. 'I didn't like the other man but I did like being magic. I'd like to be magic when I grow up and make people disappear.'

Eleanor suddenly bent down and hugged him. 'Don't ever run away again.' Her voice was breaking. 'I thought I'd lost you.'

'I wasn't running away.' His voice was muffled and he was attempting to extricate himself from his mother's tight embrace.

'I was waiting like Maggie said but I was frightened by the man with the horrid face.'

Laurence thought that on such a hot day the man underneath the mask must have been burning; no wonder he raged at a staring child.

'Where's Maggie?' Laurence asked. 'Did she say?'

Nicholas looked at them as if they were stupid.

'She went to see somebody. She's probly not coming back today. She said she would soon be back or she'd write a letter and you wouldn't mind if I sat still and waited and not to be cross.' His face fell. 'I wish she hadn't gone.'

The others, standing by Tutankhamun's Tomb, looked up and caught sight of them. Frances rushed over. She too seemed close to tears and tousled the boy's hair with a false insouciance.

'Oh I'm glad to see you,' she said.

'Maggie left him to meet someone,' Laurence said, and saw concern on Frances's face.

Nicholas said, 'It was a secret before.' He smiled shyly up at Patrick. 'That's why she was looking nice. Like a film person. She'd saved the pretty ribbon Mr Easton gave her for special.'

Frances stared at Julian in surprise but it was clear he was puzzled.

'He means me,' Patrick said, after a second's pause. 'I gave her the ribbon, for God's sake, to try and make her feel pretty. She's fifteen years old. She's got nothing, not even a future.' He looked angry. 'No wonder she's run off at the first sight of the real world, or of any damn place but Easton.'

PART TWO

CHAPTER NINE

*L*aurence got back to his London rooms late and grimy after the abortive day at Wembley. Relief had exhausted him and he almost slept through the clattering of his alarm clock the next morning but he was just in time to catch the train back to Swindon. All his connections went smoothly. A very subdued David was waiting at the station. He drove in near silence, answering questions in monosyllables. Only when they arrived at Easton did he speak properly.

'I never dreamed for a minute she'd leave him alone,' he said in an agitated voice. 'It was the sun, I wasn't feeling right. Couldn't be doing with the crowds. I thought they'll be quite safe. She'll only have gone off as girls do, won't she?'

He wouldn't look Laurence in the face.

'I was talking about her dad – I knew him a bit as a lad.' His words tumbled out. 'Not her mum. I was married meself by then and had gone away. I knew that he'd been a brave man. Maggie seemed to like my talking about him. I never meant to upset her.'

Laurence crossed the courtyard and went in through the stable door. It seemed as if nobody was at home except Mrs Hill who was disconsolately dismembering rabbits.

'Young Maggie,' she said, 'turned out to be just like her ma. Susan's gone back home – she's in a proper state about it.'

He walked on through the house; the doors and windows were thrown wide. From the terrace he could see the wide hose now leading to the yew plants which showed a deep green in contrast to the parched lawn. William, wearing a white hat, sat supervising the watering, with Julian standing next to him. For once even Scout looked subdued by the heat, her tongue lolling.

'I've been to the river. It's worse each day,' Julian said, looking perplexed. 'Thousands of dead fish. It stinks down by the Mill. The narrower stretches are scarcely more than mud. I've never seen it like this. It could be from drawing too hard on the aquifers to provide for Swindon. I always said it was going to cause problems. We'll have to shut down the generator, close the sluices. We can't take water out when there's so little of it.'

His face creased with worry as he surveyed the new hedging.

'Don't use more than you have to here for the time being,' he said. 'Still, it's looking very fine, Bolitho. It's good that Lydia can see it from her room.' He took off his hat and ran his fingers through his hair. 'She's taken Maggie's disappearance very badly. But I don't see what else anyone can do.'

'Keep on pushing the police?' William said.

Julian nodded. 'The Wiltshire chaps are speaking to their colleagues in London, trying to make them see a fifteen-year-old country girl isn't like a young woman from the city.'

'David tells me he was feeling unwell in the heat,' Laurence said.

Julian regarded him levelly. 'It's stuff and nonsense,' he said. 'He's outside in the sun every day. He's a good man but this sulking because he didn't want to drive to London has had a catastrophic outcome. Not that he intended this mess but he's responsible for it.'

When Laurence returned to the house, wondering whether David's position was at risk, he met Frances coming up the passage.

'Just the man,' she said with what he sensed was forced enthusiasm. 'Patrick and Eleanor have gone to Stonehenge to take their minds off everything. Do you fancy a walk?'

'Fine.'

He was amused by the feeling he'd been ambushed.

'I thought that while we're out we might pop by Walter Petch's, see if we can get a feel for where Maggie might have gone.' She gazed at him so seriously and unblinkingly that he knew this visit was the sole object of the proposed walk.

'Somebody has to do something,' she said.

Walter Petch's cottage was the last house in the village at the furthest point from the Hall. The nearest dwelling to Petch's was a newly painted cottage with cut logs stacked up against the porch. Running alongside it was a sparse orchard, with small, gnarled apple trees and two beehives to one side. A few scrawny brown hens were pecking about

Frances nodded towards the well-ordered cottage.

'That one is Mrs Kilminster's,' she said, 'a very nice, sensible woman. It's Ellen Kilminster's cousin by marriage who survived with Julian and who's coming home. Victor. He's been farming in New South Wales.' She hesitated. 'Ellen's sister was Kitty's nanny.'

Walter Petch's cottage was a gloomy contrast to his neighbour's. The ridge of the roof sagged, the windows were grimy and opaque, and the path to the porch was so unkempt that the place felt derelict. The impression was reinforced by the long silence that greeted their knock. The porch had been built in rustic style: once the lattice of branches must have had charm but now, the wood slimy and several struts missing, it added to the sense of utter neglect. Laurence thought back to how excited and uncharacteristically voluble Maggie had been three days ago and felt sad.

'Poor girl,' Frances whispered. She was looking up at the chimney and the thin line of yellow smoke that rose from it.

He knocked again. There was a scuttling in the eaves above their heads and then, almost as if a larger version of whatever was in the roof was approaching from the other side of the front door, a heavy scratching noise. A bolt was drawn back, with some muttered curses, and the door opened. Walter Petch, whom Laurence had seen many times working in the gardens and on the church floor, and who must have known Frances since she was a child, stared at them suspiciously as if they were strangers. He looked as unkempt as his house and bleary-eyed with sleep.

'We've come from the Hall,' Frances said. 'My sister — Mrs Easton — wondered if we could speak to you about Maggie?'

Walter Petch showed no sign of having heard her. He was still a big man and his bulk filled the doorway. He continued to stare at Laurence. His face had dirt ingrained in its heavy folds.

'May we come in?' Laurence asked, finally.

Walter stood for a few seconds more, then turned and walked back into his cottage. His broad shoulders blocked their view but as he made no attempt to shut the front door, Laurence assumed they were meant to follow.

The door opened directly into a dark room with a low ceiling, shiny and brown from years of pipe smoking. The smell was almost tangible: of tobacco, tar, beer and damp, and over it all a slight ammoniacal tang. Clinker lay on the tiny grate and even on an summer's afternoon an oil lamp provided nearly all the light. A deal table, with the greasy remains of a meal, and some hard chairs occupied a third of the space; two armchairs, of indeterminate colour, stood on either side of the fire. The floor was covered in oilcloth. The only decoration was a calendar picture of the King and Queen – not the current year, Laurence noticed – on the narrow mantelpiece. By the closed back door was a framed tract with the words 'Every Good Gift Comes from Above' surrounded by birds and blossom.

'Mr Julian spoke to the police at Marlborough,' Frances said. 'They feel it is very unlikely that anything serious has happened to Maggie.' She spoke firmly, as though trying to convince herself as much as the old man. 'As she is fifteen they don't feel it's a job for them unless there's anything indicating she's come to harm.'

Walter grunted.

'But we,' she turned to Laurence as if to make it clear that they were a team, 'we wondered if we could ask a few questions, just so that we can keep a lookout.'

'Did she say anything at all about staying in London?' Laurence asked.

Walter looked at him again, this time with clearer eyes. There was something else in his gaze too, almost as if he and Laurence both knew where she was and it was a private joke.

'Little missy from the Hall had th' whole county after 'er.'

Frances looked puzzled but only for a second before realising he meant Kitty.

'As they would if Maggie was only five,' she said firmly.

'Bad blood,' Walter muttered. 'I did my best but it seems she were just like her ma. She run off. Left my boy.'

Frances looked at Laurence. It was extraordinarily unlikely that Maggie was involved in a love affair, he thought, and he could tell from Frances's face that she didn't believe it either.

Whatever the police view, Maggie was much more of a child than a young woman. When she was getting ready for Wembley, with her hair brushed and wearing a pretty dress, she had looked attractive – he had never seen it before – but not fully adult.

'Did she say anything?' Frances was asking.

Laurence suddenly thought, what if the dressing-up and the excitement hadn't been about Wembley but had been to do with some other plan? Was it possible that Maggie, stuck out here, had seen some opportunity in her first trip to London?

'Never says much,' Walter replied.

Laurence thought angrily that it was hardly surprising. Life had abandoned this young girl to live her life in this hovel with this gruff, slovenly man. But then again, he didn't have much choice after Maggie's mother had left and her father had been killed in France. It wasn't every grandfather's choice to have the responsibility of a growing girl foisted on him. He might simply have refused and sent her into service elsewhere once she reached twelve or so.

Walter seemed to soften slightly. 'She's never been much trouble,' he said. 'Daft at times but until now ...'

'Mr Petch,' Frances said gingerly, 'could we possibly look at Maggie's room? Just to see if there's anything that might help us find her?' She paused, watching the man's face. 'We miss her, you know. I'm sure you do.'

Walter's shoulders dropped and all his aggression seemed to leave him. 'It's up there,' he said, indicating the far door with a lift of his chin. 'Top on the right.'

Frances went up in front of Laurence. The walls either side were grimy where years of hands had brushed them while climbing those narrow stairs. There were only two rooms at the top. On the left, a door half ajar gave on to the same

152

depressing mixture of neglect and spartan disregard for comfort as downstairs. The door on the right was closed. Frances lifted the latch.

To Laurence's surprise this room was much lighter than the rest of the house. Its thin curtains were cleaner than anything else they'd seen in the small cottage and a rag rug on the floor had once been bright. A metal bed with chipped paint was neatly made up. A crocheted blanket lay diagonally across it and the wall above it had been decorated with pictures. A glazed pottery bowl and zinc jug were on a washstand. By the door a coat and a couple of dark-coloured garments hung on a peg. Two other pegs were empty.

Frances moved to a painted chest of drawers. Laurence was rooted to the spot; he felt like an intruder into Maggie's life. Frances held up a framed photograph, a faded shot of a young woman. The girl, not much older than Maggie herself, though noticeably prettier, was poking her head through a painted backcloth of a woman in a crinoline and bonnet.

'Her mother?' he said quietly. Frances nodded.

The other photograph was of a stiff-looking man in uniform. Maggie had placed a paper poppy in the papier-mâché frame. The only other ornament was a Coronation mug. Frances made a face and pulled open a drawer. All it contained was a toffee tin, a pair of fabric gloves and something in folded wool. It was a matinée jacket for an infant: old and slightly felted. Frances looked puzzled.

'Hers?' he guessed. 'From when she was a baby?'

Underneath was an album with cardboard covers. She handed it to him. Inside, on the first pages, the pictures were missing, sticky corners their sad memorials. On the third page was a picture of what were almost certainly Maggie's parents at the seaside, about to go bathing; opposite was a picture taken in a studio, again of Maggie's parents, her mother holding a baby, presumably Maggie, and a smiling older man.

As Frances and Laurence bent over it, Frances said in wonderment, 'It's Walter,' then stopped and listened, self-conscious, her hand over her mouth, but they could hear nothing from the room below. The man wore a white shirt, a jacket and trousers and a flat cap. He looked trim and handsome, probably in his early forties. The younger man was dark like Walter but in this picture it was still obvious that Maggie now looked more like her mother than either of her male relatives.

Frances laid the album back in its place and opened the drawers below. The third held a cardigan, a figured blouse, a flannel petticoat, a couple of other undergarments, some lisle stockings and a long-sleeved nightgown. Frances crouched down and touched each item, then moved them minutely as if searching beneath the clothes, her expression thoughtful. He turned away, feeling uncomfortable, and looked out of the window towards the Hall whose chimneys could just be seen behind a clump of trees.

Behind him he could hear Frances get to her feet again and reopen a drawer. When he turned, she had in her hand the decidedly battered toffee tin. On the front was a picture of two puppies. She eased off the lid and held out the tin to him. He took out a service medal that had *J. Petch* inscribed on the back. There was a French coin, which perhaps Maggie's father had brought back on leave, and an irregular piece of terracotta stone with incisions in some sort of rough pattern. At the bottom of the tin lay a small photograph that was obviously of her mother as a very young woman, with her married and maiden names on the back.

Beneath were a handful of letters. One was a Valentine card decorated in violets with *To Rosaline from her ever faithful, J.* Maggie's mother in happier times, he thought. Two were written to 'my dear old dad'. From the military addresses he judged they were from Joe Petch's time as a soldier. The third began 'My Dear Joe'. The signature was 'Rosaline'. More fragments from Maggie's lost childhood. He didn't want to intrude further on the family's privacy and he handed the tin back feeling uncomfortable. Frances replaced the lid and put it away in the drawer.

'Look,' she said, pointing to the wall with a rueful expression. Immediately above the bedhead was a print of a radiant Christ, feeding small birds and animals, and around him a vast array of unlikely acolytes: cuttings from magazines in which bow-lipped, doe-eyed film stars melted before the camera, or were caught in role. He recognised Lillian Gish and a blush-tinted Mary Pickford in velvet and white swansdown. However, he had no idea of the identity of the actress in eighteenth-century dress who cowered before a villainous-looking bewigged nobleman, nor of the girl in a blazer, draped over a Crossley shooting brake. Maggie had also stuck advertisements on to the brown wallpaper. Instant transformation was promised to the user for brightening lotion and cold cream.

He was still taking in this modern pantheon as Frances picked up from the bed a small stuffed rabbit with all its nap rubbed off, gently put it aside, then raised the counterpane and single pillow. Nothing.

There was a bible on a milking stool by the bed and beside it a jam jar with some twigs of dried-up apple blossom. Laurence imagined Maggie picking them from the orchard next door and the thought of her setting them carefully by her bed in this sparse room made her loss seem more acute. He picked up the bible and opened the soft black cover. There was a printed Sunday-school sticker on the flyleaf that said *Joseph Walter Petch, St Barbara's, Easton, 1891*.

'Her father,' Frances said as he tipped it towards her. Just above the bedhead was a tinted picture postcard of Calais. He pulled out the rusty tack with a thumbnail and turned it over. The postmark was January 1917. It was to Maggie from her father: a few brief words in big letters.

'Im glad your learning to read,' he'd said, 'so soon you will be able to read to gramps because his eyes are bad. But where I am you couldnt read any books because they dont talk English. Be a good girl and when I get back to Easton you can have that puppy. Heres a hug to his favourite girl from your old dad.'

Frances sighed as she read it. He replaced it over the dark rectangle of wallpaper that marked its place. She was still looking at it, biting her lip.

'We ought to go down,' he said.

The silence unnerved him; was the old man just sitting downstairs, listening to them picking through his granddaughter's things? Did he understand why they were doing it or did he think it was gratuitous curiosity?

'Do you think she's all right?' Frances said and then, 'Sorry, stupid question. Stupid. Stupid.'

As they left the room she turned, hovered in the doorway, and then went downstairs. Laurence feared Walter would question them but he was sitting at the table, filling his pipe, and hardly seemed to notice their reappearance.

'Did Maggie have any friends?' Frances asked. 'In the village, say?'

Walter looked at her as if surprised to find her in the room.

'Not a young man I knew of, if that's what you're coming to. I wouldn't ha' allowed it. Not after her ma.'

'A girl friend?'

Walter drew on his pipe and coughed, his gaze on the fire, which still smoked with no visible flame. It was obvious he'd had enough of them and Laurence turned to go. Walter tapped his surviving teeth together against the pipe stem before saying, 'There's Ann Hobson's girl. Ruby.' He fell silent again. 'Bit simple.' Another pause. 'Sometimes when Maggie were younger she used to mind the Kilminster children. Their girl ...' He paused, obviously thinking. 'Edna, no Ethel, she's a bit younger. Sees a bit of her. Likes their dog.' It was a long speech for the old man.

'Is there any family?' Laurence asked. 'Or other relations?'

Walter seemed to consider, scratching his chest. 'My sister's gone. As for her ma – Maggie's ma, not that she was any kind of mother to her – I don't know.'

'Thank you,' Frances said. She paused. 'I'm truly sorry about Maggie. I'm sure she'll soon be back.'

'I didn't want her to go but she set her heart on it. I thought as she'd be safe, being with the party from the Hall.'

Frances's head dropped a little. Laurence said, 'We'll do everything we can to find her.'

Even as he said it he thought how meaningless his words were. Walter didn't bother to respond.

'She was at me to have a dog,' he said, still staring at the fire. 'I told her it'd be too much trouble. Mebbe if she'd had a dog she'd have come back to see him.'

Once they were clear of the house Frances said, a desperate note in her voice, 'Why didn't we ever talk to her? She obviously had dreams, however improbable, and she'd tried to make her room nice, kept her things neat and treasured those pitiful few mementoes of her parents.'

'Not knowing really what became of either of them,' Laurence reflected, wondering whether Maggie might have gone in search of her mother, although it was unlikely she'd know where to begin to find her.

Frances looked almost on the point of tears.

'We never really thought of how things were when she wasn't bringing in tea or polishing the floors. Patrick saw it more because he hasn't just got used to her being here.' She seemed bewildered by her own blindness. 'Her mother had abandoned her, her father had been killed, yet we thought, if we thought at all, that she was lucky to still have a home and to stay in the village.' Her words came fast. 'That awful smelly house. And none of us ever saw, or thought whether she wanted any of the things other girls had. She was just a plainish child to us but she was growing up. Perhaps she did have a young man. I rather hope she did.'

Laurence nodded, though it seemed unlikely. Over the last weeks he had come to think their collective sense of loss at Easton Hall had rendered the family insensitive to any other grief. As long as Maggie came back eventually, perhaps her going would have done some good.

They walked on and reached the small village green; its duck-pond looked almost idyllically pretty in the sun. Half a dozen ducks were basking on the bank.

'Shall we sit for a bit?' Frances said, crossing to the bench under the tree. She settled on it with her legs stuck straight out. He couldn't help but notice that the wrinkles in her cotton stockings and her dusty lace-up shoes only emphasised rather fine ankles. She exhaled noisily and when she said, 'What a rotten situation,' he didn't ask whether she meant Maggie's disappearance or the whole shadow of misfortune that seemed to lie over Easton Deadall.

They sat together with their backs to the old tree, gazing at the handful of cottages in front of them. Some were obviously being repaired, their new thatch yellowy gold. It was quiet with the older children not yet back from school in the neighbouring village. They could just hear a woman calling to a child or perhaps even to chickens, but not clearly enough to make out what she was saying. Laurence rested his hand on the arm of the seat, his hand smoothing wood so old that it was more like warm stone. Feeling some ridges, he glanced down to see some old initials and wondered whose long-dead love they spoke of.

Almost as if she sensed his thoughts, Frances said, 'Easton was so full of life once. I don't expect you can imagine it. In the early days – before Kitty went – there would be pranks and sudden decisions to go on picnics, or play poker in the drawing room, or have a tennis tournament, or force guests at their house parties to put on these dreadful plays. When Digby was dancing he'd pick Lydia up right off the floor.' She smiled in recollection. 'He had a really fine voice, whether singing along with his own playing on the piano, or booming out in church. He played for the village cricket team. The men loved that; he was their best bowler. He should have had a son, really. Kitty was gentle like Lydia and she was frightened of loud noises and the dark.'

She turned to face him as if eager for him to see how it was.

'But he still used to walk around the estate with her on his shoulders.' She paused again, looking away. 'He was never the same after Kitty. He went through the motions but the boyish fun was gone. It became a bit desperate; after all, who would want to make up a jolly house party when the couple had managed to lose their only child?' Her voice had an edge of hardness to it.

Laurence had noticed how everybody who talked about Kitty had trouble finding the right vocabulary. They would describe her as 'lost', 'gone', 'taken', or 'disappeared', or just the phrase he'd heard two or three times, 'before' or' 'after' Kitty, her diminutive name expressing the avalanche of fear, uncertainty and misery that had settled on the Hall.

'It must have been hard for Julian too,' Laurence said, hoping that in the change of subject she didn't think he wasn't taking in her words. 'To have such an older brother.'

Frances was nodding in agreement before he'd even finished the sentence. 'On the other hand it's hard to imagine it the other way round, if Julian had been the heir, solid, decent and second-best at everything. Perhaps he was not a man who could have led the village to war?'

To death, more like, Laurence thought. He had come across men like Digby at Oxford: on the river, at college balls, following a beagle pack. Men so handsome and so physically able that it was hardly surprising they glowed with confidence. He had never felt he knew any of them; did they exist when they weren't performing? Instead he said mildly, 'Is Julian better for the estate perhaps?'

Frances smiled, the slightly asymmetrical smile he liked so much. 'Much better in some ways, with better accounts, perhaps, better plans. Sensible, if not so much fun.' Then she sighed. 'If only Julian hadn't been very much in love with Lydia. Once Digby brought her home, Julian never had eyes for any other woman.'

'Was there ever any other woman?'

'Oh yes.' Frances looked surprised. 'I mean he's a nice man, nice looking too. But he fell for Lydia.'

'Not so sensible, Julian, then?'

'No. I suppose not.'

It seemed to Laurence that the silence between them stretched on for ever. She was leaning forward, her arms resting on her thighs, he face almost hidden by her fall of hair. He rested his head against the rough bark of the tree. Through the leafy tips of the branches, the sky was a rich shade of blue, and small birds – swallows? swifts? – swooped high above. His eyes closed; it was the sort of peace he had once taken for granted.

'I don't mean to be disloyal to Lydia in any way,' Frances said suddenly, startling him. 'But you must feel as a relative newcomer, looking in on us all, that we are obsessed with the past?'

He made a noncommittal face, but she was looking at him so intently that he said, 'All this,' he indicated the small cottages beyond the green, with their half-repaired roofs, 'this is looking to the future in a good way, I think. Perhaps bringing William in, who had no connection with Easton Deadall, helped. He could only look forward because he wasn't familiar with its past.'

He didn't say that he thought William had a determination to look to the future because for him the past was not, as it was for Lydia, a place of sorrow. Rather it held life and opportunity and certainty that had been removed from him for ever in a single mortar explosion in France.

'Sometimes,' Frances said, 'I feel as if Easton will never recover until we —Lydia, Julian, Patrick and me — are dead, and all our memories with us. Kitty dominates everything we do. A little girl who has been gone for over twice as long as she was with us, whose strange afterlife leaves a sort of smothering blanket of guilt over all of us. Even Patrick, who can't bear to come here more than once every few years.'

'Why is everyone so angry about Patrick being absent?'

'The war,' she said. 'He couldn't fight but he could have run the estate for Digby and then for Lydia. But he wouldn't. He was only at Oxford while we were struggling and the place slid into rack and ruin.'

It was so unlike her to sound bitter that he wanted to take her hand and tuck her into the warmth and safety of his arms. The moment passed. He asked whether she felt that Maggie was in danger.

'I did at first, because of Kitty, of course. It seemed like fate repeating itself. But when Julian had spoken to the police I realised how it looked to them. Still . . .'

'Still what?'

'Still, why would she suddenly take off? She seems fond of us, very fond of Nicholas. She never caused any trouble.'

'As her grandfather said.'

She nodded.

'Patrick's right: there wasn't a lot of fun in her life,' he said. 'Though in his own way Walter seemed to care about her. He cares about her now she's gone, even if he didn't when she was there.'

'Did anything strike you when we were in her room?'

He thought for a second. 'Her belongings were pretty paltry, yet she'd tried. It was a funny mixture of childhood and adult curiosity.'

'What about her belongings?' She looked almost eager.

'Shabby? Sentimental?'

'Her clothes?'

He shrugged. He'd tried to look away when she was going through the girl's possessions. 'There weren't many.'

'They were winter clothes: woollens, a coat that I think Lydia had given her. A warm dress, a flannel nightdress, a shawl. She probably has very, very few clothes, but there was no underwear, no dresses. No handkerchief. No hairbrush, for heaven's sake.'

He thought he could see where she was going with this but was temporarily distracted by four or five children walking into the village: a tall girl in a pinafore holding a little boy by the hand, and three other children with school bags who were shouting and pushing each other. A woman had come out from the nearest cottage and was standing at a gate. The girl stopped to talk to her and the two of them both glanced towards where they were sitting. One of the boys ran at the ducks, causing them to scurry into the water, squawking loudly.

Laurence turned back to her. 'You think she's taken some of her things with her, that she'd planned to go?'

'I think it's possible. It's better than the alternatives.'

'The most likely person she'd try to find would be her mother, don't you think?'

'If she knew where she was. But how would she? They wouldn't even recognise each other now.'

He thought back to Maggie in the kitchen, preparing crockery for the picnic, a picnic she was never going to share. She had unquestionably been excited; like her grandfather, she was a girl of few words but she'd been positively chatty. She had looked pretty with the ribbon in her hair and a print dress, which, while a bit old-fashioned, had made her look smarter. He had put it all down to anticipation of seeing the Wembley exhibition. Even at the time he'd been glad they were taking her, thinking there wasn't a lot to do around Easton. Now that he'd seen how she lived, her eagerness had an added poignancy. She'd had a bag on a chair next to her as she directed Nicholas. Laurence had nearly teased her about it. It was the sort of bag his grandmother had had: black, capacious and ugly.

'I think she could have had things with her,' he said. 'Her bag was big enough.'

The four smaller children were all standing only yards away now. One of the younger girls tucked her frock into her knickers and did a cartwheel in a flash of blue and white, then stood and regained her balance, adjusting her plaits.

'I think we're going to keep our audience as long as we sit here,' Frances said.

Saying good afternoon as they passed the children, they were about to set off for Easton when Laurence had a thought and turned back to the small group.

'Are any of you Kilminsters?' he said.

A smallish, curly-haired boy put his hand up. 'He's not a teacher, Johnny,' the girl with the plaits said. 'Stupid.' She looked scathingly at the boy and then at Laurence in a businesslike way. 'He's one and that's his sister.' She pointed at the tall girl talking to the woman by the cottage. 'Ethel. Their Sidney's got a quinsy.'

Frances said, 'And what about a girl called Ruby?'

One of the boys sniggered and even the girl with plaits looked amused. 'You won't get sense out of Ruby.' She tapped her forehead with a finger. 'Her ma was frightened by a bull when she was carrying.'

Two taller boys, eleven or twelve perhaps, had come up the lane and joined the group. One had a face covered in freckles and reddish-blond hair. The other was sturdy and reminded Laurence slightly of someone.

'Are you talking about Mags?' the freckled boy said eagerly.

'She's been taken by white slavers, my auntie says,' the girl in plaits retorted. 'It comes of going to London.'

The two smaller boys had stopped scuffling and were listening intently.

'She's been kidnapped,' the same older boy volunteered.

'What makes you think that?' Laurence asked.

'Stands to reason. People up at Hall go missing.'

'But that was a little girl and before you were born,' Frances said.

The older girl was walking towards them and Frances wanted to get the younger children's opinions first, in case her presence inhibited them.

The girl in plaits struggled to retain her authority. 'And they'd think old Walter could give 'em pots of money to get her back? They'd have to be soft in the head.'

The boy was ready for this. 'But them at the Hall have got plenty—'

The older girl interrupted. 'You don't know anything,' she said, with a slight wobble in her voice.

Laurence was surprised. Perhaps Maggie did have friends in Easton. The older girl put her arm out as if to herd the smaller children back towards the cottages. When the girl with plaits stood her ground, she said, 'Annie, your ma'll have tea.'

'Not my ma, she won't.'

'What's your name?' Frances asked the older girl.

The girl looked at her, only tiny movements of her facial muscles indicating that her silence wasn't rudeness.

'Eth,' she said, finally. 'Ethel Kilminster.'

'Ethel, we could do with your help. Could we talk to you, just for a minute? We won't keep you from your tea.' Frances indicated the pond, the bench and the tree. 'We could talk out here.'

It was obvious she wanted to get the girl away from her companions. Ethel looked doubtful, while the two smaller boys had lost interest and were wandering away. The older ones were murmuring to each other. Only the girl with plaits was still concentrating on every word they were saying.

Ethel glanced back towards the cottage where she just been chatting but the woman had gone inside. She tucked an imaginary strand of fair hair behind her ear, then rubbed one black-stockinged leg down the back of the other. The thick fabric had a large hole in it. She was fine boned and already showed signs of being a good-looking woman, Laurence thought.

'Might Maggie have run away?' Frances said.

'She didn't say to me.' Ethel's expression was sad. 'She said old Walter needed looking after. But my ma says he's an idle—'

'So Maggie said nothing about leaving Easton?'

Ethel shook her head, looking bewildered and suddenly younger. 'Her grandad wouldn't even let her go to the Mop Fair,' she said plaintively, 'in case the man who took her ma, took her too. Though sometimes she crept off. He wouldn't let her do anything, go anywhere outside of Easton. But because it was the Hall he couldn't say no to London.'

'What did Maggie say about it?'

Ethel looked down, describing a circle on the grass with the toe of a scuffed shoe.

'Don't know.'

When she looked up, Frances raised an eyebrow, which appeared to make Ethel uncomfortable.

After a bit she said, 'We wasn't speaking.' She fell silent but Frances didn't push her. 'She didn't talk of nothing else when Mrs ... the red-haired lady with the little boy ...'

'Bolitho,' Laurence said.

'When she said first Maggie could go to London. I said to Maggie to see if I could come too but she wouldn't.' She rubbed her nose vigorously. 'She said she was going along to help and I was too young and they didn't want another child with them and it wasn't for the village.'

'So you'd had a bit of an argument?'

The girl nodded miserably, her eyes on the ground.

'We'll try to find her,' Frances said.

Ethel looked up. 'You don't think she's dead then? Or with slavers?'

Her eyes filled with tears and this time she wiped her nose on her sleeve. Frances handed her a small folded handkerchief. Ethel stared at it and touched the border of tiny forget-me-nots, her expression doubtful, but eventually she used it to wipe her nose, then kept it clutched in her hand.

'I thought she might have run off because I said I didn't want to be her friend ... And that only would've left daft Ruby.'

She appeared to be studying her shoes, wrapping the handkerchief round her fingers as she did so.

'But I didn't mean it,' she said eventually.

'Of course you didn't. Everybody says things they don't mean when they argue.'

'If she's dead it's my fault ... and I miss her. Because now I've just got the little 'uns.' She looked towards the playing children with resignation.

'When do you leave school?' Frances asked gently.

'I could leave now. I'm just helping Miss with the small ones.'

'What if I were to ask Mrs Easton if we could find a place for you at the Hall?'

Ethel looked up sharply. 'Instead of Maggie?'

'No. As well as Maggie. When she comes back. She has too much work. Maybe that's why she wanted to go away for a bit.' Frances faced Laurence. 'Don't you think that would be a good idea?'

'I think Ethel would be a huge help to Mrs Easton. Would your mother allow it?' He could see the eagerness in the girl's eyes.

'And you wouldn't have to sleep at the Hall. You could stay at home and still help your mother with your brothers and sisters,' Frances added.

'Brothers,' said Ethel, wearily, then added, 'Would I be paid? Just it would help my ma.'

'Of course you would. Not very much but you'd get your dinner too and sometimes there'd be bits you could take home.'

Ethel smiled, and was transformed from pretty to beautiful. Just for a second Laurence felt uneasy. Easton had not been a happy place for so many who'd lived there. But at the sight of

Ethel's face lit up with excitement, the thought vanished as swiftly as it came.

'I'll get Mrs Easton to speak to your mother, then,' Frances said and turned to go. Ethel held out the crumpled handkerchief.

'Why don't you keep it?' Frances said.

As they walked on through the village towards the Hall, Laurence said, 'Do you feel as positive as you sounded?'

Frances shrugged. 'Probably.'

He nodded.

'On one ridiculously superstitious level, I feel that Easton is a benighted place from which people disappear or die, but more rationally, inasmuch as any utterly innocent country girl would be all right in London, I suppose I think Maggie thought she knew what she was doing.' She didn't sound entirely convinced. 'Realising that she probably planned to go surprises me but it's infinitely better than her just wandering off.'

'You don't think it was an assignation, then?'

'No. I mean, who with? Her grandfather scarcely let her out of his sight. Her mother's been gone ten years or more without a word. Who knows if there are really any other living family? There are no young men here and, anyway, I don't quite see Maggie as an object of lust.'

'So you think she ran away?'

'She didn't seem the type. It sounds cruel now, but I wouldn't have thought she'd have that sort of initiative. She's always been a bit awkward, but diligent, and she loves Mrs Hill. But until today I'd never been inside the cottage.' She made a grimace of regret. 'Now I can see she might have become desperate to get away.'

CHAPTER TEN

 Although they kept doing their work, there was a tension in the house over the following weeks that was not helped by the sweltering heat, Lydia's continuing non-appearance, and Julian's obsession with the water levels. He was always alone now, Laurence noticed, trudging back and forth to the river, as David kept his distance. Now that Nicholas was back in London, it was Eleanor who helped William into the garden and into the village. The one time that Laurence had bumped into David as he crossed to the church, the man looked preoccupied and was thinner than ever, with dark smudges under his eyes. Laurence was more and more convinced that Maggie had gone away deliberately but the toll on David was heavy. Even the cheerful Susan seemed fretful.

When Laurence passed the kitchen a week or so later, Mrs Hill, at least, seemed to have cheered up. The first thing she told him was that it was St Swithin's Day.

'And look what a day it is,' Susan said. 'Flaming July. And if it's fine today it'll be fine for forty days. That's nearly the end of August. And in my state I'm too hot to move. David likes walking at night when it's cool and nobody's about but I'm frightened of the dark and all the noises.'

Then she looked more solemn.

'I hope by then we'll have found Maggie. It's six weeks away. She's a good girl. I'm sure she didn't mean to worry her grampa, but she must miss her ma and pa. I was an orphan so I know.'

Her hand instinctively cupped her stomach.

'And David's taken it so bad,' she said. 'He knows what it's like for the Eastons. He came over from West Overton – his ma was dying – when they were searching for the little girl, Kitty. Ever since Maggie went, the first days he was just upset and talking of it all the time, but now he won't hardly eat. I wake up and he's just staring up like he's dead. Won't talk at all.' She suddenly looked embarrassed. 'Sorry, sir, I don't know what come over me – you don't want to hear all our troubles.' She started busying herself at the sink. Even Mrs Hill looked startled by her outburst.

Only William and Eleanor were at breakfast. Julian, aiming to travel in the hours when it was cooler, had already left early to see the police and then attend an agricultural meeting and dinner in Devizes. With obvious reluctance he had decided to stay the night afterwards. How rarely anyone left Easton, Laurence thought, as Julian had announced his plans the day before. Laurence had himself planned to go to London in a day or so to see if he could find out more about St Barbara's in the archive. Now, even as he wondered if his timing looked clumsy, he knew he had never wanted to get away more.

Tiny storm flies circled overhead. Eleanor was uncharacteristically quiet but William hardly waited for Laurence to help himself to his poached eggs and bacon before he opened a letter that was lying by his plate.

'They're finally coming to prepare for the window installation next week. Two of them. That's something positive, don't you think?'

Eleanor said sharply, 'When there's a child missing, it's hard to think anything's very positive.'

William put the letter down, the excitement fading from his eyes. 'Yes, selfish of me. It's just been a long time arranging it all. Do you think we shouldn't go ahead right now?'

'No. I'm just being peevish,' Eleanor said. 'I feel responsible for Maggie as it was me that was so keen she should go.'

'And Patrick,' William said. 'The whole thing was Patrick's idea.'

'Her being in the car was my idea. I can't help thinking that she never intended to be left with Nicholas, that she thought she might be free to explore alone.'

'She'll come back,' William said and he reached for her hand, but she made no attempt to clasp his.

After breakfast Laurence walked out into the garden, hoping to find David. He thought the man needed a specific task to take his mind off recent events and it was easier to talk to him in Julian's absence. He made for the overgrown kitchen garden, where David had cleared a patch and begun to grow vegetables. David wasn't there but Laurence liked the tidy way the man had put straw under the marrows, and had staked the peas and the runner beans, in even rows. Raffia ties secured each stem to their canes and their bright-red flowers reminded him of allotments seen in his childhood. Between the rows, David was growing flowers for cutting for the house. He had repaired one of the glasshouses and when Laurence opened the door, the green smell of tomatoes was almost overwhelming. The heat was already building and there was a greyish tinge to the cloudless blue of the sky.

As he came along the terrace he saw David coming uphill

from the generator shed. He appeared deep in thought and started when Laurence greeted him. His face shone with sweat.

'Oiling the parts while the generator's off,' David said defensively. 'Can't see it'll be on for a while. With no rain the water's too low. The mill up river, that's closed too. Should be all right at the Hall as it's still light late and it's full moon tomorrow. They can do without electricity.' There was something desperate in his tone. He scanned the horizon. 'Mind, I reckon the weather'll break any day soon. You can feel it coming.'

'Your wife thinks it's going to be dry until August.'

'St Swithin's Day.' David forced a smile. 'She's a superstitious one.'

'Actually, I came to find you because we need to clear the west end of the church soon,' Laurence said.

David's expression was wooden. 'But we finished the floor.'

'That's the east end. We need to clear the other side.'

'It's the window,' David said. 'I forgot all about the window.' He seemed to be speaking to himself more than answering Laurence.

'If you're free tomorrow it would be good to get a clear space for them to take out the old glass. Then they can assemble the new. I am afraid it will make the most fearful mess however careful they are.'

'I didn't think Mr Julian would be wanting all that with Mrs Easton ill and Maggie gone.'

He could see David was unhappy. He had worked hard on the old floor, asking William's advice on how to bring it to its best condition without damaging it. Now attention would move to the west window and the exposed area would unavoidably get covered in debris. But mostly he was still bearing the burden of his poor judgment at Wembley, Laurence thought.

'Well, he's away and Mr Bolitho says the glaziers are coming next week. Tomorrow at eleven, then? Unless you've got other chores?' Laurence said briskly.

David nodded but he wouldn't meet Laurence's eyes. As Laurence walked away he had the feeling David had not moved. But when he reached the terrace and looked back, David was gone.

'Thirteen and a half hours of sun,' Mrs Hill said as she served up the haddock that evening, as if the weather was something else she had laboured over. She set down a tureen of disintegrating potatoes with a crash. 'David grew 'em.'

However, it was not the sun but the heat that was extraordinary. When Laurence went to bed, he lay in his pyjama bottoms on top of his blankets until they irritated his skin and he pushed the whole mass of bedding to the floor. He had thrown open both sash windows and left the heavy curtains slightly apart but the room still felt airless. After a while he thought he'd read and felt for the light, forgetting the generator was off. It clicked uselessly. He lit the oil lamp instead, but heavy-bodied moths were soon thudding against the glass shade. Eventually he turned it out, expecting darkness, but the moon was almost full and the bedroom was surprisingly light. An owl hooted. He looked at his watch: it was one-thirty.

He got out of bed and gazed out at a monochrome landscape of white grass and grey trees. The moonlight transformed the garden. The curves of the maze cast shadows which made it look much more substantial, as if he was looking into the future. For him, Lydia's dream, William's vision and David's labour had created something magical.

Behind the darkness of the shrubs around the lake, the barer ground rose to the south. Even standing at the window, he felt sweat on the back of his neck. He was wide awake now and

173

thought that, as sleep seemed impossible, he would go outside and walk in the strangely altered landscape. He pulled on his trousers and yesterday's shirt, and, carrying his shoes, opened his door. He went downstairs, stepping as near the wall as possible so that the treads would not creak.

In the hall he found the front door unlocked. Julian had claimed he always locked the door at night but clearly this was not the case. Laurence put the key in his pocket just in case Julian should come down later and secure it while he was outside. He was relieved the door opened smoothly and he stepped barefoot on to the terrace. Stopping to put his shoes on, he set out across the lawn. He had thoughts of walking right out towards Silbury Hill, driven by a feeling, which he knew Patrick would regard as fanciful nonsense, that to see it in a nocturnal landscape would be to feel closer to the unknown men who created it. It would also be extraordinary to be there in the moonlight. He made his way slowly down towards the dark mass of foliage surrounding the lake.

He was quite close when he heard a splash and then a stifled giggle. He stopped and then went forward again without thinking, amused that others had had the same idea, but something made him pause and move more slowly. He was deep in the shadow of the evergreens when the lake came in view. Now he could see a figure in the water; a man he thought.

"Come on,' the man said – it was Patrick, 'better to jump than walk in through the mud.'

He took one more step and saw the whiteness of a woman, naked, on the edge of the black water. She raised herself on her toes, her arms thrust back as if to dive, then stepped back and laughed.

'If I jump I'll wake the whole house up,' she said in a loud whisper. It was Eleanor.

Just as he recognised her, she sat down on the water's edge and slipped in. She gasped, then struck out smoothly towards Patrick. When she reached him, he drew her to him and kissed her, one hand cradling her head. She put her arms around his neck, then let go and floated backwards with her legs hooked around his waist.

'What a night,' he heard her say. 'I could float here for ever, looking at the stars.'

As Laurence turned to retreat as quickly as he could, he must have trodden on a twig. Whether or not they heard it, something alerted the swimmers. Eleanor broke free and swam to the side. Both fell silent.

Laurence's heart was pounding, his legs suddenly clumsy, and he felt like a voyeur, however inadvertent his interruption. He knew he could not return the way he'd come because he'd be in plain view, although, looking up, he saw cloud had now covered the moon and the night was much darker than when he had set out.

Once he heard them relax their vigilance and talk again, he followed the ha-ha to just below the generator shed, came up behind it and went round the far side of the church. At this point his only option was to walk along the terrace and enter by the main door. He looked back across the grass but nothing moved, although a breeze had got up and the leaves were rustling. Somewhere a window banged.

Up on the downs a single flash of light caught his attention but when it was repeated he realised it was lightning – the storm was approaching. He had no idea whether Patrick and Eleanor were below him still at the lake or had already returned to the house, but he put the key back and left the door unlocked. He crept upstairs and was overwhelmed with relief when he shut the door of his room.

His mind was teeming with questions. How long had this

been going on? What was going on? What had he actually seen? Had they seen him?

As the thunder grumbled some way away, he replayed the scene again and again in his head. Above all, he felt a terrible sadness for William.

CHAPTER ELEVEN

When he first opened his eyes, freezing cold and lying uncovered, the grey light made him think that it was only dawn but in fact it was nine. He surfaced from sleep vaguely aware of noise. Outside trees roared in the rain and the gutters were already gurgling with more water than they could cope with. The long spell of dry weather had finally broken. He jumped up to close the windows but the billowing curtains were already wet. Outside the ground was so hard that rainwater lay on the grass in shallow pools.

Laurence felt tired and ill at ease. Although relieved that by the time he got up nobody else seemed to be about, he couldn't bring himself to drop in and see William as he usually did.

After breakfast he sat in the library reading a book on Wiltshire hill forts. It was too wet to leave the house although at least he had the arrangement with David later. He had his torch with him, knowing he would need it in the church. Water had seeped under the library windows and somebody had laid down rolled-up cloths to soak it up. He dreaded seeing Eleanor or Patrick. It was inevitable, sooner or later, but he wanted it to be in a room where any embarrassment would be diluted by the presence of others. When the door opened his heart sank, but it was only Frances.

'Am I disturbing you?'

'No.' He stood up. 'Of course not.'

'You look pretty glum.'

He forced a smile.

'You were out last night,' she said.

He was about to deny it when she added, 'I saw you from my window. Don't look so surprised. I saw you. You weren't the only one unable to sleep.'

'No,' he said, more firmly than he intended.

She looked at him intently. 'Ah,' she said. The single syllable was heavy with meaning and as she held his eyes he realised she already knew about Eleanor.

He said, 'It's none of my business,' and looked away.

'It obviously feels like your business. You're horrified. It's written all over your face.'

'I can't understand how they could be so indifferent to William. So cruel.' As he said it he realised how desperately he felt this.

'And are you angrier with Eleanor or Patrick?'

'It's not a competition,' he said. 'Here we are, with tragedy unfolding all around us and there they are, frolicking about without a care in the world.' He knew what he was saying was ugly and unfair.

'Don't you think that's part of it?' she said. 'To escape all that?'

'I don't know.'

He felt wretched, not least because part of his response when he saw Eleanor at the lake edge, passionately embracing Patrick, was envy.

'You're probably right,' he said less angrily, 'but William will never have that choice.'

When she didn't answer but just kept looking at him, with more understanding than he deserved, he said, 'I'm not naive, and I know relationships are infinitely more complicated than they seem to onlookers, God knows I should, but they didn't even seem to like each other much.'

He knew he was being disingenuous but he was also annoyed. Were the uncomfortable dinners that had been forced upon them by the couple sniping at each other just a charade?

'To start with, Eleanor was jealous, I think,' Frances said, and it was obvious she had known of this relationship for a while.

'Who on earth of?'

'Patrick,' she said. 'He represented freedom. Eleanor isn't like most women who live in the wider world through their husbands. You should have seen her before the war. She came to Girton all on her own, with just a trunk and a few books, in a trap from the station. She was extraordinary at Cambridge – even though we couldn't get our degrees; even though the male undergraduates thought we were there for their amusement and nearly all the professors despised us. She was very young to be by herself but her mother was never very interested in her. She lived in Switzerland, I think, with Eleanor's stepfather.'

Laurence thought how little he had really known Eleanor. Since he had first met her, three years ago, he'd seen her as an ideal of a free-thinking independent woman, someone quite different from his dead wife, Louise, and the girls he had known before the war, whereas growing into adulthood without a proper home, without belonging, was something he and Eleanor shared.

'She fought as a suffragist,' Frances said, 'and she went to France as a nurse, as you know. She gave up a life she loved, didn't complete her degree. She made these decisions all by herself. She was never a follower. And now ... what? She's still a nurse. That old life's been taken away. So *she* doesn't get many choices either.'

'But I thought she was happy.' He corrected himself, 'Or content at least.'

'She was. She probably still is. She loves William and adores Nicholas,' Frances said, almost pleading with him.

'And does she love or adore Patrick?'

For the first time Frances looked irritated. 'I would have expected better of you, Laurence.'

'I'm sorry. I'm being a prig. The truth is that I'm just desperate for William. And as for Patrick Easton—'

'I suppose most men we knew fought, then they returned to their old lives, or they died, or, like William, they came back scarred, but Patrick was different,' Frances said. 'He couldn't fight, not because he didn't want to, but because they wouldn't have him. But unfairly that means he's had an interesting life.'

Laurence tried not to feel resentful or to let vague thoughts that it wasn't just the chance of seeing the world, of having some kind of option about which dangers might be worth pursuing, crystallise into speech. Patrick had had the advantage of escaping a world of lives either lost or ruined. But then he looked at her face and knew she thought these things too. After all, the evidence was right here on her sister's estate.

He had never really dwelled on the limitations that William's injuries placed on Eleanor. He had so wanted to believe that she was different and this meant she saw her situation as something positive. But he was being naive. Of course it was a compromise. She was still a relatively young woman, and perhaps that compromise had become an intolerable burden in the years since the war and her marriage.

'I don't think she wanted to be *with* a man like Patrick necessarily.' Frances held his eye. 'My guess is she wanted to *be him*.

Just for a while, to be free, to explore, to feel, to . . .' She paused. 'To have an unknown future. Whereas you think it was simple desire.'

Laurence didn't protest that he thought it was a great deal more than that, or that, in his experience, desire was seldom simple. Instead he said, 'Patrick desires *her*, though, whatever she feels about him.'

Frances made a face, but she nodded agreement.

'I don't understand Patrick,' he said.

'Eleanor's a beautiful woman and a spirited one.'

'But there are plenty of women these days, God knows.'

'She's not like most women. She's more like him. She's curious about everything, and brave.'

'She's a wife and a mother.'

'Patrick's used to wanting things he can't have,' Frances said, simply.

'Do you mean Easton?'

'I think he wanted to be the oldest, yes, in a way that Julian didn't. And instead he made himself the cleverest. And he couldn't be the bravest because he couldn't fight. Digby had it all and, until Kitty was born, Julian was his heir. Patrick was just the spare. But Patrick's seen more of life, more of the world, than Julian ever will.'

She leaned forward. She spoke quietly but vehemently.

'Easton Deadall is a prison. For Lydia, first of all because Digby possessed her, and now because she holds it for Kitty who, as we all know, has been dead for over ten years. For Julian, because he's the heir apparent and because he's got a thing about Lydia and he loves Easton. For me, because I don't want to leave my sister who is not strong.' Her face was bleak. 'For William, because the only work he can get, let's face it, is Easton. Don't look like that, Laurence. I'm not being unkind, I'm being honest.'

She drew breath. 'But Patrick is free. He can come and go as he pleases. Easton hasn't trapped him yet. Everything lies ahead.'

'Eleanor would never leave William.'

Laurence hoped it was true and hoped, too, that Nicholas would be part of the glue that held them together. But if Frances's and Julian's horizons did not stretch far, William's were only as wide as Eleanor made possible.

'The thing is,' Frances added after a long silence, 'Patrick has the makings of two people: a good man and a very selfish man, and one day he'll have to make up his mind which he wants to be.

'And you, too,' she said, 'only you have a different choice.' She smiled sadly. 'Your heart and thoughts are elsewhere, far, far away from Easton. Back in the past. But do you want to be the decent chap, always responding to the needs of others: the one who waits, who watches? Or do you want to make a life for yourself, take some chances?'

For a few seconds he couldn't look at her. Had Eleanor told her about Mary or was she thinking of his dead wife? Whatever she knew, her assessment of his character was accurate and painful.

Just as he struggled to find the words to reply, the door opened and Julian came in with Scout at his heels. He looked tired and worried.

'Lydia's not quite the thing.' He looked at Frances. 'Could you come up and see her?'

He left at once, with Frances following. Laurence jumped to his feet, realising he was five minutes late to meet David. It had stopped raining but the front door was almost blown back on him as he opened it and he ran along the terrace, trying to avoid the deepest puddles.

The church was gloomy. Little light shone through the

stained glass but it was peaceful and dry, except for wet foot-steps down the aisle. David was sitting by the floor maze, leaning forward, his head bent. For a minute Laurence thought he was praying and waited; but some movement alerted David. He stood up fast and, just for a second, Laurence thought there was alarm in his eyes. But he realised it was just surprise; David evidently hadn't heard the door open because of the downpour outside.

'We should all thank you,' he said to David. 'You've done a fine job on the floor. When this window is in, I think Mrs Easton will have a really impressive memorial.'

'Mr Bolitho showed me the design,' David said, obviously trying to make an effort, pushing his damp hair out of his eyes. 'It's a downright shame he can't be making buildings everywhere.'

'You like it here, don't you?' Laurence said.

'It's the best place I ever lived,' David said, with urgent inten-sity. 'Like it was waiting for me, just a few miles away, but I didn't know it. And I have to learn it – learn to work with it, winter and summer, day and night – because it changes all the time.'

'I envy you. To find a place that feels like home.'

Laurence turned and moved to the back of the church, sud-denly awkward. He hoped there was no question of Julian dismissing David because of one mistake. He walked to the west window, pulled off the cloth that covered the heavy table and laid it on a pew. David hung back, still looking down at the labyrinth. Laurence took hold of one end of the table.

'David . . .'

Together they lifted the massive piece to one side, staggering in their efforts to manoeuvre it round the pews. He must have winced because David said, 'All right, sir?'

'Bad back. Nothing.'

He was sweating from the exertion. The carpet underneath

showed a clear rectangle of brighter colour where the table had stood for years.

'It's old but it looks quite good,' Laurence said. 'Let's roll it up.'

As they did so, it was not more stone floor that was revealed but a wooden door, set flush into the stonework with two inset metal rings.

'What now?'

Laurence took hold of one of them. It lifted up the door a little but not enough to raise it fully.

'You want to be careful of your back,' David said, his expression solicitous. 'Me and the Kilminster boy can do it later.'

David was right. There was no need to see where it led now. It was probably a store room or just possibly the entrance to a crypt. David looked relieved as Laurence let go of the ring and stood back. He obviously wanted to get on with his own tasks.

Then Laurence's eye was caught by the odd column and brick-work he'd pointed out to Patrick. What if there were foundations from an earlier church here? It would be something to surprise William.

'No, damn it. Let's have one good go and if we can't raise it we'll come back with another pair of hands and some timber to use as a lever.'

David's shoulders slumped but he took a deep resigned breath and moved into place. They stood either side of the door, each taking a ring.

'One, two, three, pull . . .'

David closed his eyes and paled with the effort but with both of them pulling, the door rose surprisingly smoothly. Laurence was just registering that the hinges moved easily, and that it had obviously been used in the not-too-distant past, when he was hit by the overwhelming impression of something vile coming up out of the hole they'd revealed. He let go of his side of the weight, almost crushing David's foot, and looked up, about to apologise, when he saw David's ashen face. They stood frozen for a few moments and then, grimly, without a word, they picked up the rings again. The door finally fell right back with a muffled thud, splintering across two planks. The wood came away from one of the hinges. A short flight of stone steps led downwards but there was no mystery as to what they would find. The smell told them everything.

It never entered Laurence's head that it might be merely a rat rotting in the blackness. David's gaze had met his, almost frightened, yet whatever was down there was long past doing them any harm. Unlike Laurence, who could not look away from the gaping hole, David averted his eyes. He too knew what they had found, Laurence thought.

'I'll go down,' Laurence said.

He took out his handkerchief and tied it over his nose and mouth. It was little better than useless. Grateful he'd brought his torch, he now turned it on, although the batteries were flickering, at the end of their life. As he forced himself to descend through the opening, he put his arm over his lower face as additional protection against the smell.

He didn't even have to go right to the bottom. Beyond the steps lay what might have been a heap of old bedding, but with one bent, purple leg thrusting outwards still in its buttoned shoe, to assert that this had once been a woman. He held the torch out to get a glimpse of her face. A glance was enough. The uneven torchlight somehow added to the horror. The features were swollen but had once been human. Darkish hair fanned across the ruined face; beside it, one arm was raised almost defensively. He moved the light: there was some kind of dust scattered over the body, like fine plaster, and the splayed, blackened fingers were reduced to stumps. A few bones protruded, pale and shocking.

He drew back slightly and this time he heard something small move in the dark. He had seen enough.

In the time it had taken Laurence to climb back, David had moved away towards the open door and was leaning against it, wiping his mouth with the back of his hand as if he'd been sick. He was grey-faced.

At that moment Laurence heard a noise. Julian came in from the porch with Scout whimpering at his feet.

David said urgently, 'Mr Bartram wanted ...' Then, 'There's a body. We've found a body.'

'We need to tell the police,' Laurence said.

For a second they seemed frozen in time: Julian framed in the church doorway, David still leaning against a pew, staring at Julian, and the dog behind Julian's legs, whining, while Laurence himself crouched just feet away from the pit in the floor, trying not to breathe.

'Who is it?' Julian said.

CHAPTER TWELVE

*L*ater he couldn't remember returning to the house. His first instinct was to find William but when he reached the gun room he could hear talking inside. Eleanor was saying something in a low voice but he could pick up distress in her tone.

William looked up sharply when Laurence came in as if he knew at once that something terrible had happened. But Eleanor just seemed surprised at his interruption. Bright spots burned in her cheeks and her eyes were bloodshot.

'I'm sorry,' Laurence said. 'I'm terribly sorry,' he repeated, 'but we've found a body.'

For a moment neither William nor Eleanor spoke. William seemed frozen with his pipe in his hand.

'Maggie?' he said.

'I can't tell. It's female.'

His eyes went from one face to another. William had spent two years fighting in France, Eleanor had been a nurse behind the lines. Neither was any stranger to death.

'A girl?' Eleanor began and he could hear that her nose was blocked, as if she had been crying. 'A skeleton?'

'Not a child,' Laurence said, as he realised what she was thinking. 'A woman.'

Before he could go on, he heard footsteps running down the corridor. Frances burst in, agitated.

'Lydia's coming,' she said hurriedly. 'Susan came up to the house when Julian sent David off for help. We've had to tell Lydia.'

She radiated alarm and fear. William was shaking his head gently as if to rid himself of the news. Eleanor was standing, rigid, holding on to the back of his chair with both hands.

Lydia now stood in the doorway with Julian supporting her. For a moment she didn't speak, but looked urgently from one face to another. Laurence found his eyes slipping away from the intensity of her gaze. Her hair was loose and slightly tangled, and she seemed dazed. Had she been asleep, Laurence wondered. For a second she stood there, her hand clutching the door handle, Julian's arm around her waist. She was so thin these days that her bare white legs below her faded silk wrapper resembled fleshless bones.

'I've sent David for the police,' Julian said. 'It may take a while.'

Lydia finally spoke. 'Is it Maggie?'

Another silence. 'It's a woman,' Laurence said eventually. 'Not old, I'd say.' He paused. 'They'll need a doctor.'

'Where is she?' Of course, she didn't know.

'Below the church.'

Frances looked confused. 'Then it could just be an old burial ...'

'It's not. I'm sorry.'

Lydia blinked a few times. Her hand rose vaguely to her head, in an almost theatrical gesture, but her pallor made it obvious that it was genuine. She swayed slightly and while Julian held her tighter, Frances pulled a chair towards her. The scraping of its legs on the old brick covered the arrival of Patrick.

'Have you found her?' he said as soon as he came through the door. He looked at Laurence.

'We don't know.'

Patrick's whole posture seemed tense, almost excited. He glanced at Lydia, then at Julian, and looked away.

'Was she . . .?'

Lydia's hands were stiff in her lap, her fingertips touching.

Frances was crouched beside her sister. 'Murdered? Is that what you think?'

'How could she have got back to Easton?' Eleanor said. Her face was puzzled. 'I mean, without anyone seeing?'

Patrick's head shot round and he stared at Eleanor uncomprehendingly. 'Because she never left, presumably,' he said sharply, but he looked at her as if in pain.

Laurence realised that, while the others were assuming the body was Maggie's, Patrick was talking about Kitty.

'It's not a child.'

Patrick appeared shocked, if anything more so than when he'd first come in.

'My God, it's Maggie? You're saying it's Maggie?'

Slowly he had arrived at the same point as the others. Laurence shook his head. He hoped the police or doctor would come soon.

Frances was twisting the end of her sleeve.

'What's under the church? I've never seen a way in. Was she just in earth or was it a . . . place?'

'A vault of sorts. Under the west window.'

Patrick was frowning. 'How did she – or anybody, come to that – know it was there? How did *you* know?'

'It was only covered by a carpet and the table. We were clearing it for the new window to be installed.'

'We?'

'David helped.'

'Did you know about the vault?' Laurence said, turning to Patrick, and realising too late that it might sound like an accusation.

'No,' Patrick said. 'Of course not.'

Frances seemed to gather herself together. 'I think Lydia and I should go back upstairs. Lydia's cold. I suppose we'll all need to see the police later?'

Laurence was surprised that Frances had got straight to the point. It began to dawn on him that the police could ask questions that he was unable to ask himself, but of course he was the one they were most likely to question first. Frances was already helping Lydia to get up when Lydia spoke.

'You didn't say how she died.' Her eyes were fixed on Laurence. 'Did someone kill her?' Her voice sounded urgent.

'I'm sorry, I just don't know.'

'But did you see her?'

'Yes, but only briefly. I really have no idea.'

He couldn't tell her of the terrible, familiar smell, the mouldy fabric, the mess of hair and the blotched, blackened face where every feature was losing its boundaries, melting into one soft and ghastly mess of tissue. As soon as they'd started to lift the door, he'd known what was in there. With that first wave of corruption, a host of associations and fragments of memory had overwhelmed him.

'I'll come up and tell you if there's news,' Eleanor said.

When they'd left, Julian taking Lydia's other arm, Patrick seemed less edgy.

'Bloody hell,' he said, 'that's just what we needed.' He sounded angry but seemed close to tears. After a moment's silence, he added, 'You do think she was murdered, don't you, Bartram?'

'She could have been trapped, I suppose.'

Eleanor looked at William. 'Somebody needs to tell Walter Petch,' she said. 'It isn't right that the first inkling he should have of this is seeing policemen all over the place.'

'Look, I can't just sit here,' Patrick said. 'I'll find Julian and go and see Petch.'

He got up clumsily, knocking over his chair, and they all jumped. He picked it up, made a rueful face at nobody in particular and left the room.

Laurence took a deep breath. His back was painful and his head was throbbing. He pressed his tender temples with his fingertips.

'I'll make us some tea,' Eleanor said.

The usually affable William seemed unwilling to engage in any conversation, and Laurence was glad when Eleanor returned with a tea tray.

'We're all assuming it was Maggie,' Laurence said slowly. 'Maggie is missing, ergo, a body in the village is Maggie. But I suppose it doesn't have to be. As Eleanor said, we can't even account for how she got home from London, if so, or where she went.'

Eleanor regarded him without speaking, pushed her chair further back from the table and swung her feet up to rest on it. The pleats of her skirt fell away like a fan, revealing pale stockings and muddy buttoned shoes. William was tapping his pipe on the arm of his invalid chair. Eleanor's eyes narrowed.

'If it's not Maggie, then who?'

Laurence moved to a window and opened it slightly to gaze at the yard outside. Patrick's car was tucked away in the open barn and the Daimler was just pulling in. A stout suited man stepped out, carrying a Gladstone bag. Laurence guessed him to be a doctor. David rushed round to him with an open umbrella. A second car came into the yard. The driver and his passenger stepped out and, despite the rain, stood and looked up at Easton Hall's bleak north face, before following David and the other stranger towards the church. He could see Julian come forward to greet them and then all five disappeared from view.

'Might it be her mother?' Laurence said, half-heartedly, knowing as he said it that it was far more likely, if far less easy to accept, that they had found Maggie.

'Only locals would conceivably have known about the vault,' William said. 'Could you tell whether she was Maggie's sort of age?'

Laurence shook his head. He had hardly been able to tell she was female.

'No idea.' And then he made himself linger at the memory. 'I think it's just possible someone had thrown quicklime over her.'

William frowned. 'Then it would certainly be murder,' he said, 'and the quicklime would be in the hope of speeding up decomposition. There's lime in the village, of course, for the cottage repairs. The villagers all know what it is and what it does because we warned them not to touch it.' He looked anxious. 'We should never have left it out there.'

'That wouldn't have stopped anyone murdering anyone,' Eleanor said. 'The quicklime must have been just an afterthought, surely?' She turned to William but, without waiting for his response, went on briskly, 'I don't know why we're talking like this.' She fixed Laurence with an accusing stare. 'It's going to be Maggie, however hard it is to take that in.'

She paused and Laurence tried to fathom her troubled expression.

'It would be easy to discount Kitty,' she said, almost with relief, 'because she has extra digits.'

'Kitty?' William looked astonished.

'It's an awfully long shot, but she could, just, be Kitty, couldn't she?' Eleanor said slowly, obviously still thinking. 'If she had survived when we all, except Lydia, thought she had died? And somehow – who knows why – come home?'

She glanced up suddenly. Julian stood in the doorway. He had a bottle of brandy in his hand but he didn't put it down. He looked even worse than he had earlier.

'I've been over to the church. The police are taking her to Swindon,' he said hoarsely. 'Maggie ... They think she was ... Her head was injured. The doctor's come to see Lydia now. She's in a bad way. A very bad way. They've informed Walter. Patrick was there. And David's completely rattled. And some police chap is coming up to speak to us after he's had some words with David.'

He had an air of bewilderment, the man of order who found himself in chaos.

'They know it's Maggie, then?' William said, his eyebrows raised, when the footsteps had faded away.

Eleanor didn't answer. She stood up straight almost as if she were bracing herself for a fight.

'Come on, William,' she said. 'I think we should join Julian.'

'I'll push,' Laurence said, but she seized the wheelchair as if it were a prized possession and he a potential bandit. Laurence just followed her out into the dark hall.

'I was going to check the yews,' William said fretfully. 'David was going to come down with me. I need to check them. They shouldn't stand in water. They're prone to root rot.'

'I'll go down,' Laurence said. 'I'll do it now – it will only take five minutes.' He wanted to be outside in the fresh air and away from the stifling atmosphere of the Hall.

As the wheelchair rumbled unevenly away on the old brick, William tipped his head back. 'Thank you.'

Laurence didn't want to go through the library or the drawing room in case he had to stop and talk. He stepped out through the garden door and instantly the smell of growing things hit him. The sky was still grey with unsettled clouds but the worn paving stones of the terrace were already drying after the most recent downpour. As he passed down the side of the house, he noticed the jasmine was wonderfully abundant. He stopped for a second and breathed in deeply but it too carried the scent of decay. He felt soiled, although he had washed his hands with coal tar soap as soon as he got in. He wanted to wallow in a bath of scalding water and scrub himself until he had removed every taint of death. He walked to the end of the terrace. All the rain that had fallen over night was already tinging the heat-scorched grass with green, and the borders were heavy with drooping and broken blooms.

David had just staked the fallen delphiniums and had moved the ramps that allowed William to reach the maze, so that the grass wasn't damaged. He was sorry that David had taken on himself so much of the blame for Maggie's disappearance at Wembley. It could only get worse now. Laurence had hoped that once the baby was born things would change, not just for David but for all of them. It would be the first child to be born at Easton since the war. But now, with the grim discovery of the morning, any change seemed likely to be for the worse. He hoped Susan was not a fanciful woman.

For a few seconds he thought of Louise. The last time he had seen her, she had been womanly in pregnancy, her face half hidden under a deep-crowned summer hat, her arm, in palest blue, tucked through his, in khaki, and her delicate ankles peeking out beneath the swooping hem of her dress. He remembered her pleasure when two soldiers had saluted him as they walked on to the crowded platform to the train, carrying him back to the front. Yet he had been embarrassed by her affection and her delight, even by her swelling belly. He had never seen his child; he had never seen Louise again. But that last image and that last shame would stay with him for ever.

He descended the shallow steps. The maze plants looked healthy, the water well drained around their roots. He bent down and touched them; the needle-like leaves smelled resinous. They were all healthy enough.

He passed through what would be the entrance, framed by the two graceful nymphs, and walked along the paths. Beyond the curves of the embryonic hedges, Aphrodite stood, her stone draperies touched with lichen like yellow gauze. He made himself follow William's pattern to the centre and sat down on the bench David was building around the goddess. It calmed him. A faint wind caught the nearest trees. The sky was dark, with more rain approaching beyond the stand of elms at the field end of the garden. They would soon be able to run the generator again.

He was bracing himself to go in when he heard a voice. He looked up. It was Frances, waving. She walked across the lawn towards him as he stood up stiffly and retraced his steps. He could still easily have stepped over the lines of yew but he conscientiously followed the route of the maze. She reached him as he stood in the entrance, her hair blown around her face.

'There's a policeman,' she said. 'Inside. He needs to speak to you as you were the one who found her.'

They were walking fast now and the first fat drops of rain caught them as they reached the door.

'The doctor's seen Lydia. She was too weak to send him away. He's given her some medicine but he's worried about her, not just because of this latest collapse. He says she needs a thorough examination, probably with a specialist. He thinks she may have bleeding into her brain. Susan's coming down to help us with her.'

She left him at the library door. He had expected to see everybody else gathered in there but he found only Julian and a police sergeant.

'This is Sergeant Stevens,' Julian said, 'of the Wiltshire Constabulary.'

'Sir.'

The man had the stocky and florid look of a music-hall comedian but his expression was serious.

'I just need to ask you a few questions about how you came to find the deceased.'

He held a notebook in his hand, with a pencil attached by a string, and now he turned over a page as if it were a ritual. Then he looked at Julian.

'If you don't mind, sir ...'

'Oh yes. Of course. You'll want to speak to Captain Bartram by himself.'

When he'd left, the room was very quiet. The rain spattered against the windows and Laurence felt chilly. He shuffled slightly to ease his back.

'Please feel free to sit down, sir.'

He subsided into an upright chair. The sergeant seemed to be studying him.

'May I take your full name?'

He gave him his name, address and occupation.

'You're not a schoolmaster at present, then, sir?'

'No. I am taking up a new position in September.'

'Are you Mrs Easton's house guest, sir?'

'Well, I suppose I am. Although I came to advise my friend – Mr Bolitho, the architect – with the restorations.'

'So I understand.'

The man looked up from his pad, and the official note dropped from his voice.

'Unfortunate village, Easton Deadall. Lost too many good men.' He paused. 'And I was newly in the force when the child went missing before the war.' The noise of his pencil moving laboriously over the paper was clearly audible.

Abruptly, Laurence said, 'Do you know how the woman died?'

'Early days for that, sir.'

Laurence nodded, aware that his question had been foolish.

'Can you tell me how you came to find the body of the deceased and may I ask you if you moved her at all?'

'Good God, no,' Laurence said, louder than he intended. He couldn't imagine how anyone who didn't have to would be prepared to touch the sad bundle of decayed flesh and hair that had lain at the heart of Easton.

'You were sure in your own mind that she was dead?'

'Yes, of course.' Perhaps this policeman had not actually seen the body.

'You saw service in France, I gather?'

'Yes.'

His eyes met those of the police officer and the other man's glance dropped to his page. He knew.

'So, sir?'

He started to explain the whole circumstances of his discovery. Occasionally the officer nodded and Laurence assumed what he was saying tallied with the account he'd already had from David.

'Who else but you knew of this entrance?'

'Nobody. I mean, I didn't even know myself. I found it that day. That's why we opened the door.'

The policeman looked down and turned back some pages.

'You were with David Eddings, who is employed on the estate as a man of all work?'

'That's right.'

'The architect, he's unable to move about?'

'He has a wheelchair. He can move it himself for short distances if the surface is smooth, but usually someone has to push it.'

'He was absent when you were in the church?'

Laurence nodded.

'And Mr Patrick and Mr Julian Easton?'

'They weren't there then. Mr Julian Easton had been away but he arrived in the church shortly afterwards.'

If anything, Julian had taken it best, Laurence thought. He could have sent Patrick for help but instead he had sent the shocked David, removing him from the vicinity of the corpse.

Laurence couldn't understand why he had himself been so unsettled by the sight of the pathetic remains. It was not because they were of a woman. Two or three times he had seen the corpses of women in France, one of whom was still holding her baby, also dead. Perhaps it was a good sign that he was shaken; maybe enough years had elapsed for him to have regained a human response to death.

'You thought it was a young lady straight away?'

'Yes. Female anyway.'

He was about to add that he had thought immediately that it was Maggie, when slowly something began to dawn on him. He could visualise Julian standing in the church doorway, and David in that oddly stiff posture out in the aisle. He himself was hunched by the descending steps, below the statue of Magdalene, his mind unable to move fast enough to let him respond to the enormity of finding the body. As he'd heard the door open and looked up, Julian's face had been cast in relative darkness with the light behind him. As he moved towards them, and his expression could be seen, it was one of concern, which shifted to alarm in response to David's shout, 'We've found a body.'

He had not been close enough at that point to see the remains himself and yet, after years of looking for Kitty, now that they had finally stumbled across a corpse, he had simply said, 'Who is it?'

Stevens asked a few more desultory questions: whether Laurence had seen any strangers, male or female, in the vicinity, and, inevitably, about the circumstances in which Maggie had gone missing. Laurence thought that he was himself the stranger here, but it was obviously unlikely to be a stranger who had placed the body in the vault below the church. The church was never locked and services were rarely held there, so somebody had to know not only that the vault existed but how to reach it.

'How soon will we know?'

The policeman, putting his notebook away, shook his head. 'It depends whether there's any personal possessions with the deceased. Any kind of identification. That would make it easy. Otherwise if the body isn't recognisable it's up to the doctor.'

Laurence nodded. 'It's very hard for Walter Petch.'

'Indeed, sir.'

He realised he was supposed to leave. There were other more useful observers of life at Easton.

CHAPTER THIRTEEN

*I*n the early hours of the morning, three days later, Laurence was woken by noises on the landing: whispered voices and footfalls. He listened for a while but there seemed to be no urgency in the exchanges, although later he thought he heard a car. But when he came down to breakfast nothing was laid up in the dining room. Only Eleanor was about, sitting in the kitchen, clutching a cup of tea in both hands, huddled up to the range. When he saw her, his first instinct was to leave but she said, 'Don't be such an ass, Laurence. We've known each other too long for this show of propriety. I know you saw me the other night. I saw you. But it's all right. It's over.'

'I'm not judging you,' he said, knowing it was not the truth.

'Maybe not,' she said. 'Anyway, probably not as much as I judge myself.'

'Was it serious?' he said.

'Yes,' she said in a small voice and her lower lip trembled. 'For a few brief days. But impossible.' Her eyes met his over the rim of her cup. 'You know all about impossible.'

'Yes.'

'It only began when we went to Stonehenge.'

'You don't have to explain.'

'And Lydia's so ill. She got much worse in the night.' She was on the verge of tears. 'The doctor came back. He's spoken to some man in London – she used to consult him apparently. She hasn't woken up. I'm not sure they expect her to. Julian says the doctor told him her heart is weak and she's had some kind of apoplexy. She'll stay here, though.'

She glanced up as Patrick came in and then turned away quickly, her chair scraping the floor as she got up.

'I'm going to help Frances,' she said, leaving her cup on the table.

Patrick looked boyish, his hair ruffled, but there were dark circles under his eyes.

'Yet this is hell, nor am I out of it,' he said. 'Poor Lydia.' His sigh was almost one of exasperation. 'Nobody can say her name without "poor" before it any more.'

Laurence looked at Patrick, thinking that there was nothing on earth he wanted to say to him now, but the sound of a car distracted him from a sharp retort.

Patrick was gazing out of the window. 'Good Lord,' he said, 'it's an actual Black Maria. I hope they haven't come to arrest us.'

They watched Sergeant Stevens get out, followed by another, younger man who was not in uniform. Nobody moved until Frances appeared.

'The police are here again. They want to see us. All of us.'

They passed Mrs Hill in the passage.

'Here they are again,' she said. 'Might as well make them up a bedroom.'

When the three of them entered the study, the new man was standing by the fireplace with Julian across from him. William was already in the room, with Eleanor behind him.

'This is Inspector Thomas, from Devizes,' Julian said.

Laurence found himself trying to read the inspector's expression. Was it the look of a man who had solved a mystery, who might, even, be about to say he'd arrested somebody? He knew he was watching for him to play a part from one of Mrs Christie's novels, but what he saw was not a genius of detection but an alert public servant: tidy, upright, conscientious. He could have been a senior NCO, a man with work to do, who would do it thoroughly. He seemed neither suspicious nor eager.

The inspector stepped forward slightly. To Laurence, it seemed more a gesture than a requirement, or perhaps he too had read a detective novel in his time.

'I'm very sorry to hear of Mrs Easton's health,' the man said to Julian. 'But I have some news. The deceased was not, as we first assumed, Margaret Petch.'

He made no pretence of doing anything other than watching their faces.

Eleanor looked sharply at Laurence.

'What?' Patrick said. 'How many vanishing girls can one house and a few cottages sustain?'

Julian frowned at him. 'Who is it?' he said slowly.

'At this time we have absolutely no idea who she is. A woman rather than a girl.' He regarded Patrick steadily, then read from his notebook: 'Aged between thirty and forty. Medium height. And she had borne children. She had also consumed a very large amount of alcohol shortly before death.' He looked up.

'No wedding ring,' the sergeant said, and just for a second Laurence thought the inspector's lips twitched.

'Indeed, a mother with no wedding ring. No possessions at all, in fact, bar the clothes she wore and a patterned hair ribbon found near the body. It may not have been hers, of course.'

Eleanor caught Laurence's eye again and he looked away immediately.

'Maggie had a ribbon,' Frances said. 'She didn't usually but she'd dressed up specially . . .'

Laurence sensed, as much as observed, their glances fall away from Patrick.

Patrick said, slightly flushed, 'I gave her the ribbon, you might as well know this, given it's causing moral agonies for everyone else not to reveal the fact. Even though this body is not her.'

'Yes, sir. So I gather from Mr Petch.'

This obviously caught Patrick by surprise.

'Mr Petch said you were in the habit of giving his grand-daughter small gifts.'

'I was trying to be kind.' Patrick voice went up slightly as it always did when he was upset. 'I saw a lonely child. When I came home I gave her some magazines and the wretched ribbon. I gave her a small piece of carving on a little stone I'd found in my work in Greece. I gave her cigarette cards of Hollywood stars. I didn't know she'd vanish and these paltry things would become sinister.'

'Not to us, sir. We just want to find Margaret.'

Patrick fumbled for his cigarettes and looked fixedly away from them all.

'But my priority is identifying this dead woman and bringing the killer to justice,' the inspector went on.

'She was definitely murdered?' Julian asked.

Before the inspector had time to reply, Patrick retorted tetchily, 'Well, it's hardly likely she'd stuff herself in the cellar and block the entrance, is it?'

'She had an injury to her head,' the inspector said, and Laurence felt he was gauging their reaction. 'It might have been an accident, but for the concealment of the body.'

Julian shook his head and looked down.

From the window seat, Patrick asked, 'Are you sure? I mean, from what Mr Bartram said, the body was pretty far gone.'

Laurence threw him an angry look, both for the cavalier tone of his voice and for implying Laurence had found the discovery worthy of gossip.

'I'm afraid so, sir. The post-mortem confirmed it. Quicklime was thrown on her body. There's lime in the village, we noticed.'

'I had it left there,' William said, 'for the building works. There's a small quantity in the stables too for repairs at the Hall.'

Laurence looked away. William hadn't mentioned the residual lime at the house before.

Inspector Thomas again studied his notebook. 'What about Mrs Petch, Margaret Petch's mother? She left the family home when her daughter was quite young, didn't she?'

Julian seemed to draw himself up as if personally responsible for the burden of Easton history.

'She went off with a showman from the Mop Fair, the year before the war. The child was five.'

'Her father is dead?'

'Yes. In 1917. He was one of our NCOs in the war. A good man and a fine soldier. We lost him at Bapaume.' Julian spoke as if he had been personally careless.

The inspector nodded. 'Of course.'

He seemed to allow a silence to fall on the room. Patrick coughed a few times. Eleanor had pulled her chair closer to William but he gave no sign he was aware of her, except, if anything, to lean his body minutely away from her.

'Before I go,' the inspector said. 'I want to ask you all one question. Later I may need to talk to you individually.'

Laurence watched Julian. His hand, holding his unlit pipe,

moved in and out of a pocket, as if he had forgotten where he usually kept it. Then he caught Laurence's eye, gave him a look of regret and shrugged, perhaps because, of the people in the room, they were the only two who had seen the body. A body the police obviously now believed was Maggie's mother.

'Did any of you know there was a room under the church?'

Patrick was already shaking his head.

'Do you mean a vault?' Frances said.

The inspector moved back to the fireplace.

'Rather more than a vault, as it turns out. It appears to be a small chapel. I am told it is possibly a chantry. In Roman Catholic practices it is a place,' he cleared his throat, 'for remembering the dead. To pray for their immortal souls.'

'Good Lord,' Patrick said. 'I mean, us not knowing it was there.'

'It's not particularly odd in itself,' Laurence said. 'All our old churches were Catholic once, but it is odd that its existence should have been forgotten.'

Julian spoke slowly. 'My mother was a Roman Catholic, although my father was very much against her practising her faith.'

'That's interesting. Because certainly somebody had lit candles down there at some point. There were two candlesticks – not so very old, I'm told, and an altar with a cloth on it. There was also a picture of the Virgin Mary and ... a ...' He looked down again. 'Missal.'

Julian was pale and it was to him that the inspector addressed himself.

'Did you know of this place, sir?'

'No. I had no idea. We had no idea.' He appeared to be thinking. 'We searched the house before—'

Patrick broke in briskly. 'I think my brother is trying to say that when our niece, Katherine, vanished, every nook and cranny was explored. If we had known about this vault, if it could have been found easily, we would have found it then.'

'So none of you knew of the chapel?'

'No.'

'No,' Frances echoed.

Eleanor was shaking her head. 'I don't really know the house that well,' she said. 'I've been in the church only a couple of times and I probably wouldn't have noticed if there was an entrance to a vault. I mean, it's the sort of thing you expect in churches.'

The inspector wrote briefly.

'Mr Bolitho, you are an architect, I gather from my sergeant? You were restoring parts of the house and church. Did you not suspect such a place existed?'

William was slower than the others, who had seemed almost impatient to answer, but then, Laurence reflected, the question had been slightly different.

'If anything, I was surprised there was *not* a vault. The family seem to have been buried outside the church.' He looked at Julian, who nodded.

The inspector turned to Laurence. He felt a strange mixture of nervousness and eagerness. He wanted to say his bit and have it over with.

'Were you surprised, sir? Given your knowledge of churches?'

'There are usually some interments – burials – below the floor in churches like this. Most often, of the family and their priests, perhaps under a monument – sometimes quite elaborate ones, even in country churches. But not always by any means.'

But as he said it, he wondered whether the person or – he realised with a shock, given the weight of the entrance door – persons who had put the body in that dark place, knew what it was. Was that why they chose it: to give the unknown woman's burial some dignity?

He had missed the inspector's next question and Eleanor was looking anxiously at him.

'I'm sorry?' he said. 'I was just thinking that I wasn't really looking hard for a vault because all our energies were going into some changes above ground. I suppose I might have wondered if there were old burials near the altar and access had been lost in the last renovation. There'd been some work on the church floor.'

'My mother,' Patrick said. 'It will have been my mother's so-called improvements.'

'Captain Bartram,' the inspector said as if Patrick hadn't spoken, 'how was it that you didn't notice this cellar entrance all the time you were working in the church and yet you found it last Tuesday?'

'Oh, that's easy,' he said, surprising himself with the degree of relief he felt. 'All the time I'd been working, there was a small secondary altar under the west window. A large table, really, covered in a damask cloth and standing on a carpet. It had a small wooden cross on it.' His voice was steady. 'We weren't working in that bit of the church – and you don't think of moving that sort of thing unless you need to.'

The inspector appeared to be puzzling over this. Laurence looked up and caught Patrick's eye. There was something embarrassing about being questioned in front of the others, even only about practical details, but presumably that was why the inspector had organised it that way.

'But you did move it. You and the handyman.'

Laurence glanced at William.

'We needed to clear the area. The window above is being replaced. Mr Bolitho had heard the stained-glass window craftsman was coming soon and they'd need space to put up ladders and a trestle.' He knew he was speaking too fast.

'Had David Eddings seen the entrance before?'

'No. Why would he? I doubt he was ever in the church before we started work on it. It's more or less unused.'

'Was there anything else remarkable about the entrance you found?'

'No, nothing. We were just surprised to find it at all.'

He thought for a minute.

'With hindsight, I suppose it was very clean, and there were no bolts, but the hinges weren't rusted or anything, given at that point we presumed the vault had been under there unopened for decades.'

The inspector wrote slowly. He turned over a page. Laurence found his fists were clenched. He pushed them into his pockets.

'Thank you, sir. We'll have a few more questions for you but that's been most helpful.' Inspector Thomas gave a polite nod. 'Mr Easton, thank you for your time. The doctor says there's nothing to be gained by us speaking to Mrs Easton?'

'She's not conscious,' Frances said.

'I'll show you to the door,' Julian said wearily. He gave Frances a warm smile as he moved to do so, but his face was still creased with worry. Eleanor leaned across to Frances and murmured something Laurence didn't catch.

'One thing, sir.' It wasn't clear whom the inspector was addressing. 'Regarding Miss Katherine. I am told Mrs Easton never sought to have her declared dead. That she believed, *believes*, that the girl is still alive.'

Julian looked infinitely sad. 'A mother's instinct, she says.'

Patrick was still gazing out of the window again as if trying to disconnect himself from the scene but Laurence observed he was coiled like a spring.

'Of course. Not unusual, I'm told.' Inspector Thomas cleared his throat. 'Thank you for your time. We shall leave you in peace for now, unless you have any questions.'

'I had intended to go to London tomorrow,' Laurence said, 'would that be all right? Just for a couple of days.' He knew he was as much motivated now by the need to escape as to do research.

'Just leave your address, please sir.'

'May we go back in the church?' Patrick said as they were leaving the room. 'It would be helpful as things stand, with Mrs Easton and everything.'

Julian shot him an angry look.

'Yes. We might want a further look, of course, but we're not seeking any further evidence there.'

Finally, Patrick and Laurence were left alone.

'I didn't mean to take Lydia's name in vain,' Patrick said, 'nor to make Julian cross.'

'I was more surprised you wanted to find solace in the church.' Despite himself Laurence still found Patrick's quick wits engaging. In his heart of hearts, he knew that, were he Eleanor, with Eleanor's choices, he might have succumbed as she had.

'There's solace and there's solace. Anyway, when I said helpful, I didn't mean to my immortal soul.' Patrick looked wryly at Laurence. 'Which you think is compromised to all hell, anyway.'

He held Laurence's gaze and it was he who eventually broke away.

'It's not my affair,' Laurence said.

Patrick walked over and shut the door.

'You don't mean that. Of course you think it's your affair. There's your friend William, who did his bit in the war, horribly injured. There's little Nicholas, the light of their life, and there's Eleanor, the linchpin of that happy family.'

His words were bitter but his tone was not.

'Eleanor, your confidante, who helped you unravel that sad

business with your friend after the war. Eleanor, whom you opened up to but who also rewarded you with secrets.'

Laurence snapped back, 'I'm not jealous, you know. *I* wasn't her lover.'

'And I was. But do you mind because of poor William, which leaves you camped on the moral high ground, or because Eleanor's not quite the woman you thought she was and wanted her to be, in which case you've got at least one foot in some decidedly boggy territory?'

Before Laurence could retort, Patrick stood up. 'She is all the things I know you admire. She's strong and clever and she cuts through cant and she's the equal of any man. But she's also beautiful, passionate . . .'

'I don't want to know all this.'

'I'm not about to tell you *all this*.' Now Patrick had lost his own composure. 'I'm asking you to consider whether she might have liked a day, a day or two, of fun, of normal life. To have someone look after her for a change. And I'm telling you, just in case you think I'm a total cad, that I love her. I love her more than I would ever have thought possible. If she would come away with me, with Nicholas, if she chose, I would be the happiest man on earth.'

Laurence looked at him, astonished. He had assumed Patrick was a serial seducer and that Eleanor, despite her apparent worldliness, had been one of his victims.

'But she and I both know it can't be,' Patrick said, feeling in his pockets.

'I'm glad,' Laurence said, drily.

'I expect, having lost your wife, you're the last person I should expect any sympathy from,' Patrick said, jiggling a cigarette out of its case.

So even in Patrick's arms, Laurence thought, Eleanor hadn't

told him everything. Laurence remembered, as he rarely did these days, the sense of claustrophobia that had overwhelmed him in the early days of his marriage. How suffocated he felt by Louise's determined creation of domestic bliss and what opportunities for escape the war seemed to offer. He shook his head wearily.

'I'm afraid all marriages are more complicated than they seem.'

He remembered wondering back then whether all married people got more lonely as their marriage progressed, as their spouses became more familiar but less known.

Patrick had lit a cigarette and inhaled deeply. 'Nicholas loves William. Eleanor loves Nicholas. All very simple. Except that Patrick loves Eleanor and Eleanor also loves Patrick.'

'Does she?' Laurence realised his tone had sounded mocking.

Patrick paced to the window.

'Yes, she does, actually. I may not seem much of a man to you, but she sees more in me and yes, she loves me.'

'And you were proposing to take her where? To Crete to live on a backward island with a child?'

Patrick wheeled round, now obviously furious.

'My God, I was a fool to think you'd have the sensitivity to understand, even if you didn't approve. No, to Oxford. I would have taken her to Oxford, where she could have shone, been among her intellectual peers.'

Laurence felt a brief and astonishing ache in his chest. The life Patrick could offer Eleanor was so much more than she could ever have while married to William. He could imagine her arguing over dinner tables, attending talks, listening to the Fabians: all the things that fired her. Having more children. Of course, Patrick could give her children.

But instead of conceding all this, he fired back, 'Garden parties in the quad, drinks with the master? Watching all the clever young men have a life she can never have? Knowing the women gossip about her abandoned husband? That's if anybody would receive her at all.'

'You're quite the knight in shining armour,' Patrick said. 'I'm sure Eleanor would be touched to hear of your concerns.'

'The thing is,' Laurence said, quietly, 'Eleanor is passionate, about injustice, about people she loves, but she is also ... dutiful. She was a nurse in appalling conditions in France. She gave up her academic life, swapping quiet libraries, summer punts on the river and tea parties for blood, pus and vomit, caring for boys turned into leaking carcasses for a war she didn't even damn well believe in. That she didn't even have to be part of. So don't think you could have rescued her from a life of duty, Patrick, because all you could ever have offered her in exchange would be a life of guilt. And once the grand passion wore off, what then would she have made of you and of herself?'

He could hear his own voice, loud and accusatory.

'I know you would have taken a commission if you possibly could, I accept that,' he went on. 'But once you were rejected you couldn't even come back to look after your brother's estate. He and most of Easton's men were being slaughtered and, for all you knew, Julian too, while poor stricken Lydia was here trying to keep the place going with old men. And all the time you were ... oh yes ... in Oxford, not so far away, with the men of ideas, with your research. You have no idea of duty. So what kept you away? Envy? Pride? Tell me. I'd like to understand.'

For a moment he thought Patrick was going to hit him. He had stepped closer, his fists balled. He was ashen faced with greyish lips. His pupils were dilated.

However, he spoke in a whisper. 'No. *You* have no idea. You live among us, eat our food, give William a helping hand, be the thoroughly decent, if bruised, chap you are. Make judgments about us – of course you do, you watch, you catch subtleties of tone and behaviour, you make connections, you're that sort of man. An observer. More a man living on the edge of other people's lives than at the centre of his own.'

Patrick was watching to see whether the comment, clearly meant to wound, hit home but Laurence felt more exposed than injured.

'Eleanor says you are perceptive,' Patrick went on, 'but inclined to see the best in people.' He looked momentarily amused. 'I think she sees that as a strength. So you probably feel desperately sorry for Lydia – who wouldn't? You're rather keen on Frances – perhaps have a few hopes there?' He raised an eyebrow. 'And at the very least you wish she could escape and build her own life. You find Julian a bit dull but, in his way, admirable. You think that I'm a bit of a waster but probably good in my own field. You share the collective hope that Easton can live again. You get frustrated, possibly even irritated, that all we ever do is look backwards to our losses while the small ghost of Kitty flits over our lives, casting her gossamer shadow.'

It was so close to the truth that Laurence couldn't think of any reply.

'And all the time you have no damned idea.'

Patrick moved away, turning his back to Laurence.

'You must think I'm a monster,' he said, 'leaving my doubly bereaved, fragile sister-in-law to manage Easton, returning only to seduce the married wife of a mutilated officer.'

He had turned back again and was watching Laurence very carefully.

'I'll tell you why I shirked my duty, as you call it. You, being such a man of honour, will, I am sure, keep it to yourself.' He paused as if reconsidering. 'Although it's history now and nothing good can come of returning to it.'

Laurence didn't answer, yet one part of him wanted to stop

Patrick. He had a sense that whatever Patrick was about to tell him would be something he might not want to know, yet he had made a vile accusation and the man was entitled to respond. Laurence had long realised that Patrick smiled when he was nervous. He did so now.

'Lydia killed the child,' he said, very quietly. 'I didn't want to be part of the lie.

'I think we nearly all said to the police afterwards that it was a day like any other. Oh, it was certainly that, apart from the dance we were giving for Digby's birthday the next day. It was a hot day. There were cracks across the lawn. It was summer: Easton Hall, idyllic in its pastoral calm. Lydia was out with Bert and Fred – he used to be head gardener – choosing flowers for the party. Kitty was with her nanny. Kitty had become quiet in recent weeks – it's hard to remember now when that had come about. She was growing up, I suppose. A governess was coming in the autumn to replace the nanny.' He looked up, suddenly calmer. 'It was a long time ago, Laurence.'

'I know,' Laurence said. 'Increasingly I find I can't remember much very clearly before the war.'

'Ah, *the war*,' Patrick said. 'The war. Sometimes it's as if I'm on a Gregorian calendar and everyone else is on a Julian one, or vice versa. Time for me is marked by incidents like the wet summer I spent in Ireland, or the August when I fell in the Thames, or my first term at school, or first was sweet on a girl, but you simply have before the war and after the war: BW and AW. Commission. Attack. Home leave. Injury. Decoration.' He looked up with friendly ruefulness. 'You have joined the heroes of legend. I just dig them up. But at least as a man you know what war is really like.'

'I served for only three years,' Laurence said. 'And a lot of that wasn't anywhere near the real fighting. I wasn't a natural soldier.'

'Back then,' Patrick began again, 'or should I say once upon a time? Once upon a time a handsome king married a beautiful rich queen from faraway lands and they lived in a fine palace, surrounded by wonderful gardens, with their pretty little golden-haired princess. All their courtiers and servants loved them and even those who didn't wished they could be them. Now one day they decided to give a ball so everyone in the kingdom could see how lucky they were to have such a king ruling over them. But just then an evil witch, flying past on her broomstick, saw their happiness and cast a spell on them and their court. In the morning the witch had stolen the princess away and ordained that the flowers should rot and the servants should be cast out and the courtiers should never laugh again. The brave king died, fighting wolves in the forest, and everyone else lived unhappily ever after.

'So,' he continued, 'Digby and Julian were larking around on the tennis court. They'd had another flaming row the day before so everyone was relieved to see them working it out with a ball. Walter and Joe Petch were putting up Chinese lanterns around the lake. We all met up for lemonade in the rose garden. Lydia came down with Kitty and Nanny and they had daisy-chain garlands.'

Patrick stopped and ran his fingers through his hair.

'It was the last I saw of Kitty. She'd got a bandaged arm, but she had the flowers clutched in her funny little hand. Lydia used to tell her that six fingers made her special. So it hadn't been a day like any other at all, it had been the last day we were happy. The day the fairy tale ended.

'That night I stayed up with Digby and Julian who were both drinking. I was feeling very much the man. Digby was on especially good form that evening. He liked being the centre of attention, Julian less so. Lydia had gone very quiet, didn't eat much. When she and Frances had gone up to bed, Digby was going on about the arms race and the perfidious French. Julian went to bed a bit later and I followed Digby up. He was pretty drunk, to be honest, and I walked behind him in case he fell down the stairs, but Lydia was obviously awake as I could hear him say something to her as he went into his dressing room. I went to my room and then of course I couldn't hear much at all. I fell asleep fairly quickly, I imagine. I'd had some port and anyway I always slept well back then.

'Sometime in the early hours, I woke up with a start. It was completely dark and I lay there listening. Nothing. But you know how it is when something's woken you – your ears seem twice as alert? After a little time I thought I'd heard someone moving past my door. I stayed put. I guessed it was Digby, gone down for warm milk for his dyspepsia or to help him sober up. But I couldn't settle back to sleep so I got up. That side of the house was lighter as the moon was shining in. I walked to the top of the backstairs. From there, there are four steps up to the nursery wing and you can see along the nursery corridor from the lower one. Julian had moved his bedroom down there ages ago. He used to sleep opposite me. But once we lost our indoor servants he shifted and took two rooms right at the end. He still has them – a bedroom and a study.

'As I stood there, his door opened, or perhaps it had always been open. Lydia came out. She was a shocking sight. She was in her nightdress, with her hair loose and a blanket over her shoulders, but her arms and her nightdress were covered in blood. Then Julian came out behind her, half dressed. He took her hands, stroked her face and then helped her down the corridor. I was barefoot. I went down the backstairs until I thought she'd had time to go past. I think she went to her bathroom, I heard the pipes gurgling. I crept up, wanting to ask Julian if she was hurt, when I saw him come out of his room again, and he was carrying sheets in his arms. He laid them down carefully by the laundry chute, opened it and pulled on the cords. I remember thinking how quiet it was; the shelves usually squeak like anything when they come up, but everything seemed silent that night. Then he picked up the sheets or whatever it was – you know, I've been through this in my mind a thousand times since then – did he have to strain to pick the bundle up? Was it Kitty wrapped up in there? Over the years imagination imposes its own versions of memory. But the sheets were bloody, I remember that. And he was crying. In the silence, there were just his tears.'

He stopped abruptly. He didn't seem to be waiting for any response; indeed, he seemed lost in the recollection.

'Are you sure?' Laurence said. 'I'm sorry, that's a fatuous question.'

He spoke slowly, all anger long dissipated, knowing what he was about to say could cause offence.

'Are you certain it wasn't a dream?'

They both heard footsteps in the hall and turned to the closed door, but the steps, whosoever they were, went off in the opposite direction.

'I don't understand it all. But I do know that something terrible had happened and that my brother helped my sister-in-law cover it up. I like to think that Julian, ever the honourable gentleman, always with a thing about Lydia, was just trying to help her out. That he didn't do anything himself. In the morning they both claimed to have slept peacefully the night through.'

'But why? Why would she hurt Kitty?'

'I don't know.' It was almost a cry. 'Because she wanted to punish Digby for something? There were rumours about a village girl but they were only that. Because she'd gone mad? She was always a bit fey long before she was ill and her father hanged himself. I don't imagine Frances has told you that. Perhaps it was an accident. Or did she plan to kill herself and take the child with her? She had seemed unhappy in recent months.'

Laurence didn't respond. None of the scenarios made any sense.

'But she and Julian watched Digby go frantic as the days passed,' Patrick said, 'and there was no sign of Kitty. At first he was just cross, sure that she'd wandered off, furious at the nanny whom he accused of dereliction and sacked on the spot. Then, slowly, the enormity of her disappearance began to dawn on him. Within the hour he sent the chauffeur to fetch the police. Then in the weeks to come he railed and raged and wept drunkenly and went out hunting for her night and day until he collapsed with exhaustion. He had been powerless to protect his own daughter in his own house.

'And Frances. Poor Frances, still young herself, trying to be strong for her sister, shut indoors with her day after day as Lydia refused to leave the house. Frances never looked out of the windows. She told me once she was frightened of seeing them coming across the grass, carrying something in their arms. They let her endure that.'

First with his expression of his love for Eleanor and now, even more, in his thoughts of Frances, all pretence was gone. Patrick's slender fingers fumbled at his lighter.

'And what a house it was. Everybody was searching: the indoor staff were banging through cupboards, calling, looking in pantries, storerooms, wardrobes: anywhere a small scared child might hide. Moving through the attics, looking up chimneys, checking the wash-houses. Outside, the hunt started in chaos and became more methodical as more men joined the search. At first we just ran here and there, wasting our time by looking in places other people had already searched, and,' he looked bitter, 'of course I ran with them. In many ways it was easier than thinking about what I'd seen and what I knew. But by the time a day or two had passed, I was part of their lie. I never spoke up. I chose Julian over Digby. By default, perhaps, but that's how it worked out.'

He drew deeply on his cigarette and it made him cough. He wiped his mouth on the back of his hand.

'The police went door to door in the village and West Overton and Lockeridge. Nobody had seen hide nor hair of her. Nor have they ever.'

Laurence had started the day at least trying to hate Patrick, but now he felt only compassion, as much for the boy he had been before the war as for the man now, who still held this secret.

'Have you told Eleanor?'

'I think Eleanor has enough troubles of her own to deal with, without handing her a few of mine, don't you?'

Laurence wondered for a second if Eleanor had told Patrick of any of her own sad mistakes or of the compromises she had made. On balance, he thought Patrick knew little of Eleanor beyond what she offered to the world.

'So where was she?'

Patrick looked puzzled. 'Kitty?'

'What happened to her body? If it was still night when you saw all this and the nanny didn't discover she was missing until morning, what did they do with her body in those hours and how did they do it?'

Patrick shrugged. 'They put her in the laundry chute. After that, heaven knows. Julian must have retrieved her body downstairs before any servants came in to set the breakfast trays. Perhaps he went down as soon as Lydia was back in her bedroom and things were quiet.'

'There's something that bothers me,' Laurence said. 'The nanny. Why didn't she wake up until morning? You're implying some brutal and bloody murder. Even a small child would cry out, surely? The nanny slept in the next room. She was there to listen out for her charge.'

Patrick tapped his fingers on the arm of his chair.

'I don't know. I can't account for it. I felt sorry for her because clearly she adored Kitty. She was local, she'd been with the family since Kitty was a baby, she was forever cuddling her and singing to her. Everyone felt sorry for Lydia but nobody gave a thought to the nanny, Jane. She can't have been part of it. Nothing would have persuaded her to keep quiet.'

'Not even sympathy for Lydia?'

'No, not if Lydia had hurt Kitty. Digby dismissed her, but of course she couldn't go at once, because the police wanted to talk to her. Eventually she moved down to the village to stay with her sister. The police went hard on her. She was obviously a suspect, for all the reasons you've just suggested. God knows what became of her. It's unlikely she would have worked as a nursemaid again. She was unofficially engaged to the chauffeur but even he seemed to take against her. She disappeared eventually, to London, I think.'

They sat in silence. Laurence was unconvinced but Patrick seemed oddly calm after this outburst. For the second time they heard footsteps in the corridor but this time they were coming towards them. Before the inevitable intrusion, Patrick said hurriedly, 'I want you to do one thing for me.' He looked urgently at Laurence. 'Well, *with* me. I need you to come down into the vault. I want to see what's down there.'

Laurence felt a wave of nausea at the thought of descending right down into the place where he had found the dead woman. But instead of refusing outright, he said, 'Why?'

'Two reasons: one, I think I know where Kitty might be, and two, if you do I'll leave Easton Hall within the week. You have my word I'll never contact Eleanor again.'

Chapter Fourteen

As Laurence crossed the churchyard he looked up at the metal image of the lightning flash of St Barbara on the squat church tower. It was dripping. Since the day-long sunshine of St Swithin's Day it had rained almost continuously. Julian had said he intended to have the generator switched on again on the next day.

Patrick was already in the church, sitting near the pulpit. He held up an oil lamp.

'See, it's the archaeological training.'

Laurence pulled out his torch. 'See, it's the modern age. Brand-new batteries too.'

Patrick got to his feet as Laurence said, 'Come on, let's get this ghastly job over with. If you're still determined to look.'

Neither of them moved, then both started forward at once. They both paused by the table and when Laurence held Patrick's gaze, Patrick appeared as apprehensive as he felt himself.

'Given my behaviour and what I know you must think of me, and that revisiting this place must be the last thing you want to

221

do, well, I just want to say thank you,' Patrick said. 'It means a great deal to me.'

He didn't look at Laurence.

'The place is cursed,' he said. 'Barren. Nothing good ever happened here.' The strength of his bitterness surprised Laurence. 'Each time I come back, I think things might change. But nothing ever does. It's a rotten place, Easton Deadall, although mostly for the Eastons. I shan't return again.'

'But what do you expect – or is it hope – to find?'

Patrick didn't answer, just gave him a complicit smile.

'Or not to find?' Laurence said. 'Kitty's bones?'

But Patrick still didn't answer. He was standing at one end of the table, his hands under the top, ready to lift it. Laurence went to the other end, braced himself and heaved. Pins and needles raced down his leg. David had been stronger than Patrick when they had moved it before. Patrick obviously noticed.

'Your back,' he said.

Laurence shook his head. 'It's fine when I straighten up.'

Patrick nodded and they shuffled sideways with the table. When they'd rolled the carpet up, he examined the damaged hatch beneath.

'No wonder no one suspected,' he said. 'It's been beautifully done: set into the floor absolutely smoothly. Even the rings are cut smooth. If you didn't know it was here, you wouldn't suspect it.'

Laurence remained standing, massaging his leg. 'My guess is that originally there were flagstones here and that the wooden door was a eighteenth-century or later replacement,' he said. 'It was probably a crypt originally, rather than a chantry, being right at the back of the church like this.'

Patrick looked at him. 'Will you be able to tell, inside?'

'Perhaps. If it is a chantry, there might still be a lavabo – where the priest rinses the chalice, or a stoop—'

'I know what a stoop is,' Patrick said. 'My mother . . .'

'Of course. Well, they often remain.' Talking about architecture made him feel calmer.

Patrick nodded, took hold of one ring and lifted it clear of its shallow niche.

'It's too heavy,' Laurence said.

Patrick appeared not to hear him but he let go and stood back. His voice became tighter.

'My niece is the reason I come back as little as possible. I don't want to think about her. I don't want to think about Julian or Digby or Lydia. I don't want to think about my bully of a father or my poor compliant mother. Yet here I am, back at Easton, hovering over the entrance to what I assume may be my niece's grave.'

Laurence was not particularly surprised by Patrick's words. He was about to point out that Julian, too, whom Patrick assumed to be implicated in her death, had almost encouraged them to search for anything that threw light on Kitty's fate, when Patrick suddenly took hold of one of the rings again.

'But at the very least I can see the evidence of my mother's one small rebellion. Quite a big rebellion really: making herself a Catholic shrine at the heart of Easton.'

Holding his breath and with his head slightly averted, Laurence took hold of the other and pulled hard. The door rose painfully slowly and at last fell back. Patrick didn't hesitate; his jaw was set but without pausing he let himself backwards down the steps.

'It'll be fine,' he said, as much to himself as Laurence as he disappeared from view. The lantern light jerked about. 'Bigger than I expected.'

Trying not to hesitate, Laurence descended the steps. The smell was primarily earthy, mildewy and organic, but with no gagging sweetness of decay. As swiftly as possible, he moved off the bottom step and away from the place he remembered the body lying. The floor was scuffed. He rubbed at it with his foot. It appeared to be stone with a fine covering of earth probably deposited over a long period of time. He bent down to pick something up, afraid, even as he did so, that he would come across some small evidence the police had missed, but it was simply a tiny metal ornament, curved and smooth, with a short spike. He buffed it on his sleeve. It was brass he thought. Looked around again. The whitewashed walls were grimy with cobwebs but reflected back some light. The sense of horror and con-tamination he'd expected had faded away.

Patrick had placed his lamp on a low stone altar. He made a whistling noise as he looked around him. Laurence was focusing on clues in the structure of the room. The ceiling was vaulted. He looked up and down both sides of the room but there was no sign of a ritual basin carved into the rock or anything that made it feel like a chapel. It was obviously a man-made space but too crude even for a early chantry. No priest had prayed for souls here, he was sure.

Two shelves ran for a few feet along the side of the chamber opposite the altar, which was itself just a hard-edged slab of rock. Some greenish brocade had collapsed to the foot of the altar, bundled up like some unnatural vegetation. He nudged it with his foot but there was nothing beneath it. In front of the altar lay large fragments of broken candle and a heavy metal can-dlestick. He set it back next to its fellow already on the altar. He guessed it had been thrown down with some force as its base was deformed, making it stand crooked. He picked up a broken pic-ture frame, with shards of glass still clinging to it. It enclosed the remains of a mouldering print of the Virgin Mary. It was pos-sible to see the crown of stars around her head but not her face;

that, and the face of the child she was holding, had been crudely punctured.

Had the police caused all this damage? He held the picture out to Patrick.

'Deliberate?' he said.

'My father,' Patrick said. 'This has all the signs of his handiwork.'

'Really?'

'My mother finds this little place where she can continue with her popish practices and my father finds out and follows her or simply explores for himself. He would have been furious at her betraying him.'

'Betraying him?'

'You think it's too strong a word? Believe me, he flew into mighty rages for far slighter acts of disobedience. This is him, all right.' He looked sad. 'My poor mother. On her knees in some frowsty cellar and then even this was destroyed.'

He took out his cigarettes.

'She'd think this terrible blasphemy, no doubt.'

He made two efforts to strike a match, before removing the glass and lighting it from the flame of the oil lamp.

'I think this is simply a crypt,' Laurence said. 'A surprisingly small one but that's what it is. The stone recesses and, indeed, the altar, they're just mortuary niches. Coffins would have rested on them long, long ago. This,' he held out the small brass object he'd found on the floor, 'is a stud, an ornamental one, which fastened a cloth covering on a coffin. We could probably find others, two, three hundred years old. The only thing left.'

He put it on the makeshift altar.

'Your mother probably turned this place into a small shrine because there was no sign of its original use and because it looked as if it had an altar and it was directly below what I'm

225

certain was originally a Lady Chapel. Probably it was incorporated into the church at the time of the Reformation, but she may well have seen the statue in the church and recognised some Roman Catholic remains.'

Patrick looked excited. He was letting the ash drop from his cigarette to the floor.

'And, for what it's worth,' Laurence said, 'the floor under here, although it's got loose dirt on the surface, is solid stone, not earth. It would be almost impossible to dig a grave through it. Kitty isn't buried here.' He could tell from Patrick's face and his uncharacteristic silence that he had gauged his suspicions correctly.

He ran his hands over the wall and the one at right angles to it. Eventually he said, 'I think this,' he touched the wall next to him, 'is much more recent than the rest of this structure.'

He switched on his torch, held it in one hand and traced the lines between the stones with two fingers.

'It's less solid. This mortar is relatively modern and clumsily done. The stones are a different size from those over there.'

He waved vaguely at the opposite wall, then stood back, picked up a candlestick and tapped the wall with it. He repeated the action, glanced at Patrick and said, 'There's space behind here. It's resonating.'

Patrick looked as if he'd had a revelation.

'Of course. I was wondering, back there, how on earth my mother moved the table, let alone lifted the door. She was slight and it was damn heavy with two of us. A strong man could lift it at a pinch but not a woman. Anyway, what was she going to do: leave it open for anyone to find who happened to walk into the church? Close it and risk being entombed? Unlikely. But if she entered from another direction,' his arm swept out dramatically, 'from somewhere in the house, it's not impossible. Perhaps something survived of the old house that gave her access to this.'

'So how is it that nobody except your mother ever found another access? And who blocked it up – your father? And how do we know there's anything behind here anyway? There might just be a few inches between the stone and the earth. It might just be to buttress the floor above. I should think far and away the most likely explanation is that the crypt resurfaced, as it were, when the church was restored.'

'Well, archaeologists have learned to formulate a theory and test it against evidence,' Patrick said. 'A German intellectual idea, I'm afraid.'

Almost before Laurence had taken in what Patrick was about to do, he'd picked up the candlestick and swung it hard at the centre of the wall, making grit fly everywhere. The noise in such a confined space made Laurence's ears ring.

'For heaven's sake,' Laurence said, although he was amused by Patrick's impetuosity. 'When the police return they'll have us both in for questioning.'

'It's family property,' Patrick said. 'They've had their chance.'

He was breathing heavily even as he picked up the shaft again.

'No. Let me.'

Laurence took out his pocket knife and dug away at the mortar around a single stone.

'It's soft,' he said. 'Damp? Badly mixed? Who knows?' He rotated the knife blade. 'Damn. The tip's snapped off.' He managed to scrape out most of the mortar with the broken blade. Over his shoulder he said, 'You're thinking someone could have brought Kitty underground from the house?'

'I don't know.'

When Laurence turned round to take the candlestick from him, Patrick looked uncertain and, in the shadows thrown by the lamp, the bones of his face stood out even more than usual.

'I don't know anything,' he said.

Laurence swung the candlestick at the centre of the stone he'd freed from its mortar. The familiar pain was streaking down his leg, but as the metal hit the wall the stones shook; they both felt it. Laurence aimed slightly higher, at an area where there was more mortar than stone. This time the blow dislodged a chunk and the base of the candlestick broke off. He looked at Patrick.

'This whole wall may fall on top of us. But it's been here longer than ten years, I'm certain.'

He looked back at the steps and faint light coming from the entrance.

'You don't want to get someone else – David, perhaps, to help?'

But even as he spoke Patrick had taken up the candlestick again.

'Don't,' Laurence said.

It was obvious that extreme physical exertion was no good for Patrick, but his face was set. This time he edged the fractured end deep into the mortar. Laurence put pressure on the metal body and almost fell over when a single stone shifted with a grinding noise and fell back into the void beyond. As he jumped back, Patrick moved forward and, picking up the slender length of wood that had been part of the broken picture frame, he eased it into the hole. It went through and fell down into the darkness on the far side.

He looked triumphant and for a second they stood there like schoolboys looking for treasure. Laurence could imagine the young Patrick, searching old sites with his elder brother: he and Digby digging fearlessly in pursuit of warriors' gold.

Patrick beckoned. 'Can I have your torch?'

When Laurence handed it over, he bent to look through the gap into the dark, the torch held close to his face.

'My Howard Carter time at last,' he said and again he laughed.

Was he always this volatile? Laurence wondered. Unlike the other Eastons, Patrick's interest in finding Kitty seemed to derive more from a wish to find support for his convictions than a continuing grief at her loss. Patrick whistled again.

'Gold beyond your wildest dreams?' Laurence said.

'Darkness. But there's another room. A passage.'

Patrick backed away, stood for a second, looking almost bewildered, and then felt in his pocket. He pulled out a handkerchief and tied it round his mouth and nose.

'You'd better do the same,' he said.

As Laurence covered his nose and mouth, Patrick again lifted the broken bit of brass. Instinctively Laurence stood back. It still seemed like folly but he had only two choices: to leave Patrick alone to investigate in his own way or to stay and hope the two of them could deal with anything that went wrong.

Patrick smashed the shaft of the candlestick against the break in the wall and, miraculously, the stones around it crumbled backwards into the dark. Patrick turned away coughing and leaned against the altar, but when he looked up his eyes were full of excitement.

Laurence reached up and felt the ceiling. It seemed stable enough. He took his torch back from Patrick, shone it into the void and saw what Patrick had seen. He knew instantly that it was the further, and larger, end of the crypt. To the left were three stone shelves, divided into niches about eight feet long; to the right was a single, larger one. Some niches had been boxed in, some bore a small heap of debris. He calculated that the crypt could have held a dozen or so interments if it was full.

He shone his torch higher. A few rusty objects, which he assumed were oil lamps, hung between some niches. The ceiling seemed to be partly natural bedrock and partly man-made. Encrustations of white blotched the edges and a few black tree roots snaked down like capillaries from the living world.

His heart was beating fast. He inhaled deeply. The air still smelled fresh. This place had once held the dead, but long, long ago and every trace of them was now gone. He aimed the beam of the torch directly ahead. The chamber appeared to come to an end but there was a dark fissure to the right, which angled away from the light.

He turned around. Patrick was still getting his breath. Again Laurence wondered about the wisdom of all this.

'Do you want to go back up?' he said. 'We can come back later.'

'Not a chance, old chap. If we leave now it's possible that the police will return or that the whole damn thing will fall down. We're going on.' Then he saw Laurence's expression. 'At least, I am.'

Laurence nodded. 'I don't think there's much to see. It's a medium-sized crypt – a continuation of this chamber; the wall was erected across it. It probably hasn't been used for hundreds of years.'

'Do you want to go first – as the church expert?'

Laurence stepped over the remaining courses of stone, bent stiffly and ducked his head. Patrick, slimmer and more agile, got through more easily.

'I'm sorry,' he said straightening up. 'I shouldn't have got you to smash the wall. We're a pair of old crocks, really.'

He walked over to the niches and ran some of the accumulated soil through his fingers.

'My ancestors,' he said. 'Ancient Eastons, all their hopes, their catastrophes, all their vainglorious deeds, turned to dust.'

'If you're right about your mother having entered this way

originally, wouldn't she have been nervous of the dead? Not many women, or men, for that matter, would have the stomach for it.'

Patrick looked around. 'Not like you and me, then, who know death as a companion, if not a friend?'

When Laurence didn't answer he went on, 'But it's most likely she never even realised – I didn't when I first looked through – and, on your estimate, some of these are Catholic Eastons. But if she did realise, well, she was a religious woman. She would probably have prayed for them.'

'Presumably they stopped using the crypt when the Eastons finally turned away from the Roman Church?'

'I haven't a clue.'

Patrick had set his lantern on the floor but now lifted it up to inspect the sealed niches.

'Do you think this is anything?' he said. 'Blocking them up?'

Laurence shook his head. 'Normal practice.' He moved the beam of light swiftly over the remaining three sealed alcoves. 'No, it was all done a long time ago and not interfered with. Look, there's your coat of arms on that one.'

Patrick walked down the whole length of the space, occasionally touching the wall, but when he reached the far end, his voice suddenly changed.

'Laurence, it goes on. There's a doorway, well, not so much a doorway as a gap, and I can feel a very faint movement of air. It's pitch black, though.'

The fissure was uneven, with a wide base. While the left side was almost straight, the right leaned in steeply. Patrick moved towards the opening.

'May I have the torch?' he said, and edging sideways he slipped through. On the other side he turned around cautiously but then, as he shone the torch ahead, he called out, 'It goes on. Both ways.

Hand me the lamp and come in, there's plenty of room.' He moved to the right.

Laurence found himself in some kind of corridor. Apparently identical passages led in both directions and after a short distance both angled away so that it was impossible to see where they led.

'Do you want to go on?' Patrick said. It was obvious he intended to. 'Left or right, do you reckon?'

'From the position of the church, which has its altar not at the east but north-north-east, we must be facing south, more or less, and so if we go right, we should at least be going roughly towards the house, which, if you're hoping for some connection, makes sense. It's not unknown for a passage to join up a big house and a church.'

'Good stuff,' Patrick said, as they started walking. 'Do you want to lead? You'll be used to being in confined spaces.'

There was no reply Laurence could give. Until now he had been surprised to have passed so easily the place where he had found the corpse. Then he had been engaged with the puzzle of the architecture, but now, moving underground, with no idea where they were going or the nature of the passage that they followed, he felt deep unease, acutely conscious that the way ahead could peter out any time and his exit route was blocked by another human being. He wanted to tell Patrick that it was a stupid idea but resisted only because he knew his impulses were born more of fear than good sense, that and the knowledge that the distance between church and house was not great.

The beam of his torch picked out a rock floor and pale walls that might be limestone or even chalk. The light from Patrick's lamp cast shadows from every protuberance and moved unevenly up and down the stone. Laurence began to feel faintly sick and focused on what he could tell from his surroundings. He wasn't sure if the structure was entirely a geological formation or man-made, although it appeared more or less to run level. He held on to that; at least they weren't descending deeper into the earth. But he couldn't shake off the fact that, to arrive here, they had entered through a place of death.

He could hear Patrick breathing heavily behind him. Soon he lost a sense of time, even though they had probably been walking for only a short while. For the last few minutes the tunnel had seemed to be curving slightly to the right. All of a sudden he noticed that the passage was narrowing ahead. Then, stopping dead, at which point Patrick nearly ran into him, he saw that there was an opening to the right about five feet high. It had a stone lintel, with a tall stone to either side. This was unequivo-cally man-made.

'Do you want to go on?' he said, doubtfully.

Patrick, looking over Laurence's shoulder, held up the lamp. 'Yes. Absolutely. Do you want to change places for a while?'

As Patrick squeezed past him, Laurence checked his watch. It was over an hour since they'd entered the church, but then it had taken them some time to decide to attack the wall in the crypt.

Patrick ran his hand down the stone portal, then he stooped slightly to get under the lintel. Laurence knew that if the ceiling beyond was as low as the lintel, he would simply be unable to make himself continue.

CHAPTER FIFTEEN

*A*t first he felt relief when the archway simply revealed another chamber but this was followed by dismay as he now had no real justification for turning back. As they came into it they were able to stand side by side. The ceiling was higher than in the previous passage. On either side two smaller archways offered a choice of exits. Perplexed, Patrick looked briefly into each, then returned to swap the lamp for the torch. He shone it over the walls, through first the left-hand, then the right-hand doorway. Just as Laurence was gearing himself up to refuse to go any further, he said, 'D'you know, I think we could be in some kind of prehistoric structure. Where we were before was obviously part of the church, but now this reminds me of nothing more than a major long barrow.'

Laurence thought back to the expedition to Silbury Hill and the barrow he had been eager to leave after spending only minutes inside. Now he was in a subterranean one and he had no idea how long it might take to get out of it.

'I wonder how deep underground we are?' Patrick mused. 'Probably not very; we seem to have kept more or less level, though you never quite know. But still, was this always underground? Around the world there are plenty of ancient remains that are underground, but around here I've only ever seen them on hilltops.'

'But you said nobody knows what these ancient peoples were thinking.'

By talking, Laurence could hold on to a sense of normality. Patrick seemed unaware of any problem.

'It could once have *been* on top, of course, land shifts over the millennia.' Now Patrick was almost talking to himself. 'The old Easton Hall and its church were built on a rise to take in the view, I suppose. Perhaps the rise they chose concealed this barrow.'

'It's perfectly possible early Christians took over a pagan shrine right here,' Laurence said. 'Perhaps Eleanor's right and St Barbara was a god of thunder in some earlier pagan incarnation.'

'Ah, the architecture of the true God, crushing the rustic stones and mistletoe groves of the superstitious ancients.' Patrick laughed, the sound echoing off the walls. 'Well, let's explore. Perhaps it will make us both famous.'

Had he forgotten about his search for his niece's bones, Laurence wondered, or, once she evidently wasn't in the crypt, had he been able to relax?

'We've come a long way already,' he said. 'We could come back better equipped. It may not be safe.' It sounded weak, even to him.

'We might never get back at all. Or we might have to tell people.' Patrick gave one of his boyish smiles. 'I'm not very good at sharing. I like secrets. It comes of being the youngest child, I suppose. Or learning not to trust anybody.'

There must have been something in Laurence's look which communicated doubt.

'Not you, strangely. You seem to know all my secrets. All the ones that matter. The best and the worst. The stranger who reveals our hopes and fears.'

He paused, pulled out a cigarette and lit it.

'An archaeologist of the soul.'

His odd, embarrassed grin offset the intensity of his words.

'Eleanor tells me you have no family. I'm sorry. But then again, it may be why you give off this sense of being unaligned. You move through the world, uncorrupted by the demands of blood and history.'

Laurence's first reaction was that it was blood and history that had taken what life he once had and had hoped to have, but these feelings passed in a second and were replaced by amusement.

'I'm afraid my soul, if I have one, is much murkier and much less ascetic than your fantasies,' he said. 'Perhaps that's because in reality I actually have a rather bossy older sister and more nephews and nieces than one man should bear alone.'

Patrick laughed again, this time entirely naturally. He clapped Laurence on the back.

'I hope all this,' he waved around the chamber, 'gives you a taste for my sort of business. I'd like to get to know you better, away from Easton damn Deadall.' He took one last draw at his cigarette and surveyed its tip: 'Burning beautifully – at least there's plenty of good air down here. It's getting in somewhere. Anyway,' he said, examining the two further portals, at which Laurence's heart sank again, 'left or right? Or shall we toss for it?'

Again they turned right, although the path swiftly split in two. Instinctively they took the right-hand fork and continued for some distance. When they entered a chamber similar to the previous one, Patrick simply muttered, 'Curiouser and curiouser. This must be utterly unique.'

This time he didn't even ask Laurence but just kept on, taking the right-hand passage. It led away at a sharper angle and Laurence thought it was descending slightly but after a while it forked again. This time a roof fall had blocked the right-hand side. Laurence felt the back of his neck prickle and his nausea returned.

'Patrick,' he said, much more urgently than before, 'we should go back. We're God knows how many feet underground, nobody knows we're here, and we don't know what sort of system we're in or where it leads.'

'But look,' Patrick said, 'the side that fell has been constructed out of dry-stone walling. On this side, the roof is bare rock. It's safe.'

He plunged on. After what might have been fifty feet or more, they reached a T-junction. Patrick took the right-hand passage, saying breezily, 'This should bring us back in the sort of direction we were going.'

Laurence started to fall back. He was tired and began to worry about the far frailer Patrick. Then he heard Patrick cry out, 'Damn.'

The right-hand turn had ended in a blank wall. It had no crevices or mortar.

'Shine your torch in the corners,' Patrick said, but there was nothing.

For the first time he sagged, visibly.

'We'll have to turn back,' he said reluctantly.

They both leaned against the wall. The silence around them fell heavily.

'Let's retrace our footsteps,' Laurence said and started more slowly back the way they'd come. He turned sharp left and walked on.

After a while Patrick said, 'I think we missed the fork. It's all so shadowy.'

Laurence shone the torch downwards, but there was no sign of footsteps in the fine layer of silt. They turned and retraced their steps until they found a disturbed surface.

Patrick said with what sounded like forced cheer, 'We'll reach the second chamber in a sec.'

It took them longer than Patrick's sec, and much longer than Laurence remembered, to regain the chamber and it was as much a relief as it had been oppressive the first time.

'Let's stop for a minute,' Patrick said. Laurence couldn't see his face or its pallor but he sensed him tiring.

They sat on the floor with the lantern burning in front of them. Patrick pulled his knees up to his chest. Laurence leaned back against the rock. His head throbbed and he was beginning to feel thirsty.

'Eleanor said you were quite the hero back in France? MC and so on?'

'I was just about the only living chest left they could pin one on.'

'Digby's chest was shot all to hell but they still gave him one.'

Laurence nodded. Dead heroes were always popular. No medal for Julian, though, who had to watch men cut down all around him.

'Though Victor Kilminster – our soon-to-be-returning son of Easton – got the Military Medal,' Patrick said. 'Perhaps that's why Julian is so cross about it.'

'I gather he helped him settle in Australia with a bit of money. Maybe he doesn't like his charity being thrown back in his face.'

'Perhaps.' After a pause Patrick said, 'You don't believe Julian and Lydia killed Kitty, do you?'

'You were there, not me.' Laurence tried to clear his head, glad to have something to focus on. 'But for me there are too many unanswered questions, too many alternative interpretations for what you saw. As you said, archaeologists formulate a theory and find evidence to support it. I don't think you have that evidence. You think Julian may have helped murder your niece. I don't, can't, see him as any kind of killer.'

Patrick didn't seem offended. 'I assume he might have fired his gun in the war?' he said mildly.

Laurence didn't bother to answer.

After a moment or two Patrick said, 'Julian's not the man he was back then. All the same, I don't believe he killed her either, but I do think he covered up. That's the sort of thing Julian would do: cover things up to keep everything nice at Easton. If he'd found this dead woman you stumbled across, you can be sure he would have popped her in the car and taken her on a ride to Chippenham. Then the police could be picking over Chippenham families and Chippenham houses, not Easton. And for Lydia he'd do almost anything.'

'I think he half hoped William and I would find out what had happened to Kitty,' Laurence said.

Patrick shrugged. 'Safe enough if he knew she couldn't be found.'

'You never saw your niece, nor any weapon. You saw Lydia with blood-stained clothes and with your brother. Both looked distressed. It could have been an accident.' He flailed for a few seconds. 'It could have been some female affliction.'

Patrick looked up. 'It could have been. But when you see your brother and sister-in-law sneaking around in the middle of the night, covered in blood, carrying bundled bedding, and in the morning a child is missing and both claim to have remained in their rooms all night, then I think you might come to the same conclusion as me.'

His voice was firm.

'If it was an accident, Lydia would have gone to Digby. If it had been a female "affliction", as you call it,' he raised his eye-brows, 'surely she'd have woken Frances, or even the nanny, Jane Rivers. She'd hardly go first to my unmarried brother.'

'When you say they claimed to have slept in their rooms all night, do you mean that's what they said when questioned by the police?'

Patrick nodded.

'But presumably their rooms were searched? Finding traces of blood is something police are trained to do.'

'They did find a tiny bit of blood,' Patrick said, 'in Julian's handbasin, but it was little enough to be accounted for by a nosebleed. He does have nosebleeds, by the way, something to do with his war injuries.'

'But where's the linen you saw? Where's the child's body? You don't really think she's down here, do you?'

Patrick shrugged. 'I thought she might – *might* – be buried in my mother's hidey-hole. It felt right. To anyone who knew it was there, though God knows who did know, it would have been easily done. She was a very slight child, not heavy.'

His voice was emotionless, but he rested his head on his knees as he spoke.

'But the floor was solid and untouched,' Laurence said.

There was no response for some minutes.

'We should go on,' Patrick said eventually. Laurence looked up. From where they were, he could see one further exit ahead. He shone the torch along the wall they were sitting against.

'I don't think we're in the same chamber we were in before,' he said, trying to keep his voice steady.

Patrick's head shot up.

'Of course we are. It's only minutes from the junction.'

But Laurence, watching him in the faint glow of the lamp, saw his eyes dart from one exit to another.

After a few seconds Patrick said, 'Well, we can retrace a bit. Our footsteps will be clear on the floor.' He got to his feet and pushed himself away from the wall. Holding the lantern high, he carried it to the nearest exit and then, wordlessly, to the other.

Laurence's mind was reeling but he tried to reason sensibly. 'I think we should mark this place so we know if we return,' he said.

Patrick was silent. They both knew it was an admission that they were lost.

Laurence dug the broken knife into the rock beside the exit, moving it backwards and forwards, then repeated it in the opposite direction, making an uneven cross. He hoped it wasn't an omen. As they walked on, he switched off his torch. Its batteries were new but they needed to conserve light.

They moved much more slowly this time. He didn't know how long the lantern might burn for. Had Patrick even filled it right up before his impulsive adventure? He couldn't bear to ask.

As they trudged on, Patrick said, 'I could do with a drink,' and once again Laurence had to take deep breaths to calm his barely suppressed panic.

He had supposed that he would never feel naked fear again, once he had come back from France, but now it returned to him with full force. In the dark, with only Patrick's lantern to light the way, he began to think the air smelled less sweet. Strange shapes were thrown up on the ceiling and Patrick's shadow, made huge, shambled along with them. Now he began to hear noises. Not just their footfalls and Patrick's laboured breaths but something behind them, something that also breathed. If he stopped, it stopped too, but when he walked, the thing followed. Twice he whirled around, but, beyond their small glow of light, there was nothing.

They came to a fork.

241

'Right,' he almost shouted.

The passage was narrower, he was sure of it, and he thought the roof was slightly lower. There were no roots here. Did that mean they were deeper in the earth?

His heart was crashing in his chest and his mouth was sticky. He swallowed with difficulty and licked his lips.

They went on in silence. Then, ahead of them, stood another of the stone doorways and with relief they collapsed into the larger space beyond it. It seemed to Laurence that the lantern was growing very slightly dimmer and when he looked up Patrick was staring into space.

'We should have brought string,' Laurence said.

Patrick turned his head very slowly and even in the soft light the strange expression on his face, half wonder, half fear, made Laurence uneasy.

'Bartram,' he said, 'you're a genius. How could I not have seen?' He shook his head as if trying to clear it. 'I can't have been thinking. Too busy trying to find a way out.'

There was a catch in his breath.

'Easton Deadall. Daedalus. The famous Easton maze that your chum's trying to re-create. It was never just a bastardised Latin name, never a pretty row of bushes.'

He was speaking so fast that Laurence had difficulty understanding him.

'Not even a pattern on the church floor. This is the maze. We're in it. Under the house, or pretty close to it. This is Easton's maze, old as the hills, right in the middle of all the other prehistoric remains. A giant barrow or system of connected barrows. Or perhaps something else.'

He sounded excited.

'Built to hide something or for the burial of a great chief, or who knows what, but here it's been under Easton all the time.

The pavement in the church was a representation of what lay beneath. Perhaps even a map – it was a pretty damn convoluted thing.'

He laughed, but it turned into a cough.

'Of all our little secrets, this has to be the best. The one we never knew we had.'

He had run out of breath. The lamp flickered but Patrick, apparently miles away, didn't notice.

'A maze. Think of Knossos. The Minotaur. Think of Ariadne, with her string. You saw it. String. You realised.'

Laurence's ears were ringing. He passed a dry hand over his face. Even in bush mazes, he had a yearning to kick through the close-packed hedges. Early in the war, when he was on home leave with Louise, they had gone to Hampton Court. Although there was a constant flicker of passing visitors on the far side of the yew and voices rose all about them, he had wanted to hurry through and was reassured by places where the yew had thinned.

The purpose of a maze was to confuse or to remove man from his material world on to a path where he was in the hand of God. Mazes had never been a game. He was angry, both with Patrick and with himself, and suddenly very sad. He put his hand in his breast pocket to find his handkerchief, when suddenly, with a feeling approaching joy, he felt something hard.

'My compass,' he said.

He had used it so often in the church and out on walks, yet here, where they most needed it, he had forgotten that he had it. He opened the battered khaki case.

'When we left the church we were heading almost due south, I think. So if we head north whenever we can, we …' He thought 'might' but said, '*should* get back to the church.'

He stood up, switched on the torch and examined the dial. It pointed north.

'There,' he said, 'if we take the left-hand exit and each time that we're forced to deviate we return north as soon as we can, we should make progress.'

They got up slowly, Laurence leading the way as they entered the passage. It turned increasingly to the west but at the next fork they were able to go almost due north. He began to relax. The next crossing was an angled T-junction, where they were forced to choose between south-west and north-east. The passage curved round and widened out before arriving in an almost circular chamber, its ceiling shaped like a beehive. There were three exits. The compass reading indicated that one led due north, but even as he consulted it for guidance, the needle spun abruptly, almost to the south. He tapped the compass but the needle seemed to take on a life of its own, trembling between east and west. He turned the case to line the needle up with magnetic north, but the needle veered away. He frowned and tapped it again, even as despair hit him, more coldly than before because of his brief flicker of hope.

'What's the matter?' Patrick said.

'We must be further underground than I thought. It's not working.'

'Ferrous oxide in the soil,' Patrick said. 'That can pull it away from north.' He stopped. 'But it's all limestone in these parts.' He sounded more attentive but puzzled. 'Let's see.'

Laurence handed the compass over. Patrick too tapped it, then exhaled.

'Damn odd. It's hovering around east,' he said, turning it in his hands.

'All we can do is follow it,' Laurence said. 'Maybe we're deep enough to distort the reading but the needle may actually be pointing north.'

Laurence switched off the torch again. He hated walking in

the semi-darkness but the idea of being trapped down here with no light at all if the lantern burned out was enough of a horror to persuade him to keep the torch in reserve.

They walked on, no longer speaking. When the inevitable next fork loomed, Patrick followed the compass needle.

Laurence tried not to look behind him, where fat Pollock had been following him for some time, lurching in the rear. Always last, Private Pollock. He remembered seeing an NCO push Pollock up the ladder with a hand on his huge bottom. 'Pollock, yer arse is in the way of the whole British Expeditionary Force,' he'd said. Carrying so much weight made Pollock seem old. But when he'd held the man's head in his lap, he'd noticed how smooth and young his skin was, and he could see that this soft hulk of a man had once been some woman's child. Pollock's bloody teeth were straight and even. He wiped mud away from Pollock's half-closed eyes. His feet were sinking. The ground was sucking at his boots.

Suddenly he was more alert. He was walking through mud. That must mean they were moving towards a river, presumably a tributary of the Kennet. Briefly the idea that they might be close to a location connected with a world he knew lifted his spirits. At a pinch they could suck a little moisture from the mud.

But then Patrick said, 'Good God,' and turned round to hand the compass back to Laurence. 'Set your torch on this.'

Laurence took the compass, switched on the torch and saw the needle quivering minutely.

'It has to be iron,' Patrick said. 'Could there be a cache of iron-age weapons down here? Funerary goods?'

'It wouldn't be big enough to affect it,' Laurence said. 'I'm afraid we're simply too far below the ground for it to work properly.' But then, slowly, he said, 'This mud. Either we're somewhere near the river or rainwater's getting through.'

He walked forward a few paces. It was definitely wet now, not just muddy. He put his fingers to the ceiling. Water dripped on to his hand and he sucked his fingers gratefully. He switched off his torch again, even though Patrick's lantern now cast a very small circle of light.

And then he realised.

'It's the generator,' he said, trying not to let any note of hope enter his voice. 'It must be the generator.'

'But it's off until tomorrow,' Patrick said.

'Yes. And if it wasn't off, my guess is we would have heard it working. It's been off because of the drought, because they closed the sluices. But what the generator has is magnets. Lots of them. I think the compass is reacting to the magnets.'

'Of course. Of course.' Patrick looked around him as if he might see wires hanging from the ceiling.

'It doesn't mean there's any way out.'

'But it might,' Patrick said. 'The generator was installed at the same time that the church was restored. They might have found two entrances.'

Laurence didn't articulate what he thought Patrick might soon remember: that mazes invariably had just one entrance. He took the lead again and they walked on, more briskly. Even Patrick, although he was coughing a lot, seemed to have regained some energy. The sound of water splashing underfoot was quite audible now and Laurence's feet were cold. He thought he could hear a faint sound, different from the noises that had come to him in the tunnel. Something brushed his face, making him leap back, almost colliding with Patrick.

The lantern flickered on green-streaked rock and cobwebby tree roots that had insinuated themselves through the great pale rock above them. Laurence reached up and touched it, then looked at his white fingertips.

'Chalk,' he said.

But roots meant they were nearer the surface again. The passage divided. It seemed a long time since they'd had to choose a direction. He kept his torch on and followed the direction of the trembling compass needle to find himself in a chamber, so much bigger than anything that preceded it that he must have made some expression of astonishment.

'What? What?' Patrick said. He sounded alarmed but as he drew level with Laurence he simply stopped and stared.

They were in a vast cavern. It was perhaps forty feet high and too wide for their lantern to illuminate the far side clearly. The floor was wet and dark. When Laurence shone his torch on it, tiny ripples indicated a small current of air. He could hear constant drips and the faint sound of water running more swiftly. Where he stood the ground was firm, probably rock, but he was loath to cross a large space of opaque water. He started to edge round the side very cautiously. After a while they seemed to be walking on to some sort of natural platform. Halfway along the beam of his torch caught a jagged incline. As he followed it with the beam, his heart leaped at what he saw and for a second he felt faint. He squeezed his eyes shut, then opened them and focused again. About halfway up the rock face, unbelievably, was a hatch: a square, closed, undoubtedly man-made door about two feet high. Patrick saw it too. His faint 'Thank God' was scarcely more than a breath.

They reached the bottom of the incline easily. It was rough enough to permit handholds. Although it left them in danger of falling into the water, it offered hope where there had seemed to be none so little time ago. Above them the small doorway appeared to have no visible handle. It was hard to tell from below, but Laurence already wondered how it might be secured on the far side.

'You try first,' he said to Patrick. 'I know you're tired, but you're much more agile than I am.'

Patrick put down the lantern, leaned back against the wall, rested for a minute to collect himself, then wiped his hands down the sides of his trousers. He looked for a foothold, then reached up and pulled himself into a position where his foot could get a purchase. Laurence kept Patrick in the torch beam, moving it to help him find a way up. Patrick again waited for a while and then climbed higher. Finally he dragged himself on to a ledge by the hatch. He lay slumped for a few minutes, then began to recover.

Laurence placed the lantern on the rock below. Despite the light from the torch, it was still inadequate to make out the handholds, so he had to feel his way across the rock face, searching. Once his foot slipped and he froze, pressing his head into the stone and stopping himself from looking down, until his arms stopped trembling. At long last he crawled up behind Patrick, heavy with fatigue.

Patrick pushed the wooden door and, as Laurence had expected, it stuck fast. He took the torch and examined the wood.

'It's in pretty poor condition,' Patrick said. 'I think we can unscrew the hinges and with any luck it will come off completely. Give me your knife.'

Laurence didn't say that, since they had descended into the crypt, luck had been against them almost all the way. He sat back, his feet dangling over the drop, his eyes closed. The wall behind him was wet. Either Patrick could ease the door open or they had reached the end. That was assuming that there was more than a further cavern beyond, of course. He heard Pollock give his lucky belch out in the blackness. It had always made the men laugh.

Patrick cursed, then cried out 'Yes' triumphantly.

'It's all so rotten,' he said, 'almost sodden, that I'm not bothering with the screws. I'm just levering out the whole hinge. This one's nearly out.'

Laurence could hear him gouging at the door. Suddenly there was a startling crash and the whole hatchment fell away from them with a loud splash. Beyond it, all was in darkness.

They both peered through. As their eyes got used to it, they saw that this time there was a small amount of natural light. Before them lay what seemed to be a small lake, whose surface was a few feet below the sill of the door and into which the door itself had disappeared without trace. Laurence shone his torch onto brickwork and took in its regular sides. In the far corner, under the opening, he saw the bottom of some piece of machinery. Next to it were a projecting piece of concrete and a short metal handrail. He realised immediately that they had reached the generator house. The rail was most likely a fixing for men to descend and repair the sluices, but for now he thought it was their one chance to get out.

Patrick said, 'Bloody hell, Bartram. You were bang on. It's the holding tank. Shine left. See, the sluices are closed, thank God.'

Water was trickling through the gates.

'We'll have to swim,' Patrick said. 'But because the water's so low it may be a bit of a struggle to get out.'

Laurence looked across to the far side, where the faint light was coming from, and nodded. 'Let's rest a few minutes.'

His limbs were juddering with cold and exertion. They sat with their backs to the rock, facing the cavern and the way they'd come.

Laurence felt deathly tired now that safety was so near. Although his jacket and shirt were soaked and he was chilled to the bone, he was close to falling asleep. He bent forward to unlace his wet boots. He wouldn't be able to swim in them. As he did so, his torch caught the edge of something monstrous out in the dark cavern.

He switched off the torch. In the army he had learned to extinguish lights swiftly in the face of an unknown foe. His heart pounded. Within seconds he turned the torch on again and held it steady with both hands. He moved his beam back and forth, and there, straight ahead of him, was a vast horned beast. After a moment's puzzlement he realised it was painted on rock. The natural topography had given it the contours which had made it seem so real, looming out of the dark.

He nudged Patrick, pointed and shone the torch on it again. There was the creature – a mammoth, he thought, pawing the earth. Moving the beam from side to side, he found men. There were hundreds of stylised figures: men with spears and rocks, men with shields and a phalanx of galloping horses. Men on heights, hurling missiles at those below; men lying flat, with weapons protruding from their stick-like bodies; dismembered men or bodies tumbled awkwardly into high piles. Clouds of falling arrows and spears.

Patrick took the torch. Although its light was too dim to add any clarity, each time he passed its thin beam from side to side, up and down, wider and wider, it illuminated more animals, more weapons, more men. They were only basic stick figures but seemed alive as they teemed across the rock face. As he moved the light up, the men swarmed out on every side and herds of beasts emerged from crevices in the rock.

Still Patrick hadn't spoken. Then, to his astonishment, Laurence felt as much as saw him lift his arm and wipe his eyes. The man was weeping.

'How old is this?' Laurence whispered, hardly wanting to break the spell. 'Is this to do with Avebury and Stonehenge? The long barrows?'

'Much older.' Patrick sounded bewildered. 'Twice, three times as old. More, maybe.'

'What is it? Who did it?' Laurence felt like a child.

'There's nothing like it known in England. In Spain, in France, but never here. And never on this scale. I don't know what it shows. Hunting perhaps?'

After a very long pause, in which all he could hear were drips of water falling into the blackness below him, Laurence said, hoarsely, 'No, not hunting. This is war.'

CHAPTER SIXTEEN

*I*f at any time in the past someone had asked him to swim across a pool in near darkness, Laurence would have said he would never be able to do it. He was not a strong swimmer and he had always needed to know what was under him and how far below.

Now he struck out, just behind Patrick. Patrick was probably a good swimmer but he was already exhausted and when he reached the tiny jetty he seemed to have trouble pulling himself up. The bar was eighteen inches above his head. Grabbing the bar, he pulled himself up a short way, then fell back in the water. For a while he just held on but made no further attempt to climb out. Laurence was treading water, his legs hanging down into the unknown depths. He tried not think of creatures coiling in the water under him.

Patrick's hands slipped a little. His face, turned upwards to the light, was waxen. Laurence tried to position himself to help when Patrick suddenly lurched back with the weight of his body against Laurence's. They both went under. Laurence came up spluttering. Patrick clawed for the bar and closed his eyes as if summoning up all his strength but they did not open again.

Laurence looked up at the bar. It was only a short distance away. If he hauled himself past Patrick, he might be able to drag him up the rest of the way, but he was frightened the weaker man would simply sink, once he wasn't being supported.

He made a rapid decision and started to undo his belt underwater. The wet trouser loops were tight and the leather belt sticky. His hands were clumsy with the cold. Several times his exertions made the lower part of his face sink below the surface and water went up his nose. He was coughing as the belt finally came loose. He reached forward to Patrick and slipped the belt around both his wrists, intending to secure him to the metal bar, but the belt slipped through his clumsy hands. Although he snatched at it, it sank beneath the surface.

'How deep is it in here?' he said.

For a moment he thought Patrick was incapable of answering but eventually he said, 'Ten feet, now the sluices are shut? I'm not sure.'

'You have to hold on,' Laurence said, 'whatever you do. Please.'

He felt around Patrick's waist to see if he was wearing a belt, but there was nothing.

He held the edge with one hand, and felt the side of the tank. It was slippery. He undid his trousers, kicked a few times and they sank slowly away. Finally he let go of the side and, turning face down, plunged towards the bottom, holding his breath. The water made his eyes sting, but he reminded himself it was not so deep and if he rose quickly he would return to the surface in a second. When his hands touched the silt of the bottom, he felt along near the wall, hoping it was the right one, although his lungs were aching. He came upon the folds of what were presumably his trousers, although the shock of finding something

253

soft down here made him start. Almost immediately he touched a loop of his belt but when he lifted it on to his arm it turned out to be something else: a bag, he thought. He put his hand out again for the last time, his chest feeling about to explode and, there, thank God, was his belt. He raised his arms to help himself rise, brushing past Patrick's legs, and reached the surface, gasping and feeling giddy.

Taking in great gulps of air, he put the belt and the bag on the side next to the bar. Patrick scarcely seemed to notice as Laurence secured his wrists to the bar, buckling the belt tightly. Now at least Patrick wouldn't slip away and if Laurence couldn't pull him out himself, there was a chance he could fetch help in time. He placed as much of his forearms as he could on the concrete to lever himself up and took a deep breath. His heart was thudding in his ears and he felt sick. He raised himself but fell back painfully. With all his might he pulled himself up again and lay, half on, half off the hard stone rim, trying to catch his breath.

With a heave, and grazing his naked legs, he finally got enough of his body on land to be able to crawl forward. He lay for a few seconds, his cheek against the rough stone, his body shocked by the pain in his back. Then he moved to squat at the edge of the water. Patrick had sunk down and his face was only just above the water. His tethered hands were turning blue. Laurence didn't dare leave him. He had to get him out soon.

If he untied Patrick and failed to pull him up on his first effort, he thought the man would simply sink away, but the belt didn't allow enough slack to pull him out while still secured. There was a bell on the wall, clearly marked *Hall*, but with the generator turned off it would not work. By the door was a fire bucket and an ordinary bell on a rope. He rang it again and again as vigorously as he could. Even Patrick opened his eyes at the sound. Massaging Patrick's hands, he waited but heard nobody.

When it seemed clear that no one was coming, Laurence undid the belt and reached forward under Patrick's arms. Bracing one foot against the rail, Laurence put all his weight into lifting the semi-conscious man. The pain that lanced down his braced leg was somehow detached from him. His other foot began to slip and Patrick's wet clothes made him heavier. He was clutching handfuls of Patrick's shirt but then it began to come away and he was afraid he was losing him.

Unexpectedly, Patrick's eyes opened and one hand came up and grasped Laurence's arm. With an almighty heave, the top of his body was out. Somehow Laurence hauled them both through into the generator room and lay on the floor gasping with pain. Patrick's eyes were closed, his face shiny and colourless, his lips a little grey, but his chest moved up and down, evenly if very fast. Laurence lay gazing up at the wires, pipes and dials. His legs were shaking uncontrollably. After a few minutes he rolled on his side.

'Patrick.' He picked up a limp, icy hand and rubbed it. 'We need to get warm. We need to get back to the house.'

The fingers closed on his. He put his arms under Patrick's and slowly dragged him out into the light. Patrick lay in the grass, his eyes open now, curling and uncurling his fingers. Laurence found himself blinking. It all felt unreal. He knew he urgently needed to get help for Patrick. He tried to rise to his feet but felt suddenly faint.

At that moment they both heard a cry from near the house. Laurence found himself laughing aloud and trying not to weep.

Patrick looked at him, more alert. 'It's funny?'

'I just thought how typical it is of my life that I should emerge from the underworld and its ancient mysteries, through a damn hydroelectric station.'

'I'd do it all again to see what we saw,' Patrick said so quietly that Laurence almost missed his words.

He looked at him to see if he was serious but Patrick had closed his eyes again.

'You're mad,' he said.

'I lied,' Patrick whispered as people ran towards them. 'I'm finished with Crete. Sent back. My health's shot.' He was labouring for breath. 'That's why I'm home. I didn't have any other place to go. I'm no use.'

It was the first time Laurence had ever heard Patrick call Easton home.

Eleanor was running down the slope, level with David, with Julian just behind.

'For God's sake,' she said, looking scared but sounding angry, 'where have you been all this time? What on earth's happened?' Looking at Laurence's bare legs, she called back to Susan who was hovering at the top of the slope, 'Get blankets, put hot water on; they've been in the river.'

Then she turned and kneeled down.

'Patrick,' she said. 'Patrick.'

She touched his cheek and moved her hand to his neck.

'Eleanor,' he whispered, his eyes opening again. 'It's all all right,' he said, as if he were comforting her, rather than the other way round. Eleanor's head was bent low, her face hidden by her hair, her shoulders trembling. She pushed Patrick's wet hair off his face and wiped her eyes with the back of her hand. He reached out and stroked her arm.

'Eleanor,' he said again.

'Can you stand?' David said, squatting down next to Laurence.

'I don't know. It's my back.'

David said, 'Can you move your legs?'

Laurence looked down at his dead-white feet and saw his toes curl.

Out of the corner of his eye he saw Frances running towards

them with blankets over her arm. Eleanor let go of Patrick's hand. 'Try to sit up,' she said.

As he pushed himself up on to his elbows, he was racked with coughing. She put her arm round his waist and he leaned on her for support. Laurence managed to get to his feet without help but his legs had become like lead and the house seemed impossibly distant. Julian helped Eleanor raise Patrick to his feet. Eleanor took one blanket and wrapped it round him. He was leaning heavily against her. Julian, breathing heavily, moved to take Patrick's weight, slipping his shoulder under Patrick's arm. Eleanor took the other side and they moved off slowly.

Frances laid the other blanket around Laurence's shoulders and he moved awkwardly towards the house, grimacing as pain returned to his leg.

David held his arm. 'Take it easy, sir.'

But almost immediately Laurence said, 'Wait a minute.'

He stumbled back into the generator shed and barely suppressed a shudder at the sight of the water. There on the edge was a sodden bag. Black, not very big, with a thin strap, which, underwater, he had mistaken for his belt. He picked it up, dripping wet, and when he rejoined an anxious-looking Frances, he had tucked it away under the blanket.

They went slowly, but the gradient seemed steep to Laurence. Eleanor, who was waiting for them by the French windows, said swiftly, 'David, could you go for the doctor? Patrick needs care. And anyway Lydia needs to see him and . . .'

Frances was about to protest, Laurence thought, when Eleanor took both her hands in her own.

'She's restless,' she said. 'Agitated. You don't want her going downhill like this with no help, nothing to ease any discomfort. Nobody's going to take her away.'

Frances nodded and left the room. They could hear her footsteps going quickly upstairs.

Eleanor looked at Laurence, at his bare feet and then at the floor. His muddy footprints were clear on the carpet nearest the windows.

'You need tea,' she said, 'and actually you'd do best in bed too. But perhaps a bath first?' She raised her eyebrows. 'You smell,' she added.

'I'm supposed to be going to London,' he said, almost mechanically, though he could feel himself trembling.

'Don't be silly, Laurence. You're not going anywhere except Marlborough Cottage Hospital if you don't get your wet clothes off.' She climbed the stairs beside him. 'You're exhausted,' she said, 'and you don't even like swimming.'

They had reached the landing.

'That's why I didn't *go* swimming,' he said. 'Not deliberately. We were in the water tank under the generator.'

She almost stopped dead, then shook her head as if to clear it and opened his door.

'Go on in, take off all your clothes and I'll go and run a bath.'

Alone in his room, Laurence took out the sodden bag from the enveloping blanket and pushed it under the bed. He looked out of his window at a landscape he had thought he knew. William's new maze had intentionally united the house and garden, the village and the big house, the dead with the living and now, in an extraordinary way, the world of Easton – with its seasons and fortunes always turning – with the unchanging underworld.

He thought he heard Eleanor return but he didn't turn around. However, it was Frances who materialised beside him.

'I've brought tea,' she said. 'You need to take off your wet things. Eleanor's run you a bath but Julian wanted her to be with Patrick until the doctor comes – he's worried about him.'

'Is he all right?'

'I think so. It's Julian who needs reassurance more than Patrick, I think.'

He took a sip of the tea; it was extraordinarily sweet and strong – the way his soldiers had liked it best – but the warmth was welcome. Frances eased the blanket from his grip.

'Come on.'

He resisted, embarrassed for a split second, but then surrendered. He wanted to sit down but was aware how dirty he was. He fumbled at his shirt buttons, but his fingers wouldn't work properly. She bent forward, her face very earnest, and undid them for him. Then, while he removed his shirt himself, she fetched his dressing gown and laid it over a chair. She showed no sign of leaving the room but kept her back turned to him, looking out of the window, while he removed his vest and fastened his dressing gown. His clothes were filthy and she seemed to sense his uncertainty as to where to put them in this pretty room.

'I'll take them,' she said. 'Now the bath. Leave the door ajar as we don't want you passing out in there.'

'You're very kind.'

And then, suddenly, she was in his arms, her head against his chest. She was so warm and her hair smelled good. He held her head to him while she clasped both her arms around his waist. He was trembling, as much with cold as surprise or emotion, and aware that he smelled far less good than she did.

'When Julian said you'd both gone in the river and I saw you lying on the grass, I thought you'd drowned. Julian was frantic but my first thought was that I'd never said how much I liked being with you. But you're safe. Safe here.'

He could feel her heart beating and he stroked her hair, instinctively tucking it behind her ear as he had once done with Mary. He felt as if, somewhere in this odd and unexpected embrace, she had stopped comforting him and, instead, needed consolation herself.

'I'm sorry about Lydia,' he said and thought how clumsy that sounded.

She broke away. 'It's all right. Eleanor was right. Lydia is slipping away from us. Sometimes she seems conscious but she doesn't know who we are. Currently she's thrashing about rather.' Then she said briskly, 'Tea. Bath.'

She watched him drink, then went before him, carrying his clothes. He shut the door behind her, reached under the bed and pulled out the small bag. He opened it with difficulty and the first thing he saw were three horseshoes. Puzzled, he pulled them out but realised immediately that they were intended to sink the bag to the bottom of the cistern, where in time, being made of cheap fabric, it would have rotted. Their presence instantly made the bag's disposal more sinister.

He pulled it as far open as he could. There were some wet papers, all stuck to each other, which he wasn't about to try and pull apart. There was a comb, some hairpins and a tiny tin, with a label he could still read: *Violet Cachous*. Two keys on a bit of string. A tapestry purse, with very little money in it. Finally he brought out a grey handkerchief.

The significance of the find was not lost on him. Frances had told him ages ago that the sluices had been closed, the rivers dragged and the lake emptied when the child vanished. No doubt, the holding tank had been searched too. But the bag he'd found had been put there deliberately and, he judged by its condition, a lot more recently. Somebody had dumped it in the cistern and it seemed likely it was connected with the dead woman. Its disposal there was another indication that someone from Easton was involved. He knew he would have to give it to the police, but at the same time he feared whom it might incriminate.

He tucked it away in a cupboard, then went stiffly along the corridor to the steamy bathroom. The walls ran with condensation. He slipped into the water, his skin stinging. He sank down with his head underwater. As he rubbed his tender scalp with his fingertips, he remembered that at one point, which seemed like hours ago, he had hit his head on a piece of rock. He soaped his hair, his grimy feet. He lay back, his pain eased by the heat. There was even a folded towel laid over the back of the bath. With his head cushioned by it, he thought about Frances and the strange shift in their friendship.

He had found her attractive from the first time he saw her but not with the sort of physical hunger he had once felt for Mary Emmett. He had not wanted to kiss her when she held him; he was more anxious in case, even weary and cold, he would become aroused and she would notice. With Mary he had felt a consuming abandon, but he knew in part it had been driven by the knowledge that he was not her first lover. There was no sense in which she had been merely tolerating him, as his wife Louise had, bewildered and even repelled by his desire. Mary had wanted him just as urgently as he wanted her. He feared that if she came into the room now, he would still desire her as much as he had three years ago.

Frances was cooler, less easily known. He had sensed something about her that was untouched and perhaps untouchable. Her sudden emotional response had taken him completely by surprise. He knew Eleanor had seen two lonely people who would suit each other well, but could he settle for a companion rather than a lover? Would it be fair?

He drifted, his mind still veering away from the narrow passages underground in which he had believed he would die, and the extraordinary cavern with its unknown artists. Was what they depicted a truth of what had happened to them or something

261

symbolic? One thing he was sure about. Although at some point in the last century someone had made the hatch that led to the cavern, once water was running through the sluices to the generator there was no way that Julian and Patrick's mother could have entered her chapel by that route. Neither could Kitty's body have been brought that way, across the flowing water, and the link to the vault in the church had undoubtedly been walled up long before her birth.

He must have slept because he found himself in cooling water. He pulled himself out of the bath and on to the cork mat. Even on a summer's afternoon the north-facing bathroom was chilly. Instead of the glorious views of gardens and downs from the other side of the corridor, it looked over the stable yard, the workshop and the garages. Beyond lay the low roofs of the village. It wasn't surprising that this side of the house had been laid out so that the kitchens were below, with only dressing rooms, cupboards and bathrooms on the upper floor.

He dried himself quickly, standing by the window, holding back the thin linen curtain, though the black-and-white tiles were cold beneath his feet. Outside, only Patrick's car was parked across the yard. Laurence eased himself into his dressing gown and walked slowly back to his room.

Somebody – Frances, he had assumed – had turned back his bedspread. Although he couldn't bring himself to get right under the covers, he lay down and pulled the bedspread over him. He fell into tumbled dreams: his father clipping his moustache, while his mother looked on, her face anxious, seeing every act of grooming as a sign of potential philandering. Then Mary was astride him, flushed and soft, but she turned into Louise. Suddenly he was climbing a rise but ahead of him were a band of Uhlan lancers. As he turned to retreat, they saw him and, with great whoops of joy, bore down on him, levelling their lances and bending low over their saddles. He knew these were dreams when Pollock appeared, grinning affably beside him, failing to see the danger, as Laurence struggled to escape the horsemen. As the first weapon whistled towards him, he stopped running and threw his arms wide.

His eyes opened and Frances was sitting by his bed. She smiled.

'You're restless,' she said. 'I brought you another cup of tea, but it's almost cold. It seemed best to let you sleep.'

'Thank you.'

He pulled himself up on to an elbow. He felt uncomfortable at the thought that she had been watching him as he dreamed of violence and lust.

'Eleanor says you need a powder. It will relieve the pain in your back.' Picking up a glass, she added water from his night jug and stirred it. The liquid turned cloudy. He drank it down, its taste bitter-sweet. 'It's aspirin,' she said. 'Lydia used to take it for her joints.'

'Has the doctor been?' he said. 'How is she?'

'David's just taking him back,' she said. 'He saw Lydia—' She stopped, as if overcome with weariness. 'We've telephoned for Lydia's London specialist who will be here by train tomorrow. We should have done it before.' She took a deep breath. 'Dr Smallwood thinks she may not have very long.'

'Oh, Frances, I'm sorry.'

'But you're not surprised,' she said. 'None of us is in our hearts.'

'Is Patrick all right?'

She smiled. 'Yes. Smallwood says he must stay in bed for three days and have plenty of nourishing food. He doesn't at all approve of Patrick's adventures this afternoon and Eleanor clearly believes you led him on.'

Her face became more animated.

'Dr Smallwood says that if Patrick looks after himself he could have a perfectly normal life. However, if he goes abroad and is exposed to heat and foreign germs and – especially, I think he felt – foreign doctors, he would be taking grave risks with his health. The same goes if he makes a habit of swimming in cisterns.'

She paused.

'I don't think Dr Smallwood holds with electricity. He was very relieved it was off. He told Julian studies had shown the deleterious effect of invisible electric discharges.' She smiled a little. 'The thing is that Patrick's idea of a normal life is all the things the doctor advises against.'

'Patrick's impulsive,' Laurence said. 'That's his charm. He's a risk taker. But he knows he can't work abroad any more.'

'He does love Eleanor, though,' she said. 'He loves her enough that he'll give her up. Go away somewhere, despite his health.'

Laurence wondered whether Patrick might feel differently, now he had found the extraordinary painted cave.

'Well, anyway, William and Eleanor would always have gone back to London soon,' he said. 'They've got Nicholas to look after.'

'And you'll go to Italy?' Her face was inscrutable.

'Probably. I have another week to make up my mind.' More and more he knew he *would* go. He would live with the della Scalas and see for himself how things were changing in Rome. The eternal city. The words excited him. Perhaps he would stay only a year. Perhaps Eleanor was right and Signor Mussolini was a tyrant – the British press didn't seem to know what to make of him. Perhaps the country was becoming less safe, not better organised as Patrick believed. But he could see Italy, its great churches, its ruins, its art, its piazzas and fountains. Maybe travel to the lakes and the mountains.

She nodded. 'And Julian and I will stay with Lydia until …' She didn't sound unhappy, just matter-of-fact.

'It must seem unfair,' he said, 'that she was born to ill health, when you are so strong.'

'She wasn't *born* to ill health,' Frances said and stood up abruptly. 'She was born healthy, and healthy she stayed until she came to Easton.' Her expression was fierce. 'I'm sorry, I'm not cross with *you*.'

'I misunderstood,' he said. 'Losing her child … that might make anybody ill.'

'Digby Easton made her ill,' she said quietly and determinedly.

'I imagine he was quite a difficult husband.'

He had known men who were courageous, full of life, popular, but who he knew would have made perfectly deplorable husbands. They were men's men, happiest in the mess or their club or planning some kind of lark. He suspected his own father was such a man.

'When I say made her ill, I mean it specifically. He made her perfectly happy, at least at first. But he gave Lydia …' She stopped and turned her face towards the window. 'A disease.' She turned around, challenging him to look away.

He took a few seconds to process what she was saying. He thought back to scared soldiers and the MO's stern lectures, the padre's moralising, so wrapped up in metaphor that he doubted any man grasped that they were being advised not to prejudice the day of final judgment by consorting with French women. His first CO used to insist that magic-lantern slides of the Lake District or talks on Anthony Trollope would keep the men out of the brothels and free from venereal infection. Yet towards the end of the war, small boys in ruined towns would sidle up to straggling soldiers and offer them their sisters. Where there were soldiers there was disease. It had been so for hundreds of years. He found himself hesitating in case he'd misunderstood.

'In France, in the army . . . lots of men . . .'

'Not in France. Not in the army. Not lots of men,' she said. 'This was years before. He infected her. And so for Lydia, after Kitty, no babies, or only sickly ones that died. And so her steadily deteriorating health and happiness. And as she became frailer, Digby became angrier — more desperate, maybe more guilty, who knows? — at his lack of a male heir. And he was really horrid to her sometimes.'

'Oh God,' he said. 'I never realised.'

She moved back to the chair by his bed. 'It's all right. Even Lydia never realised for years. Or if she did she wasn't admitting it to herself. Or to anybody else. Julian still tries not to know.'

'When did you find out?'

She shrugged. 'I suppose only after her Harley Street doctor saw her last: eighteen months or so ago. I'd wondered if she'd got a cancer or some kind of consumption. I insisted on going with her; she was already too weak to go alone. The consultant veiled his comments but Eleanor explained it to me later — she'd suspected it from when she first arrived here last autumn. I wrote to him again two weeks ago, said I was the one who was caring for her. He said it appears she now has the terminal form of the illness. Her heart and other organs are damaged as well as the joints that have bothered her for years. Dr Smallwood says there's slow bleeding into her brain.'

'How long does she have?'

'He wouldn't commit himself. Maybe weeks, maybe a month or two, Eleanor says. She's being a brick. When she leaves, we shall have to employ nurses.' She looked more weary than distressed. 'I had hoped we could avoid Lydia being looked after by strangers.' Then she said quickly, 'I suppose you think I'm surprisingly sanguine?'

She had almost read his mind. He did not reply.

'Well, my heart breaks for her tragic, wasted life and it rails against the fact that she wouldn't stop loving Digby. That very love was a disease.' She shook her head. 'All the excuses she made for him. That his father had bullied him. That mostly he was a good man. That it was only drink that turned him into a maniac. And of course she had nowhere else to go. So I'm glad she knows nothing now and that she'll soon be at peace. And when she is, then I'll be sad.' Her voice wobbled.

He said nothing. Her hand had taken his early on but she seemed to have forgotten she had it. She gazed out of the window.

'I don't know whether it would have been better or worse if we'd found Kitty's body,' she said. 'That's what you and Patrick were doing, wasn't it? Looking, still looking?'

He was surprised Patrick had obviously said nothing much about their ordeal, the cavern or what they'd found.

'May I ask you something?' he said.

She nodded. 'About Kitty?'

'I'm not sure.'

She raised an eyebrow.

'Can you tell me how long it was until any help was sent for, after Kitty was found to be missing?'

She screwed up her eyes. 'It's a long time ago. I could be wrong. Everything was such chaos. Her nanny was half asleep, and her sister, Ellen Rivers, as she was then – one of the maids – was trying to comfort her, and Jane – that's the nanny – kept wailing that she loved Kitty more than anything in the world. Digby was in Jane's room, raging at her. But that's when he suddenly said it. "Send for the police." It was to frighten Jane, I think, as much as anything.'

Laurence let her think.

'Half an hour?' she said, hesitantly. 'A bit longer? They'd already checked she wasn't in obvious places in the house or in the immediate garden.'

'And who went?'

'Robert, Digby's driver.'

He tried not to look over-interested.

'Did you ever think the driver had something to do with it?'

'No.' She was too quick.

'Yes. You obviously do. Is it possible?'

She sighed. 'Would I like it to have been him? Because if it had to be an Easton person I liked him least? Yes, probably. But he almost never came into the house. He lived over the garages. Outdoor staff were never seen upstairs. I don't think he was suspected any more than the rest of us. Less, probably.'

'Right. But when it happened nobody was about that night anyway?'

He meant it as a statement but she looked away. He thought she had taken it as a question and one she didn't want to answer.

But then she turned around and said, 'Patrick was up – I saw him on the back stairs.' She gave a small smile. 'Looking more scared than murderous. And the corridor lights had been turned on.'

'And Digby?'

'He certainly wasn't up. He was dead drunk.' She looked uneasy. 'Once he was in bed.'

'What about Lydia?'

'Digby had been perfectly foul to her all evening. Beastly. Teasing with a nasty edge. So Lydia went to bed early. She was pregnant again, although she hadn't told Digby. He went up after her. Heaven knows what happened. There were odd movements in and out of rooms but then there often were. I went to see if

Lydia was all right. Sometimes if Digby was very drunk, she'd sleep in her dressing room; occasionally she'd get in with Kitty. As long as he wasn't likely to wake up and find her gone from his bed.'

Her look was one of resignation.

'But Lydia wasn't there. That's when I saw the back of Patrick's head at the top of the back stairs. He wasn't looking my way, but along the servants' corridor, so I tiptoed back to bed.'

'You never thought that Patrick——'

'Heavens, no. I thought Patrick was probably sneaking off to Jane Rivers' room. She was a very pretty girl and she clearly liked Patrick, though I don't think she would have welcomed him in her bedroom. Julian, who had rooms at the end down there, would have been furious. But I imagined that's where he was off to.'

'Furious?'

'Well, jolly cross. He hated that kind of thing. His father . . .' She waved her hand vaguely. 'However hard his mother tried to employ plain girls, older women, Colonel Easton always treated them as if they were his property.'

'What about Lydia?' he asked again.

'She'd hate me to be talking about this but what does it matter now? She was having a miscarriage. She was losing the baby. Again.'

'I'm terribly sorry. My wife lost two babies like that. It's hard.'

She looked at him oddly. 'Probably not because you'd shaken her or deafened her permanently with a hard slap to the side of her head. Or taken her by force.' She went very pink. 'His marital right, of course.'

He couldn't look away from her, her eyes shining now with anger and distress. He was stunned.

She said, 'Yes, he did do all those things. And that's just what she owned up to. Not necessarily that night – she had trouble with all her pregnancies – but that's how she lived: always making excuses. Everybody trying not to see. Julian taking the furthest room away from their bedroom. Patrick going abroad at the first opportunity.'

'And you?'

She looked at him with tears in her eyes. 'Digby was so charming – genuinely, I mean. Such a huge character, who made things happen. He was funny, made you feel special. People would do anything for him. But sometimes when they didn't – later on – then he wasn't so nice. It was so subtle you'd have to have known him well to see it at first. He had a couple of fits, which Lydia tried to keep secret.' She made a face. 'Recently I've wondered about the way he changed, the way his charm and energy slipped away and the anger grew. Was that the infection too? Who knows? It changed Lydia, but with Digby it might just have been drink. He was always a frightened man underneath, I think – even the best of him was all about trying to keep people amused and loving him.' She pressed her fingertips to her eyes. 'I'm sorry. I'm just tired. I don't mean to be melodramatic.'

After a pause, which he hoped was long enough, he said, 'When Lydia was ill that night, how did you know? Did she tell you?'

Despite her earlier frankness, he thought he might have asked her something she felt uncomfortable with, because she was a long time answering and she didn't look up when she did.

'No. But you have to understand how it was. The next morning, Lydia was embarrassed, but she was also frightened. Her child had disappeared. At some point she must have been cleaning herself up, but anyway Digby had woken and found her gone. When we couldn't find Kitty, he had Lydia by the arm, saying,

"And where were you when someone was stealing our daughter?" As if it would have made any difference if she'd been asleep next to him. He was mad with anger and mostly fear, I think.' She screwed her face up a little. 'Usually he was so careful but he didn't even mind that I was watching. His fingers were digging into her. So I said, "She was with me. I didn't feel well."'

'But she wasn't?'

Frances shook her head. 'When he'd gone she told me about the nightdress she'd been wearing and she begged me to get rid of it. She was distracted and ashamed but I expect she knew how it might look, and even if it didn't look that way she didn't want the humiliation of the police going through her soiled linen. She couldn't get out of the house but I was unimportant. I could. Before the police had even come, she gave it to me and I cut it all up into tiny strips and I walked over to the kitchen garden incinerator and burned it all, bit by bit, so the fire wouldn't be damped down. I waited until I was certain it was all gone. Then I burned the dead cuttings and leaves that were waiting by the incinerator, on top. Everybody was so frantic, looking for Kitty, that nobody noticed me.'

She started to shake her head to a question Laurence hadn't even posed yet.

'Of course it entered my head – more how it would look than that she could have done something. But she would never, never have hurt Kitty.

'However, there was one odd thing. She said there were stained sheets down in the laundry, too, that I'd need to deal with. But there weren't any. They'd gone.'

CHAPTER SEVENTEEN

*B*efore going out the next day Laurence went in to see Patrick. He was in bed and awake but lying back on his pillows. He seemed delighted to see Laurence.

'You saved my life,' Patrick said, sitting up and putting out his hand to shake Laurence's. 'Thoroughly embarrassing. First Julian has to be saved by David, now you save me. Easton men all thoroughly in debt to heroes. What does one say? Yet I hope you might suspend my promise to you to leave Easton for ever ... the cave paintings you see ...'

'We got out of there together,' Laurence said. 'Frankly on my own I'd still be down there gibbering. How are you feeling?'

'Bodily rather wrecked and mentally rather mad. I keep thinking it's a dream, what we saw. I can't even tell anybody because I haven't got the words straight yet. I want to go back and check in case it was a hallucination.'

'It was real.' Laurence smiled. 'Please don't go down there again. Not without proper assistance and certainly not with me.'

'It's a promise, old chap.' He lay back. 'I hardly know where to start with it but I think I'll ask Sir Arthur's advice. Then try to get a team together from Oxford.'

'Get better first.'

'Yes. I've been pretty reckless, suicidally so at times, but I'm going to see a decent man in Harley Street – one that dreadful old buffer Dr Smallwood recommends – and lead a more temperate life. No doubt you'll congratulate me on this conversion.'

Suddenly he looked slightly discomfited.

'It's as if Easton finally gave me a gift. Something terrible and beautiful and mysterious. My life's work, I suppose, stretching ahead.'

Laurence said, 'I'm glad. And glad I was with you to find it. I'll never ever forget that moment.'

He sat for a few minutes watching Patrick, who seemed close to sleep. When Patrick opened his eyes again, Laurence said, 'I'm still off to London, tomorrow now, but I wanted to ask you something.'

'You'll be back?' Patrick looked anxious.

'Of course. In two days.'

'Now I'm in your debt, I am bound to reveal all.'

'What was Digby's chauffeur like?'

Patrick looked puzzled. 'Good God, that came out of nowhere. Eleanor said you'd been involved in some sleuthing before.' He shook his head in mock admonishment. 'I think you've got a taste for it. You'd be a damn good archaeologist.'

'Thank you.'

'He was an out-and-out rotter, if you ask me. Handsome fellow. Digby liked him. Digby liked rogues. But not a man you could trust. And I'm not sure he wasn't a bad influence on my brother, bizarre though that may sound. The rest of the servants and estate staff didn't care for him. Except for the poor nanny, of course, who was sweet on him from the day he arrived.'

'Was he sacked?'

'No. He saw the way the wind was blowing. I think he wanted to escape any commitments to the nanny, Digby was probably impossible, the other servants had never liked him and life as he'd enjoyed it at Easton just stopped. No jaunts, no glamour. Nothing for a man like him. Went off to London.'

Laurence nodded. 'And did what?'

'Without sounding like a member of the *ancien régime*, I really don't keep a list of where servants go after they leave Easton. Probably to pimp for his expensive sister.'

This time it was Laurence who was surprised. 'I'm sorry?'

'You would have been if you'd met her. Before his marriage, Digby was keen on the odd night at one of London's more discreet establishments. Well, we were none of us averse; even Julian came along.'

He watched Laurence with the odd focus that he sometimes had, as if Laurence was an interesting artefact that he couldn't quite place.

'You don't look as shocked as you might,' he said.

'For God's sake, I do know what the inside of a brothel looks like.'

Laurence thought of the queues of cheerful soldiers, supervised by military policemen and surprisingly unembarrassed, waiting their turn in a French *estaminet*. The ladies inside, despatching men with admirable speed, were reputed to be as old as most of their mothers – grandmothers, one soldier had said. The same man said it reassured his wife to know his needs were being looked after. Officers went to Paris, paid a great deal more, stayed a great deal longer and enjoyed younger and more versatile girls. The outcome was much the same: anticipation, disappointment and, afterwards, anxiety.

He had once joined three other junior officers at a place on the rue Chabanais where the girls were exquisite, the champagne real, the Moorish rooms elegant. Afterwards he was relieved that he had been too drunk to perform; two of his friends had to see the MO within a week. The third had been killed the day after their return. His lasting memory of vice was of a gloriously comfortable bed, and hot and cold running water.

'Robert's sister or so he called her — I was always doubtful — was the madame at a house in Chelsea,' Patrick said. 'Perhaps Digby met him there, I never quite knew. But a nice man? No. Once he saw the world had turned against Kitty's pretty nurse-maid, any engagement there'd ever been was off.'

'Nobody suspected him of being involved?'

'No. In some ways he was Digby's rock. In fact ...'

'In fact?'

Patrick looked thrown for a second. 'Nothing — speculation.'

'I'd still be interested to know.'

Patrick exhaled. 'You never give up, do you? Dogged Bartram. I was only going to say you probably know a letter was delivered, wanting money. Digby was furious, yet both hopeful and afraid. He seemed paralysed by indecision. The letter had given him four days to find the amount they demanded. Julian went to the bank for him. Lydia wanted him to tell the police but in the end she gave him some of her jewellery to sell. The evening of the deadline I was in the bathroom and saw him cross the stable yard to the car. Robert was waiting. Not Julian, not me, Robert. Digby had a Gladstone bag. Robert had the car's engine running. I wondered later whether Robert, who always had some scheme going, had persuaded Digby they could catch them, whoever they were, rather than hand over the money. Whatever happened, it failed. The next day Digby had changed. Before, he could be up and down ... Afterwards, something had broken in him.'

'And the police?'

'Quite obviously he hadn't told the police. Not until later.

They were not best pleased. That was very much Digby's style: acts of derring-do and the terrible need to win all the time, even faced with a missing child.'

'Did you think the demand for money was—?'

'Julian? Lydia? No, not for a minute. Whatever they'd done that night was a catastrophe but not an attempt at gain. It was somebody cruel or greedy, taking advantage. It was all over the newspapers. It could have been anybody in England or simply a particularly malign hoaxer.'

'I'll leave you,' Laurence said. 'I don't want to exhaust you.'

As Laurence left the room, Patrick said, 'Thank you. I would never have got as far as the paintings on my own. But I'd rather not tell people while Lydia's ... you know?'

Laurence nodded.

He was glad to get out of the house. He remembered when his mother was dying that there had been a sort of limbo when she was unconscious and sinking slowly towards death. Occasionally he had felt impatient, even bored, and then, swiftly, guilty. But his mourning had begun weeks before she finally breathed her last. The emotion he felt afterwards was at least partly the product of relief.

He had been up to see Lydia earlier. The windows were open and Susan had got David to cut some delphiniums and stocks. She was setting them down by the window as he entered. Lydia, who had loved flowers so much, lay unaware of all this. It seemed to Laurence that the vase of flowers really served to camouflage the stale smell of the sickroom. The slight body in the large bed was that of an elderly woman now. Her hair was greyer since he'd last seen her, her collarbones protruding through her nightdress. Her lips, slightly parted, were dry and her yellow skin was stretched over her facial bones. Frances had sat next to her, tenderly unfolding her swollen fingers and rubbing cream into her dry hands.

There was nothing to say and nothing that needed to be said. He just sat on the other side of the bed, watching the two sisters. It was peaceful and he thought Frances was glad to have him there; his presence was largely for her. An hour or so later, Eleanor came up to relieve him and as he left the room he knew he might not see Lydia again.

The first time he had seen Ellen Kilminster's cottage, Frances had been with him. This time he went alone and he took Julian's bicycle. He jumped off when he saw Mrs Kilminster standing in the garden. She was feeding hens. Her youngest child was clutching a cat and sitting on a simple swing. He could tell at first from her apprehensive expression that the mother didn't recognise him.

'Laurence Bartram,' he said, keeping his distance and then pointing, needlessly, in the direction of the Hall.

She smiled, her face relaxing. 'Mr Bartram, I'm sorry, I'd seen you but I didn't know you close up.' She paused, uncertain of what to do. 'Do you want to come in?' She had a pleasant voice softened by her local accent.

'No, thank you, but I'd like a quick word if I may.'

Her look became wary again.

He put his hand on the low gate and eventually she nodded.

'I don't know what I can tell you,' she said.

'May I sit down?' Laurence said. A small bench stood by the house. 'My back's not very good.'

She nodded again. 'Maisie, you run off and play,' she said. The girl made a face but tipped the cat off her lap and wandered off behind the cottages, hitting flowers with a stick.

'Have they found her?' she said, suddenly.

It took him a second to realise she meant Maggie. He shook his head.

'Did you think the body was Maggie when you first heard?' he said.

Ellen Kilminster sighed. 'Well, it made sense. Maggie had gone, a dead woman was found in the church.' Then she said, sounding distressed, 'I'll box her ears for worrying us so when she comes home.'

He wanted to take her hand and tell her it would all be all right. Instead he looked across the small, well-kept garden, the vegetables and bright flowers, some slightly battered after all the rain, and knew he could never promise her that.

'She was growing up,' Ellen said. 'There was no life here for her, not even in service. And she was all talk of the pictures. She'd never even been to a picture house but she was daft about actresses. Thought she could go to America.'

She looked exasperated, as if Maggie were still a small child.

'But she was an ordinary girl. Her mam, now, she was a beauty. Joe met her in Swindon. Cycled over twice a week. She had books and a piano. He thought he was marrying above himself, which he was, probably, if she'd not run off. And she, poor woman, I think she did love Joe at first. But she can't have reckoned on living with old Walter and being stuck out here. She had the look of a trapped animal.'

'She went off with a gypsy, though? That wasn't likely to be much more comfortable?'

Ellen shrugged and looked into the distance.

'You were brought up at Easton, did you know about the vault?'

She shook her head. 'The police asked. No, I don't reckon nobody did. Not living, leastways, and I never heard talk of it before. I haven't been in the church for years. Not since the old vicar was here and that would be before the little girl went.'

She paused.

'Don't think I'm bad, but I can't do all that any more. I don't know what I believe, but it's not that. Some women here, they go and they say a prayer or leave a bunch of flowers for their sweethearts, but it's not for me.'

This time her sigh was audible.

'Bert was so proud to go. The lads, we all went to see them off from Salisbury after training. Mr Easton hired a charabanc.' She pronounced it 'charabang'. 'Even old Walter came along though he was moaning about being left to do all the work while they were gallivanting.'

A bee buzzed past Laurence's face and she lifted a hand to sweep it away from her own.

'They were on parade. Ever so smart. Mr Easton and Mr Julian on horses – Easton horses: Lightning and Ace of Spades, which Mr Julian called Ace. They never came back either. Poor horses.'

When she screwed her eyes up, lines ran deeply from their corners.

After a while she said, 'B Company, them and lads from West Overton and a couple of other villages round here. Bert was made up to NCO in training and had a section. Joe Petch did too and Ivor Baines, and Fred Deacon as had been footman when Mr Easton married.'

She sat very still. He could hear children playing a short distance away. A breeze ruffled the leaves of the apple tree and spun the jam jar of honeyed water she'd hung to catch wasps. He looked at her sideways, trying not to stare, but she was gazing into space. She was still young despite a few grey strands in her neat hair.

'Of all of them it was Baines that I couldn't believe was

gone. He was the strongest man you ever saw. Known for it —
cow-tipping or tug-o'-war. He was in the team that beat Pewsey
and Marlborough, and they'd got some big lads and more to
choose from. My Bert now, he wasn't built large, I could see
things could happen, but Ivor ...' She looked at him almost
accusingly. 'How could that be?'

Laurence thought of Pollock. Pollock was vast but it was all
blubber; it just made him a bigger target. The hopeless soldier
had fought under him for two years, and finally he had fought
for Pollock, lying back on a steep, wet slope, holding him in
his arms, trying to keep them both from the stinking yellow
water of a shell hole. The stretcher-bearers had wanted to leave
him.

'He's buggered, 'scuse my French, sir. Hop on the rig, let's get
you to the aid post — we'll never even get him off the ground. Do
us all an injury. He's stone cold, sir. No point to it.'

But he'd made them take Pollock, both stretcher-bearers
straining and cursing, while he'd limped behind, shuddering, his
arm around an orderly's shoulder and the man's grip firm around
his waist. He assumed Pollock went into the great pit waiting
behind Rosières.

'Mr Julian said Bert didn't suffer. A bullet just like that. Didn't
know anything.'

She turned towards him and a beautiful smile lit up her face.

'And that's what he's told all the other women. The way Mr
Julian's told it, not a man in B Company ever knew a second's
fear or pain. One minute they were here at Easton Deadall,
next minute they were in France, doing their duty, the next — in
paradise.'

He smiled back at her. She was no fool.

'I expect your husband wrote?'

She made a wry face. 'Never much of a one for letters,' she

said. 'There was this army form you could tick – things like: all well, am shot, am in hospital, am coming on leave soon. That sort of thing. He always just ticked it.'

She looked amused. 'We got our news at first through old Walter. There's a joke – Walter can't scarcely read his own name. Yet his boy Joe was always good at his books. Me and my sisters were at school with him. He was the first to read. So anyways, Joe wrote his dad letters from France. Well, old Walter never let on he couldn't read, always said his eyes weren't too good. So Joe would write and Walter would come trotting over and I'd read them to him. First couple of months it was all news. Then the letters got shorter and then they stopped. And Walter was the first to get the telegram, same day as Mrs Easton, postie said. He didn't have to read that. He knew.'

He felt he was watching a display of emotion, only just controlled, yet all around was peace.

'I wanted to ask you about your sister.' He had expected her to tense up at a personal enquiry but instead her hand flew to her face.

'Oh no, it's not Jane, is it? They don't think that woman's Jane?'

He'd simply wanted to see whether Ellen Kilminster had any information on Robert the former chauffeur, but realised instantly what she was saying. Even as he started to reassure her, he was thinking, what if it *was* her sister? It was as likely as any other solution. The body was of a woman who had given birth but it was not impossible the nanny had had a child since leaving Easton Deadall. Why hadn't he thought of it before? Jane Rivers had been brought up on the estate and had worked at the Hall. If anybody knew about the church, she might well, given her familiarity with the inside and the outside of the big house.

'No. No. The police think it's a stranger,' he said, thinking that it wasn't entirely a lie because he hadn't been told otherwise.

'But nobody from here saw the body.'

'The police have measurements, physical details.'

'But then they'd need Jane's to compare.'

'Do you want me to ask?' he said, knowing that he was giving the impression he might be some kind of conduit to the police. 'When did you last see her?'

'See her? Not for years. But we write once or twice a year. Not recently though. She's had it hard since she left here.'

'Do you think she was badly treated?'

She didn't answer for a few seconds. 'Not really. With Kitty gone she didn't have a job. She was leaving in the autumn that year to get married, and anyway, Mr Digby thought she was molly-coddling Kitty. Wanted her to have a governess. I can see why the police and Mr Easton were suspicious. She couldn't say why she didn't hear them take the child, only that she'd not been feeling well that week. But she loved Kitty as if she was her own. Used to bring her here sometimes, lovely little thing. So polite. Shy. If Bert spoke to her she'd bury her head in Jane's shoulder. I don't think Mrs Easton thought Jane had done anything amiss but Mrs Easton always did what Mr Easton said.'

She rolled her eyes, like a schoolgirl.

'But then there was Robert,' she said.

'Robert?' He gave no sign he knew about Robert.

'Her fiancé. Robert Stone. The Eastons' chauffeur. He must of known she had nothing to do with it but he kept his distance. It broke her heart. When she got to London she kept thinking he'd come, that perhaps it'd been difficult for him here, him wanting to keep his job and everything, but he never did.'

'One last question – and I'd be very grateful if you could keep it to yourself. Did your sister ever think anyone in the family was involved in the little girl's disappearance?'

This time Ellen Kilminster gave him a long, appraising look.

'Like who?' she said quite boldly, but when he just shook his head, she backed down.

'No. Jane said she couldn't bear to see Mrs Easton in such a state. Once the police said she could go, she was off. Found work as a machinist. But then she was too ill with her nerves to work.'

Distress returned to her face.

'I do hope they can be sure it's not Jane. I'll write but she doesn't always answer quick.'

'Look, if you like, I mean, I'm going back to London,' he said. 'If you want I'll look her up. I won't bother her, just make sure she's all right.'

She looked dubious for a second.

'Where she lives isn't exactly ...'

'No. Absolutely. I'll go there when I arrive.'

Suddenly she became brisk. 'I really need to go now, Mr—?'

'Bartram. Laurence Bartram.'

'I need to get up to the house to fetch the mending. And Ethel's starting today. But I'll get you Jane's address first.'

He stood outside the door as she went inside, listening to the gentle clucking of her hens, and feeling it had been somehow underhand to get the address he had originally wanted, but feared she wouldn't hand over, by making her anxious about Jane. In minutes she returned wearing a faded hat and a cotton coat. She handed him a bit of paper.

'Thank you.'

Then she said, 'It's been nice having someone to talk to, funny as it seems.'

'Your cousin's coming back soon, I gather?'

'Not mine,' she said. 'Bert's. Victor is Bert's cousin. Mr Julian was very kind to Victor.' She looked reflective. 'I'd've liked to've seen him after the war. To talk to him about my Bert. But before I knew it, Mr Julian had given him some money and set him up with some farmer he knew in Australia, and it was as if my kiddies were the only Kilminsters left. But still, I'll be ever so glad to see him.'

Her whole face lit up. 'Mind you, Mr Julian's none too pleased that he's coming back, though he's given him a cottage. Will Victor have to pay him back, do you think? He says he never settled, always felt homesick for Easton. He's got a girl – a wife – an *Australian* one.' She looked as if this was extraordinary in itself. 'He'll be coming back for good, he says, and he can be a real help on the estate. Victor was a hard worker.'

She put her hand up and tucked a stray lock of hair under her hat.

'And his wife's expecting so that will be company for Susan.'

'How did Susan meet David?' Laurence asked, hoping that, in the context, his question seemed like a bit of a distraction.

She smiled. 'Biscuits. She was in a factory made biscuits for our boys in France. The way she tells it, the girls used to put cheeky messages in the tins, sometimes, if they were unmarried, with their names on. Susan being Susan, she doesn't put anything a bit ... Well, you know what these girls can be like, all egging each other on. Susan just writes she hopes the man who eats the biscuits goes on all right and she's put good luck in with the ingredients and hopes God will take care of him. A whole year later he finds her at the works. He was a widower – married a London girl and lived there before he was a soldier. But he'd kept the note and everything. I've seen it, Susan's got it now.'

'Golly,' he said, wondering unromantically what sort of less happy surprise might have been waiting for David in the biscuit factory.

'She never put a note in before, she says, just the once – she says it was fate.'

'And he was a sapper?'

'I think so. Not with our lot, anyways.'

She looked uneasy and he thought he was asking too many questions. She was clearly an intelligent woman.

He picked up his hat from the seat beside him.

'I'm sorry about Mrs Easton,' she said. 'They say she's not got long?'

She watched his face. He hesitated briefly but he didn't think she was an idle gossip.

'No, she's in a coma. I don't think she'll recover. She's been ill for much longer than any of us realised.'

And at that she nodded, said goodbye and headed off in the direction of the Hall. She didn't wait to see if he was going her way, Perhaps, he thought, she didn't want to be seen with him.

In fact it suited him that she had gone as he didn't want her to see him going from cottage to cottage, seemingly interrogating the villagers. Yet he also wanted to speak to old Petch — he had been at Easton the longest. And he wanted to look at the letters he had been too foolishly fastidious to pore through last time. Now that it seemed likely Maggie was alive, surely her most likely destination had been to find where her mother lived. It was just possible she had discovered her address.

He was glad Petch opened the door fairly swiftly and relieved that he evidently recognised him. Petch himself looked older but more alert than when he'd come before.

'You got news about Maggie?' the old man said. Laurence cursed himself, as he had at the Kilminsters', for not realising what Petch's first thought on seeing him might be.

'No. I'm sorry. I'm sure she'll be back soon. It must be a tremendous worry.'

The old man looked at him sceptically. 'Leastways, she's not bin rottin' in the church. You want to come in?'

'If I may.'

Petch shrugged.

They sat on either side of the cold fireplace in the small room.

'I bin finishing the old chimney at Kilminster's. Mr Julian wanted it done before Victor comes back.'

This was the longest sentence he'd ever heard Petch speak.

'I done a good job.' He was nodding his head.

'Is that what you did here as a young man?' Laurence said.

Petch stared at him as if uncertain whether to trust him with the information. Eventually he nodded.

'Did all sorts but stone's my trade. Was apprenticed mason over at Salisbury.' For a minute the loose folds of his face seemed to ease. 'But my pa died and my mam needed me home. Mrs Easton – old Mrs Easton – she had me carving little creatures like I done there.'

'You did the ones on the terrace? But they're beautiful.' Laurence was astonished.

Walter straightened up and looked directly at him. 'She says that. She says they were better than ones she'd seen in London. She loved flowers and animals, she did. Joe never had the feel for stone – he preferred the gardens – and Mrs Easton took him on when he were a lad o' fourteen. But Joe could lend a hand: we did the new privy and wash-house out back before he went.'

'You must have known Mr Julian's mother well?'

Petch's face lightened further.

'You liked her?' Laurence said.

'She was a fine lady. When my wife died having our Joe, she was kind.'

'All the building back then must have kept you busy?'

'Easton men did it all.'

'You must have helped with the electric plant?'

'That's right.' Petch had picked up a clay pipe. 'Big job. Cutting through from the river. Mrs Easton – old Mrs Easton – had an engineer man down from Scotland who liked giving orders.' He suddenly looked unnaturally cheerful. 'I heard as he electrified himself back north.'

'When you were building the shed for the cistern and the generator, did you come across anything unusual?'

'You'll be meaning the cave?' Petch said, matter-of-factly. 'As you and Mr Patrick got stuck in, I expects.'

Now Laurence found he too wanted to smile. So much for secrets.

'Well, yes.'

'You should've seen the Scotsman when we found it – he were jumping about shouting. Livid, he was. Carrying on like it's our fault because we live there and should've known. Because the water might break through, he says we'll have to reinforce the whole wall.'

'Did Mrs Easton see the cave?'

'That were funny,' the old man said. 'Mrs Easton, well, between you and me, she was a bit of a left footer. Couldn't help it – she were brought up to it. Colonel Easton wasn't having any of it but a fox is a fox even in britches. And the Scotsman was one of them killjoy types whose God's against everything. If Mrs Easton wasn't paying his bill, he'd have had her burned, I don't wonder, back in his Scotland. But the cave ... well, they both agreed on that. It was full of them pagan drawings. Least, she says it's pagans and he says it's witchcraft. They blocks it up and tells us men never to tell a soul.'

'But you left a way through?'

Petch frowned and appeared to be thinking, biting on the stem of his pipe. After a while he said, 'I reckon we did. The Scotsman. To allow water to run off if the sluices failed. For floods. I shouldn't think he told Mrs E.'

'Did you tell anybody about the hatch?'

Petch shook his head. 'She was a good lady. If she wanted her secrets, that was all right by me.'

While Petch was talking, it had slowly dawned on Laurence that there was one other matter he might be able to help with.

'In the church, did she ask you to cover the floor in front of the altar with the bitumen?'

Petch seemed to be thinking again but Laurence could tell he knew what he was being asked and was simply deciding whether or not to lie.

'Right. She did. Mighty quick.'

'Why? Did she say?'

'There was patterns under there. Roman patterns, like she'd seen with the colonel in some big church on their honeymoon in France. He was for digging it up. She asked me to cover it. We was going to put boards on top, ordinary like, but she got ill with her next babby. Poor lady.'

Then he came close to laughing.

'I put it all on and now I been taking it all off. If I live long enough, perhaps them Eastons will want it all put down again.'

'You walled up the vault under the church, too, didn't you? For Mrs Easton? Back when they were restoring it? To make a private chapel for her?'

Petch obviously hadn't expected this and looked even more uneasy. Eventually the man grunted.

'I didn't see what harm it would do. She believed what she believed. Colonel Easton wasn't an easy man. She found this little place she said had been holy but she didn't like the tunnel.'

This time he did laugh but his face was transformed by gentleness.

'Thought them pagans might find a way through from down the hill. Me, I thought it was more like dead people'd been put down there.'

It occurred to Laurence that Walter Petch had been closer than he knew.

'When I thought it was Maggie they'd found ... I were glad if it had to be that she'd been left in that place. Mrs Easton had me put up a wall – mind, it wasn't much. One good push and it would have gone through, but although the colonel was in London at the time, she didn't want tittle-tattle on the estate. I didn't have much stone either. Put distemper on the walls to brighten the place up for her.'

'But how did she get in and out?'

'I fixed her a pulley system. Like we had at Salisbury for lifting stone up the cathedral. Didn't look like much. I put it near the bell rope so it looked like part of that. They only had a little table then and the carpet was laid over the door – surprising they'd forgotten it was there. She just had to thread a cord through it and pull it up. She could shut it behind her and thread the cord through to make it lift from inside.'

Laurence thought nothing would induce him to go down and shut himself in a vault under any church.

'Mind, she mostly went when the colonel was away and then she'd just lock the church door and leave the hatch open. Told me never to say to a soul but anyway the colonel caught her in the end. Broke it all up in a fury. Tore down the pulley. Put that great table on top. He must've wondered how she done the pulley but she never said. And I never told. All them years. Not even Joe.'

'Not even the police?'

'Didn't figure I should. It was a long ways back and I'd never told, so no one else knew. And they found it now anyway.'

The logic, although impeccable, was flawed by the fact that the unidentified woman had also been found down there.

'Not even Mr Julian or Mr Patrick?'

'What're you suggesting?' Petch gave him a sharp look. 'But no, I don't reckon they ever went down there. And it would have to have been both of them. They'd never get in there alone without the pulley.'

Laurence remembered the struggle he and David had had with the massive oak table and the weight of the door.

'Are you going to tell them, then? The police?' Petch said.

Laurence shook his head, feeling he had stayed long enough. More bits of the puzzle that was Easton Hall were falling into place. But, as with a jigsaw without a guide image, it was impossible to know how big the whole picture might be.

'You didn't tell your son?' he persisted.

'I didn't tell no one.' Then after a pause Petch said, less irritably, 'Why would I?'

Laurence let a silence fall while he decided whether his questions might have left the old man less amenable to the request that had brought him here in the first place.

'I was wondering if I could look at a postcard in Maggie's room?'

He waited for a refusal, but instead Walter Petch looked hopeful. Laurence hated himself for raising any expectations that he could find his granddaughter, while at the same time hoping Petch wouldn't either offer to fetch it himself or ask him specifically what he was looking for. But the old man seemed resigned to strangers picking their way through his life.

'You know where it is,' he said, turning his face slightly towards the stairs. 'But she likes it left nice.'

Once in Maggie's room, Laurence went straight to the drawers and pulled out the one he wanted, trying to ease it gently so that it didn't creak. He lifted out the tin and took the letters from underneath the keepsakes. As he had thought, apart from the Valentine card there were three. Two were in identical handwriting, but the third was quite different. He flicked to the signature to confirm the first letter was indeed from the dead Joe Petch. The first time he'd seen it, he had recognised it, by the size of the paper and the deletions by the censor, as having been sent from a military unit. As a junior officer he had gone through innumerable soldiers' letters, performing the task: removing details that might identify where they were serving or battalion strength or any operational details. Some officers deleted critical comments about senior NCOs and officers, but he had always felt the men were entitled to gripe, given the conditions they tolerated.

Of the two, one was long for such a letter and he was not surprised that it appeared to date from a period before Joe Petch had seen action in France. He read it quickly and had an immediate sense of the man who had written it.

Dear Father,

I hope this is finding you well. We are well. I wish I had my mouth organ and my thicker socks. It is warm but my boots rub something awful. We have not seen any Jerries yet face to face only to lob artillery at and have them lobbed back. None has landed on me yet youll be pleased to hear. Mr Easton who I forgot to call Captain yesterday says we shall be in there and do our business and out again and home before spring.

This is not a bad place. We walked as far as it would be to go to Marlborough and blimey I hardly dared take my

291

boots off for fear Id never get them on again. Tomorrow we go up the line but this is allright. The officers are in a chatau, which is not so much a castle as a grand house. It is not much bigger than the Hall not that we poor sods are let in. It is a shame for the gardens are mostly ********, 'scuse my French. Ha ha. My joke. There are French camped at one end of the park and have made a right mess of it. They eat horses Captain E says. Though he is always teasing and their horses are scraggy beasts better for carrying kit than for chopping into stew. Theres lime trees in straight lines buzzing with bees and hives that are ruined and the grass near the house is very long. But the kitchen garden has all kind of queer things growing as well as weeds like you cant imagine though carrots too which the Frenchies eat raw but we cooked up for dinner. The roses and carnations are a sight and they have these little hedges which dont do anything much along the gravel paths except the men dont want to take the longer way round so they blunder about breaking up everything. There are snapdragons gone wild. I dont know who was gardeners here before we come but when weve done they arent going to be too pleased.

Our officers are more decent than the others. One sapper captain keeps coming over and borowing us he says for this and that. Digging latrines. We wasnt too keen until some old lag from the Bedfords said filling them in was a whole lot worse. This officer hes all complaints, we dont salute quick enough, and or hes going to have us on charge if we dont fall in. Captain E has at him for sticking his nose in. Says we Easton men got our own ways and fightings our business not digging pits unless he says so. Then he says that officers a schoolteacher and is doing his officering out of a book. The sapper heard because his ears went pink.

The Bedfords are coming with us when we go forward. They seem like decent boys. Them thats been there say the Jerries send over whole foundries of iron not just shells. One platoon their officer got blown to bits and all they found was his lip with his tache on. They put it in a matchbox.

Captain Easton is a card. We had a sing song on Wenesday and he did a turn. Then we made poor Peter sing and all he knew was hymns. The lad hes been right homseick. First week the older lads thought hed been crying not that I saw it and were taking the rip but Mr Julian told them to leave off. It was mostly Harper and you know what hes like. Captain Easton had found a ladies scarf and with that covering his hair and a flower from the garden behind his ear and some French drink in him Peter looked like a girl and it quite made us laugh. Even Ivor cheered up. Mr Julian wouldnt take a turn said he was too busy.

He doesnt like the plan of attack I think and he worries about stores though he is not the QM. He always wants us to march further so that we get to where were headed which I cant tell you on account its secret. Captain E says it will be hard enough and no point us being used up before we get anywhere near the real fighting.

Bert takes himself very seriously now hes got his stripes. Drills and orders and exercises when theres no sign of fighting. Bert must be loving this war and being able to order us about. Bit of a change from back at Easton where he has to ask us nicely and Mrs K has at him for lighting his pipe indoors. He and Mr Julian are like two old aunts

fussing and making rules. But its all for the best and the
boys are all good lads. Its like weve got Easton right with
us.

Anyway on account of Bert and Mr Julian being so keen
we got to go and do drill. I hope all is well with you and at
Easton and little Maggie isnt giving you any trouble. You
tell her her Pa'll soon be home and I might bring her a bit
of French cheese if shes <u>not</u> a good little girl. The stink of
it you wouldnt credit.

Your loving son

Joe

Laurence's first thought was how innocent and cheerful the
letter was. Only weeks had passed since the Easton men had
joined up, although they'd been through training and had already
joined their regiment. Perhaps it was the wisdom of retrospec-
tion or his own war-weary cynicism, but he could read the seeds
of disaster in Joe Petch's excited account. This was the gardener
at war, not a soldier. And Digby Easton a landowner courting
popularity, not a professional officer. Not even that for long.
Within the year they were all dead.

The second letter might have been written by a different man.
By that date, they were within two days of their end. The censor
had let the letter go through and he wondered whether it had
simply been among Joe Petch's effects when they were parcelled
up to be sent home. It might never have been read at all.

Dear Old Dad,

What a day weve had. Youll hear soon enough that we
lost Bert and Peter. Theres hard feelings about it. Were
only about — from Jerry trenches. We came forward
Thursday and yesterday Cpt E wants Peter to do a recce. It

was bad weather but too light and Mr Julian said we shouldve gone out before dawn only the captain was late waking and Bert wades in and thinks its too dangerous and slow going in the mud and even if the Jerries cant see us we cant see if were about to walk into them. Captain E laughs at him and says the whole wars b***** dangerous and its not just mending pigsties these days. He said if Bert had got the wind up hed see to it someone else got his stripes. Bert goes white but not because hes a coward but because he hates Cpt E now and his fists were clenching.

Weve had a bad run of it. Fred got hit by a Jerry sniper and Dennis Ames the new miller from West Overton was hit by shrapnel. Them two brothers up at Vale Farm are both gone too. One got hit and the other went back for him the silly b****** and they got him too. Its always raining.

Cpt E's wound up something rotten since we got stuck here. He and Mr Julian are hardly speaking. The Cpt takes a drink at night and Mr Julian he doesnt like it not a bit. Were stuck in this hell-hole it stinks and you have to sleep sitting up. Theres a mist youd think had glue in it it sticks to you so. We couldnt see much anyway but daylights daylight.

Mr Julian says dont be a fool Digby and we hear and Cpt E pushes him away and he falls in the mud. Bert says the lads too young and they should take one of the older men but Cpt E says no Bert can take Peter if he wants to be his nursemaid and then things youd never believe and Id never tell. Anyway cant say more here. But it turns out bad for Bert and Peter like I said. All us lads that once were friends and enemies but always talking are sitting around quiet as the grave not even looking at each other now. Easton will never be the same place we left. Dad if things go bad for us you will tell Mags I love her wont you and take care of her forever. Ill write more after but Ive got to go now. Business to do as they say.

The letter ended abruptly. Only as he finished it did Laurence remember that Mrs Kilminster had told him that Walter Petch couldn't read and she would read Joe's letters to him. It wasn't hard to imagine her feelings if she'd read this terse account of events leading to her husband's death. But had Maggie read it, he wondered? The first letter had conveyed some resentment at Albert Kilminster's higher rank, which Joe Petch might not have included if he had realised Ellen Kilminster would see it, but in this account Kilminster had clearly tried to protect the men — and from their own officer. None of it had saved them.

He was still mentally with the 6th Wilts as he picked up the next letter, the one he had hoped might be from Maggie's mother. Now that he saw it again, he found that it was indeed hers. Her writing was tidier and more fluent than Joe's.

Dear Joe,

You always thought I would be off. Used to say you could never believe your luck. Now you'll think your luck's run out. But you were always good to me and I loved little Mags. See I am crying as I write that. You are a good man and I know you will look after our little girl. I don't want to go but I have to. Please try and understand. Well how can you when I am not telling you anything. You were too good and loyal a man for me and you will always have Easton which never took to me. I don't know where I'll be. On the move I expect.

Your wife. The last time I'll write that.

Rosaline

There was no address. He almost banged his fist on the chest of drawers. The next thing that struck him was that both letters carried the shadow of unexpressed knowledge. Both were from individuals who knew that everything about their lives was about to change.

He had been in Maggie's room too long – he was only supposed to be looking at a postcard – and he put the tin away as quickly and quietly as he could. When he went down, Walter was in the garden, digging apparently randomly in a patch of weeds, perhaps to discourage any further conversation. Laurence called out his thanks and Walter raised a hand as if in salute. Laurence did not look back but felt the man was watching him to make sure he was well away.

As he walked back to the Hall he reconsidered what Walter had told him and whether it changed things. It was not Colonel Easton but Mrs Easton who had had the maze blocked off. More importantly, Walter, at least, knew of both the cave end of the maze and the vault. But had he told anybody else? On balance, Laurence believed him when he said not, but that made Walter a suspect for leaving the body. And if the body should turn out to be Maggie's mother, Rosaline, he had a motive. However, he was an old man and the door was heavy, needing two men to lift it, not to mention the physical force needed to subdue and kill a much younger woman.

As he came in sight of the Hall he reflected that although it was extremely unlikely that Walter was involved, he felt uneasy nonetheless about colluding in Petch's withholding of information. He decided that if the body was identified as Rosaline Petch, then he would urge Walter to speak out. He knew too that soon he must hand the bag he'd found in the cistern in to the authorities.

The rain had held off and he veered left to the church. The

door shut behind him. The hatch was closed but the table was still to one side, presumably awaiting the delayed installation of the new window. He paused for a minute, looking up at the glass where Lydia Easton's vision would soon be turned into William's explosion of light. She would never see it now.

He ran his hands over the nearest walls by the west window. The whitewash was a consistent colour, repainted reasonably recently, although, under the paint and close to the bell rope, he could see the shadow where the pulley Walter Petch had set up might once have been screwed to the wall. He made a careful check of all three walls. They were rough but he felt no irregularities. He stood back and examined them closely, up and down, higher than his reach, but of the one thing he had expected to find, there was not a trace.

CHAPTER EIGHTEEN

David was out in the yard. As well as taking Laurence to Marlborough station he was fetching the London doctor off the down train.

'Could you drop me off in Marlborough a little early? I need to do a couple of things,' Laurence said.

'Mrs Bolitho's coming too,' David said. Since the discovery of the body he wouldn't meet Laurence's eyes.

Eleanor had tried to persuade Laurence her journey was pre-arranged. She was so wrapped up in herself, so silent for once, that she never even asked him why he wasn't going straight to the railway station. He was relieved not to be travelling all the way to London with her.

The officer on the desk at the Marlborough police station evidently thought Laurence was mad. He took the bag gingerly but politely and promised to hand it on. A part of Laurence hoped it might never reach the inspector. They couldn't have much experience of murder in Wiltshire.

*

Most men who came up from the underground station at the Oval were probably thinking about cricket but Laurence was considering churches. For him, London's history and geography were arranged around them. He had never seen the supposedly fine church of St John the Divine. The great spire was unmistakable but when he reached it he felt no urge to enter the building, however beautiful its interior and windows were supposed to be. Although it was only half a century old, there was something over-insistent about St John's. Was it possible to feel a sense of wonder, even if uncertain about God, in such a place?

For some reason he thought again of the hundreds of planned small streets he had seen at the exhibition, spilling out across the acreage to the north-west of London. In those intersecting lines and plots, had they left a place for a church? A church, even more obediently built than St Johns, unequivocally facing east, with nothing to surprise in its vaults or on its floors, and all its shadows falling evenly? Or was modern living about tobacconists and butchers, factories, public houses and infant schools? Despite his own beliefs or lack of them, he hoped there would be a church.

It would be a dull place to start with, testing even the ardently devout. When the houses had been lived in for a century or so, and their gardens and trees had grown, and been cropped and redug according to fashion, and some of the houses had fallen, and some factories had failed and been turned into studios for moving films or dance halls, and the place had gone up and down in the world a few times, then the church might be interesting. When it had seen a thousand men, women and children come from their small, neat homes to pray or weep or give thanks in the dark, then this as yet unbuilt church would speak for the place around it. He hoped the area would have no need for a memorial as St John's now had, carrying the names of so many of its sons. In Metroland – he remembered now that was the development company's name – he felt lives should have a guarantee of safety in return for the settlers' courage and enthusiasm for this new world they were creating.

It was the events of the last few days that had flung him into such melancholy reflection, but at least it had brought him closer to Jane Rivers in Holland Road. He passed some meagre but tidy shops. Men and women, respectable but shabby, walked and spoke quietly. A coalman's horse ate peacefully from its nose bag. Were Mrs Kilminster to come and visit her sister, he thought she would be reassured.

He found Holland Road easily but, judging by the numbering, Jane Rivers lived at the far end. His journey had reminded him of traversing London in early-winter snow nearly three years ago, on a similar, slightly quixotic mission. The result of those enquiries, when they bore fruit, merely revealed that his instincts had been wrong all along. But at least that time he had been asked to act and, through a combination of love, boredom and loyalty, he had almost accidentally come upon a resolution, rather than a solution. This time, only finding out what had happened to Kitty could be said to be any kind of result. At the Hall they still talked more about the child than about the newly murdered woman. Had he become infected by their obsession?

He thought some more about the woman he'd come to see. All he'd heard of the nanny, Jane Rivers, was that she loved Kitty as if she were her own and that she had never stopped protesting her innocence. It didn't take a great brain to see that she would come under suspicion, despite being unwell before the abduction. Lydia had not been well either. Now as he approached Jane Rivers' house, he realised what a fool's errand this was. If she was there, all well and good; he might ask her some questions *if* she let him in. If she answered the door, then obviously the dead woman was not her. If she did not, it proved nothing.

He checked the number again. This end of the street was darker than the other. Three-storey buildings in dirty brick crowded in on both sides. Flights of steps, once white, went mostly unscrubbed, with weeds growing in the cracks. An old man with a white beard nearly to his waist sat on a step, smoking a pipe, a contented look on his face. He nodded to Laurence. A battered perambulator stood outside another house.

Seventy-seven was at the end of one of these tall terraces. Clearly the whole building couldn't all be hers. A washing line with men's clothing hung below the open second-floor windows, dripping on the pavement beneath. The first-floor windows were shut, even on this warmish day, and discoloured lace curtains obscured any view. If she were as poor as her sister said, she'd be on the top floor or in the basement.

There were no names on any of the bells. He rang what he hoped was the second-floor bell but heard no sound. He rang another at random and then another. Above his head a window went up. A woman's face, round and red with a scarf over her hair, appeared, almost comically framed in the arch of a man's wet long johns.

'Who're you wanting?' she said, apparently not bothered at being disturbed.

'Miss Rivers, Miss Jane Rivers,' he said.

'Wait a tick. I'm coming down.' Was she going to tell him Jane Rivers had gone?

The door opened.

'You could've come in. It's not locked.'

She had a washing basket under her arm as she led him through a passage with three or four doors, each belonging presumably to a different habitation.

'Church outing,' she said over her shoulder. 'For the kiddies. St John Div. Taking them to the exhibition, Gawd help them. They said, did I want to go. I said, no, it'll be more of a holiday for me back here without them all.'

He thought she was quite young, but she waddled as he followed behind her, only just squeezing herself and the basket through the narrow space.

'Miss Rivers is out the back,' she said. 'Lovely lady but lives on her nerves. Hasn't been well lately.'

'She's been around recently?'

She turned and looked back at him as if suddenly suspicious.

'Well, of course she has. Where else'd she be?' She had stopped completely now and put down the basket. 'Why d'you want her, anyway? You're not some sort of copper, are you?'

He almost laughed at the idea but could see she needed persuading. Her eyes appraised him carefully.

'No. Absolutely not.'

'See, she had a hard time before I knew her. A bad business at the place she worked.'

He nodded.

'She had trouble with men,' she said. 'Her sweetheart broke his promise and there was some trouble with one of the men in the family where she was in service.' The woman had lowered her voice. 'Then things went missing – something really valuable, diamonds or some such – and some people thought it was her. Coppers on to her night and day. The family let her go of course.' She looked outraged on Jane Rivers' behalf. 'As if she would. Kind to her heart. And anyway if she'd got hold of diamonds or rubies or something, she'd live in a darn sight better place than this. Mind you, she'd probably give it all to St John's. She's a bit ...' She put her hands together, closed her eyes and moved her lips in a mock prayer, then her eyes flew open. 'She wasn't so much when she came, but she is now.' She raised her eyebrows. 'Can hardly blame her, though.'

He was relieved she was such a talker that she'd forgotten to clear up the issue of who he was or why he was there.

Right at the back, the house had been extended into what might once have been a garden. Now a narrow alley ran alongside the one-storey, slate-roofed building with ground elder growing through the dividing wall. At the end of the alley he could see and smell the wash-house. Beside him was a faded front door.

She tipped her head towards it. 'I'll be off then.' She continued down the path to the copper, from which steam was rising in a fragrant column.

He knocked self-consciously. A single window was shut but he thought he saw the curtain move. He stepped back, although there was precious little room to do so. As he did so, the door opened. The woman who stood in the doorway, still clutching the door handle, might once have been pretty, but there was little trace of it now. She was very thin. Her skin looked dry and she was lined about the lips. A tiny cross hung on a chain around her neck and a modesty panel filled the V-neck of her print dress. Despite the relative warmth she wore a cardigan. He couldn't read her expression but it didn't seem to be hostile.

'Miss Rivers?'

'Yes. That's me.' Immediately he could hear her west country accent.

'I'm sorry, it must seem very odd, my turning up like this. Your friend' – he turned to where the large woman was putting linen through a mangle – 'she showed me where you were. I'm sure she's keeping an eye on me.' He hoped to put her at her ease.

'You've come from Easton,' she said.

304

'Well, yes. I mean, I don't live there. I live here, in London. But I have been at Easton, yes. Working on the church.'

The look she gave him was grave and calm. From all accounts of her, he had expected to find an older version of an emotional, defensive girl. But Jane Rivers, although obviously in reduced circumstances, had a dignity of her own.

'You've got the look of Easton,' she said. 'And the voice.'

'May I come in?'

She made no protests but opened the door wider, allowing him to go in before her. The door gave straight on to a sitting room. Behind a curtain he could see a small stone sink and some pots and pans. There was one further closed door, which he assumed was her bedroom. The wall in the alley outside kept out much of the light but the room was tidy and clean, with faded floral curtains at the window. Two prints hung on either side of a small tiled grate. One was of St Francis feeding birds and small animals; it was the sort of image he remembered sticking in his attendance book at Sunday school. The other was of three crosses in silhouette on a hill against a sunset.

A single chair stood by a small, black-leaded fireplace, with pristine white antimacassar trimmed with crochet. Next to it was a round table with a cloth over it, its edge embroidered with cheerful daisies. A pile of what looked like embroidered bookmarks, perhaps twenty or thirty of them, sat in a shallow cardboard box.

He smiled. 'They said you and your sister were good seamstresses.'

She turned to look at the tablecloth and when she faced him once more, a slight blush made her look younger.

'I take in sewing,' she said. 'Sometimes my ladies let me keep oddments. I make little bits for the church bazaar.'

She spoke quickly and earnestly. He had the impression she wanted him to think well of her, yet she hadn't asked what on earth had brought him from Easton to her doorstep.

'I get by,' she said, to an unasked question.

'Your sister will be pleased to hear you're well.'

'Ellen?' This time she did smile and her pale-blue eyes opened wider. 'I miss Ellen. We were never apart as girls. Irish twins, they call it. Born the same year. Went into service at Easton together.' Her smile faded a little. 'Would you like tea?'

'Yes. Thank you.'

'I don't have any cake.'

She pulled up a heavy dining chair from the table and disappeared behind the curtain, to return with a tray, a clean cloth neatly laid under the china. They sat solemnly drinking tea, almost like a dumbstruck courting couple. Her knees with the dress drawn tightly over them projected towards him. Her ankles were still shapely in her unfashionable shoes.

'Is everything all right at Easton?' she said politely, although he sensed it cost her to ask. 'I haven't heard from my sister for a while.'

He found he didn't want to tell her there'd been a murder at the Hall. No doubt her sister would tell her soon enough.

'She's well,' he said. 'The children too.'

He knew he had to get to the point and he plunged in.

'I know you had a hard time of it when Kitty Easton disappeared,' he said.

Immediately her face closed up. 'It's only to be expected,' she said rather primly, 'being a servant.'

'I'm sorry,' he said, and he was. She seemed an eminently decent woman, whose life would never amount to more than it was now.

'It wasn't my fault,' she said.

'Mrs Easton is dying . . .' he began.

The effect of his few words caught him by surprise. She gave a small, restrained cry and stifled it almost immediately but her eyes were suddenly full of tears. She blinked a few times but eventually fumbled in her sleeve for a neatly pressed handkerchief. As she unfolded it, he remembered the name of the tiny stitches on its hem: lovers' knots. His mother used to do them.

'She was such a lovely lady.' She gulped and lifted the handkerchief again to her eyes.

'I'm dreadfully sorry,' he said. 'I didn't mean to upset you.' But then before she could regain her equilibrium, he asked gently, 'What do you think happened when Kitty went missing?'

She gave him an appalled look.

'Mrs Easton?' he said. 'Might it have been her fault in some way?'

She was shaking her head so violently that she nearly dislodged her cup and saucer from the tiny table by her chair.

'No, not Mrs Easton. She lived for that little girl. She would have done anything to save her.'

'Save her?'

'If she was in danger.'

'Was she in danger, do you think?' He kept his voice relaxed.

'No, of course not. She was in her own home. Everybody loved her.' But her eyes slid to the bible and for the first time he had a sense she was lying.

'Yet she vanished.'

Jane Rivers didn't pick up on the implications of this but went on, 'She was the dearest little girl – skipping about, singing her little songs. And she had such an imagination, with her picture books, and playing outside, and she had her own little bit of garden where she grew pansies and forget-me-nots and nasturtiums and radishes. Except she'd always pick the flowers as soon as they showed, for her mama.' She looked up again. 'She had a kitten, called Polly. She . . .'

She began wringing the handkerchief and her face was full of pain.

'She trusted everyone.'

He felt contempt for himself. He had sought out this harmless woman and distressed her immeasurably. Yet he pressed on.

'Mrs Easton – she always believed Kitty was still alive. Do you believe that?'

She gave him a steady look. 'Yes,' she said very quietly. 'I do. I hope it and I believe it. I pray for her every day.'

They both fell silent. From outside the window he heard the washerwoman brush past.

'I'm going to leave you in peace,' he said. 'But there's somebody else I want to talk to and I've no idea how to track him down.'

He could see alarm creep back into her face.

'Robert Stone. I think you were engaged to be married once?'

He cringed inwardly at disturbing her further but in fact her face took on a harder look.

'He was a bad man,' she said. 'A liar and a greedy man and a betrayer.'

He didn't respond to the sudden passion in her voice but simply said, 'I gather he came to London?'

'So they say. But if he did, he kept a long way from me.'

'So you've no idea where he is or what might have happened to him? Did he join up, for instance?'

'I have no feelings left for Mr Stone,' she said. 'I wish with all my heart I'd never met him. I don't know if he's alive or dead. Nor care. Maybe he's with his sister. He had a sister in London. His only living relative, he said.'

She drew breath, audibly.

'But I have no idea where she lived, or whether she was married or still called Stone. He didn't give much away. I don't think she was a respectable woman.'

Her hand moved towards her cross but fell away without touching it.

'He might not even have a sister at all. He was all stories. Always trying to shock people.'

Two purplish spots burned in her cheeks. Her level of anger after so long was, he imagined, provoked not so much by the broken engagement, as by Stone's failure to support her when the world was against her and she faced leaving the only home she knew.

Eventually he decided that his visit and all its alarms deserved some explanation.

'Actually something bad has happened at Easton Deadall. Apart from Mrs Easton's decline.'

Her eyes opened wide.

'Not to anyone you know. But a woman was found dead.'

She looked, if anything, more anxious than either indifferent or intrigued, which surprised him as, although the discovery of the corpse was an atrocious event, she could have no love left for the Easton family.

'It's not ... Do they know who it is?'

'No.' He wondered who she had thought it might be.

This time her hand went up and held her cross. All of a sudden words came tumbling out.

'It wasn't Kitty, was it? It wasn't Kitty come back? Can they tell? She'd be quite the young lady now. Her birthday's in March. She'd be eighteen. They might not recognise her. She had lovely silver-gold hair but it probably went darker – they usually do when they grow up.'

'It wasn't Kitty,' he said gently, wanting to take her agitated hands in his. 'But for a while they thought it was Maggie Petch.'

'Maggie?' She was clearly thinking. 'Oh, Joe Petch's girl? She was just little when I was there. Didn't her ma run off with a gypsy?'

Not for the first time, Laurence noticed how there was a single tale of Easton told by everybody connected with it. The same accounts, the same reasons for things, the same phrases.

'That man was another devil,' she said.

He didn't know how to reply. Everyone else had said Joe Petch was a good man. But perhaps they simply spoke well of the dead.

Before he could reply she said, 'So it's not a young woman?'

'No. Older.'

She seemed to relax.

'Is that what you came to tell me?' she said, puzzled. 'Or just, like everybody used to, to ask me about my Kitty?'

He felt embarrassed but decided to tell the truth.

'Actually, I was worried it just might be you.'

'Me?' she said, astonished. 'The dead person? Why would I go back to Easton Deadall?' She seemed almost amused.

'You might have gone to see your sister.'

'I might.'

She didn't speak for a while.

'I'm sorry to have disturbed you,' he said. 'And sorry about what happened. I think you had a raw deal, back then. From everybody.'

'They were upset,' she said calmly. 'But thank you, sir. Where was she found? The dead lady?'

'In the church.' He avoided telling her the woman was probably murdered.

'I'm glad. Her being in a church. Not in a ditch or some wood where foxes might find her. At least she was in a proper place.'

He got up to go and she let him into the alley. She glanced towards the empty wash-house.

'You won't say here, will you? Nobody knows I was part of all that.'

'No. Of course not.'

He tipped his hat to her and walked through the house into the street once more.

Later, as the train ran deep into the underground tunnels, he thought back on Jane Rivers. In a way he had learned a lot from the conversation, without gaining any obviously useful information.

He was certain she had not been involved in Kitty's death. It was not so much because she had echoed Lydia's belief that the child still lived, but because of her almost instant terror that the dead woman might be a grown-up Kitty.

Her religious sensibilities had given him one further insight. Like Walter Petch, she had thought of the church as being a 'proper' place to leave a body. He had merely assumed it was the most convenient hiding place for somebody who happened to know of the crypt. The fact that whoever had done it also knew that quicklime was being used to restore the cottages meant it was almost certainly someone connected with Easton Deadall. Now, however, he wondered if the murderer was either possessed of the same sort of sensitivity as Jane Rivers, or whether there was a relationship between murderer and victim that contained, even in anger, some residual respect.

In the end, he was unable to make anything of it. Each scenario was possible, but none suggested a single individual as a perpetrator, nor a single obvious victim.

It was good to get back to his rooms in London. As he walked upstairs, carrying a pile of letters from the hall table, he felt an overwhelming sense of relief. His flat was on the top floor of a corner building between Great Ormond Street and Lamb's

Conduit Street. He had moved here from a much larger house in a much smarter area, after Louise's death a few years earlier. He had wanted somewhere with which he had no connections, where the shadows of a past which had been cut from behind him, could not reach. Of course they came with him; it had been folly to believe otherwise. Sometimes he thought that, when he first got back from France, he was at least partly mad; a quiet sort of madness: of insomnia, inertia, a wish to avoid surviving friends.

It had taken a woman – Mary Emmett – to free him. Certainly he had loved her, even after he realised she could not be wholly his, but he had also come to feel comfortable in his new life. He had come to enjoy the views over London from his eyrie, the small shops and the untidy history that lay all around him. He liked the way the light moved round the rooms. He had had two very happy years teaching at Westminster School. Although the master he had replaced, temporarily, had returned, Laurence thought, if he made it clear he wanted it, that a permanent job there might be found. He might live this easy life, marry a nice young woman like Frances, have children, see generations of boys pass through his classes, see London grow and enjoy all it had to offer.

And yet there was Italy. The less sensible option, wonderfully seductive. Unlike so many of his friends at Marlborough and Oxford, he had never been abroad until fate sent him to France. By the time he had crossed the Channel, the war had been waged for well over a year and whatever beauty he might once have found in the landscape and its treasures had long since been destroyed. He had seen medieval churches – places whose architecture he had once studied and which had taken generations of master craftsmen to build – obliterated in a day's bombardment. Although he had found leave in Paris exciting, it was a different Paris to the one he might have explored, were he not conspicuous in his uniform, as well as uncertain whether this might be the last week or month of his life. Italy was unknown. Literally unknown: apart from the della Scala boy and his father, he knew not a soul in the country. As he stood on the cusp of middle age, Italy's unknowns seemed magically alluring.

His rooms were stuffy. He went round and threw open all the windows. He made himself some tea and taking his cup to his desk, he slit open his letters with his paper knife. He had not bothered to arrange for them to be forwarded to Easton Deadall, knowing he would return regularly.

One was an invitation to a gaudy at Oriel, his old Oxford college. Three years ago he would not have considered it; the idea of a feast, where so many of the faces from his cohort were missing, would have seemed entirely melancholy, but now he thought he might go. He still knew several of the dons; one, indeed, had been a contemporary, and three or four old Westminster boys, taught by him, were now undergraduates.

He felt his spirits rise as he opened the next envelope with its ebullient, but rather childish writing. It had been franked in France and was from his oldest friend, Charles Carfax. The wealthy but rather idle Charles was currently in the Hôtel Bristol at Le Touquet with his car, the love of his life. Rather like a man hopelessly smitten with a temperamental and demanding mistress, for Charles the unreliability of his car and its constant need for a mechanic's care seemed to be part of its attraction.

The last letter was from Mary. He had all her letters; although he had never told her this, even the ones written in her unhappiness after her brother's death, three years ago. For a while they had written quite often, but slowly the letters became fewer, though still as warm. When he finally opened the most recent, he held it for a second before reading it.

10 Warkworth Street,
Cambridge, 16 July

Dearest Laurie,

   I hope your stay with the Bolithos' friends has been jolly. I could have written to you there addressing it to: Laurence Bartram, investigator of churches somewhere near Stonehenge. I'm sure it would have found you, but I prefer to be able to think of you somewhere I know — back home sitting at your old desk — because you will read it at your old desk, won't you?

   Or perhaps you'll read it in bed, your very big for one, very small for two, bed. (Who do you think it was ever intended for?)

   I think of those rooms as our small world. I think of them, and you, often. You don't want me say 'if only' so I won't.

   As for me, well, you can see I am still here with Mother and Aunt Virginia. I don't seem to have become that independent girl in London.

   I have been down seeing Richard the last few days. He has been quite unwell and it was touch and go several times but at the minute it's go, or as go as things can ever be with Richard. I stayed with his old doctor. Very decent people. Richard's so thin now; you can see the skeleton within the man, and he has these sores on his heels and back. However wonderful the nuns are, I sometimes think his body is disintegrating. He smells — it's not about washing or clean linen — he smells as if he is already dead. I couldn't tell anybody but you.

What is the meaning of it all? What is his life? I can't ask the nuns because they believe every life is sacred and suffering has purpose, and because he believed all that, he might still agree with them, but it is hard not to think how he would have hated all this. But he can neither believe nor hate, of course. Sometimes I've been beside him and I've thought, if I really loved him, I'd pick up a pillow and end it all now. Would they hang me, do you think? But then I realise it is all about my discomforts, not his. And he goes on all right at present.

Poor Richard.

And just a bit poor me. Am I allowed? I am sorry to be such a misery.

M.

He put the letter down. He had started off by smiling, because he was indeed at his old desk, but his brief pleasure in her proprietorial take on his rooms, and her sense of humour, was soon dispelled by her news of Richard's condition. That, in turn, was superseded, fleetingly, by hope: that Richard was finally dying and that Mary would be free. To his shock, he recognised his own disappointment, as he read on, that the man was again holding his own, and hated himself for it. For the first time, he knew that living like this, vaguely waiting for Mary, waiting for another's death, couldn't continue. It was not a question of trying to love someone else, it was finding his own way forward.

CHAPTER NINETEEN

*E*veryone seemed in increasingly low spirits back at the Hall. The doctor had been and had provided morphine for Lydia. He had suggested her removal to a nursing home, but Frances had refused. The doctor said Lydia had days, at most, to live.

Patrick had struggled to shake off quite a severe chest infection since his immersion, while William was subdued and scarcely ever out of his office. Lydia was being nursed by all the women in rotation, day and night, but fatigue was beginning to tell in all of them. Julian sat by her bedside for hours but according to Susan, never said a thing.

Laurence began to wish he had delayed his return. After walking up to the village to give news of Jane to her relieved sister, he returned and sat in the library, reading. His clothes were damp. Rain had been falling off and on since breakfast; gusts of wind blew the roses against the library windows and scattered leaves down the terrace. As darkness fell, William had asked for a scratch supper in his office. He was leaving in two weeks, as soon as the new window was installed.

Laurence had gone down to see him, but a barrier had come up between them.

'Are you managing?' Laurence had asked, but had received answers of unconvincing good cheer.

'Frantically busy,' William had said eventually, making it clear he wanted to be alone.

Susan had cooked and for once it was an excellent dinner but Frances ate her supper quickly and returned upstairs. Patrick went up after one glass of port. Julian drank his way through most of a bottle of claret by himself.

Laurence went to the kitchen to thank Susan. She was washing up and looked tired.

'David's coming up for me with an umbrella,' she said.

'Your St Swithin let us down.'

'My David says it's all for the best,' she said. 'It's a blessing for the maze and the fish in the Kennet, and we've got the electric back on too.'

He went and sat in the library again. The day seemed interminable: it was still only just after nine-thirty. He didn't hear Julian come in until he sat down heavily in a chair, holding a glass of port.

'Poor Lydia,' Julian said, looking round vaguely.

Laurence sensed that for Julian too the news of her real medical condition was recent.

'I wish she'd never set eyes on Easton.' His voice was very slightly slurred.

Laurence didn't think an answer was expected, but he put down his book.

'There were only two things I ever loved,' Julian said. 'I loved Lydia, who was Digby's, and I loved Easton. And that was Digby's too.' He seemed to consider what he'd just said. 'It sounds foolish probably but I always thought that if I'd been her

317

husband, if we'd had a daughter, nothing would ever have harmed her. Nobody would have taken her. But with Digby ...'

It occurred to Laurence how often at Easton conversations about Digby petered out into nothing.

'She didn't love me. Even after Digby'd gone.'

Julian contorted his features into an unconvincing smile and Laurence noticed how he'd already slipped into the past tense when talking of his sister-in-law.

'I know that. She never had feelings for me. I'm too solid. Too dull. And she had money — younger sons don't get the rich girls, they get the sensible ones. But I never wanted anyone else.'

He fell silent again. After a few minutes he said, 'Perhaps I made a fool of myself — I know they all gossip about it. But it's too late now. She's failing ... this illness ...'

'The first time she came to Easton, she and Digby were about to announce their engagement. I'd met her at a dance the year before but she'd forgotten. They'd met in London. We had a London house then. Let it go when my father died. My father had been introduced to her at the house of the American ambassador. Not my father's sort of thing at all, but I suppose Digby wanted them to see what a match he had in mind. Then she arrived at Easton. So pretty. A lovely smile — she seemed happy all the time. So did Digby. Father invited round what passed for local society to meet her and to show them how well Digby had done for himself. The local families pronounced her charming, although I expect there was some whispering about her smart clothes — she'd only ever lived in cities: New York, Paris, London.

'Two days before the wedding, Patrick, Digby and I went up to town to celebrate. It was supposed to be just a dinner, but Patrick wanted to go to see Maskelyne and Devant at the Egyptian Hall.'

He paused as if he wasn't sure if Laurence knew who Maskelyne was.

'Magic.'

'I took my wife to one of his shows just before the war,' Laurence said.

The surfacing memory startled him. The war had made old, uncomfortable memories almost irrelevant, but now he remembered Louise's excitement and fear. She was young, they were both young, but Louise was always superstitious and she more or less believed in the spectacle that unfolded on stage. At the same time her conventional upbringing left her feeling she was indulging in something risqué, merely by sitting in the audience.

Julian looked surprised, either at being interrupted or at discovering Laurence had been married. Was it possible no one had told him? Laurence rather imagined everybody spoke of it behind his back, as much to protect him as to pass on gossip.

Julian shrugged. Whatever legerdemain Maskelyne had pulled off in front of the Easton brothers that night, it evidently wasn't the dominating memory of Julian's evening. He got up and took Laurence's glass without asking if he wanted it filled. Carrying it with his own over to the drinks tray, he reached for the decanter.

With one of the rare recollections of absolute clarity, Laurence had a picture of Louise as she had been that night. She was in dark blue, he thought, with black frogging on her hat and coat. She wasn't wearing gloves. They were newly engaged to be married and she abandoned her gloves whenever possible to admire the rather small diamond ring on her left hand, moving it so that its facets caught the light. But what he remembered most was how her eyes shone and, when the naphtha lights were extinguished, how she clutched his arm. The theatre was airless, the seats cramped, and she undid her coat buttons. Louise's perfume was sweet and flowery but as she moved closer he could also detect a trace of sweat, which somehow excited him. He was conscious of her softness as she leaned against his upper arm. They were surrounded by couples just like them and the theatre was alive with a mood of anticipation. The man next to him smelled strongly of beer and shouted suggestions to the performers on stage: 'Behind the curtain,' or 'It's in the other pocket.'

Julian returned holding their drinks and set one down by Laurence. He settled himself back in his chair for a minute without speaking, then rose to put some wood on the fire. He seemed restless. He walked to the window and stared out, though there could be nothing to see so late on a moonless night. He seemed to have lost the thread of his story.

Laurence was struggling with his own memories. How could he have forgotten that evening for so long? Maskelyne made claims only to devising extraordinary delusions; he had devoted so much of his career to unmasking frauds and mediums. Yet Louise was quite capable of believing the scene enacted for them as the curtain rose again.

A young artist sat at his easel. He wiped a tear from his eye as he gazed at the painting of a beautiful girl on a swing. He was clearly a widower. Louise, at Laurence's side, held his arm a little tighter. Finding his work too painful to continue, the artist laid down his palette and brushes, pulled a curtain over his canvas, sat back wearily in his chair and fell asleep.

Suddenly an angel appeared. Laurence had observed that she was a very shapely angel in gauzy, almost transparent draperies. Her swan's wings beat gently. The angel drew back the curtain and the previously inanimate canvas came to life. Louise gave a little gasp. A living, breathing young woman slid off the swing and stepped down from the canvas. Tiny lights played on her golden hair. Her footsteps were silent as she crossed to her sleeping husband. She placed a hand on his cheek and, with an expression of ineffable sadness, kissed him. The angel looked on benevolently, her hands clasped in a position of prayer. Then the girl turned almost immediately and returned once more into the picture. The angel drew the curtain in front of it again just as the artist stirred.

The young man woke with a look of joy, jumped to his feet and ripped the curtain aside, but there was only his lifeless painting. As the desperate artist covered the canvas with kisses, the young woman reappeared. The lights had altered, Laurence recalled, so that she appeared to be insubstantial. When the artist clutched at her draperies, his hands appeared to snatch at nothing; she had disappeared into thin air. The curtain came down as the artist fell to his knees.

Beside him, Louise sniffed and took a small handkerchief out of her bag. Tears were running down her cheeks. A woman behind them was weeping more loudly.

They had gone back to the Chelsea house of Louise's aunt and uncle. Louise was quiet. She sniffed occasionally but she still held closely to him. Part of him knew she had a streak of ridiculous sentimentality but a greater part of him responded to her vulnerability. When they left the theatre, two drunks had nearly bumped into them. One was singing 'Our Lodger's a Nice Young Man'. He'd looked Louise up and down, said 'Very nice' in mid-song and muttered something to his friend. Both men had laughed. Laurence had been aware that Louise's relatives would not have thought Maskelyne an improving entertainment and wondered if he could ask her not to speak of it.

He was relieved when the maid who let them in told them their hosts were still out at dinner. When the maid retired, Laurence poured them two drinks. Louise's was Madeira, he thought. Unused to spirits, Louise drank it still standing, almost in a single go. His own brandy burned his throat. They were both still on their feet, close together but not touching. As he took the glass from her, he saw them both reflected in the vast mirror over the console table. The effect of seeing himself with her – one image, his height, her slightness, his face in the light, hers in the darkness, their shoulders only inches apart – was arousing. Here was a portrait of a man and his wife. A man and his property.

As he moved closer she bent slightly backwards, keeping her balance with her fingers splayed out delicately on the rosewood surface. He put his arm around her and pulled her to him. Part of him was conscious of her slight, warm body in his arms. Her face was damp when he kissed her. As he did so more vigorously, he was conscious of her hair falling down. He pulled out a single pin that threatened to impale him. He kissed her again and her lips opened. Coals shifted in the grate, making him jump, but Louise seemed oblivious and kissed him back.

The taste of her excited him more than he could ever have imagined. He could feel her tongue, not resisting now but soft; it seemed an undreamed-of intimacy and he could taste the sweet Madeira of her mouth. When he moved his hand to her breast, it was as if he had suddenly developed nerve endings where none had ever existed before. He felt the rough lace and tiny pearl buttons under his hand, felt her small breasts rising and falling.

They both subsided on to the window seat. Louise's eyes were closed as her lips placed gentle kisses on his cheeks. He undid two buttons of her blouse, fumbling ineptly. She made no attempt to stop him. Another two, then three more. Her blouse gaped, revealing the ribbon and tucks of a lawn liberty bodice. Her pearls lay across the hollow at the base of her neck. He kissed her and followed her hairline, lifting her heavy hair. She smelled almost animal. When he slipped his hand into her blouse, he could feel her nipples hard through the fine cotton.

The woman in his arms was so unlike the Louise he knew,

who had allowed him some kisses but who had always drawn back if they went on too long, and he had never known any other woman. Watching his hand as if it did not belong to him, he moved it again and as the cotton was pulled taut by his fingers, he could see the outline of her flesh beneath.

An ache that was almost a pain threatened to overwhelm him. He pulled her down on to the floor, still expecting that at any second she would return to her senses. Her skirt had ridden up a little, and he gazed briefly at her slim legs in their white stockings, one knee slightly raised, then followed its curve with his hand. Louise sighed deeply. Her skirt moved upwards with his cuff, exposing naked thighs. He kissed her more hungrily, even as he wondered for the first time when her aunt and uncle might get back.

After that, it was all a blur. He was touching her in ways he had only ever dreamed that he would when they were married. The textures and sensations were simultaneously strange and utterly familiar. She was making small movements against his hand, her breath coming quickly. His arm was under her head.

He fumbled at his trousers, even more clumsy with his own buttons than he had been with hers. And then he was on top of her, pushing her thighs apart and trying to enter her. It was awkward and he heard her whimper of discomfort. Yet he was like a man possessed, forcing himself on. He had a sense of being far deeper inside her than could ever be possible, as if he was totally safe and enfolded. Almost as soon as he felt himself gripped by her, the pent-up energy in him exploded and he heard himself cry out. As spasms gripped him, he looked down. Her eyes were wide open and with a look almost of horror.

The minute he'd finished, he rolled off. She seemed about to cry again.

'I'm sorry,' he muttered.

He didn't know what else to say. She was doing up her blouse with trembling hands. He wanted to touch her and assure her that it would be all right, to tell her how beautiful and wonderful she was, but the moment passed. Then to his alarm he heard the front door open, distantly down the hall. Louise had heard it too. She jumped to her feet, searched for her pins and feverishly pushed the weight of her hair back into an untidy pile. By the time her aunt and uncle entered the room, they were both sitting sedately in chairs, well apart. Her aunt looked at them suspiciously but her uncle was full of his usual bonhomie. Louise made her excuses after a few short exchanges, and she and her aunt retired to bed. Laurence went through the motions of conversation with her uncle.

Over the following weeks they never mentioned the evening again. It was as if an act that should have brought them closer together, which Laurence had found exhilarating and extraordinary, albeit shameful, had left them strangers. A month or so later she told him she thought she was pregnant. A few weeks after that, they had a quiet wedding, during which both her parents and her aunt and uncle looked at him reproachfully. Louise, though happy in her pretty dress and her flowers, was disappointed at being cheated of a big celebration and embarrassed by her own thickening waistline. He felt ashamed.

Outside their proper little world, with its rules and conventions, the armies of Europe were mobilizing. By the time Louise miscarried, shortly after their honeymoon, it was obvious that a far wider world was about to reach them. As Louise wept at Maskelyne's and Devant's dreaming widower, she had just four years left to live, while he was about to see more death, destruction and horror than he, or anyone, could have imagined that night. It seemed appropriate that that old world, and what had seemed to them like innocence, had vanished in a magician's illusion.

*

He had almost forgotten Julian's presence. It was the sound of a thud in a distant part of the house that brought him back to the present. He looked down at his glass — he had never had a great head for alcohol. Julian too had started at the faint noise and began talking as if he'd never fallen silent. Or perhaps he had been talking all along and Laurence had forgotten to listen?

'... and when we left the show, Digby was all fired up because he'd loved the spectacle, but he was irritated by Patrick explaining how the tricks worked. He changed the subject to Maskelyne's tips for winning at cards; he'd read his book and thought he couldn't lose.

'Patrick was pretty blotto, he was only eighteen and not used to it. I was less so. We went off to some gaming club of Digby's and the idiot tried some of Maskelyne's tricks there. But of course they were wise to him and, anyway, a child could have seen what he was up to. Because he'd been there before and was quite a good customer, and probably because his efforts were so crass, they simply tried to escort him from the club, but Digby started shouting and flinging his arms about, knocking chairs over.'

Julian shook his head. He glanced at Laurence almost as if pleading with him to understand that Digby was more honourable than his account revealed.

'He was as strong as an ox when he was riled. I was worried someone who knew him would tell Lydia.'

He paused. Points of firelight played on the cut glass.

'Patrick was half amused, half distancing himself, but he was trying to keep us out of a fight. Anyway, it turned out the chauffeur knew this house, in Chelsea. Run by his sister, of all things. Digby'd been before. We were welcomed like old friends. It was a very superior brothel. We're hardly through the door when two girls are all over Digby. Digby was always a man of the world but it was two days before his marriage to the most beautiful, sweetest girl in the world. I hated him then.

'Digby went off with two blowsy whores.' His voice was shaking. 'Crashing into the French furniture. Breaking a glass. I imagine it all went on his bill.' His voice was full of remembered anger. 'Patrick had gone up with a very young, slender girl – she was perhaps sixteen – red hair, loose, looked younger with all her paint on. She was giggling – I could hear her all the way upstairs. Patrick gave me his look as he went up behind her – as if he was simply amused, a spectator, not like Digby. Some swarthy girl was trying to sit on my knee. She was solidly built, with thick wiry hair. I could smell her, animal like, under her perfume. She had a strong accent – Spanish or Portuguese, perhaps. She was wearing a peignoir. She picked up my hand, pressed it to her breast. Rubbed herself with my fingers. They brushed a crucifix.' He looked almost ill, retelling it all. 'I took my hand away, she put it back. It was like that game we had in the playroom. Perhaps she took it as a slight. She picked up my hand again and then she noticed my hands and crossed herself, dropping them as if they were diseased.'

He looked down at his scars. When he spread his fingers, the deformity was more obvious and more ugly. A bony nub showed the site of the missing finger and a thick web of skin stretched between it and his index finger. The rudimentary surgery had left stiff-looking whorls and ridges.

'I pushed her away and refused any alternative girl the madame of the house tried to offer me. I sat and drank expensive champagne until Patrick and Digby reappeared.

'Two days later Digby and Lydia were married at St George's, Hanover Square. A Friday. Bad luck, the servants said. Lydia looked as beautiful as I've ever seen her – and then she was gone: to Paris and Florence.'

The door to the library suddenly swung open. Frances stood there, with frightened eyes. Laurence's first instinct was that, like him, Julian thought Lydia had taken a turn for the worse.

'The police are here,' Frances said. 'They want to speak to Julian.'

Inspector Thomas came in behind her, leaving the door open. An unfamiliar uniformed officer was standing in the hall. The inspector spoke before Julian had a chance to rise from his chair.

'Mr Julian Easton,' he said, looking Julian straight in the eye. 'I have come to ask you to accompany me to the police station at Devizes to answer questions in connection with the death of Mrs Nancy Ennals of Stoke Newington, London.'

'Am I being arrested?'

'No, sir.' The inspector's face was sombre. 'But you may wish to ask your solicitor to be present.'

'It's not necessary,' Julian said.

Frances looked horrified. 'No. Julian would never ...'

But Julian just walked across to the inspector, interrupting her.

'Yes,' he said, 'we'd better go. Could you get my hat, Frances?'

Frances made no move, as if frozen. Then she made a tiny noise of distress and went out. They heard raised voices in the hall.

'What the hell's going on?' Patrick burst into the room, breathless and untidy. 'For God's sake, it's a bit late, isn't it? Frances says you've arrested Julian.'

'Not arrested, sir. Not at this juncture. We just want a formal talk with him.'

'But he can't choose not to?'

'It would probably be unwise, sir.'

'Who on earth is this woman? Why was she here?'

'We are hoping your brother may be able to help us with that.'

Laurence expected Julian to protest but he just stood there with a half-smile on his face. Frances, standing in the doorway with Julian's hat, appeared stunned, but it was Patrick whose face crumpled.

'No,' he said. 'No. Julian would never hurt a woman or anybody, come to that. You've made a mistake. Don't take him away.'

Laurence thought he was about to grasp hold of his brother and pull him back.

The inspector turned to Julian. 'By the by, I expect you will be glad to hear, sir, that we have located Margaret Petch. She has been given the wherewithal for a train ticket home although I gather she is worried that you will not want her back here.'

At what must have been one of the worst moments of his life, Julian's whole face was filled with happiness.

'Maggie,' he said. 'Thank God.' His voice flooded with relief.

'Where was she?' Patrick asked.

'No doubt she'll explain to you, sir, and we've only had it from our colleagues down south. Apparently she had an argument with the grandfather who didn't want her to go to London. So she decided to find her mother. It seems she'd tried to look for her mother every year at the Mop Fair, despite the old man forbidding it.'

He took out and opened his notepad.

'Scudamore was the name of the fairground family your cook had it in her head the mother'd gone off with. Then Margaret saw their ride in a *London Illustrated* photograph of the Wembley fairground. The fair folk had their fun, gave her the runaround and took a bit of money off her, but of course eventually they said they'd never heard of her mother. By then she'd missed you and was scared to come back. She'd still got a little money.'

He looked pointedly at Patrick.

'Courtesy of Mr Easton. Which got her as far as the south coast but she was caught trying to get on a boat to France without a ticket.'

'*France?*' Laurence asked, astonished. 'Going where?'

'Bapaume,' the inspector said. 'Apparently her father's buried there. Your driver said he told her when they were at the exhibition. Nobody previously had ever got round to informing her he had a grave.'

Laurence thought there was the faintest accusation in the inspector's tone.

'Fortunately a sergeant at Portsmouth, a former military man himself, took pity and paid her fare home. One of my men will pick her up at the station. She's very apologetic. Very embarrassed at causing so much trouble.'

'But now,' he looked firm but sympathetic as he took Julian's arm just above the elbow, 'I must ask you to come with us, sir.'

Laurence had known as soon as he saw Inspector Thomas that it must be the bag in the cistern that had provided identification for the body. He felt as if he had betrayed Julian.

'It's better this way,' Julian said. 'Look after Lydia.'

He went out, suddenly sober and calm. He had feared something, Laurence thought, and now that it had come to pass, that fear had evaporated.

Frances stood looking at Laurence and Patrick. She was trembling.

'I gave her money to buy fripperies at the exhibition,' Patrick said, defensively. 'I didn't mean her to take off.' And then almost without pausing, he added, 'God, what a mess. They can't suspect Jules. I know he's not involved with this. What can we do?' He ran his fingers through his hair. 'Who is this damn woman? I'm going to ring old Vereker. Julian needs a solicitor.'

The door banged open and David stood there, looking wild. He hadn't even bothered to knock first. His boots left a muddy trail behind him.

'Why've they taken Mr Easton?'

None of them spoke for a second. Then Patrick said, 'They've identified the body. They seem to suspect him of ... involvement in her death.'

'They only want to ask him questions,' Frances said.

'You're a fool then if you believe that,' Patrick said, spinning around. 'He's as good as arrested. They believe he did it and they just want him to confess.' His hand shook as he opened the cigarette box on the table.

David was shaking his head so vigorously that his whole body moved with it. Rain dripped off his hair.

'No. No. No. He never touched her ...'

His voice was hoarse. Still speaking, he turned and left as quickly as he'd arrived. They could hear him crash through the back hall door.

'What on earth was that about? I just don't understand,' Frances said. 'We don't even know who she was. Why should Julian, Julian of all people, have killed her? Why do they think he did it?'

Laurence felt cold unease. 'I'm going to see if David's all right.'

'He was always thick with Julian,' Patrick said.

But Laurence knew it was more than that. In the kitchen he could hear raised voices and then shouts more of distress than of anger. As he went down the passage, a door slammed and through the laundry-room window he glimpsed David getting into the Eastons' car. Someone was screaming. He passed the gun room to see William, looking startled and horribly marooned, by his table.

'What the hell's going on?'

'I'm trying to find out. The police have taken Julian but David's going off in a frenzy.'

Then they both heard a terrible, ugly howl of pain. The hairs on his arms prickled.

'Oh Jesus,' William said.

Laurence rushed next door. The back door to the kitchen was wide open, banging against the dresser. Rain was already driving in. On the floor by the stone sink lay Susan, curled up, sobbing piteously.

He put one hand on her shoulder and the other on her arm.

'Is it the baby?' he said, although he knew instinctively it was nothing as simple as a woman going into labour. He sat beside her on the floor, stroking her back, while she took great gasps of air and continued to cry noisily.

William had hauled his wheelchair to the doorway. Frances appeared behind him.

They lifted Susan to a chair. Pregnant and half fainting, she was heavy. Her hair stuck wetly to her cheek. Suddenly she started to retch. Frances seized a bowl and the woman was copiously sick. When she seemed to be over the worst, Frances wrung out a damp cloth and wiped her swollen face.

'Try to breathe slowly,' she said. 'You'll feel better.' Frances sat down next to Susan.

'His wife. She was his *wife*,' she said.

Frances said nothing.

Susan gasped again, then wiped her nose with the back of her hand.

'He had a living wife all the time. She was no good. But she was still his wife. She wasn't dead. He wasn't a widower. He said it was an accident. She was drunk.'

'David?'

Susan nodded, then gave a mad laugh.

'So the baby's a bastard because we were never man and wife. Least, I thought we were ... We had such a nice ... But it wasn't even his name. Eddings.'

'What happened?'

'I don't know,' she wailed. 'He was racing off after Mr Julian.

331

He just said she was his wife and when she came she tried to attack him and she fell and he put her in the church and . . . the police thought it was Mr Julian.'

She began to sob again and then, lowering her head to the table, to bang it rhythmically against the wood.

'Don't, Susan,' Frances said. 'It's not good for you or for the baby.'

Susan howled and the men both jumped. She looked half deranged with grief.

'And what's going to happen to the baby and me, now David's killed that woman? Where shall we go? What can we live on? I'm not going in the workhouse. I was born there. Bastard child of a bastard child. It would be better if we died.' And then, seemingly exhausted by her own emotion, she whispered, 'He didn't love her. He loved me. He did.'

Laurence realised that in some extraordinary way Julian had gone willingly with the police, not because he was guilty but because he knew all along that David was.

As Lydia lay dying, Susan's child was born in the night in a bedroom at Easton Hall. Ellen Kilminster and Mrs Hill delivered her of her large, bellowing son. Mrs Hill sat with her while Ellen went down to make her some tea. Laurence found her weeping in the kitchen.

'I don't care what they say David's done,' she said. 'A better man you couldn't hope to meet.'

Julian arrived back in the early morning. Laurence heard the sound of an engine and went down. Julian looked stale and tired as he emerged stiffly from the police motor car. He stopped by Laurence and said, 'Bad business, Bartram. Bad business. We must look after Susan.'

'Susan says the woman was his wife.'

Julian nodded. 'Yes. Apparently. Unhappily. He deserted her, let her think he'd been killed in the war. But someone who'd known him before saw him at Wembley. Which was just what he feared and why he was so unwilling to be there.' His tone was one of resignation. 'Some wily chap followed the children from the car, bought them ices, then asked Nicholas or Maggie where they and the chauffeur came from. They gave whoever it was my name and the location of the Hall. Unfortunately for me, the dead woman, whom I suppose we should call Mrs Ennals, left it in her handbag, which someone found in the cistern.'

He smiled gently at Laurence.

'But by then the police had already discovered she had spent some time in a public house near the station, where she asked where the Eastons lived and became loud and obnoxious enough to be remembered. It was nearly enough to put a noose round my neck. It was certainly enough to connect her with us. But her behaviour should help David's case.'

Julian fell silent, but while he was speaking it had dawned on Laurence that, if David couldn't prove the death was an accident, he could hang and that hiding the body as well as the bigamy made his actions look worse. He remembered Susan telling him David had helped in the original search for Kitty. Possibly he'd found the vault then.

'I'm going to lie down,' Julian said. 'Need to think.'

'Susan's had a son,' Laurence said, as Julian started up the stairs. 'All well and currently upstairs, I'm afraid.'

'Good. Good. Exactly where she should be, poor woman. I don't think anything will happen very fast,' he added, taking each stair like an old man. 'I'll ring my solicitor. A good brief should save him from the hangman, though not from prison, I fear.'

Chapter Twenty

The cell had a low ceiling. There were bars over the windows, and a worn stone floor. David was lying on a thin mattress on a metal bed, his face to the wall. He must have heard the door being unlocked but he didn't move.

Laurence stood awkwardly. The position of the sun was such that David lay in darkness, while the light illuminated the thick, battered door. In minutes this brief ray of summer would pass by. Laurence thought that if he were confined, unlikely to be free again, he would lie watching for that sun, absorbing all he could of it. But then perhaps it became too much a marker of time.

'You didn't have to come.' David's muffled voice caught him by surprise. 'You don't owe me anything.'

'I know.'

'I'm only here for another day,' he said. 'I'll be moved to the assizes. The barrister thinks I'll get a long sentence but the injuries and the drink support my story.'

'I came to give you some news. About Susan.'

Suddenly David was alert and turned around to face him.

'She's all right?'

Laurence nodded. 'Yes. She's well. Your son was born yester-day.'

David swung his feet to the floor. His face was transformed, all the weariness and hopelessness slipped away.

'And she's well, you said? You wouldn't lie?'

Laurence smiled. 'She's very well. And your son. I've seen him.'

Frances had been holding the baby in her arms, a large boy, his skin seeming too big for him, damp-haired and furious. Laurence had struggled to contain his emotions. Had his own son looked like this for his short life?

'She says you wanted him called Stephen?'

'My father,' David said. 'I've spent the last six years denying his surname, so it's right he live again through his grandson. But Susan's all right, you say?'

'She's well. She was delivered at the Hall.'

Laurence didn't tell him how bitterly Susan had wept as she held her little boy. He was wrapped in a shawl that had once been Kitty's. Lydia must have kept it secretly for so many years.

David seemed to be fighting to absorb it all.

'And I thought you should know that the family want Susan to stay,' Laurence said. 'She and the baby can live in the lodge until you come back.'

Again David seemed to be struggling. Eventually he said, 'It was the best place I ever knew. The fields, all that grass and the garden: getting it back to how it used to be. I thought if I had a child it could grow up there, never have to deal with the city and with mean-spirited folk. I know Easton had had its troubles, but not for me and Susan. We didn't have the history, we just had the days, one by one.' His voice was slightly hoarse. 'And all that space — she'd say the Hall was like a tiny doll's house — made little by the bigness of the downs and the forest and Salisbury Plain. Susan had never seen far outside Reading, you see.'

The shaft of sunlight had already moved on and now just the top corner of the cell was lit. In a few seconds it would be gone.

'I shall miss it, you see.' And then he said, 'Mr Bolitho's yews will do all right. Mrs Easton will have her maze.'

'I'm afraid not,' Laurence said and paused. 'I'm here instead of Mr Easton to tell you about Susan because Mrs Easton died last night.'

'I'm very sorry to hear it. She's been very good to us. But she was a very sad lady.' He looked up. 'What will happen to Easton?'

'I suppose Mr Easton is the heir, as Mrs Easton's daughter has never been found.'

When Julian hadn't been sitting, holding Lydia's hand, he was out alone around the estate, the small dog at his heels. Heaven knew how he would manage without David over the next few years.

David said, 'I'm glad. He loves the place like I do, only he grew straight out of it. If anyone can make something of it, Mr Julian can. What he wants, he only wants for Easton.'

Laurence said nothing. He too hoped Julian could finally come into his own.

'He was brave,' David said, 'out in France. Not just once either. He went back under fire for his brother. Was badly hit himself. Mr Easton took both guns and saw off three Germans and then he dragged his brother close to some ruin. It was nothing – no kind of protection. Told the powers that be it was his brother saved *him*.'

David looked up.

'Captain Digby Easton, I never met him, not so as you'd count it, but he was as much a coward as Mr Julian was a hero.' His face became almost ugly. 'The lost men of Easton?' he said, mockingly. 'Well, it was Captain Easton who lost them and Mr Julian who tried make it all right. His nerve went only right at the end.'

'In what way?'

David's face had frozen again. He said, 'You'll have to ask him.'

After a while he added, 'When I'm back, that maze will be full grown.'

'Susan will walk in it. Your son will.'

They sat in silence, David leaning forward slightly, his eyes lowered, kneading his hands. They were a countryman's hands, weathered and scarred.

'In some ways it's harder to know there's a child,' he said after a while, 'that my boy will grow up knowing his father was ... Well, what I am. I used to think I was good on my own. In the war I was usually alone and I liked that best. But now I've got someone to miss.'

The warder knocked twice, briskly, on the door.

'Time to go, sir.'

Two minutes.

'What did you really do in France? What happened when you saved Mr Julian's life?'

He thought the man wasn't going to reply, but just as the warder knocked again David looked up and said, 'I was a sniper. Hiding and camouflage was my game. "No one sees me, but I see everything." In the end you start to fancy you've become the bush, the tree, the hidden place you're blending into. You know it and it knows you.' He almost smiled. 'Like me at Easton.'

'Do you want Susan to come? Do you want her to bring the baby ... ?'

David shook his head vigorously. 'I don't want her to see me like this. And if I saw the baby, well, it would be one more good-bye. Harder to leave, you see, if I'd got to know him.'

Laurence stood up. The door was opened from outside.

He held out his hand. David didn't see it at first, although

337

when he did, he held out his own without getting up. Laurence pressed the small bit of paper – the note Susan had once sent in a tin to France – into it. David appeared not to notice. Laurence hoped he wouldn't let it drop on the floor but as he left the cell, David spoke.

'Tell her . . . tell her, that the day I opened her biscuits was the best day of my life, except for the day I first met her, when I thought she was the most beautiful girl I ever saw.'

CHAPTER TWENTY-ONE

*L*ydia was laid to rest at Easton. There were few people from outside the village but almost everyone from within it stood around the grave. The melancholy feeling Laurence had that Lydia was being laid to rest among strangers, far from where she had started her life, dispersed.

He did not know all the faces, but clearly, from their proximity, they knew one another. There was the Kilminster cousin, Victor, who could only have arrived in the last day or so, his hair cropped, his face creased from the Australian sun, his wife at his side. Maggie, slightly nearer to the graveside, was supporting her grandfather with her arm. On the far side of her, Susan held her baby son, invisible in a shawl and clutched tightly to her as if someone might take him away too. Laurence could hardly bear to look at her. Her expression was fixed, her face pale. Formerly animated and cheerful, she was now gaunt with purple smudges under her eyes.

David was due for trial the following week. Julian had secured the very best criminal barrister for him. The lawyer, an almost-legendary KC, was confident that the evidence and David's wartime courage would save his client from the gallows. Nevertheless, he would be gone a long time, although Laurence knew Susan would wait for him at Easton.

Ellen Kilminster stood next to Susan, a black ribbon around her straw hat and clutching a handkerchief in her hand. The two Kilminster boys, one now nearly at manhood, stood with their heads bowed, with Ethel, in an old-fashioned grey dress, slightly too small for her, between them.

The one surprise, when Laurence entered the church earlier, was another familiar face. It was Jane Rivers, out of place in her city shabbiness, but with a strong resemblance to her sister, now that he saw them both together. Catching his eye as the coffin was carried out to the churchyard, she held his gaze for a second before glancing away.

Eleanor, her face almost hidden by the deep brim of her hat, had pushed William's chair down the stone path, and they remained there, a little distance from the grave. Laurence had talked very little to either of them since Eleanor had returned from London for the funeral but he thought William looked better, although he had already lost the colour he had acquired over the summer spent outside. There had been few on hand to push him out into the grounds over the last two weeks. It was hard not to see Eleanor's brief affair as a further demonstration of how few options William had; how weakened he was by his injuries in a way that all his wit and good humour could never disguise. As well as having to cope with the pain of losing Patrick, Eleanor had to live with the knowledge that she had also struck William a hefty blow.

In the church, the scaffolding for the new window was in place, ready for work to start. As the sun blazed through the Magdalene's draperies, the vicar said prayers not just for Lydia but for Digby Easton, then for the lost men of Easton and, finally, for Kitty. If there was an irony in Digby being mourned alongside the wife he had, in effect, doomed, no member of the family seemed to register it. As the vicar spoke of the repose of Lydia's soul, Laurence thought that, at last, a generation, their secrets and their troubles were being laid to rest.

Lydia's coffin was lowered into the ground beside those of her parents-in-law. The untidy churchyard grass had been roughly cut two days earlier and there was a smell of hay. The early afternoon was warm and completely still. A thrush sang from somewhere just behind them.

Frances stepped forward, her face pale, taking a small handful of Easton earth from the pile by the graveside. Almost before he heard it patter on the coffin below, she had thrown in a musk rose, one of the blooms that had grown so densely this summer below Lydia's window. She quickly stepped away.

Julian, looking calm, followed Frances's handful of earth with his own. Brushing the last dust from his hand, he stood at the grave and gazed down for a moment, head bowed. But as he walked away he seemed to draw breath and stand straight and he looked towards the twenty or so villagers who were now his tenants. Laurence wondered what the years of bearing Lydia's pain had been like for him. He was glad Julian was now the rightful heir to Easton and that there were now young men, young families, who might help him make the small estate viable. Perhaps in time he would even marry. When the short ceremony was over, Julian talked quietly to Susan as she held her child.

It was Patrick who had surprised him. His decision to stay at Easton, to restore the old vicarage, was perhaps the biggest change in any of them. He hoped to take up a position at an Oxford college, where he could catalogue and publish the extraordinary finds at Easton. The awkwardness between him and his brother was still there — but so, it was clear, was affection. At the point at which Julian had been arrested, Patrick's shock had been visible. He might remain angry while he believed Julian had been implicated in concealing Kitty's death, but when he thought his brother might be taken from him, he had looked bereft.

Frances too, though often red-eyed over the last week, had seemed relieved when Lydia eventually slipped away peacefully on the first really fine morning since the heat of St Swithin's Day. Laurence had had a single exchange alone with her and he thought they had both found it painful.

'What are you going to do?' he said.

'What, now I have no purpose here?'

He felt clumsy. 'I meant, what would you like to do?'

'Julian's asked me to stay,' she said, 'to set up the schoolhouse again.'

'And are you going to?'

'I might, later. But I'm going home first.'

He must have looked puzzled because she said, with a half-smile, 'America. New York. It's the only home I ever had. I left it when I was three. I can remember only shadows – vague impressions – but it is the only place I ever lived where I had a right to be. And it's the new world. I want to be part of it, for a bit at least.'

'But where will you live?'

'I have distant cousins,' she said. 'I never knew them. Some of them weren't born by the time I left, but they've invited me to stay.'

'I see.'

She took his hand. 'Laurence, you think I was falling in love with you. Perhaps I was. Perhaps you thought you could fall in love with me if you concentrated. But it would never have worked, not really. I was an antidote to loneliness. And I have compromised for far too long to be second-best now.'

He looked at her without speaking. If he had been coming to love her, and he had never really known whether he was, or whether he simply saw the potential for love, the feeling had never been stronger than at that moment. He knew that, for a split second, they had the chance to retrieve whatever lay between them, for him to retrieve her, but neither seized that opportunity.

Eventually he just managed, 'I'm sorry.'

'Silly ass,' she said. 'You've been quite marvellous. You *are* quite marvellous.'

'You'll be crossing the sea to your city of skyscrapers and I'll be going south by train through Europe to my city of ruins,' he said, 'which probably tells you a lot about us both.' Then he added, 'Thank you,' although he didn't quite know why.

Now she stood there talking to Eleanor and William. She was leaving from Liverpool in ten days, while Eleanor and William were off to London the next morning. Julian was driving them there and then seeing the family lawyers. Laurence would be travelling by train. He had two further tasks to complete and then, he thought, his life at Easton was over.

He moved to intercept Jane Rivers as she walked a few steps behind her family.

'May I come and see you later?' he said.

Her eyes on her sister's retreating back, she simply said, 'All right.' There was something resigned in her tone.

When he turned to follow the family back to the house, Patrick was waiting for him. He raised his eyebrows as Laurence caught up but said nothing.

After a quiet lunch Laurence walked up to the village. Victor Kilminster's wife was carrying a basket of apples, which she said she was taking to the Petches. She beamed at him.

'Good send-off,' she said, with a strong Australian accent.

'Indeed. She deserved it.'

She pointed towards the Hall. 'It's beautiful,' she said, 'just like the schoolbooks. Just like Victor said it was.'

'Your family must miss you.'

'My older brother was at Gallipoli. Didn't make it. But my younger brother – looks like he's coming to join us.'

She grinned again, the gap between her front teeth giving her a schoolgirlish charm.

'He's a great man with sheep. Mind you, this little place will seem like a garden to Bill. He's been working on a farm a thousand times as big as what's here.'

He raised his hat to her. 'I'm glad. Mr Easton must be delighted.'

He walked on to Ellen Kilminster's cottage. The front door was open and he could hear children and adult voices. He knocked on the doorpost. It was Jane Rivers who came to the door.

'Would you walk a little with me?' he said. 'I just wanted to ask you a few things.'

'I'll fetch my cardigan.'

He could hear her exchange a few words with her sister, then she came out again. She walked beside him silently, as they headed for the small pond and the bench.

'Mrs Easton left me something in her will,' she said. 'Mr Julian told me.'

He nodded. 'I think she felt you'd been hard done by.'

She reverted to silence for a few moments. 'She didn't have to,' she said, but it was obvious she wasn't going to be any more forthcoming.

After a while, still not looking at her, Laurence said, 'The last time we spoke you said that Maggie's mother's man was a devil. I thought you meant Joe Petch. But you didn't mean him, did you?'

344

She didn't answer, but he could sense her breathing faster.

'You meant the mother's lover. Not the gypsy everybody said she'd run off with. Because there never was such a man.'

When she still didn't answer, he decided to put it in a way that he calculated might make such a religious woman uncomfortable.

'It was a lie. I think you knew it and perhaps your sister did. Perhaps even Walter did?'

This time he looked at her. Her head drooped.

'I think it was one of the Easton brothers.'

It was a statement, not a question.

She raised her head again and looked straight ahead. 'He *was* the devil,' she said. 'Handsome and funny and a tempter. And in the end he became cruel and wicked.' In her forthrightness he could hear her Wiltshire accent more clearly.

Laurence still wanted her to give him the name.

'He started good but became like his father,' Jane said. 'None of us were safe. But some of us women were stupid. And some loved him. He was easy to love when he wanted you to love him.'

'Are you talking about Mr Patrick?' he said.

She looked at him with incredulity. 'Of course not. Mr Patrick wouldn't hurt a fly. He was a lovely young man. A bit hot-headed but well meaning. And Mr Julian would do anything for Easton folk. It was Mr Digby could be a devil. Not always, but when he was in his cups he thought Easton was his plaything and all of us with it.'

'Including you?'

Her nod was imperceptible.

'I was engaged. I did like him ... but I didn't want ... Mr Digby said he just wanted a kiss but then he didn't take no for an answer. He always got what he wanted.' Her voice was bitter. 'Said I'd been making sheep's eyes at him. It was in the room next to his own child. I was asleep. He smelled that bad of brandy.

345

Put his hand over my mouth and he . . . did it. But I wouldn't of called out anyway because of little Kitty.'

She paused and looked embarrassed.

'After, he cried, said he hadn't meant it.'

'I'm sorry.' He was so much more than sorry that he couldn't express it.

'And stupidly I told Robert. He could see I was upset, and he and I, we'd never . . . I wanted to save myself and he was angry, but as much with me, as he'd thought I was soft on Mr Digby, and although he seemed to be going to help, in the end he was a worse man than Mr Digby.' She screwed her face up in pain.

'And Maggie's mother?'

'Mr Digby played the same trick on her. She told me Maggie was his. Yet she was really sweet on him. Believed it all. Stupid woman.'

But she said it sympathetically, shaking her head.

'Mr Digby said he'd set her up in London. She told our Ellen. He made promises. But none of us ever heard from her again. She left Maggie behind because Mr Digby didn't want her along. But it was Joe as really loved that little girl. I don't think he ever dreamed she wasn't his. And me and Ellen, well, we weren't going to tell anyone. Joe Petch was a good man and didn't deserve it. And . . .' she faltered.

'Nor did Mrs Easton.'

Jane Rivers cleared her throat.

'Do you think she knew? About all of this?' Laurence asked.

'She loved him. For her dream of him — how he was. Sometimes I wondered how rotten does he have to get for her to see it, but in the end she did see it and yet she still loved him.'

She seemed to be going to say more so he remained silent.

'She was a proper Christian lady like that,' Jane said after a few minutes, but he had the feeling she'd been about to say something else. 'Always forgiving.'

'Can you keep a secret?' he asked and was surprised when she flashed him a look of contempt.

'Mr Patrick . . .'

He hesitated, considering how best to put it. Could he trust her not to gossip?

'Mr Patrick believes – he saw something that made him think – he has *always* thought Mrs Easton and Mr Julian . . .'

She was staring at him, obviously astounded, and he realised she thought he was going to say that Patrick believed his brother and sister-in-law were having an affair.

'He thought that they were somehow involved in Kitty's death.'

He knew immediately he should have said 'disappearance', not 'death', but she leaped in.

'No.' It was almost a cry of pain. 'Mr Julian just wanted things to be right. Always. And Mrs Easton would have given everything she had to keep her little girl.'

'But sometimes strange things happen – accidents. Mr Patrick has spent years with the awful thought that his own brother, now his only living relative, did this. It's why he left Easton – to avoid them.'

When she didn't answer, he turned to face her. Tears were running slowly down her cheeks. She sniffed twice, felt in her sleeve and brought out a neatly ironed, finely stitched handkerchief. As she unfolded it and wiped her eyes, he thought of all the flowers she embroidered in her cheerless rooms in south London.

She was shaking her head. More tears fell.

'But he was wrong,' she said. 'He got it wrong.'

'Mr Patrick?'

She nodded. 'Mr Julian never did anything except to help.'

'But what about Mrs Easton?'

'Mr Easton hurt her. Not at first. Not deliberately then. At first it was things – things she had from her dead mother he broke. But as it went on, he hurt her too. Usually in ways you couldn't tell.'

'Digby Easton?'

'If he'd been drinking.' Her voice was hoarse and she blew her nose.

Laurence gazed across the cottages to the hills. The trees were darkest green in late summer, the grass of the downs worn almost through to the chalk. All this had been Digby's and still he had become a man of violence. He had good health, good looks, a rich and beautiful wife, a healthy child, and yet he had become a monster.

'He bruised her. Tore her ear, pulling an earring out,' Jane Rivers said. 'By mistake, Mrs Easton said. There were worse things …'

She looked embarrassed. The handkerchief by now was a sodden rag.

'Why didn't she stop loving him? She even lost her baby.' Her voice held a note of wonder. 'She wouldn't see nice Dr Maurice because the doctor would of known.'

Then she said, very quietly, 'We all knew. Not that she said, though once or twice she'd say that she'd made Mr Easton angry, or that he hadn't meant to do this or that. Excuses. But we all knew. Her lady's maid left and she never employed another one. Didn't want anybody to see her, I reckon. Used to dress herself, despite who she was.'

There was a note of censoriousness in her voice.

'Did away with living-in staff. Mr Julian moved rooms. Mr Patrick – well, it may of been like you said, him going away, but

I bet he couldn't face her any more. Miss Frances, I think she didn't know for a while, not when she was young because Mr Easton, back then, he seemed charm itself, not a bad man most of the time. But he got worse and she grew up and even she saw in the end.'

He was ashamed by the revelations, despite never knowing Digby Easton, ashamed that a man, ostensibly just like him, could do such things.

'Did you ever see Mrs Easton hurt? Bleeding?'

'Once or twice. She was ever so ashamed. But she sent me down to ask Cook for ice. I didn't say anything below stairs.'

'So is it possible that what Mr Patrick saw was nothing to do with what happened to Kitty that same night, but an injury?'

'Of course it was. Mr Julian was always dealing with his brother's mess. And all the time, the men here, they loved Mr Digby. He had the cricket team and was its star; he had them beating for his London shooting pals and they spoke about what a good shot he was, as proud as if it was them that held the gun; how he and his horse were like one when he was hunting. How he'd tell jokes when he'd had a few, man to man. How visiting ladies or women serving beer found him attractive. It was . . .' She struggled as if trying to understand it herself. 'It was as if he was the man they all wanted to be. A hero.

'And if Mr Patrick saw blood on her, if that's what you're coming to,' she said, 'it was her own husband who'd put it there.'

'Do you think — I know it sounds incredible — that Kitty's father had killed her and the family knew?'

It was a new idea but it seemed to fit the circumstances.

'He didn't kill her,' she said without a moment's hesitation.

She'd stopped crying, but Laurence could see out of the corner of his eye that her cheeks were blotchy.

'He was like to do anything if he was drunk but he didn't do that.'

He looked up and saw Ellen Kilminster coming through her cottage gate and walking towards them. Jane Rivers hadn't yet noticed.

He said hurriedly, 'Like to——?'

This time when she turned towards him he thought she must catch sight of her sister but she appeared to see nothing at all. Her look was one of absolute misery.

'He'd started on Kitty. She was little, gentle, not a strapping lad who needs a bit of discipline.'

'Dear God,' he said and then, 'I'm sorry. I just——'

'It's all right,' she said bleakly. 'God was just watching, letting Mr Digby do what he liked and doing nothing about it. Just like the rest of us. I don't know why. I prayed and prayed. Then when I heard he'd died, I thought God had his chance in France and made sure he never came back. But why all the lads with him? All our lovely boys? And Kitty was gone by then.'

As her sister reached her side, looking at Laurence accusingly, the tears started again. Ellen sat down and put her arm around her sister. Jane sat rigidly, continuing to stare straight ahead of her.

'What did he do to Kitty?' Laurence asked. 'Help me to understand.'

Jane nodded and he noticed Ellen's expression change. He thought, she knows; whatever Jane knows, she knows too.

'He was harsh,' Jane said.

'She broke her arm,' Ellen said.

'*He* broke her arm,' Jane said, forcefully. 'He didn't mean to – he never meant to. He wanted her to get on a pony – she was trying to edge away from him to me, and he dragged her by her arm and swung her on to the pony. The arm broke, although we didn't know it straight away. She was screaming and it seemed to make him angrier. He called her a freak.'

Suddenly she stood up and started pacing back and forth, her arms wrapped around herself. It was hard to remember the composure she had displayed the first time he had met her.

'He said he was cutting her fingers off – she had extra fingers—'

'I know.'

Jane appeared relieved that she didn't have to explain. Perhaps she too had some residual discomfort about what country people had once regarded as a sign of being a witch.

'He didn't want a circus freak for a child, that's what he said before – that they were disgusting and he should have done it years ago. He'd give her brandy and it'd be done in five minutes. But this time poor Mrs Easton, she was crying and begging him not to. She took hold of his arm and he shook her off. She fell against the door and cut her face.'

Her hand went up and touched her own.

'Mrs Easton told Mr Julian and the two brothers had a fearful row that evening. We could all hear it. Cook was frightened to send the girl up with their dinner. Petch was in the kitchen – he'd been fixing something and Mrs Hill gave him his tea. He said she should put rat poison in Mr Digby's brown Windsor if he were going to do Miss Kitty's fingers. Mrs Hill said perhaps it was like puppy dogs' tails but Petch said no, he remembered when poor Mr Julian had it done when he were a lad. Awful, he said it was. What you wouldn't do to an animal.'

She seemed to be speaking more to Ellen than to Laurence.

'But Mr Julian going on, that's what made him really set on it. And that's when she knew what had to be done. Perhaps she still loved him, but what could she do? Mrs Easton? If she went away he'd have the child and then what? There would be nobody to defend her.' And I was going anyway in the autumn so there'd be nobody for Kitty.'

He felt uneasy. Was she about to tell him something that confirmed Patrick's story, at least in outline?

'She could have divorced him, surely?'

Jane looked at him as if he were an idiot.

'She wasn't English, despite seeming it. Kitty was the heir. Do you think he was going to admit what he did? He'd say Mrs Easton was a mad one. Do you think some judge in a wig would think Kitty should be brought up away from Easton Deadall? He'd probably be Mr Easton's best pal.'

Ellen put her hand out but Jane ignored it.

'You don't have to say any more,' Ellen said.

He thought afterwards that for a few minutes Jane was wrestling with her conscience. He wondered whether he should give her assurances that, whatever she told him – and he was certain now that she would tell him something – he would keep it to himself, but he wasn't sure that was true. He wanted to be able to tell Patrick that Julian and Lydia had done no harm to Kitty.

'What's done is done,' Ellen said to him as much as to her sister. 'Mrs Easton's dead now. No one can hurt her again. Mr Easton too. He's where he can never hurt anyone any more.' She was looking anxiously from one to the other. 'Bad blood,' Ellen said. 'Like father, like son.'

'We made a plan,' Jane said very quietly. 'He'd been going for Kitty for a while. She made him angry, her being so shy of him. But I think it was also to pain Mrs Easton. The first time I was worried, it was because he was trying to get Kitty to drink wine and she didn't like it. When she wouldn't, he forced some of it down her and she was scared and bit the glass and it cut her. Later, it was like the more harsh he was to her, the more timid and frightened of him she became, the more he went at her . . .'

'And then the kitten,' Ellen said.

He felt Jane shudder. 'I don't want to talk about it. It was a bad time. It was like something in him was poisoning him.'

The shock of it was still with her, Laurence thought.

'Drink,' Ellen said wearily. 'Our dad was another one for the bottle.'

'So after that,' Jane said, 'when he'd said he was going to take her extra fingers off, Mrs Easton says to me — she was that afraid — what if we arranged for Kitty to disappear? As long as Mrs Easton was at home and no one saw anything, they couldn't suspect her; it would be like a kidnapping or that she'd got lost.'

The nanny faced him, her emotions increasingly under control.

'It was how much she loved Kitty. She would never be her mother again. I would leave service — they wouldn't need a nanny, I'd just wait for them to let me go — and keep an eye on the child. I'd place her with a nice family. Look after her. I'd take her in, once the hue and cry died down. Tell her mother how she went on. Then one day, maybe long ahead, Mrs Easton could slip away from Easton and him, and start again. Change their names. Maybe take Kitty to America.'

Now she squeezed her sister's hand.

'We thought we were saving her. He was getting worse. We didn't know he'd die not so long after.'

Laurence could see the reasoning behind it, but at the same time the absolute folly of their decision. It was naive through and through, but then they were desperate. Whatever had happened, it was clear the plan had gone horribly wrong.

Jane started and stopped several times, once looking at her sister.

'It was my fault,' she said. 'My fault for trusting Robert.'

Slowly her story reached the one point Laurence had already guessed.

'I thought he'd be all for it, he was that angry with Mr Digby after. After what he did. To me. Before, he wouldn't hear a word against him. He thought he was Mr Digby's confidant. That's what he called it,' she said mockingly. 'And he thought Mrs Easton was a trial to her poor husband. "A sensitive blossom", he called her. Said it was hard for a man in Mr Digby's position to put up with a wife who had the money. Said it was humiliating. And for a country gentleman to have a city girl, a foreigner, for a wife. As if you could ever tell Mrs Easton and Miss Frances weren't English through and through.'

She sounded more indignant at this than at whatever betrayal Robert might have inflicted on her personally.

'Robert said he couldn't call him on it because we'd be out without characters and never get another job as good.' She looked bewildered.

'It wasn't your fault. None of it was your fault,' Ellen said angrily. 'And even Mr Julian was weak. It shouldn't have been you and Mrs Easton. They should have dealt with their own.'

Jane didn't appear to have heard her.

'Your former fiancé – he took Kitty from the house and then away by car, didn't he?'

This time he had both sisters' attention. Ellen's eyes were on her sister but Jane looked only at him.

'How did you know?' Ellen said after a few seconds.

'I didn't know. I guessed. I glanced out of the bathroom window not long ago and saw how few other windows looked over the stable yard. The old servants' bedrooms had views half blocked by the balustrade. Unless he was very unlucky, a man could take the child out the back, a few feet across the yard and into the car in a minute or so, and never be seen.'

Ellen Rivers kept her eyes averted as he continued.

'No one but Robert left the house until after the police had been. He took her out in the night — presumably she'd had a powder to keep her asleep — and he went off with her when he was sent to get help. He'd counted on it being him who'd be sent.'

In speaking of Robert's scheme, Laurence had a sudden insight into Julian's motives in sending David off, also to get help, after the body had been found in the vault, but he said nothing now.

Jane was wet-faced with misery, her head bowed, as she took up the story.

'Robert left her with a woman who'd come up to Marlborough from London, special. We hadn't known how to arrange that bit. A safe place for her to go to straight off, until I could be there. There was a woman that he'd paid. She'd have another child with her already so it would look natural. And we were so relieved. They were going to cut her hair off, put her in boy's clothes and leave before the alarm had even been passed to the railway station.'

'Did he fetch her from her room?'

For a second Jane Rivers seemed surprised rather than sad. 'Of course not,' she said. 'If he'd been seen upstairs he'd have been in big trouble. Mrs Easton gave me one of her sleeping powders. I gave a quarter to Kitty.'

She shot him an almost defiant look.

'Mrs Easton put one in her husband's Madeira. His brothers always took port.'

'And then?'

She made another of the odd twitching expressions he'd noticed before.

'But things went wrong?' he said, watching her face intently.

They killed her, he thought with sudden insight. They gave

355

her too big a dose in their need to make her sleep and they killed her. Everything made sense: Lydia's behaviour, Jane Rivers' and Robert Stone's speedy departures. The rupture of all those relationships. Guilt.

'First, Mr Digby'd had a big dinner,' Jane said quite calmly. 'A lot of wine, even for him. He didn't drink all the Madeira. The powder took too long and with the wine it seemed to set him off on one of his fits. He laid into Mrs Easton. He was furious with her going up early or something. Later she told me he'd shook her, she was expecting, but ... she was already ... losing the baby. He said she was disloyal, telling Mr Julian he was going to cut Kitty's fingers off. It had been a joke, he said. But now she had told about it, he'd no option, not to look a fool. He'd do it in the morning and it would be her fault.

'So we had to go on, despite she was taken unwell, it was the night we'd planned to take Kitty, and Robert was ready downstairs, and the woman he'd got to take Kitty to London – there'd be no way of stopping her from coming. Mrs Easton struggles down to get me to help her, I turn the lights on – she's bleeding – but Mr Julian hears, he's only four doors away. She needs him to go back in his room, so she goes with him and lets him comfort her. He keeps brandy up there and he gives her some. My door's ajar and I don't know what to do but she hasn't said to stop. I lift Kitty out of bed. Open the laundry chute, which we've oiled two days before and tested to see that it's quiet. All the time I can hear Mrs Easton crying. I don't know if it's partly to cover but mostly it's because she's reached the end. I tuck Kitty up with her little doll, wrapped in a blanket, and down she goes. Peaceful as an angel.'

Towards the end of her recitation her voice began to wobble.

'But just as she was going down, I thought' – she began to cry more heavily – 'she looked like I'd laid her out. Like a dead child ready for the grave.' Her face twitched with grief and incomprehension. 'I never saw her again.'

'Why not?'

'Robert was there. He did as you thought, or so he said. Told me Kitty was in London before the next day ended.'

'Tell him about Robert,' Ellen said, her voice suddenly hard.

'Robert, it turns out, had his own ideas,' Jane Rivers said. 'A week later he sends Mr Digby a ransom note. I tell him it's stupid but he says, why not make a profit. That even if Mrs Easton gives me money, keeping Kitty will be expensive and we've run all the risk. We'd go to prison if they knew. Mr Digby, he's all over the place. You'd almost feel sorry for him. Robert won't say exactly where Kitty is to me and Mrs Easton until he thinks it's safe. Doesn't trust me or her not to blab to the police. Mrs Easton's beginning to get afraid – Kitty's in London and only Robert knows where.

'And then Mr Digby and Robert between them, they make sure we never see Kitty again.

'Mr Digby confides in Robert about the note, of course. Just as he always does. You'd wonder who was the master sometimes. He says to drive him to leave the money where the instructions say and where they say Kitty will be exchanged. Robert thinks it's very funny although it means he can't pick the money up easy. But on the way Mr Digby tells him, he's bested the kidnappers as it's not all money – between is cut-up papers. Robert knows he isn't going to give Kitty back anyway. He was just trying to get more. He's furious that Kitty's pa is trying such a stupid trick on him but pleased because he's made Mr Digby suffer a bit more for it.'

'But he still wouldn't say where Kitty was,' Ellen said, as if trying to hurry her along.

'He said she was quite safe,' Jane said softly. 'And perhaps she was. Safer than here probably. He knew we wouldn't say. Not me and not Mrs Easton. If he'd found out, I'd have gone to prison and Mr Digby would either have beaten Mrs Easton to death or divorced her.'

Laurence thought there was something else bothering her but she didn't continue. Ellen was stroking Jane's arm.

'She didn't mean any harm,' Ellen said defensively. 'She risked a lot to try and save Kitty.'

'I know,' he said.

He wondered at the strange alliance of a landowner's wife and her daughter's nanny. How frantic they must have been. And ever since they had also watched Frances's and Julian's lives being over-shadowed and circumscribed by uncertainty over Kitty. But were they right about the danger or had they just persuaded them-selves that Kitty was unsafe because her father was too boisterous with his timid daughter? Would he really have mutilated his own child? In the claustrophobic world of Easton Deadall, small things might have seemed large. Or had Lydia even wanted to punish a husband who had so punished her?

'Robert had a sister,' Jane said. 'I told you. And I thought Kitty might be with her. I thought she might be the one who'd taken her to London. It had to be someone he could trust. But although he boasted of how he'd pulled it off, he never let on. And I didn't know who she was from Adam. I was dismissed. Robert wouldn't talk to me.'

'He cut her dead,' Ellen said angrily, 'Robert. Next thing, he's given in his notice. We hear he's gone to London, thinks he can get a better job.'

'He disappears?'

'I never even knew if he had kept Kitty with him,' Jane said, with huge sadness. 'Sometimes I wonder if I might pass her on some street. I loved her so much but I don't know if I'd recognise her. I never told a living soul, not even my vicar, not even Ellen until this week.'

Laurence wondered whether the child had lived long after Robert had her in his power. Had she ever gone to London with an unknown woman? She was a liability – not an infant but an intelligent child of five, a child who knew who she was. Why would Robert keep her or give her to another to keep if he was no longer being paid by Mrs Easton? But perhaps he *was* being paid, in a sort of excruciating, protracted blackmail? Any mother could probably be induced to go on paying indefinitely on the faint chance the money would reach her child. But they could never know, now that Lydia was dead.

Jane looked up. 'I pray all the time that she's all right. Somewhere.'

He didn't have the heart to respond that, in the event she was alive, it was unlikely she was in any way all right: a delicate, highly protected five-year-old propelled into a huge city through a mixture of malice and greed.

Ellen said, 'So now you know and I suppose you'll tell Mr Julian and he'll do what he has to do.' She stood up. 'It's a pity because Jane would like to stay. And she's a good worker. And we've got each other.' There was a weary air of resignation about them both.

'No,' he said, getting up.

He'd already made his decision long before the whole story came out.

'There's no point. It's too long ago. There's been a war. Robert is untraceable. Kitty would be nearly grown up by now.' He didn't add, if she ever had that chance. 'Mr Easton, Mr Julian Easton, needs to look to Easton Deadall's future.'

Then he touched Jane Rivers on the arm.

'You too. You made a mistake. But it was trying to save a child. We all might have done the same.'

359

The two sisters said nothing. He watched as they walked towards the cottage, their heads slightly bowed, Ellen's arm in Jane's. When they'd closed the front door behind them, the village seemed momentarily deserted. Then he saw, at a distance, Victor Kilminster and one of his nephews, in a field between the village and the Hall, sawing up the branches of a fallen tree.

CHAPTER TWENTY-TWO

*H*is last night at Easton was a quiet affair.

Maggie and Ethel had waited at table. Patrick, Julian and Laurence sat up in the library long after Frances, Eleanor and William had retired.

'We'll see the solicitors after the weekend of course,' Julian said to Patrick. 'But Vereker sent me a copy of the letter Lydia left with her will.'

He took a folded piece of paper from the mantelpiece and gave it to his brother.

'She encourages her trustees to have Kitty declared dead, you see.'

'She's right,' Patrick said, when he handed it back. 'Was right. Easton can't belong to a ghost.'

Julian seemed surprised by Patrick's forthright response but there was something else there: gratitude perhaps. He cleared his throat and went on, 'She says she couldn't do this in her lifetime because she had always believed Kitty was alive, but if there had been no trace of her at the date of Lydia's own death, things should be clarified.' He looked at his brother as if still anxious for his approval. 'Vereker agrees. He believes this is long overdue. I think he would have suggested it anyway. But I don't want to act without the consent of you and Frances.'

'It should have been done years ago. Certainly after Digby's death,' Patrick said.

'Thank you.' Julian hesitated and his fingers stroked the stem of his wine glass. 'She left Maggie a sum of money.' He smiled. 'Jane Rivers rather more. I have told them both.'

'The nanny?' Patrick appeared to be taken aback by this but then said, 'She was hard done by, I suppose. But still, after all this time.'

After a pause Julian said, 'There's a small amount for Susan's child.'

Patrick looked up. 'Surely she can only have added that relatively recently?'

'Two months ago. Her will remained substantially the same after she remade it when Digby died but she had added a codicil. Long before everything happened with David, of course,' Julian said.

'Do you think she knew she was dying?' Laurence asked.

'Yes,' Julian replied. 'Yes. It was I who resisted.'

'Damn Digby,' Patrick said. 'Damn him to hell.' He pushed his chair away from the table and went to the side table where the decanters stood on a silver tray. 'I'm getting some port. Laurence? Julian?'

When he sat down again he looked at Julian almost accusingly.

'You always got him out of scrapes. Why? Why didn't you let him clear up his own mess?'

Julian seemed about to speak but said nothing. He picked up his glass.

'You knew what he was like,' Patrick repeated.

Julian shrugged. 'Not always,' he said. 'Not when we were younger. Not when Lydia first came.'

Patrick looked thoughtful and slightly sad. 'No. Not always but, by God, at his worst he could be nearly as bad as Father. And you were always blind to it.'

'And you just went away,' Julian said.

The words were simple but the intensity of feeling between the brothers was massive.

'I thought he was so strong then,' Patrick said. 'But really it was only because he was older and the favourite. Now, I think he was a weak man and afraid of being found out, first by Father and then by life. Digby shone when things were going well. But when they didn't, he was lost and frightened. And so he bullied people to keep things his way. I loved him, but you were a much better man.'

Julian looked astonished but Laurence saw his expression change to comprehension and relief. The words tumbled out.

'I thought it was just drink,' Julian said. 'And after Kitty I didn't even blame him for that. And he could still be old Digby so much of the time.'

It occurred to Laurence that Digby had had the good fortune to possess the gift some people had that made men and women love them, but how dreadfully he had squandered it.

Cautiously, it seemed to Laurence, Patrick spoke again.

'Eleanor thought – of course she never met him – that it's possible Digby had symptoms of the disease he handed on to poor Lydia. But it came out as anger and volatility. Apparently that's common. A bright, intelligent woman like Lydia can become a confused, crippled invalid. An ordinary man can become a monster.'

Julian nodded slowly, looking down. 'I was never going to be a hero, not with these grotesque hands.' He spoke with loathing.

'But Digby could have been. He *was* Easton. I wanted him to be the best possible version of himself.' He thought a little and added, 'I just wanted him to deserve Easton and Lydia.'

Although Patrick was silent, he was gazing at his brother with a look of undisguised affection. Laurence recalled Frances saying that Patrick needed to choose what sort of man he would be, but he thought Patrick had always been a decent man, just scarred by believing his brother part of a conspiracy to conceal a child's murder. It was Digby Easton who had had two sides to his nature. In Digby, cruelty had eventually and disastrously overwhelmed so much that might have been good.

After a while, Julian said, as if it was bothering him, 'I helped him seem the sort of man they would follow into battle. And in creating that man I killed them all as surely as he did.'

'No,' said Patrick.

'Yes. He was no good as a soldier, you see. And I couldn't cover for him there. Not away from Easton, not in the end. Rations were short, the weather was lousy, the men were sick. Morale was at an all-time low. And Digby ... you could smell the drink on him. He'd fall asleep in his boots, still clutching a bottle. He looked dreadful.

'He was making bad decisions.' Julian hesitated. 'Stubborn to the point of folly. Bullying the men ... Peter ... the boy was just seventeen. We only took him because he wanted to come – all the other Easton lads were going on this great adventure and the pay would come in useful for his mother.'

Julian ran his hands through his hair. His forehead shone in the light of the fire and the marble scars were ridged on the taut skin of his hand. He sat, staring at the flames. The dog whined uneasily but was stilled by Julian's touch. He stroked it without really seeming to notice its presence.

Laurence realised Julian was not yet ready to give Patrick the whole truth of what had happened. It was the thing David had hinted at, the thing Joe Petch had half written of in a letter home, the thing, presumably, that Victor Kilminster had known all along.

'None of it matters,' Julian said. 'Our orders were to advance and we did advance. And most of the 6th Wiltshire were killed in the process. Ironically, Digby thought he was going away from the guns, but when I told him he had lost his sense of direction, he wouldn't listen. We had hardly started to move when they opened up. Cross-fire. It took less than five minutes, I should think. We ended up dead or dying along the Bapaume road. And perhaps it was for the best,' he said, wonderingly, 'because everybody hated him by then. He could never have brought them home.'

Julian had an odd sort of smile on his face but Patrick's expression was one of deep sadness.

'I should have died. I go over it time and again. A piece of shrapnel caught my jaw and I was on the ground with the others. But they are dead and I am . . . here.'

Laurence said quietly, 'But David was there too, wasn't he?'

'He watched it all,' Julian said. 'He was a sniper. A crack shot, about to get his sergeant's stripes. David was hidden in a clump of broken trees overlooking the road. He'd been there all day. He just sat there, camouflaged in his ghillie suit, waiting for the senior German officers to ride up once they'd secured their positions.' He smiled slightly in recollection. 'What a sight he was.'

Laurence already knew all about the men who created their own rules and disguise for this warfare of loners. They were usually countrymen, men who had handled guns and stalked prey before the war.

'They could sit there for hours and hours,' Julian said. 'Never moving, never startling so much as a pigeon, becoming part of

365

the landscape, just waiting for their quarry. I'd lost so much blood that I was hallucinating. I was just sitting by Digby's body when two Germans appeared from nowhere. Perhaps they came to see if we needed finishing off. I watched them get ready to kill me — they could take their time, I was too weak — when David gave up his hiding place and shot them. He saved my life. And that was it, I suppose.'

Julian paused, his eyes on the dog. When he raised them he held Patrick's for a long time, saying nothing. Was there something more? Laurence wondered.

But then Julian just said, 'That's it. Not a very glorious story.' He looked away, embarrassed.

'It wasn't your fault,' Patrick said. 'None of it was ever your fault — not Father, not Lydia, not France. Not David.' He hesitated. 'Not Kitty.' And there was real compassion in his eyes.

'I owed him,' Julian said. Laurence thought he meant Digby but Julian went on, 'David. I'd said to him that if there was anything I could ever do for him, I would.

'Near the end of the war he wrote to me. He'd heard Digby had been mentioned in despatches.' He faltered. 'Easton needed them to have died bravely, you see. He'd seen the shambles we'd really been in but he said nothing. He asked about Easton. Said he'd been thinking we'd need hands to replace all the losses. Said he would like to work for me. He knew the area from childhood. His family were dead. He didn't want to return to his pre-war life in London. He was a widower, he said. Wanted to marry again. Said the war had changed things. I suppose I guessed there was some petty criminality. Or money owed. But I liked Susan — I would have had it out with David if I'd known the truth. He said he was a hard worker. Wanted to start a new life. And I judged him a good man.'

Patrick looked sceptical but Laurence knew that, in war, where your life might depend on it, quick judgments might be made.

'And Victor Kilminster?' Laurence said.

This time Laurence thought Julian seemed uneasy.

'No mystery there – he'd tripped over. One of those freaks of war. Tripped, went down and stayed down as his friends were ripped to pieces about him. Came to see me in hospital while I was waiting to go back to Blighty.'

'And he knew exactly what sort of a leader of men our brother had turned out to be?' Patrick took out his cigarettes with an unsteady hand. 'And Kilminster, who'd grown up with our estate workers, whose cousin had been led to his death by Digby – he was willing to go along with it all and be sent away?' Patrick said.

'I suggested I could set him up in Australia. I spoke to him, man to man. He knew what I was offering. He wasn't very happy. I said he'd have to spend any remaining leave in London. Never go home. At first he was dead set on coming back to Easton and I couldn't have stopped him, but over the next few days I think he saw what it would be like. He didn't have living blood family beyond Ellen's children. Apart from me, he was the sole survivor. He would be the only man in the village who was not old or a child or impaired. It wouldn't have been easy.'

Patrick nodded. 'Still, I would have thought he'd want to come back.'

'Well, he did come back,' Julian said. 'He had six years of it in Australia and turned up here once more.'

'No wonder you were cross,' Patrick said.

Julian shook his head. 'Not cross. Afraid, perhaps. And I hadn't given him more than the fare and the contact. But yes, I thought if he came back he'd probably tell people that Digby had failed. How he'd behaved. And now that he's here, you know, I don't think he will. How could it help?'

Laurence was uneasy. The story still felt incomplete.

'But what about David? Who was he before? Who was Susan?' Patrick said. 'Did you ever know?'

'David was David Ennals, not Eddings. He changed his surname but to one that sounded and looked similar, so if he ever met anyone who had known him years ago, they would think they'd simply misheard. He's a clever man. Susan was just Susan,' Julian said. 'She'd met him exactly as she said she did – she sent a message in a tin of biscuits. Anybody might have picked it out, might have thrown it away, joked about it with their pals. But it was David who took and kept it. David who was unhappily married and unable to escape. David who spent hours on his own. Then this small message arrives, "full of innocence and goodness", he said to me.'

'She might have been a married grandmother of sixty,' Laurence said. But he knew himself that holding on to a dream, however improbable, might help a man survive.

'Did he tell you this?' Patrick looked perplexed.

'No, of course not. Not then. He told me the whole story only when his real wife was dead.' Julian looked away.

'You always knew?'

He hadn't just known, Laurence thought with certainty; he had helped David hide the body. Laurence had looked closely at the walls in the church on the way back from talking to Walter Petch, to see whether the practical David might have set up a temporary pulley, such as Petch had once fixed up for the former Mrs Easton. But he had found nothing. Without such a pulley, there had to be two men to lift the hatch and he doubted it was David who knew about the hiding place beforehand.

'He came and told me. He'd been spotted at the exhibition. He had been afraid it could happen; it was why he wouldn't leave the car, but he hadn't known he'd already been seen.

'His real wife turned up at the lodge. She was very drunk.

Susan was up at the Hall. David was at home. He said she was standing in the doorway, unsteady on her feet, but looking triumphant. There were baby clothes airing on a clothes horse – gifts from Ellen Kilminster and from Lydia, but at first his wife was standing with her back to them. He said she was smiling all the while, saying she would just wait for his lady friend and introduce herself, and then she'd go on up to the Hall to talk to his employers.'

Julian stood up and walked to the window.

'He asked her not to. To accept that the marriage had been all wrong, that he didn't make her happy. And then she asked for money to go. He didn't have any. He started to explain when she turned to look around the room and saw the layette Susan had been putting together.'

Julian stopped and then went on, 'I have no reason to doubt him. He was almost in a state of collapse when he came to see me. He said Susan might have walked in at any second. That woman – his estranged wife – was screaming and although their place is a way from the village he was frightened someone might hear. She grabbed some of the baby things and began to tear them apart. He took hold of her, trying to stop her, to calm her, and she spat in his face. Then she stumbled to the stairs. He tried to pull her back by her dress. He pushed past her, stood barring the bedroom door. They wrestled. She lost her footing and fell straight back.

'David said he heard the crack as she hit the stone floor. He said she was so instantly quiet that he knew it was bad. She was still breathing but oddly, and while he sat next to her there, frozen, trying to decide what to do, she stopped breathing altogether. He was trained to think and act quickly but he had limited options. He dragged her out to the wash-house and covered her with sacks. It was unlikely that Susan would go there until wash day the following Monday. But the weather was hot ... He collected some quicklime from the village.' His eyes went to Patrick apologetically. 'We used it in the war.'

'I know what it's used for.'

'The next morning, when Susan was in the village, he drove the car up to the lodge and loaded the body into the boot. If he had a plan, I think it was to take her away from the village and bury her, hoping they'd never tie her in with here. But he couldn't be gone long or we'd be asking questions. He couldn't leave her where she might be found in case she'd told someone back in London and they tracked him down.'

In a way Julian seemed relieved to finally get things off his chest.

'He'd just put her in when Susan reappeared, saying I wanted him back at the house. She looked bothered, he thought, and presumably he was quite a sight – he was bewildered by what had happened and sweating with the exertion of hauling his wife's body into the boot. So he couldn't go off straight away and he couldn't load a spade into the car with Susan watching. So he drove up to the Hall.'

'What stopped him taking her away later?' Laurence asked.

'I came along,' Julian said. 'I'd only wanted him to talk about closing the sluices because of the drought. But David was standing there, looking shifty, frankly. He's not very good at lying. And then I saw the bag, it had fallen out of the driver's door. It was a cheap handbag, but not old and it was on the ground by the car. I picked it up and was just about to ask him what it was when he started to cry.'

It seemed to Laurence that David had thought himself safe, forgetting to look behind him to see if the past was catching up. He'd woken up that day with a woman he loved, a child about to be born and a good life. He'd gone to bed that night as a bigamist, covering up a death, possibly manslaughter, possibly, a court might think, murder. No wonder he cried.

Julian's expression was desolate.

'It was his dead wife's, of course.'

'Why on earth didn't you turn him in then?' Patrick asked. 'I mean, he's a good man but a woman was dead.'

'I owed him a life,' said Julian.

It was oddly put but there seemed to be nothing much more to add.

After a few minutes, Laurence said, 'When we found the body and you sent David off to get the police, you were giving him a chance to escape, weren't you?'

'Yes. But he didn't take it. He wouldn't leave Susan.'

It got darker and the house fell silent. It was only as Laurence was thinking that he should take himself to bed that Patrick spoke again.

'And you were willing to take the blame for David,' he said, 'because he saved your life? Or because of Susan and the child?'

Julian shrugged, but said nothing.

'How did you know about the vault?' Patrick sounded matter-of-fact.

Laurence felt a surge of something like relief. Everything that he thought he would have to keep a secret, Patrick had worked out for himself. It was not so surprising. Patrick had once struggled to open the entrance with Laurence. He too knew it took two men.

Julian didn't seem perturbed, merely weary.

'Mother. When Father found out what she was doing – her chapel, her secret religious practices despite his views – he waited until she was down there and cut the pulley she had rigged up. She must have been in the dark for hours.'

He looked at Patrick in a way that suggested the easing of a burden.

'She didn't appear at dinner, or lunch the next day. The next dinner she was still absent. Father said she was indisposed. Then as I was preparing for bed I heard this noise. I thought at first it was a vixen or an animal in a trap. But it went on rising and falling out in the night. I went into Digby's room. It wasn't so loud there but he could hear it too. Eventually we got up, went outside and followed the sound to the church. I was about twelve, I suppose. I can tell you, my hair was standing on end – part of me thought it was some ghost or werewolf. Something from Digby's more ghoulish stories.'

'And it was Mother?' Now it was Patrick who looked stricken.

'After that, I swore I'd never go down there again, I'd forget about it. She was in a dreadful state. Half mad, with dirty, broken fingernails. She wouldn't look at us, or talk to us. She was just babbling prayers, going round and round and round in circles. Her candles can't have lasted long and, as far as I can gather, she'd been blundering around in the dark – things were broken. I think she believed Father was quite capable of leaving her down there to die.'

'Did he say anything?' Laurence asked.

Patrick jumped in. 'Of course he didn't. This is the Easton family – we talk a lot but say nothing.'

'No,' said Julian, 'he never referred to it. And she was dead just months later. She was pregnant at the time he shut her in. And Digby – Digby was beside himself, which is why I could never understand . . .' He stopped abruptly.

'About Lydia.' Patrick finished the sentence for him. 'I hope he came to hate himself for that, however ill or mad he may have been.'

Then Julian said vaguely, 'It felt like a good place for David's wife. Under the church. Full of Mother's spirit, not Father's.'

But they still had to shovel quicklime on her, Laurence

thought, in the hope she would soon be unrecognisable. And where was she now?

'I'm tired,' Julian said, almost like a child. 'I want to go to bed now. I've had enough.'

'Shoot me.'

He thought he must be talking to himself. But then he realised the eye below him was moving. The dead man blinked and the mouth had opened.

'Shoot me,' it repeated. 'Just — get on — with it.' Each phrase seemed to exhaust the body because it closed its eye again and stopped speaking.

He looked down, thinking it had been easier when he'd thought Digby was dead. Then it had all suddenly been straightforward. Now, apart from the mess of God knows what, sticking out of something badly adrift at the top of the leg, Digby was making demands again.

There was a hoarse noise, an almost mechanical sound. And yet although he had thought he might be mad, and although he'd thought that usually if blood was black and clotted and drew flies, rather than bright and fresh and increasing like his own, the man would be dead, he knew that Digby was still alive.

'I'm finished,' Digby said. 'They've shot my fucking balls off. And my hand.' He began to sound as if he were trying to find the energy to cry. 'You wouldn't let your bloody dog go like this, Jules.'

Julian looked down at the stump. He could see the white bone and something yellowish that had emptied into a sticky pool. So Digby's perfect hand had been blown off, yet he still had his scarred, imperfect ones.

But why was Digby still alive?

As if in response to his thoughts — or had he spoken aloud? — his brother seemed to drift into unconsciousness. For a time there was just the sound of his breath rattling and the occasional animal whimper.

'Please,' Digby said.

He tried not to think about the patrol, or about Digby emerging, late and malign, from another night of drinking.

He'd been along the line at a meeting with the CO, covering for Digby. When he returned it was all as good as over. Digby had decided to send Peter out on a recce the following morning. He was smoking a cigar. Julian couldn't reason with him. In reality they were cut off. The lines had been severed by a stray mortar. Ahead of them was a German machine-gun, behind them, German trenches. He had known all along that Digby had misread the maps.

Bert Kilminster challenged Digby. He was the NCO. And he'd promised the boy's mother he'd look after him. And it was a stupid decision to send Peter. One stupid decision after another. He'd be a sitting duck in the early light.

As Kilminster turned away without waiting to be dismissed, Digby said, 'The boy's a blubbering nancy. We don't need him.'

Kilminster had hit him then and knocked him flat in one smooth movement. Digby lay on the ground, rubbing his bleeding nose and looking amused. He'd drawn his pistol.

'Striking a superior officer,' he said, mockingly. 'You're a dead man, Kilminster.'

He was pointing it very carefully. The men had stood, frozen, as if frightened Digby would point it at them next, their eyes all averted from Kilminster.

Digby was on his feet, brushing off the dirt.

'So off you both go. Take the lad with you if his mama wants him tucked under your wing.'

'Please.' Now Digby's head had turned minutely towards him. 'Water,' he mouthed.

Eventually Julian felt clumsily for his canteen, unscrewed it and shook it gently. It was part full. He held it towards Digby, let the water trickle into his brother's mouth, down his chin and into the earth. Digby's dark tongue moved across rough lips. He seemed to be trying to focus.

'You killed Kilminster,' Julian said.

Silence. Then, 'Jerry killed him.'

'And Peter. He was only a boy. He shouldn't even have been here.'

Digby's lips moved but at first no sound came out.

'Not a dame school.'

The body was trembling.

'Shoot,' he pleaded.

'I can't.' Julian looked away into the mist.

'I had Petch's wife,' Digby said. 'So bored by Easton. The girl — plain one — mine. Turned Mrs Petch into a whore. But . . . punished.'

There must have been silence because Julian could hear distant firing and the next time he thought much about Digby it had got much colder and Julian's neck was sticky with blood as he lifted his head.

'And Lydia. Father said . . . must show them . . . who rules the roost.' Digby coughed. 'You — now you would have cherished her, wouldn't you? Soft old thing?' He choked on something and panted a few times, his face screwed up in pain. 'Always so . . . good. Lydia always so damn . . . good. Forgave . . . everything. I wanted . . . to love.'

The eye steadied.

'Not going to do it? Jules?' Digby paused between each word. 'Never quite able to take the shot — not with the ladies, not in the field. But never . . . a bastard.'

His voice faded.

'The nanny . . . just . . . bit of fun. Got out of hand.'

He coughed again and seemed to be struggling. His head moved from side to side.

'Prim little thing.' A strange vibrating noise in Digby's chest. 'I'm fucking, she's praying.'

Now Digby was having trouble drawing breath at all. He could see a small wince of pain punctuating each tiny, shallow inhalation.

'God hated me. Why Kitty? . . . Such terrible . . . punish—'

The eye was fixed on him. Such beautiful blue eyes, the one pupil tiny now. A tremor passed through Digby's body — and the thing sticking out of the mess of blood and slime quivered like a flag on a child's sandcastle in the wind.

Digby was scarcely more than mouthing words and at first Julian thought they had become meaningless but as he bent closer he heard it. 'Agnus dei, qui tollis peccata . . .'

It was decades since they had heard those words as they brought their mother, demented and muttering and filthy, out of the vault.

Lamb of God who taketh away the sins of the world, have mercy upon us.

He picked up Digby's remaining hand and held it, icy, in his own, trying to see beyond the mess of Digby's body and mind. He remembered Digby diving into the lake, white and strong. Digby teaching Julian to shoot crows or lying next to him at dusk to watch badgers. Digby and Patrick, dirty and excited as they dug for treasure. And then, pushed away for so long, Digby's face, full of surprise and joy as he turned to see Lydia come up the aisle. He remembered Digby before it all went wrong and the madness seemed to take hold of him.

'I can't do it,' Julian intended to say but his jaw wouldn't work. 'Don't ask.' But still the words were there in his head.

He thought he heard something move behind him; he smelled something fusty and damp. The iced fingers moved minutely in his. Digby's face contorted and then he realised it was meant to be a smile.

Julian had not even picked up his gun but a great red eye had opened in Digby's forehead. Digby's mouth was ajar.

He gazed down at the ruin of a man. His ears were still ringing with the shot: one great explosion ricocheting around his brain. He felt light-headed and chilly. He blinked two or three times, swallowed a thick bolus of blood.

From beyond Digby's body, two soldiers appeared, drawn by the shot, perhaps. It took Julian a minute to see that they were Germans. One sighted down his rifle while Julian was still considering how easily Digby had been silenced in the end. There was a crack and the first soldier's arms went up and he collapsed almost soundlessly. The second clutched his chest and fell backwards. Julian blinked. A voice from behind him said, 'You're bleeding. We need to get in the cover of the trees.'

'He was my brother,' he tried to say. 'I couldn't do it.'

'Yes.' The voice was odd, slightly muffled. 'But it's all right now.'

The green man stood behind him in his cloak. As a boy Julian had looked for him all over Savernake Forest: on horseback, on foot, at dawn and at dusk, and he had never found him. Sometimes he had caught a movement out of the corner of his eye; sometimes he had heard something moving purposefully in the deepest undergrowth, but the green man never showed himself. He just waited, season after season, year after year, century after century. And yet now he had found Julian and was taking him away from danger, from Digby who had been so terribly changed, from death, who would be returning for him soon.

'Did you kill Digby for me?'

There was a singing in his ears and blurred circles broke up the landscape of the dead. He thought the green man nodded but it might have been a breeze in his leaves.

'You've come a long way,' he thought he said to the creature whose black eyes shone in a face of brown bark. He wanted to reach up like a child and touch the greenery that sprouted from his gigantic head and shoulders, feel the folds of his cape. The green man was like a young woodland oak tree or a willow from the river; in his hand he carried a leafy staff. He wanted to go with him but his knees gave way and the green man enfolded him, lifting him to his feet and supporting him round the waist. The day roared and went dark.

He was being handed some cloth. 'Press your hand against your face,' said the man, 'to stop the bleeding.'

Then the man said, 'Come on, sir. No good staying here. There's more where those two came from and you need to get to an aid post.'

He could smell that strange fustiness about his saviour as well as human sweat. He stumbled and the man held him closer.

'My brother wasn't always like this,' he told the green man.

'If you say so, sir. It's all the same to me.'

His mouth formed the words, 'Who are you?'

'Corporal Ennals, sir,' the man said as Julian fell and was lifted up into the branches.

CHAPTER TWENTY-THREE

*E*aston seemed to remove itself from Laurence rather than the other way round. Eleanor and William left before him but he knew he would soon see them in London. As he stood, packed and waiting to go, he looked round his room, thinking how he had idealised Easton when he first arrived. Before leaving, he took down the small wooden frame from the wall and removed the picture of Digby and Lydia. He would return it in due course but in the meantime its loss would not be noticed.

On the doorstep he shook hands with Julian, who seemed to have grown in stature almost overnight. Although it was so soon after the funeral, an optimism appeared to have replaced his previous somewhat resigned doggedness. Maggie was nowhere to be seen, nor Susan, the one terrible casualty of the summer. Presumably she was with her baby.

The drive to the station was terrifying. Patrick obviously enjoyed hurling the decrepit motor car along the narrow lanes, while Laurence sat there willing there not to be a herd of sheep in the way. The train was slightly late. Patrick came with him on to the small platform and they sat together on a bench, Patrick slumped, his legs stuck out in front of him like a boy, and Laurence very upright. When he got back to London he would do as Eleanor suggested and get treatment. He had endured the discomfort for too many years as if it were his punishment for surviving.

Since seeing Jane Rivers, he had been wondering what he might safely tell Patrick. He had promised not to tell Julian what she had revealed, but could he trust Patrick not to pass on any information? In the end he decided to hold back, to let things be. It seemed to him that Patrick had come to terms with the past, whereas Jane Rivers could only be put in jeopardy by any further revelations. Instead he asked the one question to which he still needed to know the answer.

'Robert, the chauffeur? You told me he had a sister who ran an establishment in London.'

Patrick looked puzzled. 'Robert again? Establishment?' And then with an amused smile, he said, 'Ah, the family outing to a bordello.' He assumed a look of mock horror. 'Not wanting a recommendation, are you? Because on the whole I doubt they'd be to your taste. Young girls were her speciality, which suited Digby. Not little girls — but slender, sweet-looking ones. Not that they *were* sweet at all.'

He pulled out his cigarette case.

'I went only the once. Different man then, I hope. Wanted to impress Digby. But Julian hated it. Terribly respectable at heart, our Julian, even then.'

'Do you remember the address?'

'Why? You can't ask for all this intriguing information without giving me some satisfying reason, old chap.'

'But do you?'

Patrick exhaled smoke and then inhaled it up his nose.

'Inexorable Bartram. Can't give you an address. Doubt even

Digby knew it. Robert was organising it all. Not sure the Madame was Robert's *sister*, or whether that was a euphemism for some other relationship. Robert was an ideal pimp. We'd been to some show, clever stuff, and we were half seas over by then. But I recognised the street. Tite Street, appropriately. The "establishment", as you so decorously call it, was on a corner. Nothing to indicate what sort of place it was. Damned pricey place for a start.'

He tapped the ash off his cigarette.

'But as we were waiting for the door to open I was looking at two identical statues on the posts at the bottom of the steps. Sphinxes. I imagine they'll still be there.'

He regarded Laurence through a haze of smoke.

'Who knows the profession of the occupants these days, though? Might be a dentist or a member of parliament for all I know. The girls they had — we had — will be dead or stout or married to marquesses by now. Robert's sister? Well, she was a professional. It was a well-run house.'

'Thank you.'

'And the reason? Our quid pro quo?'

'Jane Rivers wants to know what happened to her fiancé. If he's alive or dead.'

He thought Patrick knew he was lying but he just gave him an odd half-smile and turned away. The tracks were vibrating and they could hear the train approaching.

As Laurence opened the carriage door, Patrick said, 'You must tell me what you find out. Unless it's to be a secret between you and the nanny.'

As the train drew away, he watched Patrick standing on the platform, one hand raised in a frozen wave. Laurence wondered if he would ever see him again.

*

There was nothing much in the post waiting for him at his flat, although it felt stuffy. He flung open all the windows and papers shifted in the almost imperceptible breeze.

He wondered what he should wear for the evening's expedition, while knowing it was a ludicrous situation that the most suitable outfit seemed to be either the suit he had worn to teach at Westminster School or full evening dress. He didn't want to go all the way to Tite Street and be refused entry. Thinking back to the Swindon police inspector, whom he had come to respect, he nevertheless took him as a model of how not to look for the best chance of success. He opted for his dinner jacket and searched for his father's gold cufflinks.

As he had an hour before he needed to leave, he sat down to write a letter to Filippo della Scala, confirming his acceptance of position of tutor to his son Guido. Then he stood at a window, his forearms on the sill, gazing out over the slate roofs that stretched before him above the tops of the plane trees. The single pale spire of St George's, Queen Square, rose behind the houses. He had come, finally, to think of this as home. It was what he had believed he was looking for, and yet in a few weeks he would be looking out over a foreign city. What would he do with this place when he left for Rome? He had once taken it for granted that if he accepted the tutor's job, his rooms would go, but now that his departure had become a reality he knew he wanted to be able to return.

He could feel the sun on his face. Pigeons strutted along a balustrade a few yards away and he could hear a motor car down in the street below. He had grown used to this corner of London. He could sit in Coram's Fields on a sunny day, or he could walk to the British Library.

Then a solution came to him and he felt certain of its rightness. He would offer the flat to Mary. He was being paid quite well by the della Scala family. He could continue to cover the rent. She would have the independent life she so often spoke of with longing. In two years, when he returned, either of them might have new ideas, new plans. He was almost certain she would agree if she could be persuaded she was doing him a favour.

He sat down to write to her immediately, before he could change his mind. He laid out his ideas and said that he hoped she would accept. He read the paragraph through and thought it sounded extraordinarily stuffy. Remembering what Frances had said to him – that he should choose whether he waited or whether he grasped life – he added a final paragraph.

> Perhaps I should have told you before that I was thinking of going abroad. There never seemed a right time to say it by letter while you were going through such a hard time. There are other things I should have said as well but I was too frightened of losing even what I had of you. I love you. It's quite simple. But loving you comes at a price. Your loyalty to Richard is a grand thing but I cannot, <u>cannot</u> just be your friend. I find I can't be the reasonable, honourable man I would like to be.
>
> So I am going away. I shall be in Italy and you will, I very much hope, be here, where I am now, looking out over London. You will know where I am and I shall know where you are. I hope you will understand.

Almost as he closed and sealed the envelope, the church bell struck seven. As he left the house, he held both letters in his hand so that he would be sure to post them before he changed his mind. In twenty minutes he had sent his life in an entirely new direction.

*

He wanted to reach Tite Street before eight. If the house was still operating as it once had, he hoped to arrive while it was quiet. He was on the bus and heading towards Chelsea when he realised he wasn't certain of the name of Robert's sister. Miss Stone sounded more like the headmistress of a boarding school for young ladies. He had a feeling that a madame might take Mrs as an honorific, in the manner of a household cook. But there was little point worrying about it as the address might well be highly respectable by now.

That proved not to be the case, although certainly from the outside there was nothing to distinguish it from the other houses on the street. He had walked from one end of Tite Street to the other, passing a postbox into which he dropped both letters with only a second's hesitation, before coming to the house with stucco sphinxes, gleaming white, at the far end. When he reached the door he was determined not to linger. Depending on what the neighbours knew of the house, he could only look dubious: either a man without the courage of his appetites or a potential burglar.

There was a well-polished door bell, which he pulled, but could not hear ring within the house. As the door opened he realised he had made a mistake. A formally dressed maid stood there, neat, with dark eyes and her hair in a bun. She bobbed to him.

'M'sieur?'

'I'm so sorry, my friend must have given me the wrong address,' he said.

Her pretty mouth curved into a little moue of doubt. 'I think p'haps not. You might come in and wet a little.' Like a comic actress she pronounced it to rhyme with 'beetle'.

'Wet?'

'Way-eet,' she said. 'Way-eet and have champagne? Make a new friend?'

He realised he had arrived at the right place. It was that simple.

He nodded. She took his hat and silk scarf.

'Please,' she said and led the way to an elegant, if over-elaborate drawing room. There was a muffled clang in the back of the house, at which she bobbed again and went out. He heard her open the front door, followed by a man's voice, and realised it was another caller.

He was in a large room with two displays of waxy flowers, whose scent filled the air. At the window thick folds of lace hid the sights and sounds of the street. He looked around. His surroundings were rich in gold, peach and cream, more like a boudoir than a reception room. His eyes settled on draped curtains of toile de jouy. When he looked carefully, the shepherds and shepherdesses were all engaged in some kind of sexual activity. Shepherds with huge phalluses approached shepherdesses reclining on mossy banks, their billowing dresses drawn up, their thighs apart. While naked nymphs lay caressing each other by a stream, another shepherdess had a lamb nuzzling at her breast. A milkmaid had abandoned her pails to take one rustic in her mouth while another took her from behind. He had never seen anything like the design but a bit of him thought it clever as well as shocking and, despite himself, arousing.

He had just taken in the equally obscene carved figures which held up an ornate marble mantelpiece when the door opened and another man was led in by the maid; she already had his cape over an arm. The man acknowledged him with a sharp nod. A stunning young redhead followed him in, with creamy skin and long tumbling curls, dressed in an ankle-length lilac peignoir trimmed with swansdown. As she moved, her gown briefly revealed a white stocking tied above the knee with blue ribbons.

She smiled brilliantly and clapped her hands.

'Champagne, gentlemen?'

She had the voice of a debutante. Laurence studied the other man. He was an ordinary sort of chap, in his forties, perhaps, with dark hair silvering at the sides, a fine moustache. Laurence had made the right decision to wear evening dress. The other man was obviously going on somewhere as he pulled out his watch.

'Seems a waste,' he said, more to Laurence than the two women, 'but I've only got an hour. So I rather think some champagne would be just the ticket.'

He looked at Laurence: it was clear they would be sharing the champagne and the cost.

Laurence wanted to ask for the proprietor, ask if Robert's sister was there, but the stranger's arrival had complicated things. The maid disappeared, and he thought he could hear distant voices. The redhead struck another of her poses, this time opening double doors in front of them and acclaiming her achievement with one knee bent and her hand held out, indicating the next room, as if she were a magician's assistant.

They passed through. This room was larger, with an oriental theme. Several ottoman sofas were scattered about and paper lanterns lent a glow to the dull gold of the walls and furniture. Low brass tables stood on Persian carpets. If there was a window, it was hidden behind bronze and crimson silk draperies. A picture close to him showed a kneeling woman, her hands lightly bound behind her back, her skirts raised to show plump buttocks, and a stern older woman standing over her, brandishing a cat-o'-nine-tails. He thought it was by Aubrey Beardsley.

The redhead returned with opened champagne and glasses. Laurence was alarmed to see it was a label he knew, if only as being exorbitantly expensive. While she was pouring, two other young women came in: one was dressed in a kimono painted with flowers, her hair black and bobbed. Despite her make-up, she seemed too tall to be Japanese. The other was pretty with the freshness of youth rather than beautiful, wearing a lacy chemise and stockings, her untidy waves of light-brown hair held up with ribbons.

The couple acknowledged neither man and sat side by side on a soft divan at the far end of the room. They faced each other and were talking in low murmurs. The dark-haired woman put up a hand to remove one of the younger girl's ribbons and then stroked her cheek. The redhead was sitting on the arm of a chair and whispering in the other man's ear. He drank his champagne fast and she refilled his glass, then got up languorously to fill Laurence's. Out of the corner of his eye, he saw the dark-haired girl lean forward to roll down one of her friend's pale stockings, revealing a very slender, very young leg. The girl had long calves and fine-boned ankles.

'I wonder if I could speak to the owner – or the lady who runs the house,' Laurence said in a whisper.

The redhead gave him a smile of complicity. 'You can tell me,' she said in a breathy voice. 'Anything you want we can provide.'

'No, I don't want anything,' he said. 'I just need to speak to a Mrs Stone.'

The redhead was undeterred. 'Everyone wants something,' she said, 'even if they don't know it yet.'

The door opened and a fourth girl came in, saw the other man and uttered a cry of delight. He obviously knew her already and got up to greet her as if it was an encounter at a society party. Unlike the other girls, she was wearing a high-necked, long-sleeved white dress, tied with a blue sash, which showed off her good figure but covered her flesh completely, and dark stockings. Her long hair was tied back and her face was unpainted. She could have been still at school. She took the man's hand and led him away. Across the room, the black-haired woman had opened her companion's chemise and was caressing almost perfect breasts. The girl's nipples were palest pink. The redhead had seen him watching and put her hand on his leg.

'Having another think?' she said. 'Do you like them young? We have some very nice young girls here. Convent girls, only been here a day or two. More than one girl maybe?'

He wanted to move but didn't want to offend her and he was inevitably aroused. He tried not to look at the couple on the divan or the dark head now moving slowly over the fairer girl's breasts, her head turned at just the right angle so that he could see her tongue circle the now harder nipples, but the small sighs of pleasure, or faked pleasure, were unavoidable. He realised the whole show was for him.

For a second he felt a deep misgiving. It had always been unlikely that Kitty had been brought here but what if she had ended up in what was essentially a brothel, which specialised in young girls? If he had a taste for it, just how young a girl might they procure for him?

'I really need to speak to Mrs Stone.'

He felt in his inner pocket and pulled out a wad of pound notes. She was watching him and her eyes held his. The money disappeared so fast that it was hard to know where she'd put it.

'It's not trouble of any sort. I just need to find a girl who once worked here.'

She gave him a sceptical look and he assumed a look of shame. 'Rose. My sister. She went missing in the war. My mother is failing and I need to find her.' He forced himself to look earnestly into her eyes but any appeal to sentiment was wasted.

'It's not a residential hotel,' she said. 'We don't leave forwarding addresses.' She seemed amused. 'This is one world,' her hand moved on his leg again, 'outside is another.'

'Please.' He took out a further note and shifted so that her hand slipped off his leg.

'Anyway, it's not Mrs Stone, it's Mrs Le Fèvre,' she said, the debutante's voice giving way to something harder and less refined. 'And for all I know she'll be too busy to see you.'

She got up abruptly and left the room.

Now he was alone with the two performers. The fairer girl was lying back on the cushions, her chemise around her waist. The girl in the kimono was stroking her thigh, pushing her hand higher and higher up the long pale leg. She bent forward, untied the sash of her kimono and, leaning over her, kissed her companion passionately on the mouth. As she did so her hand reached the apex of dark hair between her legs and started moving rhythmically.

Laurence looked away but there was nothing else to look at that didn't carry its own erotic charge. Although the spectacle in front of him was contrived, it still affected him. With her face hidden, the dark girl's neck and shoulders reminded him of Frances. The air smelled heavy with gardenias and musk. The younger girl's gasps became louder and more uneven, the dark girl's white hand more vigorous. The young girl's head was tipped back so that her hair tumbled over the edge of the divan. If he stood up he would look a fool but he considered returning to the previous room.

Just as the girl arched her back and cried out, the door finally opened again. It was the maid, who appeared completely oblivious to the ecstasies being played out only feet away.

'Mrs Le Fèvre will see you,' she said.

He leaped up and almost collided with the redhead leading two youngish men into the room. They were already flushed and one laughed loudly. The maid took him back through the hall and up a flight of stairs, wallpapered with gold cherubs. The maid passed several closed doors. Occasionally he could hear talking and once a brief shout, but she moved on briskly up a plainer flight of stairs to a single doorway, where she knocked and waited. Laurence heard a female voice call out, 'Come in.'

The woman before him, sitting at a bureau, apparently doing her accounts, was middle aged. She wore a dark dress and her long, thick hair, streaked with grey, was piled up on her head in an old-fashioned way. She was in the act of removing a pince-nez, rubbing the bridge of her nose between finger and thumb, an expression of vigilant doubt in her face. Behind her, an open door led into a sitting room. He could see quite a homely arrangement of furniture and pictures.

'So what you do really want?' she said. Her voice was deep with only traces of a London accent. 'Mr——?'

'Bartram,' he said. 'I'm looking for somebody.'

She looked down and rubbed the glass of her pince-nez with a handkerchief. When she met his eyes again, her expression had changed.

'You're a bit old to fancy yourself in love with one of the girls,' she said. 'I'm surprised I agreed to see you. I only did because Eugenia was pressing, which means you must be a generous man. Eugenia's affections are regulated by the number of notes in her stocking top. And also because I have had enough of figures for an evening. But as for your young lady — frankly, Mr Bartram, if that's really your name, if I had a penny for all the young men who want to find their "sisters", I could close down tomorrow.'

'But you wouldn't want to, I think?' It was a guess.

'Probably not.'

'So if I pay you better than I did Eugenia, you'll tell me?'

She shrugged, and his comment sounded crass in his ears. 'Actually it's a man I'm after,' he said.

Her finely shaped eyebrows rose in surprise. He doubted that she was often surprised.

'Not here, I'm afraid. I think – I hope – we cater for most tastes. We can be quite ... recherché.'

She pronounced it perfectly, and smiled tightly.

'But we're not a queer house.' He felt he was being scrutinised. 'Though you don't look like a nancy. I can usually tell what a man would really like.' Her face cleared. 'Or perhaps you want to watch? A nice boy with one of our girls? Eugenia said you were enjoying our little divertissement? We can arrange that.'

He was already shaking his head. 'I think he may be your brother.'

This time she looked genuinely taken aback.

'Well, you won't find him here. And he's certainly not a nancy boy.' She seemed to find the idea amusing.

'Where might I track him down?'

'Shanghai, I should think,' she said. 'Smuggling opium, for all I know.'

Relief and disappointment flooded through him. She had a brother, but she had no real idea where he was.

'He was a seaman in the Great War,' she said. 'Got a taste for a life on the ocean wave or, more like, in foreign ports.'

This took him a moment to absorb. After what he had heard, Laurence had expected the man he sought to be in some motorised section in the army, but of course they had engines on ships.

She glanced at a clock above the bureau, her interest obviously seeping away. He knew he should move fast but carefully, as he took her back into the past.

'Did he ever say anything about his time at Easton Deadall Hall?'

'George?' she said. This time she looked puzzled. 'George was never in service.'

He registered that it was not the place that was unfamiliar, nor the occupation, but that the name was wrong. But before he could tie this together, she added, 'You're muddling him up with Robert and Robert's been dead for years.'

It might have been his imagination but he thought that her expression changed minutely from tolerance to wariness.

'Was he killed in the war?'

'Killed, yes, but before the war. Stupid man. Working as a chauffeur. Crushed under his car — had it propped up on bricks. Fixing a fuel line, the coroner said. Whole lot came down. Neighbours heard screams but thought it was just trouble of some sort. Dead by morning.'

'I'm sorry,' he said.

She looked at him long and hard. 'If you are, then you're about the only one.' She sighed. 'He was a bad lot. Broke our mother's heart. Well, we all did, I suppose.'

'I had understood you were close?'

She was shaking her head slowly. 'I don't know who told you but close we weren't. Not at the end. Earlier, mebbe. He could charm the hind legs off a donkey. Him and his schemes.' She paused. 'Or are you looking for him because you're part of one of them that went wrong?' When he didn't answer she eyed the clock again. 'No point looking at me for any money. And seeing as the brother you're after is the one I haven't got any more, and it's going to get busy downstairs soon—'

'The girls here are very young.'

He could see at once that he'd offended her. 'They're not children,' she said, sharply. 'And I take care of them.'

'The girl downstairs, Eugenia, said you could provide a range of ... services.'

'I'm not running a bloody Sally Army hostel. Most men just want a change — same things they get at home but with a different face; even the girls get bored — but some men want rarer amusement. I try and satisfy them, no matter how bally odd their ideas. Most of it's acting. Some of my girls are failed actresses, like some of them are ruined housemaids that Robert foisted on me. But I stay on this side of the law. Mebbe only just, but I do. That's how I've stayed open for nigh on twenty-five years.'

'What if they want a girl? A very young girl...?'

'I tell them where to go,' she said with speed but before he could feel encouraged she added, 'There are other places for specialities and, anyway, little girls are too much trouble.'

'There was a little girl at Easton ...' he began, but she'd stood up.

'You've had your time,' she said. 'I'm a city woman, I've got no interest in west country gentry unless they ring my bell wanting what I'm offering.'

'Which they did.'

'Possibly. Probably. I'm not choosy if they've got the money.'

'And you know where Easton is?'

'Of course I do,' she said, sweeping across the floor. 'Robert worked there.'

'And he brought his master and his brothers here?'

'For Christ's sake,' she said, 'I let you come up here on some wild bull's chase out of the goodness of my heart and now you're trying to hold me to account for Robert's doings.'

'What was the name of the ruined housemaid?'

'It was years and years ago.' Her voice was indignant, her cheeks flushed. 'I don't know. I don't keep a school register. She was a looker but didn't stay — was expecting a more domestic arrangement with some gentleman as I recall — and now I'd like you to go.'

He thought it might be Maggie's mother but doubted he could ever find out.

There was a bell on her desk, presumably to summon the maid, but she had opened the door herself.

'I don't want to have to get my man up here.'

Laurence wasn't keen on meeting some backstreet bruiser himself. Of course she'd need one for the odd obstreperous drunk or for a customer who didn't treat the girls right or pay when asked.

'There's been a murder,' he said as he went out of the door, grasping at straws. 'At Easton. A young woman.'

Mrs Le Fèvre put both hands up in mock protest. 'Well, I'm not missing any of mine.'

'The police are starting to look back into the disappearance of the child, Kitty Easton,' he lied. 'To see if there's a connection. The connection they don't know about yet is between you and Robert and the Easton brothers. But I imagine you'll feel more obliged to help them than to help me. They'll want to get to the bottom of the whole business, whereas I only want to find out what happened to a small child. I don't care who took her. Her parents are both dead. But one of your brother's ruined housemaids, who was involved in this particularly stupid, cruel scheme, has suffered all her life because of it. I don't want the police involved any more than you do, I imagine. Especially as you're the only one left to blame, but you don't give me any choice.'

He turned and went down the steps, leaving her where she stood. As he reached the long corridor on the floor below, a girl came along it with one of the young men who had been in the oriental room. He was already pawing her.

Laurence suddenly felt a sense of relief at not finding out the truth, not having his fears confirmed that Kitty Easton had been brought here. On a hunch he had tried and failed to find out, and now he didn't even know why he had felt he should come here in the first place. Lydia's death, though sad, had freed them all. The stricken village of Easton where so many lives had been destroyed, including Kitty's small one, had, finally, moved on without her.

He stood back to let the girl and her enthusiastic companion find her room, then moved towards the top of the stairs. As the door closed on them, Mrs Le Fèvre spoke from behind him. He turned to find she had followed him down from her office. He could not see her face; she was a dark shadow, her profile illuminated by the light behind her. The long cavern of the corridor stretched between them. Behind thick doors a girl giggled, somebody tripped over something and he heard a man's laugh. He kept his eyes fixed on the woman and waited in the semi-darkness. The sound of music drifted upstairs.

'All right. What I know you can have. I'll deny everything if the police come round, but if you give me your word.'

She sounded doubtful that his word was worth much. For a few seconds he didn't move, then slowly he walked back towards her.

'Robert kidnapped this child. As you bally well know. Of course it's not what he called it but that's what it was. He had it her father was a cruel man despite his wealth and his position. But he always wanted money, did Robert. Two things he loved: money and motor cars. The first he never quite got hold of, the second killed him.'

'You helped him? You fetched her from Wiltshire?'

She shook her head. 'It's a long time ago,' she said. 'I don't remember.'

She said it so firmly that he knew she would never admit any active part in the business.

'She ended up here. Not exactly a bright move. She was small, frightened – she was always crying and yet almost never talked at first. This is a business of nights and grown men's desires. What the hell was I supposed to do with her? Robert said it was just for a bit and I was the only person he trusted.'

'Was she all right?' It was a lame question, he knew.

'When she stopped crying, she was rather a sweet little thing. But she wouldn't eat properly and I had to keep her upstairs.' She gestured behind her. 'Couldn't let the girls see her or word might get out.'

'And then?'

'And then Robert's killed. Leaving me with the problem and a life in prison if I was found with her.' She sounded resentful but defensive.

'She had this funny thing — I only noticed when I'd had her a while — six fingers: never seen the like. She had a bad arm, too, never quite straight even when it didn't seem to hurt her. But the fingers meant she could be identified. She knew my name, talked of Robert, needed clothes: sooner or later she might need a doctor. And then ...'

'Then?' He felt cold despite the airless warmth of the house.

'One day I left the door unlocked. I used to give her a little brandy to settle her so that I could leave her alone up here, but one day she'd wandered down. One of my gentlemen found her.' She stopped. 'He should have been in one of the special houses. It turned out his tastes did run to very young girls.'

Laurence couldn't trust himself to speak. She fiddled with some keys at her waist.

'It was no place for a child and Robert knew that, but I'd grown quite fond of her. I had a little dog — she loved that dog. I bought her a dolly.'

He still couldn't see her face but he felt her transforming in front of him to an older, more resigned woman.

'One of the girls heard her screaming. The worst didn't

happen – the gentleman was too drunk, too excited – but I knew she had to go. Now I had to pay off the girl who'd pulled the gentleman off her – and I still thought she'd blab. They don't half talk, these girls. Like a flock of geese, they are.'

'What did you do with her?' He tried to sound matter-of-fact.

'Sold her.' When she rightly took his silence for shock, she said, raising her voice, 'I didn't have much choice. She was a liability.' When he still failed to respond, she added, 'There's some would of done a lot worse.'

'Where? Where did she go?'

He wished he'd never known any of it. The image of the small child who cried a lot and said very little, brutally treated in different ways: first by her father, then by the chauffeur, then by a stranger in a brothel. And the thought of her innocent, childish pleasure in a small dog: together they created an image he knew he would never forget.

'I had a washerwoman used to come in. Shared her with lots of other houses. She'd chat on if you gave her half a chance – another one who talked. She told me of this couple she knew. He was an ostler, she'd been in service before her marriage. She said they were a nice, respectable couple but they'd never been able to have kiddies. Broke their heart.

'After a bit I asked if they wanted to take a child. Said she was Robert's bastard landed on me.' She gave him a sharp look. 'And that's what I'm saying still. Said her mother was dead not long past. She used to ask for her mama all the time, you see.

'I hear back they're interested. I say a hundred pounds for my expenses. They say they haven't got it. Then he says twenty-five. They can do twenty-five.'

'Twenty-five pounds?' he said in wonder, thinking what Digby Easton might have given to have back his daughter, the heir to Easton.

'I could have got a fortune for her if I'd sold her to a gentle-man. That gentleman who'd already spent himself all over her—'

It was the first time a note of real disgust had entered her voice.

'Or one of the other houses. She was a pretty girl once she set-tled a bit, sweet, and she had this funny, old-fashioned voice.'

'I'm glad you didn't.'

'Well, like I say, I'd grown fond. Or gone soft.'

'Do you know where she is now?'

'God knows. I mean, she'd be grown up or near. It was a long time ago. The couple didn't want to see me again. I mean, respectable didn't begin to cover it. I'd given them their little one and they still didn't want anything to do with the likes of me. Didn't want their new daughter to know they'd bought her from a woman like me. Still, I handed her over at their house, just to make sure they were all right.'

'You don't know their name?'

'Of course I do. I wasn't letting her go off with a couple and it turn out they'd sold her on like I'd considered and they'd taken the profit on it.'

She sounded indignant at his assumption of professional care-lessness, then turned abruptly to the stairs to her rooms.

'I'll give you the name. The parents might still be there. And then, frankly, you can bugger off.'

He followed her up the short flight, uncertain whether she meant him to. She turned up the lamp and, with her back to him, rifled through pigeon-holes in her bureau. Eventually she pulled out a piece of paper and scribbled something.

'Smith,' she said. 'Dennis and I think it was Elsie. Live out Camberwell way.' She handed him a bit of paper. 'She probably did all right there. Dull and decent, you know the sort?' She looked dis-approving. 'Thrifty. No drink. Methodists,' she added, as if that explained everything.

'Thank you. For telling me.'

'Go easy,' she said. 'It'll be a shock to them. I went round a couple of times to look without them seeing — well, like I say, I wanted to check I hadn't been had for a fool, but anyway I was missing her even though I was glad to be rid of her. That woman had her turned out nice. I saw her with her new dad on his allotment over the road one time. Last time I went over she was skipping outside their house. Didn't recognise me.'

She rang the bell.

'They call her Kath. Kathy.'

The maid appeared at the door. He hadn't heard her footsteps.

'Show Mr—?'

'Bartram.'

'Show Mr Bartram out,' she said. 'I think he's got what he came for. Another satisfied gentleman.'

She held her hand out.

'Think carefully about what you do next,' she said, as he shook it.

He walked out into the street between the sphinxes. Did the other impassive Tite Street houses hide secrets? he wondered, as he walked past lit drawing-room windows. In one a woman was playing a piano with a girl turning the pages beside her. The sash was down and the notes were quite clear on the night air.

As he turned into Flood Street he was hit by a wave of emotion. He thought of his baby son, whom he had never had a chance to see, of Mary, whom he was leaving. Yet in all the death and loss of the last years, the fate of Kitty Easton struck him as being inordinately sad. He had discovered her fate so easily. If Lydia Easton or Jane Rivers had not been so frightened, if either had confided in one of the Easton brothers, they might well have made the connection that he had. Even after Digby's death, the two women had kept silent through a pact of loyalty, fear and shame. For want of a single conversation, Kitty Easton had been lost to them for ever.

CHAPTER TWENTY-FOUR

*F*inally he walked into the shop. The floorboards were bleached with age and neat piles of goods were stacked up on a scarred wooden counter. It was an old shop, smelling of tar and soap, but everything was spotless, from the glass jars to the small wall of drawers. There were two customers: an elderly lady in a battered black straw hat and a small boy. The shopkeeper, a woman, was up a small set of steps, reaching for a caddy off a shelf, the white ties of an apron hanging down against her striped dress.

A noise from the corner made him look round. A fat baby — he could never tell how old they were — was sitting, gurgling happily while it bit on a rattle and then examined it carefully. A few toys lay on a blanket around it. The baby's eyes were following its mother as she descended backwards, clutching the jar. She stepped off the last rung, put down the jar and started unscrewing the lid. As she did so, she lifted her head to acknowledge Laurence.

He knew in that moment that it was her. Her face was wider than her mother's or aunt's, her bobbed hair thicker and almost tawny, her colouring much more like the pictures he had seen of her father, and she had wonderfully bright-blue eyes. She took up a scoop and measured tea on to the scales. Finally his eyes went to her hands.

'Is that enough, Mrs Jones?' she said and in those few words he could hear her London accent. When the old woman nodded assent, she checked the scale and tipped a little more in. She smiled conspiratorially at the boy.

'And four ounces of broken biscuits, was it?' She went to one of the sacks behind her, holding a brown paper bag.

The customer turned her head and regarded Laurence with curiosity.

'Good morning,' he said. She said something back that he didn't catch. Behind the counter the young woman was writing the prices down on a bit of paper, biting her lip with concentration.

'You come back when you can. When Fred's better.' Her head was still down as she wrote. 'Wait a minute, Sidney,' she said to the small boy when she'd finished, 'let's see what I got here.'

She reached under the counter, brought out a tin, opened it and tipped it towards him. The boy hesitated for a few seconds, then his hand darted forward as if she might snatch the tin away at any moment. He pulled out a sweet, looked enquiringly at the older woman beside him and then put it in his mouth. When the older woman nudged him, he muttered something like 'Thank you, missus.' She picked up her tea, a block of green soap and two other small packages, and put them in a string bag.

'Isn't your little 'un doing well?' the customer said, turning around, yet glancing at Laurence again.

The young woman came out from behind the counter and swept the baby up into her arms, its two plump feet kicking excitedly. She kissed its head.

'You are a good little girl, aren't you, Esme?' She swung her on to a hip. 'Mostly.' She looked up and laughed. 'She's getting teeth, though! So we've had some bad nights, I can tell you.' But her voice contradicted any complaint. 'Mind you, you've had plenty so you'd know.'

The older woman's face crinkled and she ruffled the boy's hair. 'It's the grandchildren makes me lose sleep,' she said. 'And now there's another on its way. Our Anne. That's three she's had since Fred got back. She'll have her work cut out. Her Ivy's a holy terror.'

Pushing the boy before her, she dipped her head to Laurence as she went out, the bell jangling.

The shop seemed suddenly silent. Dust shimmered in the sunbeams. The young woman jiggled the baby and it chortled at her. Then she met his eyes, her expression open and curious.

'Can I help you, sir?'

His gaze took in her face, her small kingdom and her fat baby. 'It's your shop?'

'Well, me and my husband's. It was his pa's but he passed away while Jim was at the war. So now we've taken it on. We've got plans to expand. Maybe.' She laughed self-consciously. 'Maybe some haberdashery, now we've got our little girl. We went to the exhibition twice; once we saw the King and Queen.' Her eyes shone. 'Close as me and you. Esme's too young to remember but we can tell her she was there.' She wiped the baby's face on a corner of her apron. 'Did you go?'

'Yes. Yes. Marvellous. I might go again. See one of the concerts.'

'There's lots of building going on up there.'

She looked eagerly at him as if testing whether he'd noticed and he nodded in agreement. He thought of the boundless expanse of flattened earth cleared of trees and bushes, and its geometrical markings of pegs and rope, the neat stacks of building materials, the digging men, and the narrow avenues cutting across the space, criss-crossing each other, just waiting for houses.

'Well, we thought we might open up near Wembley Park. They've got shops going there. People with new houses'll need all sorts, Jim says. And with Esme, it'd be better out there in the country. Better air than smoky old London. We could have a little garden. Jim'd like to grow vegetables ... have chickens.' She stopped. 'But what am I running on about when I should be serving you? Jim always says I could talk the hind legs off a donkey.' She put out a hand to stop the baby pulling her hair. 'Let me put Baby down and I'll be with you.'

He watched her set the child down tenderly; it protested but only for a few seconds. He felt in his pocket for the photographs of Digby and Lydia, the picture of Easton.

As she stood up, she smoothed down her hair in an action he recognised from Frances. Yet he was still glad he had not told Mrs Smith, the widow at Camberwell who had acted as her mother since she was five, the truth. He had, as Mrs Le Fèvre counselled him, gone carefully.

'Your husband sounds a good businessman.'

'Oh he is,' she said, suddenly looking even younger than her eighteen years. 'He's a good man. He looks after us.' She shot a glance at the baby and suddenly looked wistful. 'I didn't have much when I was little but we're going to give Esme everything.'

He paused, looking at her until he began to see slight anxiety come into her eyes.

'Could I have two ounces of rice?' he said, quickly. 'And some baking powder and ... some custard?'

She seemed amused but turned to fetch them. Cutting string from a ball on the counter top, she wrapped everything up for him. He handed her the money. She rang up the cash register and handed him back sixpence.

'No,' he said. 'Keep it for Esme.'

She looked embarrassed. 'No, you can't—'

'I want to. Really.'

Comprehension dawned in her face. 'You've a kiddie yourself?'

He nodded. 'Yes. A little boy.'

'They're everything, aren't they?' she said happily, as she passed him the brown paper packages.

For a second their hands touched. He took one last long look at her familiar, yet unknown face, tipped his hat to her, opened the door and walked out on to the street.

Two ringed pigeons were squabbling over a piece of stale bread in the gutter. Across the road a group of girls had chalked out squares on the pavement and were jumping in and out of them, following the rules of some ancient game. A stout woman in an apron watched them from her doorstep, arms akimbo. There was a breeze getting up. He wasn't sure whether it was going to rain again, but he thought he'd walk the whole way home anyway. Soon cool, rainy English streets and tidy front gardens would be just a memory.

ACKNOWLEDGEMENTS

I should like to thank my agent, Georgina Capel at Capel & Land, for ten years of support, advice and friendship; Lennie Goodings and Victoria Pepe for clear and sensitive editorial direction; and the larger team at Virago and Little, Brown for their enthusiasm and professionalism. Once again I am indebted to Celia Levett, the ideally patient and rigorous copy-editor for a rather slapdash typist.

Two inspired and inspiring gardeners, Mary Keen and Julian Bannerman, answered questions on mazes and Wiltshire soil; the Bannermans' marvellously dramatic house, Hanham Court, near Bristol, was partly responsible for my creation of Easton Hall. John Hopkins advised upon hydroelectricity and drew my attention to early installations in private houses, particularly Cragside, Northumberland, and Knightshayes Court in Devon.

Catherine Hopkins assisted me with questions of law. Louise Foxcroft, medical historian, provided details of diseases and treatments of the 1920s. Descriptions of the River Kennet – a very different river in the 1920s from the narrow watercourse it is today – were taken from a wonderfully elegiac piece in

Blackwood's Magazine, 'Passing of a River' by Dr Godfrey Maurice, a Marlborough doctor from 1912 to 1921.

Twenty-seven million people visited the 1924 British Empire Exhibition at Wembley and all bar two of the fifty-eight countries of the Empire exhibited. Only the Palace of Industry still survives, as a run-down warehouse. Of many sources *Metro-Land: British Empire Exhibition 1924* (edited by Oliver Green) was the most evocative.

My interest in the strange prehistoric landscape of Wiltshire dates from a field trip over three startlingly cold and wet days in my first term as a mature student at Cambridge. I am grateful to Lucy Cavendish College for that and so many other opportunities.

Also by Elizabeth Speller

THE RETURN OF CAPTAIN JOHN EMMETT

The bestselling Richard & Judy Summer Book Club pick

'The new *Birdsong* – only better' *Independent*

'It is 1920 and Laurence Bartram has come through the First
World War but lost his young wife and son. He receives a
letter from the sister of his old friend, John Emmett. Why,
she wonders, did Emmett survive the war only to kill himself?
Laurence begins to investigate . . . Speller's writing is gorgeous,
her research immaculate and very lightly worn. Sheer bliss'
Kate Saunders, *The Times*